Beyond the Sea
Book Three: Crystal Odyssey Series

Joyce Hertzoff

Mary!
Thanks for wanting
my books

Joyce Hertzoff
4/2018

DEDICATION

To Ira, Hilary, Andrew and Julie

ACKNOWLEDGMENTS

Many thanks to my cover artist, Deva Walksfar. Thanks to all those who critiqued this story. Your suggestions were great. All remaining errors are my own.

Other Books by Joyce Hertzoff

The Crystal Odyssey Series:

> The Crimson Orb
> Under Two Moons

The Portal Adventures Series:

> A Bite of the Apple

For Children:

> So You Want to be a Dragon

CHAPTER ONE

"Nissa, send a scream my way," Madoc instructed.

Those with any experience with mind screams met one evening in the Stronghold's solarium. We made certain no one else was there so they wouldn't be hurt, and then began to see how we could shield ourselves or even better, repel a scream from an attacker.

How could I do this to the man I loved? I took a breath, let it out, focused my mind and aimed a scream.

"You're holding back," Madoc accused me.

I was.

"All right, try it with Toren." He indicated the other mage in the room.

Madoc and I laughed. We both knew I'd have no reservation, although I no longer felt the same antagonism toward Toren I had just a few weeks before. I took a deeper breath and closed my eyes to concentrate. I tried to remember the first time I'd aimed a mind scream at him, and let go with all I had.

Toren gave a start, but it didn't have the same effect as it had the time I really needed to fight him off.

He nodded. "Have any of you ever used shields to prevent anyone from reading your thoughts?" he asked. "It's like that. Picture a door or a wall, just a short distance from your head. It keeps the scream from coming through."

We continued until late at night.

The next evening as everyone gathered in the refectory for

dinner, Oskar made an announcement. We would leave for Fartek in four days.

"We must complete all preparations for the expedition. The Planners have decided on several objectives, and they will be posted just outside the refectory after dinner this evening. If you have comments, objections or additional suggestions, please see one of the members of the committee." Up until then I thought the only objective was to make contact with any people remaining in Fartek and determine what technology they possessed. But there was more. Oskar, Col, Madoc and the others had considered what were the most important things to look for, as well as how we might approach any people we met. The objectives included looking for other artifacts that had been preserved in Fartek in addition to the machines.

"Tomorrow, several people will go to Osterbruk to show the citizens a few of our inventions. They'll first approach the leaders of Osterbruk, the mayor and so forth, and ask to demonstrate the gadgets at the town hall."

There were murmurs, mostly approval. Oskar had used the phrase 'testing the waters' several times and I began to understand what he meant. The citizens of the town would serve as a testing ground for acceptance of the machines. But I wondered whether the reception of them by the residents might influence our plans for the trip.

Kerr, Donal and Madoc asked that we bring some of the more mundane inventions with us to show the Duke when we reached the Manor, such as the lamps used at the Stronghold.

Meetings over the last days allowed those going to get to know one another even better than before.

Col would come along, and with him, Wim and Raj. Gita, wouldn't let her husband and adopted son go without her.

Toren convinced Oskar he'd be better use with the expedition than at the Stronghold.

The people who'd taken the devices to Osterbruk returned to report a mixed reaction. Some townspeople were pleased the Stronghold was willing to share what they'd made, while others wondered why they might need the machines. But no one was downright hostile, an encouraging sign.

Rani and I had made protective clothing and some covers

for the supplies from the waterproof yellow material developed for the Dulno Lake expedition. The alchemists were still trying to determine what the water at the bottom of the lake had done to it, but even with those changes, it remained waterproof.

The party would be large, even larger than the one that went to Dulno Lake, and we'd be taking at least two wagons. That would mean we'd have to go around the higher mountains rather than over them to the southern harbor town of Riesund, but Niko pointed out there was safety in numbers.

At least six of the women from our dorm were going, Carys, Morna and myself, Katya, Gudrin and Eva. Helga felt almost cheated she hadn't gotten far during the last expedition, and we'd probably have need of her skills. Ana was somewhat noncommittal.

"I wish you could all come with us," Morna told them time and time again. "I want you to meet our parents and for them to meet you."

***

We were prepared for whatever we'd have to face, or so we thought. The first parts of the journey would be through Solwintor, south of the Stronghold. Would marauders attack as we traveled to the coast? We'd fought them off in the past. Would we have to face pirates, the spiny sea ruda or storms crossing to Arrandis, or later from East Harbor to Fairhaven? We were ready for those dangers too.

The morning we were to leave, the refectory was full even though we were breakfasting early. Many people had seen us off when we went to Dulno Lake, but this time, the entire population of the Stronghold would bid us 'bon chance', as Sura would say.

There was an excitement in the air, different from that before the party. Everyone hoped for our success. The eighteen of us, who made up the expeditionary force, were the most excited of all.

We took communication devices and some of the imaging equipment, too. Donal and Kerr had improved them all, based on what they'd found on the satellite. We still didn't know how far the communication devices could send and receive messages, but that was something we would test.

After breakfast, we collected our packs of clothing and personal supplies and headed for the corrals near the cavern entrance. As we passed through the corridors of the Stronghold, we were very aware some of us might not return. People along the way shook our hands and bestowed wishes for a safe and successful trip.

People, horses, and wagons crowded the vast entryway of the Stronghold. The day had arrived for the start of our next adventure. I'd looked forward to this for so long that it was almost anticlimactic to actually be embarking for home and then Fartek.

We saddled our steeds and stowed our packs, mounted and took one last look at the people and the place we were leaving behind, and then Oskar opened the entry so we could file out. I already missed the Stronghold.

CHAPTER TWO

I sat on the wooden dock in Reisund with Morna, and Carys, our legs dangling over the side, but far above the water, even my much longer limbs. A breeze blew a long strand of my hair off my damp neck and brought the salty scent of the sea to my nose. Madoc and Col Ramin, haggled with the boat captains at the end of the pier, trying to arrange passage for all of us across the sea from Solwintor to Leara.

"Nissa, do you think we can all fit on one boat?" Morna asked. "Including the horses and wagons?"

I shook my head. "I doubt it."

"None of the boats look very big." Carys squinted her eyes in the sun.

It had taken our party three days to travel through the hills to the port on the south shore of Solwintor. The size of our party, the heavily-laden wagons, and the need to avoid the marauders who menaced travelers in the area slowed our progress.

"At least Riesund is nicer than Brenhavn was." Morna referred to the ramshackle harbor where we'd arrived in this country almost two months before. And now we were going home, at least for a short time.

"Madoc and Col will find a way to get us home," I stated.

"You think Madoc can do anything!" My sister had teased me about my faith in his abilities ever since she'd learned I loved him

"Well, he can. Right, Carys?"

Madoc's sister nodded. "He'll find a way, even if his 'magic' doesn't extend to making a huge ship appear out of the blue."

The rest of our party had set out to explore the town. Some hadn't left the Stronghold since they'd arrived, and were fascinated by the shops.

"I'm looking forward to reaching home," Morna said. "I want to show Holm Manor to our new friends."

"We'll only be stopping for a day or two," I warned. "Just long enough to introduce everyone to the Duke and Duchess and to our parents." I missed them, my parents, I mean.

In the few months we'd been away, Madoc had transformed from the Manor's science teacher and wizard to a Planner at the Stronghold.

We heard Raj's bark before he reached us and turned to see the small spotted dog come bounding over to Morna. She laughed as she caught him in her arms and he began to lick her chin. He was followed almost immediately by Wim. The ten-year-old had grown in recent weeks.

"Morna, look what Gita bought me!" he shouted as he approached, holding up a pair of boots and boy-sized trousers.

At least I wouldn't have to alter any more clothes to fit him. There were other children at the Stronghold, but I'd taken in some of the men's clothes to replace the tatters he'd worn before.

Gita walked up to us more sedately with a smile on her brown face as she looked at him. She obviously loved the orphan she and her husband had adopted. We all did. "Are they still negotiating?" She indicated her husband and Madoc.

"It would seem so."

The captains shook their heads and Col and Madoc gestured frantically as we watched. They were as determined to get to Leara as we were, even if we had to swim. Since I didn't know how, that would have been quite a feat.

"Maybe we can build our own boat," Wim suggested. "Baca built boats before." Baca had grown up on an island and learned to build boats from his grandfather before he came to the Stronghold.

"That would take forever!" Morna shook her head. "Especially one big enough for all of us."

Why had we decided to send such a large party? But the leaders at the Stronghold, including Col and Madoc, had felt there would be safety in numbers. Much as I liked everyone who was with us, I wished they'd realized how cumbersome this entourage would be.

Col and Madoc shook hands with two of the captains and walked toward us with smiles on their faces.

"We sail in the morning." Col's dark eyes shone. He and Gita came originally from Standia where many of the people had the same dark coloring, a sharp contrast to the people of Solwintor, who were blond, blue-eyed and very tall.

"Two of the captains agreed to take us, our animals and our wagons." Madoc slipped an arm around my shoulders. "So we'll split into two groups and meet up again on the other shore."

"What town will that be?" I asked. I didn't know much about the northern coast of Leara this far west.

"They sail to Melsford and we can follow the river there south to the Merchant's Road."

"So we won't be going through Dunswell on our way home." Morna frowned. "Gran will be disappointed not to see us."

"I'm afraid visiting your grandmother will have to wait for another time," Madoc said.

"Well, I'm just happy to be heading home." Morna frown disappeared.

"Where will we spend tonight?" Gita looked back at the small town. "Will we camp outside of Riesund?"

"I doubt there's a tavern or boarding house that could accommodate us all," her husband replied.

"Even if we split up?" Morna had been very good about sleeping on the ground so often during our travels, but I knew a bed, indoors, was attractive to all of us.

"We can inquire," Madoc said.

We walked up the dusty main street, stopping at one tavern after another to ask for lodgings for the night, to no avail. We met some of our party along the way, including my brothers and Baca and Dreas, the two young men interested in Morna.

"It appears we may have to camp just outside of town tonight," Morna told them. "But we have passage on two boats tomorrow morning."

"They can carry us all?" Blane looked from Madoc to Col. "That's good! And what's one more night camping out?"

"Have you seen any of the others?" I asked.

"Eva and Kerr just went into a tea shop." Baca pointed. "And I saw some of the other women coming out of a clothing shop at the end of this street."

We returned to the stable in a side street where we left our horses. The stable man had promised to guard the wagons and their contents for as long as necessary, but we wanted to retrieve one of the machines we were transporting to show to the townsfolk.

"How about the imaging device Kerr worked on?" Donal suggested. "It's something they'll understand and appreciate."

"If they don't think it works by magic." Blane was right.

Next we had to find a group of people to show it to.

We met up with the other members of our party and gave them the news about the ships.

"We can show the device to the townsfolk while we eat dinner." Kerr pointed to the nearest tavern. "They might not have space for us for the night, but it's large."

We invaded it, all of us at once.

CHAPTER THREE

The tavern was crowded so we split into three small groups and sat at the scattered empty tables. I had Madoc on one side of me and Morna on the other with my brothers and Carys across from us at a long table. Baca, and Col, his wife and Wim were also at our table.

Donal kept looking over at the table where Katya. I knew he was torn between sitting with us and with her. At that table, Dreas was frowning, his eyes fixed on Morna and Baca.

A waitress offered fish for dinner, fried or in a stew. We each chose and she left.

Col immediately began the discussion. "For our first demonstrations to the citizens of Osterbruk, we arranged with the mayor to assemble people in a central place."

We'd heard that before. "Does this town have a mayor?" Morna asked.

None of us knew. We watched as people entering the tavern greeted each other, and some even walked from table to table, shaking hands.

"This tavern seems to be a meeting place," Madoc said. "The people here tonight should be a good audience."

Col's eyes lit up the way they did when he had a new idea. "I'm going to ask the barman whether he'd let us perform a demonstration."

He rose and squeezed past a few tables to a bar that stretched along one wall. We watched him gesture as he explained what he wanted to do. The barman's expression went from confusion to disbelief, passing quickly through disapproval, but finally to acceptance. Col was very persuasive.

The barman put two fingers in his mouth and let loose a whistle that penetrated the din of many voices. "Listen up," his voice boomed followed by a sudden silence. "This here's Ramin and he's wantin' to show you some newfangled thing."

Col looked around the room and his eyes seemed to lock on Kerr's. "I'd like my young friend to help me." He motioned to Kerr to join him at the bar.

It was a good move. Col was obviously not a native of Solwintor, and even though our diverse group hadn't met any kind of prejudice, Kerr, who wasn't a native either, looked like they did, tall and blond, with the start of a mustache and beard, making him appear older than his twenty-four years. His command of Solwinish, their language, had improved remarkably, too. They'd listen to him sooner than to the shorter and much darker Col.

"This device can capture the image of anyone or anything, and then put it on paper so it can be kept forever," Col began. He held the box up so all could see it.

"Got to be the work of the devil!" one older man shouted.

Col shook his head. "It's the work of men, including my friend here."

"I wouldn't want my likeness caught by some machine!" another objected.

"It doesn't harm the person. Trust me," Kerr said. "Why, to prove it, take my picture, Col."

Col smiled. He held the small device between himself and Kerr and pressed a button. It whirred, it clicked, and finally it whirred again. A piece of paper came out of the device and Col held it up. It showed Kerr's smiling face very clearly although it was only in black, grays and white.

"And I'm still here," Kerr said, bowing slightly.

Then the questions began: How did it work? What could it be used for? Could the picture be bigger? Smaller? Can you capture my image?

Col and Kerr patiently answered everyone, but were finally allowed to sit down to their dinners once they promised to capture the images of a few of the citizens of Riesund.

The barman came to our table while we ate to thank Col for

the demonstration. "Best entertainment we've had here in a long time. Why, I just might have ta have my picture taken!" He started to walk away, then turned back. "Did you find lodgings for the night?" He'd turned us away earlier.

"No, Lors," Col answered. "No one seems to have room for so many of us."

"Tell you what," he said, scratching an ear. "After everyone's gone for the night, we could set you up out here. You'll just have to help move tables out o' the way."

"Thank you," Col said.

"Least I could do for you after you put on such a show for my customers." He chuckled as he walked back to the bar.

We spread the word to the others in our group. Somehow the food tasted better now we knew we'd be spending the night indoors. Even if we had to sleep in our blankets on the floor, it would be better than the hard ground and the vagaries of the weather under the stars.

A handful of people came by to have their images captured. When Col handed them the results they all smiled with delight. The last was Lors.

Many of the other customers made a point of stopping at our table and Kerr's to say "tek" and "have a good night". Once the last one had gone, we moved the tables to the side of the room, providing a large area in the center. Lors asked some of the men to go with him, and soon they returned with pallets and thin mattresses. "I'm not sure I have enough," he said, but they brought out all he had. Most of us had one, the rest made do with piles of blankets.

I slept well that night, certainly better than I had the previous couple of nights outdoors. In the morning, Lors provided us with hot tea and coffee, and sent a lad to bring pastries from a bakery farther down the main street. Col and Madoc added additional coins to the pile they handed Lors for his hospitality.

By the time we packed our belongings and retrieved our horses and wagons, it was time to board the two boats, the Great White and the Dolphin. Madoc said those were sea creatures, and I took his word for it. The captain and crew of each vessel were loading cargo when we arrived, but stopped to tell us where we could go and where to take our horses. We were paying well for passage. I was happy I didn't have to pay for mine by cooking for the crew, as I'd done on past voyages.

Madoc and I, our sisters and my brothers all boarded the larger vessel, the Great White. Col and his family and Gudrin followed us up the gangplank.

Many of our traveling companions had never been on a boat before. Wim was fascinated by the way the crew's quarters were arranged to take as little space as possible and fitted to prevent anything from falling while the boat was under sail.

Soon after we boarded, the anchor was raised and the boat pulled away from port. The captain of the Great White, Simon Felden, was from Leara. When he learned some of us were, too, he switched to Learic when talking to us.

"The Great White is a ship!" he stated adamantly when he heard us call it a boat. "And stay out of the way of my crew, preferably below deck, during the journey."

This far west, the arm of the sea separating Leara from Solwintor was narrower. "We'll be in Melsford by sunset," he promised.

The sea was calm at first, but Gudrin still found the motion disturbing.

"Sit on your bunk and don't look out the porthole," I advised her.

She nodded, swallowing and pressing her lips together.

Wim wanted to watch the water so we had all we could do to keep him below decks.

"You don't want to be washed overboard, do you?" Morna asked him.

The ten-year-old's eyes went wide. "That can't happen, can it?"

"It'll depend on the weather, and whether we have to contend with pirates, or sea monsters." My sister liked to tease, but that could happen, as we'd learned on previous voyages.

That only whet his appetite, and tempted him to sneak up the rickety stairs whenever no one was watching him until Gita finally put her foot down. "Wim, you stay right here where I can keep my eyes on you! I don't want to have to lock you in one of the rooms."

I'd never heard her yell at him before, but this time she had cause.

"Yes, Ma'am." He looked at the ground.

Soon, Gudrin wasn't the only one sickened by the motion of the ship as it become more pronounced. I'd expected this arm of the sea to be calm. Looking out the porthole, all I could see were sheets of rain, falling at an angle, and waves that sometimes covered the little round window. One wave rocked the ship until it tipped precariously to one side, and we each had to hold onto something solid to keep from falling, but it soon righted itself. Perhaps the weight of the cargo deep in the hold kept it stable, or perhaps our belongings were being tossed around just as we were with every lurch.

"The horses!" Morna cried. "I hope they're OK!" Leave it to her to worry about any animals. My eyes went to Raj, who sat on a bunk with Wim's arm around him. He was safe, but our horses were deeper in the ship with the cargo.

"They'll have to manage until it's safe for us to go check on them," Gita told her.

Meanwhile, Donal began to look a little green, and even I didn't feel as well as I had just a few minutes before.

"I'm going to see what's happening on deck," Madoc offered.

"I'll go with you," Blane volunteered.

"Be careful!" Carys called after them as they opened the door of the room where we'd all congregated.

I wanted to go with them, too, but thought I might be of better use in the bunk room. Helga, our healer, was on the other ship, and hopefully was caring for the people with her. The only remedies I had were some of the herbs my mother had given me before I left home. I searched through them for something to counteract seasickness and found a mixture of ginger and raspberry leaf. The instructions said it could be used in a tea to relieve the symptoms, but where could I brew anything? All I could do was add them to water and stir, then pour some into a cup for Gudrin, who was still the most affected by the motion of the ship.

"I'm sorry it's not hot," I said as I handed the cup to her.

"That's all right," she said. "It probably won't matter." I knew if she'd been feeling better she would have questioned what herbs were in the brew, but she was sweating and the color in her cheeks had drained. She sipped the cold drink and grimaced at the taste, then swallowed slowly before taking another sip.

I watched to see whether it was helping her or not before making more for Donal and anyone else who felt sick.

"The only thing that will permanently cure me would be if the ship would stop swaying!" he said. But he took the cup I handed him and drank it.

CHAPTER FOUR

Madoc and Blane burst through the door, both drenched and swaying along with the boat. "The captain and the crew are doing their best to keep the ship upright." Blane shook rain off his clothes and wiped his face with the cloth I handed him. "But they're having quite a battle. One of the masts was broken in two by a wind gust, and the other sails are battered and torn."

"What about the other ship, the Dolphin?" I asked.

Madoc frowned. "We can't see them through the downpour. We should have set up the communication devices to keep in contact with them."

"I hope they're all OK!" Morna grimaced.

"How are you faring?" Blane studied each of our faces.

"A few had a little seasickness, but Nissa found a remedy that brought relief," Gita said.

Just then the ship lurched and those of us who were standing began to fall. We reached out to steady ourselves and each other. But when everything was upright again, all motion didn't just slow, it stopped entirely.

I dared to look out the porthole. The sea was calm, the rain had stopped, and the wind had as well.

"What happened?" Carys reached my side.

"We've stopped moving," Col said.

I followed Madoc, Col, Blane and Kerr as they scrambled up the stairs to see what was happening, what the captain and the crew were doing. They seemed to be racing around but whether they were achieving anything I couldn't tell. The ship wasn't moving, not forward or backward, but also no longer sideways.

"Can we do anything to help?" Col asked Captain Felden.

"Do you know how to mend a sail?" the captain asked.

"I do," I said. Immediately Blane looked up at the rain-slicked masts. He picked the one with sails with the worst tears then began to climb. Astonished looks appeared on the faces of the captain, crew and our companions, but Blane had climbed masts before.

Before long he'd returned to the deck with a torn sail.

"I'll mend that one if you get the other." I bolted down the stairs and rummaged through my packs for needles and thread, then returned to work on the torn sail. Blane was already back with another one.

I mended one sail. But the second sail, although it had fewer tears, was more of a challenge. The rips were jagged and the edges fraying. I could fix it given enough time, but it might not be as good as new. "Can you use the sails from the broken mast?" I asked.

"That's an idea." The captain didn't say whether it was a good or bad one, but at least he considered it.

Two of the crew removed a sail from the piece of mast that had fallen on the deck.

"Repairing the sails won't be of any use if there's no wind," Col pointed out, but it didn't deter me.

"Oh, the wind will be back," the captain said. "But until it is, we're preparing the oars."

"It's unfortunate you can't bring forth the wind at will," Kerr told Madoc, grinning.

"Aye, that is unfortunate," Madoc replied with as big a grin.

A short, rotund man came up on deck at that moment. "Excuse me, Captain. Will you be wanting luncheon to be served anytime soon?"

I didn't think anyone in our party was in the mood to eat, but a few had stronger stomachs than mine. "I made some cold tea with herbs earlier but if you could brew us a large pot, I know our companions would appreciate it."

"It'll be my pleasure, mistress." He bowed.

"The crew could do with soup or stew," the captain told him. I was pleased he looked out for his men. "Their work isn't done this day, and they'll need something in their bellies afore they begin rowing."

The cook nodded. "I have a pot of soup cooking already."

The captain turned to two crewmen who were moving the broken piece of mast out of the way. "Duffy, Hastings, get below and change out of those wet clothes, then find Grant and Rusty. You four will man the oars."

"Aye, Captain," one of them said. They were young and strong, good choices to be oarsmen.

"I'll bring the cook those herbs for tea." I rushed for the stairs. Blane was already climbing one of the masts to reattach the sail I'd mended.

When I reached the room where my friends were, I found fewer people than before. "Where'd Morna go?" I asked.

"She and Gita went to see to the horses," Carys replied. "And Wim and Raj went with them."

That wasn't surprising. "I'm going to give the cook these herbs. He promised to make a pot of tea. If anyone is up to soup, he's preparing a pot for the crew."

"I'm not sure I'm ready for that yet," Donal said. "Any sign of the other ship?"

I nodded. "It's not far away. They're probably repairing the sails and preparing to row like the crew here."

"But you can't be sure they're all right," Gudrin said. She'd regained the color in her face.

"We can't be sure of anything at this point." I took the herbs and walked back to the door.

"I'll have soup," Carys said. "In fact, why don't I come with you." She couldn't resist seeing the galley.

It was larger than the one on the Flying Dragon, the first ship I'd sailed on. I was intimately acquainted with that galley because I'd had to prepare all of the crew's meals then. I didn't see any cookbooks, which surprised me.

"I've brought the herbs for the tea," I told the cook. "And my friend, Carys, is a cook herself. She wanted to see your galley."

The cook practically sneered.

Ignoring him, Carys asked, "What kind of recipes do you use?" She'd noticed the lack of books, too.

"Ones I've always used," he replied. "Ain't nothing to boiling up some meat and vegetables. When you need to have it go further, you can always add more water."

Carys had a knack for adding ingredients to soups and stews to improve the taste. Usually things most cooks never thought to use, like berries and herbs.

"May I have a taste of the soup you're making?" she asked.

"A few others in our group might want some, too," I added. I expected Wim would, and possibly my sister and Gita.

"I suppose since you be payin' customers, the captain would allow it." He found a pewter cup, a little larger than the mugs we generally used for coffee or tea, and put a ladleful of soup into it, then found some spoons. "How many more will you need?"

"Let's start with three," I said, deciding I wanted some, too.

"I'll stay here and talk to the cook," Carys said.

The cook frowned but his scowl was gone so I thought it safe to leave her with him. I took the three cups of soup back to the room. Morna and Gita had returned with the boy and dog. Their smiles indicated the horses had fared well. I handed Gita and Wim each a cup.

"The horses were happy to see us, especially since we each had carrots in our pouches for them," Morna reported. "How is it?" she asked Gita, who was eating her soup.

"A bit thin and not as flavorful as the soup Carys made day before yesterday," Gita said.

I gave my sister the last cup.

"We're still not moving, are we?" She took her first spoonful.

"The sails were damaged by the storm, but there's no wind, anyway. The captain has ordered crew members to take up the oars. They should start rowing before long." I'd spoken too soon, of course, as the ship chose that moment to lurch forward before smoothing.

Gita finished her soup. "Does anyone else feel well enough for any?"

Both Donal and Gudrin nodded, and Gita returned with me to the galley. Carys had convinced the cook to let her try to improve the soup by adding a bit of rice and some roots he was about to throw away.

"We need three more cups of soup," I told them. "But make sure to feed the crew first."

The cook lifted the entire pot and started for the stairs. "I'll be right back." He must have been stronger than he looked.

"I'll bring the cups," Gita volunteered, and we each gathered some, following him up on deck, and helping him dole out the crew's soup. The captain took some to the rowers, and Blane, Kerr, Col and Madoc took over with the oars as they ate. The comments from the crew varied from, "That hit the spot!" to "This is the best soup you've ever made!"

Once the crew was fed, and Blane, Kerr, Col and Madoc had their own cups, we filled some to take to our other companions. Carys finally took a cup for herself and gave me one. It turned out to be quite tasty, and I was sure Carys' additions made a difference. I wondered if Morna, Gita and Wim wanted another, better cup.

Before I descended the stairs, I looked out to the other ship. It seemed to be moving, too, although very slowly. How long would the trip take at this rate? Would we reach the shore before nightfall? It seemed unlikely. I hoped this was no indication of the complications we'd find throughout our journey, but no one could predict what we'd face.

CHAPTER FIVE

Once everyone who wanted it had soup, we returned to the galley for the soothing tea for those who still needed it.

The sun was setting when land appeared ahead. The wind had never returned. The efforts of the crew managed to bring us this close to shore. Another hour or two to reach Melsford, and disembarking by the light of the Evening Moon.

The ten aboard the Great White met in our room below decks to decide what we'd do once we were on dry land and met our companions on the Dolphin. We still didn't know the situation on the other ship, but assumed it was similar to this one.

"We can't travel much beyond Melsford tonight," Col said.

"Does anyone know the town?" I asked. "Will we find lodgings?"

"Captain Felden says it's smaller than Riesund." Madoc shrugged. "A farming community, with fewer shops and taverns. We should make camp just outside the town and make an early start in the morning."

After a while, a few of us returned to the deck, looking towards the old wooden buildings lining the street past the dock. We approached very slowly.

The other ship was even farther from shore. We stood on deck for over an hour. The captain no longer insisted we go below. Still another hour passed. Finally we neared the dock, lit by torches, but no people appeared. The moon was high in the sky, providing some light.

The crew brought the ship even closer to shore and dropped anchor. We returned below to let our friends know.

They were already prepared to leave. "We felt the ship dock." Morna looked around for anything she'd forgotten.

The captain and crew helped us bring our horses and wagons onto shore. We thanked them for bringing us safely to Leara. "We're happy to be back on dry land." I looked back out to the sea we'd just crossed, waiting for our friends to arrive.

Meanwhile, Captain Felden and his crew secured the ship and set off to find what taverns the town offered. After the day they'd had, they to drink some ale and relax. When they were gone, it was very quiet. The sea lapped against the pilings.

The Dolphin finally pulled into the other side of the dock from the Great White. We watched the passengers disembark. Eva and Baca appeared first, then the others slowly made their way up on deck and across the gangplank, leading their horses. We rushed forward to help them.

"Is everyone all right?" Gita asked.

"Aside from a few bruises, we're fine," Helga said. "We'll need help with the wagons."

It took a while to bring everything onto the dock. Those who'd traveled on the Dolphin agreed to camp on the outskirts of Melsford. It had been a difficult day for us all.

Judging by the darkness in the stores and houses, the town was mostly asleep as we rode through it. We reached the last buildings and found an empty field near the river to set up camp.

Blane and Kerr built a fire, and Carys quickly put together a delicious dinner for us all with help from Helga, while the rest of us fed the horses and set up our blankets. We sat around the fire as we ate, trading stories about our voyages.

Toren frowned. "I tried to use my mind to control the wind when it was at its most violent, but to no avail."

"I did the same," Madoc said. "It was too wild to harness its power. And then when it stopped, I couldn't stir up even a slight breeze."

Toren nodded. "I suppose our powers over the elements are limited."

Madoc laughed. "It has always been so."

"I wished the ship had an engine like the one you created for your father's ship," I told Madoc.

He described it to those who hadn't heard the story before. "It would have worked even better if I'd known to use crystals to power it."

Carys sat with her own food. "Perhaps Father will let us use the Queen Bronwyn to travel to Fartek."

"Or you can build another engine that uses crystals for whatever ship we voyage on," Donal said.

No one stayed up late that night, except for Baca, Donal, and Katya, who took the first watch. There were enough people in our party that the camp could be guarded each night with four teams of three without everyone having to take a turn every night.

When I woke with Madoc for the last watch in the morning, it was quiet. The Second Moon was sinking below the horizon. We were teamed with Blane and took over from Toren, Gudrin, and Kerr. The three of us sat for a short while around the low-burning fire talking quietly, but soon Blane rose to walk the perimeter. We didn't expect any trouble. Still, one never knew what dangers might be out there.

"I hope we're not camped on anyone's land," I said.

"There aren't any buildings or animals anywhere nearby." Madoc put his arm around me to pull me closer.

Blane returned. He didn't see or hear anything during his walk. Soon, the sun began its rise in the East. We heard our companions stirring and Blane added kindling to the fire so we could give them tea or coffee.

Carys was first to rise. "I'll start some porridge."

But our friends weren't the only ones making morning noises. A rooster crowed in the distance and some animals bayed. A man and a boy approached from the west, driving some cows in our direction. I watched them, hoping they wouldn't shoo us away before we'd had our breakfast.

"Who are you and what are you doing here?" the man asked in Learic, his tone even.

Madoc stood. "We arrived late last night from Solwintor and thought this to be common land where we might camp for the night."

"You don't look Solwinish," he said, then looked at the

others as they gathered near. "Well, some of you do."

"Some of us are from Holmdale in Arrandis," I said. "That's where we're heading."

"You're right, this is common land." The man nodded. "Many of us bring our herds here to graze and drink from the river."

The boy had been silent, but when he saw Wim and Raj, he smiled and tugged at the man's homespun shirt.

"We will eat our breakfast and be on our way," Col told them.

The boy whispered something to the man who nodded. Only then did the boy walk towards us and say to Wim, "Hello, I'm Dorin. Is that your dog?"

"Yes," Wim replied. "His name is Raj and I'm Wim. You can pet him, he won't bite."

Raj confirmed that by a single bark and then licked Dorin's outstretched hand.

"Would you like some milk? Or fresh eggs?" the man asked. "It won't take long to get them."

"That would be wonderful." Carys pointed to the pot she stirred. "I'm preparing porridge, but eggs would be so much better. Thank you very much!"

"A few of us can go with you." Morna likely wanted to see more farm animals.

"Thank you, Miss."

While we drank tea and Dorin ran about with Wim and Raj, Morna and Carys went with the farmer. When they returned, in addition to a large container of fresh milk and two dozen eggs, they were laden with cheese and pots of jam.

"Fenir says berry bushes grow along the river a gyrd from here," my sister reported. "You should have seen all the chickens and baby chicks!"

"How far is a gyrd?" Gudrin asked.

"Less than half a dulno," I replied, realizing we would have to get used to Learan measurements again, at least for a while.

"Four gyrds is equal to ten dulno." Donal always had to be exact.

"The road south runs sometimes very close to the river, and other times there are thick stands of trees between them," Carys said. "It should take us a day to reach Layton, where we can start east on the Merchant's Road toward Holm Manor."

We ate a filling and tasty breakfast and then prepared the horses and wagons for our journey. Reluctantly, Wim and Dorin bade each other farewell. They'd likely never see each other again, but stranger things had happened.

We put out our fire and cleaned up our camp, then waved to Dorin and Fenir and were on our way south.

CHAPTER SIX

It was a clear day, and we could see great distances. The flat land and the dirt road, well-worn by men, animals and wagons, made travel easy. Autumn was more evident here than in Solwintor. Leaves turning shades of gold and brown, with a few red ones thrown in for variety. I remembered the ones I embroidered on table linens at the Manor two years before.

We stopped to pick the berries Fenir had told us about. Wim ate more than he gathered, judging by his dark red lips, but they were very good, sweet and juicy. After three more hours of riding, we stopped again for luncheon. The cooks at the Stronghold had provisioned us well, but eighteen people and even more horses consumed a lot of food. We still had plenty of dried meat, carrots, bread, and cheese, as well as the cookies we all loved. And now lots of berries.

We washed our meal down with water from our flasks, then we fed the horses carrots and shared some apples with them, before continuing on. It had warmed considerably since the morning. The sun was high in the sky. We rode through a large grove of trees and the amount of birdsong increased, but so did the number of pesky insects.

All afternoon we rode. The path meandered first close to the river then farther away. The river became narrower the farther south we went. The water didn't appear deep, like the Tavy we'd have to cross after our stop in Holmdale. At some points you could easily walk across on stepping stones.

At times, Col or Wim let Raj down to run alongside the horses, but then one or the other would pick up the small dog, knowing he'd tire trying to keep up.

After the ordeal of our sea journey the day before, this ride was pleasant, but we'd soon tire ourselves spending so much time in the saddle. For some, the idea of this expedition must have seemed like a great adventure. Now they were finding the reality was a long, arduous journey, punctuated by real dangers, like the storm the day before.

I couldn't have picked better companions. None of them seemed faint-hearted, complaining about every discomfort. The one who surprised me most was Kerr. Before we left the Manor, I'd thought he'd be a burden, thrust on us by his father, the Duke, but after the first few days, he'd shown he could hold his own. Would his parents be as surprised by the changes in him as I?

When the sun began to set, pink and purple streaked the western sky, and we caught our first sight of Layton. I hadn't expected it to be as large as it was, a village that had grown up at the crossroads of the north-south path from Melsford with the Merchant's Road that ran east and west the entire width of Leara. We entered the town along one of the many criss-crossing streets.

We spread out as we rode, looking for a place to stable our horses while we located a restaurant or tavern for dinner. Most of the establishments were clustered around a large central square, a park with trees and benches and a small open building in the middle.

"It's called a gazebo," Madoc said when he saw me staring at it. "There are some in the parks in Fairhaven where musicians play at holidays."

I'd seen one or two when Blane and I walked through his home town to the Citadel where his family lived.

Donal, Ana and Dreas found a stable large enough for our animals. Once we knew they were being brushed, watered and fed, we walked along the streets, back to the square. We found a restaurant with an interesting menu posted near the door.

"Maybe the proprietor can point us to some place we can spend the night," Gita said. If not, we could always retrieve our horses and wagons and find another field outside of the town.

The waitresses stopped what they were doing when we walked in, but when we took seats on the benches on either side of a very long table, one of them approached. "We have roast lamb, fried fish and a fricassee tonight."

I didn't know what a fricassee was, and wondered about the posted listing. "The menu mentioned other offerings," I told the waitress.

"Oh, that," she said dismissively. "The cook makes what she likes. That list comes from the owner's imagination. So, what'll it be?"

"What's fricassee?" Morna asked.

The waitress chuckled. "It's a fancy name for chicken stew."

"I'll have the lamb." Col got us started, and the rest of us ordered, too.

The waitress left, but was back soon with pitchers of water and juice. She poured whichever we wanted into the glasses already on the table. Once more she left, and when she returned, she had three loaves of bread and knives to slice it.

We contented ourselves with the bread and our drinks until she and the other waitress brought out our dinners. "Is the owner here tonight?" Madoc asked before taking his first bite.

"I haven't seen him but he may show up later."

"Maybe you know of some place we can find lodgings." Toren stared intently at her.

"The tavern across the road has rooms, but I don't know whether they'd have enough for all of you."

A piece of bread was halfway to my mouth. "We're willing to split up, stay at more than one establishment."

"You can ask." She shrugged. "There are three taverns with rooms, and a small inn, but I wouldn't recommend the inn." She left to attend to other patrons, and we began our tasty and plentiful meals.

When we were mostly done, the waitress approached to offer dessert. We doubted we'd get anything as good as our Meecham cookies, or the gradglass we'd had a few times in Solwintor, but we asked her to bring us a variety of sweets.

She brought pies, pieces of cake, cookies with bits of nuts in them, and a pudding made with flavors I'd never tasted before. We shared them all around, as we'd often done at the Stronghold refectory.

Finally, Col and Madoc paid for everything we ate, and we set out to find beds for the night.

The best that could be said about the places we found was they were indoors. That became even more important when we heard rain, drumming on the sill of the window of our room as we drifted off to sleep.

When I woke in the morning I went to the window to see what the day would be like. The glass was so filthy I could barely see out, but it appeared to be a gray, overcast day. At least it had stopped raining.

I've never enjoyed riding in rain. But I decided to prepare myself for the eventuality. I'd made capes for many of our companions from the waterproof fabric I'd used for coveralls for those who'd dived to the bottom of Dulno Lake. When Morna saw me take mine out of my pack, she said, "Good idea!"

Once we'd dressed, we walked back to the restaurant where we'd eaten dinner to meet our companions. The eatery served breakfast and was a convenient place to find each other. The last to arrive were Eva, Ana, Helga and Gudrin. Almost everyone had thought to have their capes handy.

The breakfast was hot and included eggs, sausage, potatoes, coarse bread with butter and jam, and lots of tea and coffee.

Well-fed, we retrieved our horses and wagons and found our way to the Merchant's Road. None of us had ever been this far west on it before. We rode off toward the rising sun on a road that ran fairly straight and was wider than any we'd been on since we'd left home.

Traffic flowed in both directions, horses, carts, even people on foot. I wondered if folks were still flocking to Meecham, looking for the legendary Crimson Orb. I'd overheard some at the restaurant talking about it, but couldn't think of a way to tell them it wasn't where everyone thought.

We were on a quest of our own, not for the Orb, but part of what we were seeking was crystals like it to use to power the devices we'd created. The Orb was just one of the largest of them, crystals that had scattered across the land when the artificial satellites fell after the night of the two moons. They might be anywhere.

CHAPTER SEVEN

As we traveled the flat Merchant's Road, I pointed. "The distant hills might stop our wagons."

"I'll ride ahead and see what the road is like." Col urged his horse forward.

"I'll go with you." Donal galloped off with him.

Donal returned before Col. "The road goes over steep terrain, but we found a lower path between the hills that will be easier for the wagons. It's longer, yet would probably take the same time to traverse."

They led us to the path. It narrowed between the sheer stone walls so we rode two abreast, watching carefully for boulders in our way. The wagons squeezed through. The wheels on one side of the last wagon became stuck in a rut, and needed several people to free them. It took over an hour for all of us to reach the other side and flatter ground. By then, it was close to luncheon time.

A young man on a horse had followed us through the hills. He sped past the wagons and the rest of us to approach Col who led our party. "There's a meadow about half an hour from here where I often stop for a meal," he said.

"Thank you," Col replied. "Would you care to stop with us? We have plenty of food." That wasn't quite true, but we had enough.

I watched him warily for his answer.

He shook his head. "I'm in a hurry. I have messages to deliver to Duke Alec at Holm Manor."

I glanced at Col. "We're heading there as well. Perhaps you can tell the Duke that Master Madoc is returning with his party and eleven others. How far would you say it is to Holmdale?"

"From here? About ten thousand gyrds. If you stop for the night, you should reach it before midday tomorrow."

"Perhaps one of you from Holm Manor want to forewarn everyone there we're on our way," Col suggested.

"Aye," Kerr concurred. "I should go with him." I didn't think there would be any danger to him, but I sensed Madoc instruct him to call us with his mind if there was. Carys gave Kerr enough food for himself and the stranger, and the two rode on ahead.

Carys, Morna and I distributed smoked meat, bread and cheese to everyone. I sat beside Madoc with my food and my flask of water. "Maybe we should have gone with them," I said.

"Are you saying that because you're anxious to reach home, or because you're worried about Kerr?" He took a bite of his bread.

"Both, probably," I admitted. "Although I think he's learned to protect himself."

"We'll be there soon enough. Until then, we might be needed with this group."

I wondered why he thought so, but he must have had his reasons.

I finished my food, and then brought Gallin a carrot. He and the other horses seemed happy for the brief rest. Although we hadn't taken the more arduous path, they needed this stop, even more than we did.

After an hour we were on the road again. The rain that threatened earlier had never materialized, and the sun was high in the sky. I rolled up the sleeves of my blouse, pulling my hair up into a tail like Gallin's.

We stopped again at a brook. The horses whinnied in thanks for the opportunity to drink. We filled our flasks, took off our shoes and waded in the shallow water, then remounted to cross and moved on.

I was becoming more and more impatient. The trip was taking so longer with such a large entourage. I knew Kerr and the stranger would reach the Manor before night, while we wouldn't arrive until the next day.

The terrain changed as we rode into farm country. "Why are the fields plowed?" Gudrin asked.

"The farmers have already harvested their summer crops and turned the soil to prepare for planting winter ones," Madoc told her.

I'd forgotten what farmland of this kind was like. We hadn't seen anything similar in Solwintor, but it looked like the farms surrounding Holmdale. It made me more nostalgic for home.

We passed an orchard, the trees heavy with apples and burce, not the red fashar we'd had in Solwintor but real burce. I would have loved to stop and pick a few, even if we had to ask permission from the owner of this land, but then I remembered the Duke now had a burce tree in his orchard and we'd have some before long.

"What are those yellow fruits?" Gudrin asked. "They look like fashar but they're yellow."

I laughed. "I was just thinking about them. The first time I saw fashar I thought they were red burce!"

"Do they taste the same?" she asked.

"Similar," I said. "But under the yellow peel, burce are slightly sweeter and juicier."

"There are many things you'll eat at the Manor that you've never had before," Carys said. "Just as we had so many new things in Solwintor."

"What are those birds?" Gita pointed to several small birds, that appeared to be suspended in the air near a pink flowering shrub.

"They're hummingbirds," Morna said. "Their wings beat many times faster than any other birds and that keeps them hovering near plants with sweet nectar."

"They're beautiful!" Gita reined in her horse to watch them for a while.

"There are all sorts of birds at the Manor that I never saw in Solwintor," Morna told her.

"So many new things, and we've only begun our trip!" Gudrin said.

We stopped after another few hours for dinner, but then

continued on for a while before setting up camp for the night. The sky was clear so we didn't expect any rain, the Evening Moon shone brightly. Still, it was cool enough we needed our blankets to make up our beds.

Baca, Morna, Donal and Helga took the first watch. We were camped in a flat field and we could see far in every direction, although in the dark, who knew what might be out there.

Unlike Solwintor, where our expedition party to the lake had to fight off a group who wanted to use our crystals to build weapons instead of peaceful machines, I didn't think there was anyone in Leara who was trying to find and destroy us and our cargo. I went to sleep feeling secure, so when I heard the first shouts, both audible and in my head, I woke surprised.

They were birds, I thought, but bigger than any I knew, and they swooped down out of the sky, attacking us and our horses. I'd never seen anything like them before. The cries had come from Morna. I tried to touch her mind to tell her to aim a mind scream at the creatures, and I sensed when she took better control of her natural reaction to the creatures.

Raj barked, and everyone raced around, trying to avoid the attacks. Those of us who could focus our minds for defense were doing all we could to fight back. Others had drawn their swords and taken out crossbows. A dark form swooped towards me and I let loose a mind attack, forcing it to veer away.

A well-aimed arrow, possibly combined with a mind scream, took down one of the birds. But the others continued to dip and attack. As two were shot down, more appeared. The battle lasted only twenty or thirty minutes, but it seemed an eternity until the birds flew off.

"What were those things?" Dreas asked.

None of us knew. We'd brought three of the creatures down and could examine them. They looked like common sparrows, but were ten times the normal size, with sharper beaks and talon-like claws. I wondered if they were native to this part of the country and if they'd return.

"Is anyone hurt?" Helga, our healer immediately took out her bag of remedies, salves and bandages. Blane had a small puncture wound, and Ana had suffered several scratches. Helga tended to them as we examined our horses for any damage, finding none.

We were too awake to go back to sleep, so Carys started a pot of water to boil and took out some fruit and cookies. Wim sat very close to Gita, and she put an arm around his slim shoulders. Raj licked his face. The dog always knew when Wim or anyone else needed him. I wondered anew how intelligent he was.

No one said anything more until we each had a cup of tea in our hands. "Did you sense those things coming before they arrived?" Madoc asked Morna. "Your warning shout woke everyone."

"I...I sensed something, but I didn't know what until I saw them." She had a blanket around her but she still shivered. "I never want to see any of those things again!"

"You did very well fighting them off." I put my hand on her shoulder.

"I'd heard about what you did, but never saw it before," Gita said. "How do you do it?"

Madoc explained, starting with how he'd first taught us to use our minds, and how that ability eventually grew into what we could now do. He glossed over the first time I'd used a mind scream to fight off Toren's unwanted advances. Madoc took my hand as he went on, and some of the tension melted away. "We defeated Brun's forces and the marauders with a combination of mind screams and superior swordsmanship."

"You said this land is similar to your own, yet you've never seen these birds?" Baca asked. He sat close to Morna, occasionally casting an admiring look at her, whereas Dreas, her other suitor seemed put off by the recent demonstration of her abilities.

Madoc paused before he spoke. "Clearly something different has happened here, some source of energy that doesn't exist elsewhere."

"Why do you say that?" Col asked.

"Remember the fish at the bottom of Dulno Lake? They were similar to fish we know, but many times larger, and we surmised exposure to the energies from the satellite caused them to grow."

"Just as something in the surface water made the deer who drank from the lake strong enough to carry the Pellbers on their backs." Donal nodded in understanding.

"Exactly. I think whatever the wellspring is here, it even intensified our abilities," Madoc added.

"Or maybe that was from the energies coming from the crystals and satellite parts in our wagons," Donal suggested.

"You have a point." I felt Madoc's mind reaching out to locate the sources of energy around us. I'd learned to use those sources, but wasn't as adept at locating the strongest and differentiate it from any others nearby. He shook his head. "I can't pinpoint it."

We talked more about the energies around us, in all living and nonliving things, and about the crystals used to power machines by focusing those energies, just as our minds focused them to our will.

"So you're saying the mind can act like a crystal," Gudrin said.

"Yes," Madoc said. "Or maybe crystals act like our minds, except they don't have the will to direct the energies they focus, and need man to do that."

CHAPTER EIGHT

Gradually, everyone relaxed again. Eyes drooped from staring at the flickering flames and listening to soft voices. When Wim's eyes closed, Gita carried the boy back to his blankets and then laid down, a protective arm around him. Col soon joined his wife and adopted son, as others said, 'G'night', and wandered off to their own blankets.

Toren, Mai, Dreas and Eva took over the watch as everyone else went to sleep. There were no further attacks that night. I slept until first light.

When I woke, Carys and Blane were already preparing our breakfast. "I hope today's journey will be uneventful," Blane said as I joined them.

Carys toasted slices of bread with thick slices of cheese between each two. Everyone seemed ravenous that morning, and she had just enough bread and cheese for us all.

I prepared Gallin for the day's ride and asked him what he thought of the goings on the night before. He snorted. I was unsure how to interpret that. We rode out two and three abreast hoping to reach the Manor before nightfall. My heart felt lighter.

Were they already preparing for our arrival after Kerr told them we would soon be there? My parents would be as eager to see us again as we were to see them.

The gigantic birds didn't reappear as we continued through farm fields, past cows and occasional trees. The scenery became boring after a while, but our first glimpse of Holmdale filled me with a mixture of happiness and anticipation, just as when we'd returned from our journey to rescue Madoc.

The townspeople stopped what they were doing as we passed. I waved to some and they waved as if they recognized me and the others from Holm Manor. Somehow, everything seemed...smaller than I remembered.

The postern to the Manor was open and several people waited to welcome us back, including my parents. I grinned seeing Father's blond head and Mother's bright red tresses. They accompanied us to the nearby stables, where we dismounted and left the wagons. Then we introduced our new friends to our family and old friends.

My Mother's arms enveloped me. She didn't let go until her gaze found Morna, then she rushed to embrace her, too. We walked together to the one-story stone Manor house, and I was overwhelmed by the sense of coming back to the only home I'd known until a few months earlier.

The ancient building was huge with plenty of rooms and beds for everyone. The members of our party were assigned rooms throughout the maze and told to come to the dining hall once they'd freshened up. Mother let Morna and me take our packs to our room, which hadn't changed since we left. And why should it? Our two beds were neatly made and the floor swept.

Morna and I washed and changed from our dusty riding clothes then went to the hall.

"This place is just as you described!" Gudrin joined us on the way. "Old-fashioned and drafty, the wood and stone walls worn by time."

My parents waited for us, along with the residents of the Manor who could get away from their duties. It looked as if Cook and her staff had worked through the night to prepare for us. The tables along the side of the room were laden with roast chicken and beef, vegetables, stew and soups, rolls, fruit, and cookies. The aromas mingled tantalizingly. But I was too excited to even think of eating.

"Kerr told the Duke and Duchess a little about what you've been doing," Father said as I sat with my family and friends at one of the dining tables. "But none of us really understood everything he said."

All of us talked at once, telling him, Mother and anyone else nearby about our experiences and what we'd learned. It's a wonder they made sense of any of it, because we burst with things to say, details and the bigger picture, descriptions and impressions. Eventually, Father held up a hand to stop us. "Why don't I ask a few questions and you can take turns answering me."

His questions ranged from how we found the Stronghold to how Blane learned to swim and dive. Then Mother asked about the medicines and plants they used at the Stronghold. Helga, as healer, and Gudrin, as plant expert, answered.

I knew my friend, Glynis was watching me. I thought she wanted to ask me about my relationship with Madoc, but waited patiently for a more private moment, and I appreciated that.

"We'll hold the rest of our questions for a while," Mother said after we'd answered many. "You must all be very hungry, and the food will go cold if we don't eat it soon."

I walked with her to the trestle tables. She handed me a plate and took one for herself. "You all look well. I don't think I've ever seen Morna so happy. Even Kerr seems to have changed for the better."

I nodded. "When he arrived from the factory, we were all surprised at the changes in him. He and Donal have formed a good friendship."

"And these friends of yours, they're not all from Solwintor, are they?"

"Not originally. Col and Gita, for instance, are from Standia. And Katya, her parents and sister, who are back at the Stronghold, are from Rinaga, but they've lived at the Stronghold for quite some time." I was happy to see the vegetable stew I liked and added it to my plate.

"So what did you do while you were there?" Mother ladled stew herself.

"Don't laugh. I was assigned to the sewing rooms." I watched her face, not sure how she'd react.

"You?" Despite my admonition, she chuckled.

"But your daughter didn't just sew." Mai stood next to us. "She showed us we didn't have to accept the shapeless uniforms we wore. Before she left, she'd altered the coveralls for several women, and was beginning to add pockets and change the color."

"They were a ghastly green," I said.

"And she constructed the suits for the divers who retrieved the satellite from Dulno Lake."

"Honestly, Mai, I only did as I was told." I had filled my plate and there were still things I wanted to add.

Mother glanced at my pile of food. "It looks like you haven't eaten in weeks!"

"Oh, believe me. We ate well, even on this trip from Solwintor. Carys taught the cooks at the Stronghold how to make this stew, so I've had it recently. Even at the Stronghold it reminded me of home."

"Well, now you're here."

"But you realize it's not for long. We'll leave in a few days for the coast, and thence to the East Islands and points even farther east."

Mother frowned. "Do you all have to go? Can't you stay and send the others on?"

I smiled at her and sighed. "You know I can't do that. I have to see this expedition to it's conclusion." I set my plate down and placed a hand on her shoulder. "I have to go where Madoc goes. I have skills you still don't know about that we learned from Madoc over the years, skills my companions need."

She raised her eyebrows. "I knew I couldn't dissuade you, but I had to try. You don't know how much I missed all of my children these last two months."

"We missed you, too. You should have heard me complaining about wanting to come home and see you and Father," I told her. "I think my friends tired of hearing me talk about the Manor, and going home."

"Nissa, this is still your home, you know."

"Of course," I said, a little too quickly.

"But I can see you'll never be content here in the future. You've seen too much of the world outside the confines of this place."

"I've considered that. But who knows what might happen during this journey. I may find coming back here and staying is just what I'll need."

We returned to the table and several different conversations going on at once.

"You'll be stopping in the East Islands to see the King and Queen, won't you?" Mother asked.

"Yes. As much as we wanted to return here, Carys wanted to see her parents." I noticed the puzzled expression on Mai's face. Many still didn't know Carys and Madoc were royalty. They'd been surprised Kerr was the Duke's son, so I could imagine how they'd react to the news. We'd tell them before we reached the Citadel. "She and Madoc think their father would be willing to provide a ship to take us to Fartek, perhaps the one powered by the engine Madoc built."

"But why do you wish to go to Fartek? What's there?"

"We told you about the satellite. Much of it came from Fartek originally and we believe Madoc's books did too."

"Ah, the famous books. So you know what they are, what the language is?" she asked.

"The language is Fartekana, and they're two of many books preserved after the Night of the Two Moons."

"That's the part I don't understand. Well, one of the parts. You told us what happened a thousand years ago, and the Second Moon was made by man." She still sounded as if she didn't believe everything we'd said.

So I explained again what we learned at the factory about the consequences of the launching. I'd never thought I could astonish my mother the way I did, but I remembered how I felt when I first heard all this.

"Now can you understand why we have to go to Fartek? We have to learn what civilization and technology still exists there, and find ways to reconnect with the people."

"Yes, I can understand." She looked at her hands.

I smiled at her. "But I intend to make the best of the time we're here!"

"And I'm looking forward to spending time with you and getting to know your new friends." She looked down the table to where Morna sat, with Dreas on one side, still looking a bit wary of her, and Baca on the other, totally in awe. "Your sister seems to have picked up a couple of admirers."

I grinned. "Yes, she has, and she hasn't decided which she likes better."

"And you and Madoc?"

I wasn't sure what she wanted me to tell her, "We still love each other, although we haven't had much time alone. We met every day during the afternoon break, but instead of talking about our feelings, we talked about everything that was going on, and what was worrying me that day."

She smiled at me. "You do have a tendency to fret and complain. I think you got that trait from my mother."

"Gran?" The thought I was like my grandmother in any way pleased me. "We'd hoped to see her again on our way back, but we came a different route and weren't anywhere near Dunswell."

Mother nodded. "She was here ten days ago, worried about the lot of you. And like you, she worries about something until she comes up with a way to resolve the problem or change things to better suit her."

"Oh! What did she do?"

"She sent inquiries to friends in other parts of Arrandis. Some of those she asked about your whereabouts hadn't replied yet, and that's why she made the journey here. We'll have to send word you're safely home, although I'm not sure I want to tell her you're going on another perilous venture."

I leaned back, finished with my huge helpings. So had many of the others. Gudrin and Helga came over together to talk to Mother about healing and plants.

"I'd love to show you my workroom,"Mother offered.

I felt so comfortable and safe here at the Manor. It might be the last time I'd feel that way for a long time. I looked across the table and caught Madoc's eyes. He smiled at me, but continued to talk to my father.

Mother was right. I wouldn't be content to remain here, not after all I'd seen and heard. I couldn't begin to predict what new experiences were in store for me. But I was happy to spend a little time here again.

CHAPTER NINE

Before I left the dining hall, Glynis stopped me. "It is so good to see you!" She hugged me. She'd been my dearest friend since we were children. "We really have to catch up! What's happened to you over the past two months? I do want to hear about you and Madoc!"

She'd realized we had a relationship on the night of her wedding, but the next morning she left for her wedding trip with Adair, and we'd never had a chance to talk.

"Let's go up on the hill so we can speak without being disturbed."

As children we'd climb the hill overlooking the Manor to share secrets. Now, on this cool and crisp autumn day, we walked up there once more. We found a spot near the top and sat, our knees pulled up in front of us.

"So, how does it feel to be an old married woman?" I asked to forestall her curious questions.

She chuckled. "It feels wonderful! Adair is the sweetest, kindest husband. And also quite sexy!"

"Glynis!" But I wasn't as shocked as I sounded. "How was your trip, and I mean the days as well as the nights?"

"We had to have luncheon with King Niall and Queen Isla. Boring!"

"Yes, Carys said the same when she and Gareth lunched with them on the way home from Meecham. But you did your duty, I'm sure."

"Oh yes. And the rest of the days we spent in the marketplace and seeing the sights of Arris. Of course, the nights, well, I won't go into detail, but they were quite pleasurable!"

I grinned at her. "So, you're enjoying that aspect of married life." I was jealous, in a way, because Madoc and I had never been intimate. I wondered if we ever would.

"Nissa, it's glorious!"

"I'll take your word for it!"

"So, no more stalling. What's happened between you and our resident wizard?"

"Well, I've been in love with him for quite some time..."

"Only since he arrived here ten years ago!"

"After we rescued him in Meecham and while we traveled home, I learned he loved me too." I thought about some of the things he'd said and how they made me feel. "During all of our journeys, we sat together during the night, just holding each other and occasionally kissing. The closeness felt wonderful, but I've only imagined how it would be if we..." I couldn't go on, couldn't voice my innermost desires, not even to Glynis.

"Nissa, it'll happen. And I think you'll love him even more once it does."

"I...I hope so."

She looked away, out over the fields, her voice softening. "You know, with all your new friends and experiences, I thought, well, I worried you'd forget about me."

"What? No, never! Glynis, you're my oldest, dearest friend. We've had so many shared experiences." I chuckled. "Remember the time we hid Cook's wooden spoons and only returned them when she couldn't make our favorite stew? But now we're grown, we no longer have to do everything together. We'd be clinging to our childhood and I surely don't want to do that."

"No," she concurred. "But I'm afraid we'll never share anything again. Not ever! And you'll find me dreadfully boring."

"Oh!" I hadn't thought about it. At that moment though, I realized there had to be a way to maintain the connection we shared. "Glynis, I never told you much about my lessons with Madoc, the way he taught me to use my mind to capture the energies around us and then focus them to help us do things."

"Like he taught the boys," she said with a nod. "Adair told me something about that. He was disappointed he never mastered the lessons the way your brothers did."

"We've also learned how to reach out our minds to each other, a way to communicate, even over long distances. It's better than the devices they've built. If you could learn to do that, we can 'talk' even when we're far apart!"

It was her turn to say, "Oh!" She was silent for a while, twisting a blade of grass in her hands. "You've changed," she finally said. "Not in a bad way, but you're not the same person who left here. The others have, too. I really don't know what you've done with Kerr, and I don't just mean the beard and mustache."

We both laughed. "There are so many new things we learned, about ourselves, our abilities, and the world we live in. It's much larger than I ever imagined. You've seen the people with us. They're all so different, and come from different places, but they want the same things."

"You make me want to go with you to this Fartek," Glynis told me. "Adair, too, of course. I wouldn't go without him. But..."

"Oh, Glynis, wouldn't that be wonderful?"

"Except the Duke won't let Adair go, not since Kerr is already going."

"If we could devise a reason you and Adair have to go, perhaps Col and Madoc could convince the Duke to allow you to come with us!" I suggested.

"Well, I won't get my hopes up. And meanwhile, why don't you show me how to use my mind."

I worked with Glynis for a little while. She was a quick student. I wasn't surprised since I'd seen how quickly she'd learned all her life. By the time we headed back to the Manor, she could do some simple things and, when I let her, to touch my mind, but her thoughts still didn't come through very clearly.

I'd forgotten certain things about the Manor, but they came back quickly as the day progressed. Like the black cats that were so prevalent. A few used to climb into my lap when I sat on a bench, watching the boys practice swordsmanship. Or the way the shadow of the Manor grew across the eastern fields as the sun set. Or the ringing of the chimes signaling the hour, time for breakfast, luncheon and dinner, time for lessons.

I was thinking about what I'd proposed to Glynis when Madoc called to me. "Nissa, I want you to come with me and Kerr when we show some devices to Duke Alec."

"Donal might like to be included, too," I said.

"Yes, he's helping Kerr unload them from the wagons." Madoc took my hand and we walked together to the Duke's chambers.

He had a room he called his office. It was where he kept the Manor's records and where he held meetings with visiting dignitaries. I'd never been there before. Heavy drapes flanked the three tall windows along one wall and floor-to-ceiling shelves lined the opposite one. The remaining walls held doors and were paneled with fine wood, covered with portraits of the Duke's parents and grandparents.

Kerr and Donal arrived soon after we did, carrying three devices, ones they'd carefully selected because the Duke might find them useful, and they were easily explained: the imaging device we'd shown the people in Reisund, the communication device, and a light smaller, but brighter, than any torch.

"Father, this is the first thing I worked on," Kerr said proudly. He explained how the image was captured and then reproduced on special paper. Then Madoc demonstrated it by taking a picture of Kerr and the Duke.

"If we'd had devices like this when your parents were alive, we could have even more lifelike images of them than the ones on these walls," Madoc pointed out.

The Duke seemed impressed, but not enough to want to try using the device himself. He didn't understand the need for the communication device, even when Kerr told him it could be used by our group to keep in touch with the Manor.

On the other hand, he wanted to know whether we could leave some of the lights at the Manor. Could I use that request to bargain with him to allow Adair and Glynis to come with us? I hadn't talked to Madoc and Col about it yet, so I didn't say anything.

We left the Duke feeling as if we had been at least partially successful. "We'll take everything back to the wagons," Donal offered.

He and Kerr headed to the shed where we'd left them, and

Madoc and I continued on.

"Madoc, I was talking to Glynis earlier, and..."

"And she wants to join the expedition."

"How did you know?"

He chuckled. "Glynis has always admired you. She's her own person, but she also wishes she could do some of what you can."

"She's afraid the Duke won't let Adair go."

"You're assuming Col will approve adding them to the expedition."

"Well...yes! He wouldn't keep them from coming, would he?" I put a hand on Madoc's sleeve.

"Probably not. So you want help in convincing the Duke."

"Maybe if we left him the lights he wants..."

"What did you tell Glynis?" Madoc asked.

"Well, first, that we should convince the Duke they'd be invaluable to the mission. And then, if he still refuses, that she and I could stay in contact with our minds."

"But she doesn't know how..." he stopped. "You already started showing her, didn't you?"

I pressed my lips together and nodded, then looked down, hoping he wasn't angry.

He just rubbed his forehead and breathed deeply. "Well, no harm that, I suppose. Yes, it would be a solution that wouldn't require cooperation by the Duke."

"He's not completely unreasonable," I said, then thought about his response to the machines, and some of the times Madoc or my father had to find ways around his prohibitions. "Not always," I finished lamely.

Madoc chuckled. "I'd forgotten how he's always thwarted our plans."

I shrugged. "He's set in his ways. Maybe he's afraid if things change too much, he'll lose his position."

"You may be right." The chime for dinner sounded. "Let's go eat, and then we'll talk to Col. Will Glynis talk this over with Adair?"

"Yes." I walked toward the dining hall with him. "I think he'll want to go."

He kissed my forehead before we walked into the dining

hall and took seats side-by-side at the table.

It was nice to be served dinner, for a change. Of course, we'd been at the restaurant in Reisund, but at the Stronghold and for breakfast and luncheon here at the Manor, we selected our food from the side tables. Dinner at the Manor was different. Cook and her staff served us whatever roasts and stews she'd made that day, putting plates piled high with food in front of everyone.

I wasn't too surprised to see Carys helping Cook. I'd expected she'd find her way to the kitchens. So I wasn't shocked either to find a stew on my plate I'd last eaten in the refectory at the Stronghold.

My mother, sitting across the table from me, asked about the ingredients, and Carys obligingly told her. "Very tasty!" Mother took another forkful.

That afternoon Father had taken Blane and the other defenders in our entourage out to the practice field. He said he was impressed with the skills Holt and Eva displayed. I wondered if Adair had gone with them. If so, it would be easier for Glynis to convince him to ask to join the expedition.

Morna had taken Gita, Wim and Raj to see the newest animals in their pens. The colt that had been born just weeks before we left the Manor was now much larger and stronger. The spring lambs and piglets had grown too.

Gudrin and Helga had seen my mother's workshop, but also the flower gardens, tended by Glynis' mother. Neither could stop talking about both. "I'll take them out to the place where I gather my wild herbs tomorrow morning," Mother said.

After dinner, Madoc went off with Col, and Toren to discuss our departure, and what they might ask of the Duke for our journey. I hoped they would be willing to add Glynis and Adair to the party, even though it was already so large to be unwieldy.

CHAPTER TEN

It felt good to sleep in my own bed that night, not that the beds at the Stronghold were bad. But the room Morna and I had shared since we were little was a sanctuary for us.

I woke feeling refreshed and ready for a new day. My bare feet touched the floor, reminding me with a shock how cold it could be in the autumn mornings. I reached for foot coverings in my nightstand drawer and drew them on before pulling on a robe and walking to the nearby bathing room.

I'd also forgotten that the Manor wasn't equipped with the kinds of pumps I'd used in my travels, pumps that brought warm, even hot water, whenever it was needed. The water in the basins from the night before was cold and so was the water someone had brought in a huge pot for the morning. I lit the fire in the corner stove and put the smaller pot on it.

Once I'd washed, I returned to my room and dressed in one of my long, heavy skirts and a blouse. Morna was waking and I left her, easling a cloak around my shoulders to ward off the chill in the drafty corridors.

A few others were entering the dining hall when I arrived, but many fewer than the night before. I expected they all wanted to sleep a little longer in the comfortable beds they'd been given after our busy day. I filled a plate and took a seat next to Madoc, who was always an early riser.

"So, what did Col say?" I knew whatever our leader

decided, Toren wouldn't argue against it.

"He wasn't totally opposed to adding two more to our group," Madoc replied, knowing exactly what I was asking.

"So now all we have to do is convince Duke Alec."

"If Adair even wants to come," he cautioned.

"If, as I suspect, he was out on the practice field with Father, Blane and the other defenders yesterday, I think it's highly probable."

"We can always use more people who are good with a sword."

I nodded. "So, what else have you decided? When will we depart?"

"Are you ready to leave?" One eyebrow went up.

"Well, no, but I'd like to know how much time we'll have here." I bit into a piece of grainy bread with cheese smeared on it.

"Toren was pushing for tomorrow, but we finally agreed on the next day. We need to ensure we have enough food to keep us until we reach East Harbor. And two of the horses need to be re-shod," he added.

"Mother will supply Helga with salves and remedies. She was taking her into the fields today to gather herbs so they could brew them. Do you think Glynis' parents will object if she and Adair want to go with us?" I knew how my parents felt about us all leaving again, and imagined that Adith and Gewain would feel the same way about their only daughter.

By the time we'd finished our food, our table had filled. Morna finally arrived, along with her two suitors. Neither one, it would seem, wanted the other to get the upper hand with her.

"Well, I promised to show Toren my library, such as it is." Madoc rose to take his leave.

"I thought I'd wander down to the sewing room to show Jannet what I've been doing with the skills she taught us." I chuckled.

"I'm sure she'll be utterly astonished!" He kissed my cheek and then looked around for the other mage in our group while I took the familiar corridor to Jannet's domain.

It seemed strange to find the class going on without me and Morna. We'd been part of it for so long. The girls and young women were working on winter projects, quilts that would be filled with feathers.

"Narissa, you're back." Jannet stood from her high stool and walked towards me.

"I'm sure you've heard we won't stay long, but I wanted to come and tell you that I've been using the skills you taught me." I knew she'd long lamented my lack of ability as a seamstress, until I began direct the energies to improve the motions of my hands. "In the place we've been, I was assigned to the construction of garments for everyone who worked there, and was then asked to make clothing that divers used to explore the bottom of a very deep lake."

She stared at me. "So my efforts with you weren't wasted after all."

"No they were not. I even learned to alter clothing to fit the wearer, and to make practical additions, such as pockets." I wasn't certain she believed me, but I'd said what I'd come to say and turned to go.

"I'm proud of you, Nissa," she said. I never thought I'd hear those words from her, just as I expected she never thought she'd say them.

I turned, smiled at her and said, "Thank you," and walked away.

I wasn't sure where I should go. It seemed that everyone was busy. But the decision was made for me when Mai called my name. Katya was with her.

"Good morning," I said. "Are you finding your way around the Manor all right?"

"Oh, yes," Mai said. "Everyone we've met has been very friendly and helpful."

"We hoped to find a classroom or somewhere to begin teaching a little Ministic," Katya said. Mai's native language was one of the five or six Ministic languages. Based on documents in the satellite we retrieved, the two of them had confirmed that Fartekana, the language used in Fartek the last anyone knew, was similar. It sounded like a few Ministic languages, even though it was written using a completely different set of characters. And none of the languages were written like Learic or Solwinish.

"Katya and I are willing to do all the talking when we reach Fartek, but we both think there should be others who understand at least a little of the language," Mai said.

"You want to start the lessons before we leave the Manor?" I was surprised.

"The sooner the better," Katya said.

I thought for a minute. "There's a room where we had some of our geography lessons when I was a kid," I said. Thinking about those lessons, I realized how limited they were. There was so much of the world that wasn't included, and the maps we had were not very accurate. After we returned here, someone would have to write a new geography book for the children of Arrandis. "It's this way." I led them down a corridor that ran between the sewing room I'd just left and the kitchens.

"This is perfect!" Mai stated when she saw the room. There was a board at the front and sticks to write on it, several chairs facing it, and a table on one side.

"Who did you think would make the best students?" I had my own ideas, but I was curious what they thought.

"Col is fluent in many languages," Mai said. "But he's busy planning what we'll do next. I'll leave it up to him whether he wants to be included. I think Ana would be good, and possibly Baca."

"Baca?" I hadn't thought of him. He was a carpenter, and he came from an island so he was good with boats and swimming. My sister knew him better than I did, but I'd never learned anything that might suggest to me that he'd be good with languages.

"And you, of course," she added.

"Me?"

"But of course! Nissa, you picked up Solwinish quickly."

"So did my brothers, Morna and Carys. Even Kerr did. It's not that different from Learic."

"Well, who would you suggest?" Katya asked.

"How about Gudrin?"

Katya nodded. "Yes, she's a possible."

"And, well, maybe my friend Glynis?"

"Glynis?" Mai asked.

"That's Nissa's friend, the blonde who's married to Kerr's younger brother," Katya explained. "But she's not part of the expeditionary force!"

"Well..."

"Nissa, what do you know?" Katya asked.

"Glynis wants to come with us, and I think Adair does too."

Katya and Mai exchanged surprised looks, then both glanced back at me and Mai said, "I have no objection to including her."

"I understand we'll be leaving the day after tomorrow, so we should start this afternoon," I said.

"I'll go find our students," Katya offered but turned to me. "Perhaps you should tell Glynis about this, and see whether she's willing."

I nodded my agreement and went looking for Glynis. She hadn't been in the sewing room. Presumably, now that she was married, she no longer had to participate. I found her with her mother in the gardens, gathering autumn flowers for the dinner tables.

"Mai and Katya are starting lessons in Fartekana, the language of the land where we're going, and I thought you might be interested." I didn't know how much she'd told Adith about her wishes to join us.

"Oh! How interesting!" she said. "Mother, would you mind if I went with Nissa?" she asked.

"No, dear. Go ahead. I can manage the rest myself."

As we walked back inside she said, "Thank you for not saying anything in front of my mother. I haven't thought about how to tell her, especially since it's still so uncertain."

"Col has giving his approval, or rather, hasn't disapproved. Have you talked to Adair?"

She beamed. "He wants to go as much as I do."

"I'm not surprised." I led her down the corridor saying, "They're using the old geography classroom."

She chuckled. "And how wrong was our teacher about other lands?"

"Very wrong!" I chuckled myself.

Katya had already returned with Gudrin and Baca. Dreas was also with them. I would have thought he'd take the opportunity, with Baca occupied, to monopolize my sister's time. Perhaps he thought that learning Fartekana would give Baca an advantage. When she saw me, Katya said, "Col says he also wants to learn the language but right now isn't the best time. He did suggest we try to teach Wim and he was going to send the boy along as soon as he could find him!"

"He's probably out in the stables with Morna," I said.

But just then, Wim came skipping in with Raj right behind him.

We all took seats except for Mai who began by reviewing what we all already knew, that Fartekana sounded like the Ministic languages. "We won't be working on the written language, at least not yet. But if you can learn to say a few words and understand when someone is talking to you, it will help us communicate with the people we'll meet."

Most of the words they were able to decipher had to do with the machines. So we learned that *anu* was a push button, *bowpan* was a dial, and *bazi* a handle. "Since so many of the words sound like my language, Miranese, I'll teach you some common words in that language," Mai went on. "'Hello' is *wa* and 'how are you' is *niho*." She had us practice all the strange sounding words until she was satisfied we were saying them correctly.

"How do you say 'friend'?" Wim asked.

Mai smiled at him. "That is *pengu*."

He repeated the word several times, liking the sound of it.

"Since I don't know what we'll find in Fartek, it will be important to be able to ask what they call anything we'll see. A useful phrase is *shen meshi nige*, which means 'what is that one'."

We spent about an hour on our lessons. I hoped I'd remember all of the vocabulary I'd learned. Mai told us she'd want to spend time with us again later that day and twice the next so we'd have a good start before we left the Manor. I hoped our efforts wouldn't be wasted, and that they still used the same language in Fartek.

CHAPTER ELEVEN

We walked together from the classroom to the dining hall, talking about the lesson. When we arrived, my gaze sought Madoc. He stood with Blane at a trestle table along the wall, so I picked up a plate and joined them. They'd finished whatever they'd been discussing, and were starting to select their food.

"So, what did you do this morning?" Madoc asked me.

"I'm learning Fartekana and some Miranese as well," I said proudly. "Mai and Katya are holding a class."

"Good idea." He followed me along the table. "And who else are they teaching?"

"Gudrin, Baca, Dreas and Wim. And Glynis."

"Why am I not surprised?" He grinned.

"How did the planning meeting go? What were you and my brother discussing?" My focus swiveled to Blane.

"You think the two are related?" Madoc asked.

"Well, aren't they?" I put two slices of cheese on my plate.

He chuckled. "Yes. With such a large entourage, we might want to send a smaller group ahead to make arrangements."

"Oh, that's a good idea!"

"Yes, we do have them, sometimes." His eyes flashed, and the corners of his lips turned up.

"I didn't mean that!" We both laughed. "So you want Blane to be involved in the scouting party?"

"I like that term for it," Madoc said. "Yes, we do. We'll

send three or four others with him, including Toren."

I nodded. "And Carys won't let Blane go without her."

"She might have to."

I looked at him thoughtfully. "Why?"

He didn't answer at first. "Your brother needs to focus on learning all he can about what we might encounter, and then communicate back to us."

I stopped filling my plate. "With his mind or with the communication device?"

"Both, I think."

"You must realize he'll be able to concentrate better if he knows what's happening with Carys, and the only way he can be sure, is if she's with him." I decided I'd taken enough food and started for the table where our friends sat.

"Aye, that's true," he conceded as he followed me.

"So, who else will go with them?"

"Hasn't been decided yet. Who would you pick?" he asked as if he really wanted my opinion.

"How about Donal, or maybe Kerr?" I suggested. There were many reasons why the others should stay with the main party, but I thought Blane's group might need someone who knew how the device worked. "And, mmm, what about Ana?"

"Good choices. We'd have to ask if they're willing, of course."

"Of course!" I thought about the road between Holmdale and East Harbor. It wasn't an easy or short trip, but it also wasn't particularly hazardous. "What kinds of dangers do you expect them to face?"

"Unless things have changed drastically, there aren't many. But one or two people can easily find shelter in places where eighteen or twenty would find difficulty."

Twenty would include Glynis and Adair.

"Yes, I can see that. There's no way the Oaken Bucket could accommodate all of us." I pictured the rough tavern. "Not with people still flocking south from there to Meecham."

Madoc nodded. "I'm also concerned about getting the wagons across the River Tavy."

"Perhaps the advanced party can build a bridge," I teased. "Oh, I know it would take too long, but it would be nice. What else did you talk about with Col and Toren?"

"Only that we can't stay here beyond the day after tomorrow," he replied. "Once winter starts, the weather will deteriorate and there's no telling how that will affect our travel."

Storms at sea would probably be even worse than the one we faced crossing from Solwintor to Leara, although some of the ships' captains knew ways around them. "Perhaps we can find a ship that has plied the waters of the sea past the East Islands. The crew of the Flying Dragon implied they voyaged widely, so they might know the waters well."

"I'm hoping to find a ship like that," Madoc said. "I doubt that Captain Trahern and the Queen Bronwyn have ventured far."

"Have you given any further thought to constructing an engine using crystals for power?"

"It comes up in all our discussions." He sighed. "Let's eat and find out what everyone else has done this morning."

We took set our loaded plates on the table where Gudrin and Glynis were telling Kerr and Adair about the language lessons.

"Madoc, I've heard we're sending an advance party to ride ahead," Kerr said. "Who's going?"

"Are you volunteering?" Madoc countered.

"I suppose. It might be better than plodding along with the rest of the party."

Just then Blane and Carys joined us. "I'm going with Blane," she said in that 'don't argue with me' tone she rarely uses. But when she does, we let Princess Carys get her way.

"I guess that's four, then, with Toren," Madoc said.

"Did you want us to wait until the rest of you leave, or go tomorrow?" Blane asked.

"There's probably no reason for you to wait. In fact, getting a head start might prove helpful." He nodded. "After lunch, we'll talk to Col and find out whether he has any objections."

"We need time to gather supplies," Carys said.

"Don't forget the communication devices, and some money," Kerr said. I could see he was becoming excited by the prospect.

"Are you going to ask Ana to go, too?" I asked Madoc.

"Yes, I believe we will." He looked down the table to where she sat, talking to Eva and Holt and laughing, then stood and walked towards them. I saw him lean over and ask Ana something, and the surprised look on her face, replaced quickly by a smile and a nod. There were now five in the scouting party.

That settled, we talked about what everyone had been doing. I was surprised Gita hadn't spent the morning with Morna and the Manor's baby animals, but in the town, exploring the shops. "They're not very different from those in Osterbruk. I found some lovely wool to make Wim a new sweater."

We finished eating. Much like luncheons at the Stronghold, but it felt odd since none of us had jobs to get back to. Instead, we returned to the classroom for another lesson in Fartekana.

Mai had come up with several more phrases that would serve us well, and everyone had a few words they thought they should know for our first encounters with the people living in Fartek.

Our teacher wrote them on the board. She wasn't planning to teach us to read Fartekana or any Ministic languages, but this was a way of reminding us all the terms we'd learned.

That afternoon she added:

> my name is
> may I have some water
> I come from Leara (or Solwintor, for those who did)
> help me
> excuse me, please
> good evening

as well as the words for horse, some basic foods like bread, apples and meat, road, river, house, hill, mountain, town, sea, ship, today, tomorrow, yesterday.

It was almost too much to take in at once.

"We'll go over all this again tomorrow," Mai said. "We're making faster progress than I originally expected."

"What about numbers? And colors?" I asked.

"Yes, we can cover those tomorrow, too."

As we left the classroom, Glynis asked, "Do you think Madoc has talked to the Duke about us yet?"

"I don't know." We were prepared with some good arguments if the Duke refused, but still I said, "Did Adair talk to him at all? I think he should give his father a chance to agree without any pressure from anyone else."

"That's true. I'll go find him and ask."

I smiled as I watched her go, but then I wondered what to do next. The best place I knew to think about it was the rose garden. The roses were already gone for the year but it was still pleasant to sit on a bench and smell the fresh air. Sure enough, one of the cats came to join me. I didn't recognize it, and from the size, I decided it was a baby.

"What's your name?" I asked it. It had one white-tipped ear, so maybe it was related to Velvet.

"Your sister's supposed to be the animal lover."

I smiled. I'd sensed his presence before I turned and saw Madoc. It was like old times. He sat down beside me and ran a hand over the small animal in my lap.

"Just don't ask to bring him...no, it's a her, isn't it?...her along too."

"No, the cats belong here, with their families." And that one had enough petting. She leaped off my lap and ran off. I leaned against Madoc and said, "I thought we'd have more time alone together here."

"I did as well, but there are so many demands on both of us. Someday, Nissa, we can go off somewhere, just the two of us, without an entourage, without our families and friends."

"I won't hold my breath until that day," I said.

"I promise you, Nissa." He kissed me, softly at first, and then more passionately. That only increased my desire for more, but he was right. It still wasn't the time.

"There you are!" Glynis said as she and Adair approached us. They were both frowning.

"What's wrong? What did the Duke say?"

"He said I couldn't go!" Adair announced.

Madoc sighed. "I suppose it's time for me to argue your case."

CHAPTER TWELVE

We followed the newlyweds, walking hand-in-hand, to the Duke's office. I'd never been there before, but in the space of two days, this was my second time.

Duke Alec seemed to be expecting us. "I told Adair he cannot go, and that is final!"

"With all due respect, Duke Alec, I request that you change your mind." I swallowed hard. "We'll need his assistance as a swordsman, since two of our defenders will go ahead."

"If I could, I'd forbid Kerr from going too." The Duke turned to Madoc. "And you seem to have forgotten you are in my employ, brought here as my wizard, and expected to train the boys and young men in your mystical arts."

"At least three of those young men are traveling with me, so I will continue their training," Madoc said. "The younger boys have plenty of time to learn, and I expect when I return, I will be bringing you a replacement for myself, someone who is quite capable of performing all of my duties, for I have...other...duties that require my skills."

Listening to him, I wondered who he expected to propose as his replacement, but what he said next told me. His 'other' duties were a lot more important to him than passing on his knowledge, but he couldn't tell the Duke that.

"That is, if you will allow Adair to travel with us and continue his instruction."

Adair and Glynis would have no desire to go to the

Stronghold with the rest of us once this mission was over, and if Adair could concentrate on learning more than he ever had from Madoc, he would make a fine instructor for the younger boys.

"Adair is newly married," the Duke continued to argue. "Surely you would not separate him from his young wife."

"We'd like Glynis to come with us as well," I chimed in. "She knows some of the language of Fartek and will be an asset to our group." That was a stretch, but he didn't know it.

"Narissa, I'm sure your parents have taught you to speak to me with more respect than that!" Duke Alec shouted. He didn't have an argument for what I said.

"Begging your pardon, my Lord." I dipped, hoping he didn't see the smirk on my face.

The Duke sighed, but Madoc had one more salvo. "Your sons' education will come to naught if they are not allowed to practice what they have learned. Time has passed when we can ignore what is happening in the rest of our world and cling only to what we know." He was treading on dangerous ground and he knew it. Duke Alec wasn't open to change, as was evident from his reaction to the devices. But he went on anyway. "The communication device that you dismissed yesterday will be used to allow the advance party to stay in contact with the rest of our group, and then to let you know at all times where we are and what is happening to us."

We hadn't tested it over such great distances, but it certainly sounded good. I knew the Duke wanted to talk all of this over with his advisers, but that would be Madoc, my father and Glynis' father, and he knew what at least two of them would advise.

"All right," he finally said, all but admitting defeat. "Adair may go. But you had better bring my sons back in one piece!" He shook his head. "I still don't understand what is so important about traveling to Fartek. We've had no contact with them in a thousand years, and there is no reason for that to change."

"That's where your mistaken," Madoc said. "It can mean that this world can move forward again. We've recovered machines that were built there over a thousand years ago and they may still have the technology to build more."

"I thought your travels were quests for the source of those

two books you treasure."

Madoc said with finality. "Those books come from Fartek, too."

The four of us left the Duke's office together. Adair and Glynis were grinning. "Wait until I tell my brother!" he said.

As luck would have it, his brother was just coming in from the practice field with Donal and Blane.

"Father's given permission for us to go with you!" Adair told them.

They grinned at the news. "Why don't we show Adair how to use the communication device?" Kerr suggested to Donal. "Since I'll be with the advance party, he can help you with the receiver end."

"Good idea," Donal agreed.

Kerr and Donal went off to assemble the various components of the system with Adair in tow, but Glynis stayed with me and Madoc.

"That went better with the Duke than I'd expected," she said. "Now I just have to break the news to my parents."

"Did you want me to go with you?" I asked. "Or better yet, why don't we ask my mother to convince yours?"

"I'll go inform Col about the Duke's decision." Madoc kissed my cheek and walked off.

Glynis grinned at me and I tried hard not to grin as well.

It took a while to find my mother. I knew she had more to show Helga and Gudrin, but they weren't in her workshop, nor out in the herb garden she'd planted the spring before. In fact, they were with Adith, examining all of the shoots she'd collected so that she could start some flower plants indoors during the winter. Her soft cheeks were pink and her pale eyes blazed as she explained what she was planning.

Would Glynis want to tell her mother her news with so many people around? I wondered if she wanted me to take Helga and Gudrin off somewhere.

"Mother, I have something to tell you," Glynis said before I could act on my thoughts. "The Duke granted permission for Adair and me to join the mission to Fartek."

Adith didn't look at all surprised, nor even resigned. She smiled at Glynis and said, "If that is what you want to do, I'd never stand in your way."

Glynis could do nothing but embrace her much shorter mother and kiss her cheek.

"Adith and I will miss you all when you are gone," my mother said. "But we know this is something you have to do."

"We're arranging one of communicators so you can talk with us as we travel," I said. "Donal and Kerr will have to show you how to use it."

"A machine can be used to do that?" Adith asked. That surprised her. So we tried to explain the devices and the way we understood they worked.

"Fancy that!" Mother said. "The machines they are creating at your Stronghold are truly amazing."

"Remember the book Madoc had with the pictures of strange contraptions? There are many books like that, written in many languages, and that's what they're using to recreate these things."

"Madoc's books were from the place you are going?" she asked.

"Yes. That's one reason we're going there," Helga told her.

"I'm glad you can appreciate the usefulness of everything we're doing," I said. "I'm afraid the Duke is not so open to change."

"He's set in his ways," Adith said. "But if anyone can prove to him he's wrong, I think it's you young folks."

"Oh, we expect to," I agreed.

"We'll be sad to see you go, though," Mother said.

"We'll be here another day, although Blane and a few others are leaving tomorrow to smooth the way for the rest of us."

"I would imagine finding lodging for so many would be difficult."

"We divided into smaller groups before," Helga said. "Even finding a large enough area to camp can be a problem. But it's solvable."

"I'll have your herbs and salves ready before you go," Mother told her. "It's been a pleasure for me to talk with you and to compare practices."

"It was my pleasure, as well," Helga said. "Nissa told us so much about you. She and Morna used many of the remedies you gave her."

I hadn't told my parents about the battles we'd fought, with Brun's men and with the marauders, nor about the injuries some of our companions endured. It would only make her worry more when we left. So I said, "They came in handy now and again."

"I'm sure there is much you haven't said. The important thing is that you survived all you endured and I know you'll survive the coming journey as well."

"And we will endure the absence of our children," Adith added. "And await the day you return safely to us."

CHAPTER THIRTEEN

The sun approached the horizon and a breeze picked up, blowing the yellow leaves that had fallen from the tree in the center of the garden.

"Let's go indoors." Mother gazed at the clouds rolling in from the north. "Looks like a storm before nightfall."

We entered the Manor through a side door and strode to the dining hall. The bell chimed the first of six, time for dinner.

Now that Glynis and Adair would officially accompany us, the mood was more festive. Ana and Eva gave Glynis additional suggestions of what to pack, and Kerr, who'd never been close to his brother before, introduced Adair to everyone.

When Cook and her staff brought out dinner, she asked what provisions the advance party would need to take. Carys and Blane agreed to tell her after dinner, and also suggest food for the rest of us the next day. "Just as long as there are plenty of Meecham cookies," Blane said, and everyone laughed.

She'd made some of our favorites again. We all had plenty to eat, since we didn't expect to eat like this while we were on the road, or on whatever ships we found to carry us east.

After we finished eating, we remained in the dining hall, discussing our plans for the trip to East Harbor. After that, we'd improvise, but the members of our group were used to that. I was very optimistic. I had to be, because if I thought about the unknowns ahead, my fear emerged, and I couldn't have that. So I focused on what I knew would be fine.

Madoc must have been watching me, and saw something in my face. When we left the table, he walked with me, his hand on my shoulder, steering me down the hallway toward his quarters. Once we were alone in his workroom, looking just as it always had, books strewn across every surface, he turned me to face him.

"Nissa, we've faced danger before. How many times have you told me that you were brave and resourceful, and could deal with whatever happened?"

I nodded. "But the enormity of what we're trying to achieve...the more I've seen, the more I realize how little I know about what else might be out there! Anything could have happened in Fartek over all of those years!"

"It's good you realize the dangers are real and completely unknown. It means you'll never become complacent, you'll always be alert." He squeezed my shoulder. "I have faith that you'll face whatever we find and take care of yourself and everyone around you."

"It's good to know you have so much faith in me." I echoed what he said. His comforting touch and words helped.

"I do. And we have a formidable group working with us. There's a reason for each of them to be here."

"Our skills and abilities have grown!" I smiled. "I worried about some but they've proven themselves."

Madoc nodded. "I, too, wondered how they'd all fit in and whether we could count on them. So far so good!"

"And I promise that Glynis and Adair will do their part as well."

"No doubt!" He ran his fingers over my cheek. "I take it Adith didn't have the objections the Duke did."

"She was very encouraging. And I doubt Glynis' father will disapprove. We still haven't heard from the Duchess, but she's always done whatever the Duke tells her."

He shook his head. "She's not completely under his thumb." He cupped my chin and kissed me. "I've wanted to do that again since Glynis and Adair interrupted us this afternoon."

It wasn't as deep a kiss as the one they'd cut short, but there was something in it that excited me in ways I couldn't describe. We kissed again, more passionately.

***

I practically skipped down the corridor to my room, but composed myself before opening the door. One last check to make sure everything was in place on my person, and then I walked in.

"Oh, hello Nissa," Morna said from her bed. "Where'd you go off to?"

I was sure she could tell just by looking at me where I'd been. I muttered something about talking to Madoc, grabbed my nightclothes and rushed off to the bathroom.

I washed thoroughly and pulled on my nightgown, then headed back to the bedroom. Morna had already fallen asleep, saving me further discussion, at least until morning. I stretched out and closed my eyes. All I could think about was how wonderful it had felt to kiss Madoc.

All anyone could talk about the next morning was the advance party that would leave just after breakfast. Carys and Blane were their usual selves, but Kerr and Ana seemed excited, and as usual, I couldn't interpret Toren's expression. Cook brought them several packages of food and spoke to Carys about what was in each, since she'd be the cook for the group.

We all rushed to finished our breakfasts so we could see them off. "We'll call you when we stop for luncheon," Kerr said. He and Ana would be in charge of the communication system at their end.

"And if something untoward happens, we'll let you know," Blane added. "But I expect it will be an easy day of travel."

"If all goes well, we'll meet you in East Harbor in two or three days time," Col said.

There was a lot of handshaking, and even some hugs, and then they were off.

It seemed odd not to be going with Blane and Carys and their group, but we'd leave the next morning. We still had preparations to make.

I walked to the classroom with Glynis and Gudrin, trying to remember what words and phrases I wanted to ask about. But it was Wim who got the class started.

"How do you say, 'sit down' and 'roll over'?" he asked.

"Why do you want to know?" Mai asked.

"Because Raj has to learn Fartekana, too!" he said, and we all laughed even though he was right.

"Of course!" Katya said. "Sit is *zoshi* and roll-over is *zhan*."

The boy repeated those words softly as if to memorize them, then turned to the dog and repeated them. Amazingly, Raj responded immediately to each command.

"He really is a very smart dog!" Glynis said.

"You haven't seen him control horses!" Baca said. "He's fantastic! So what's the word for dog?"

We learned that one *gou*, and then went on to counting, *yi*, *er*, *san* and on from there. Then I asked, "How do you say, 'I don't understand'?" I could imagine having to say that a lot.

"Yes, and 'speak slower'," Gudrin added.

"Another good one would be 'I don't know'."

So we learned those phrases, and moved on to some foodstuffs, because we'd have to eat, wouldn't we? We learned apples are *ping*, and chicken is *ji*.

"But you must realize that, even in the Ministic languages, depending on where you're from, there are other words for the same things," Katya pointed out.

The lessons were fun and Mai and Katya promised to help us practice all we'd learned. "You made more progress than I thought," Mai said again. "But there's so much more."

CHAPTER FOURTEEN

We finished the Fartekana lesson in time for luncheon and headed to the dining hall, more interested in what the scouting party reported than in any food. Donal and Adair had the receiver unit set up on a table, along with another device so we could speak, too.

At twelve chimes, we heard the crackle signaling a message was coming through. Soon, Kerr's voice clearly said, "We've reached the Dalton Plain and we've stopped for luncheon."

"Any problems?" Col asked.

"No, none. Although you might have more trouble going through with the wagons than we did on horseback. Just to the right of the road after you pass the first hills, is a more level path that should be easier to navigate. Ana and I went that way. It was longer, but also much easier."

"Good to know," Col told him. "That's the kind of information we'll need. Go eat your luncheon. We'll talk again when you've camped for the night."

"Very good."

As Madoc said, so far so good. The advance team had been an excellent idea, and the communication system worked well.

Cook and her staff had put out luncheon on the trestle tables while Kerr was reporting, so we selected food. The spread included the usual sliced meats and cheese, bread and salads.

After lunch I returned to my room to pack. My laundered wide-legged pants and other traveling clothes sat on my bed. There were a couple of things I'd added at the Stronghold, including the waterproof cloak and a nightgown. One of my blouses was torn beyond my ability to repair it, so I replaced it with another. It didn't take long to collect everything I'd need, no matter what weather conditions we'd find along the way.

As I was closing my packs, Morna came in. "I guess you had the same idea I did." She began to go through her own things. "Do you think we need any summer clothing? I mean it's almost winter."

"But the seasons, or at least the weather, may be different where we're going," I pointed out.

She nodded and put in both long and short skirts with her wide-legged pants. "We should probably tell Glynis what to take."

"So says the experienced traveler," I said with a good-natured laugh.

Morna laughed too. "Well, more experienced than Glynis."

Once we finished, we searched out our friend. Our traveling companions must have been packing, because we didn't see anyone except the Duke's daughter, Larena. She'd been avoiding us since we arrived but I had a question for her.

"Where are Glynis and Adair's quarters?"

"You convinced my father to let Adair go with you wherever you're off to now." Her voice held the superior tone she tended to use with us. "Why he should want to go is beyond me!"

"Their quarters?" I wasn't going to argue with her.

"And I really don't know what you've done to Kerr. I hardly recognized him!" She still hadn't answered.

"I guess I'll ask someone who knows where their rooms are." I turned in the other direction.

"Wait. So what do I get if I tell you?"

"Larena, with your brothers gone, your parents will dote on your every wish."

She shrugged. "They do that already."

"We can bring back something for you," Morna offered.

"What?"

"If I knew what we'd find in Fartek, we might not have to go."

She thought that over, then shrugged again. "Father gave them the rooms at the beginning of the corridor leading to Kerr's old room."

"Thanks, Larena. That wasn't so hard, now, was it?"

We didn't wait for an answer, but walked toward the corridor she'd mentioned. We found Glynis and Adair going through their clothes.

"You two are just the ones we need." Glynis ushered us inside. "We have no idea what to take."

Glynis was already off on her honeymoon trip when we'd made our wide-legged pants at the beginning of the summer. "Sturdy pants and skirts, and simple shirts and blouses to start."

It didn't take long to help them select appropriate clothing. The bell over the gate to the Manor chimed three and Glynis said, "It's time for our next Fartekana lesson."

"I want to check on all of the horses," Morna said. "Especially the newest colt."

"And Donal promised to show me some more of the devices in the wagons," Adair said excitedly. He seemed as fascinated by them as his brother and mine.

"We'll see you at dinner, then." Glynis kissed her husband's cheek and took my arm to stroll down the corridor toward the classroom.

That afternoon, Mai and Katya reviewed what we'd learned so far. Baca and Wim had retained more of the words and phrases than anyone else.

The afternoon went by quickly and before we knew it, it was time for dinner. But none of us wanted to eat the delicious meal Cook placed before us until we'd heard from the forward party.

The bell chimed seven and our food was getting cold, yet there was still no word. "What could have happened to them?" Gita asked worriedly.

"If there was any trouble, Blane or Carys, or even Toren would have tried to contact us," I said, more to convince myself than anyone else.

Many agreed, but Madoc warned, "Depends on what predicament they found themselves in."

I frowned, knowing deep in my heart he was right. We tried to eat, mostly just pushing the food around on our plates. It was probably delicious, but the few bites I took tasted like straw.

Finally the receiver came to life, but it wasn't Kerr's voice that came through. Instead, it was Ana's. "We've been set upon by a group on horseback, trying to steal our supplies. Luckily they didn't recognize the importance of this device, but Kerr is injured and Toren has disappeared."

"Where are you now?" Col asked her.

"We're in the woods and we can see Holden in the distance, but we dare not go there tonight."

"Are Blane and Carys alright?" Madoc asked.

"Just minor cuts and bruises. We learned a lot about fighting in our battles with Brun's group and the marauders, and these ruffians weren't as organized. We sent them off fairly quickly."

I glanced at my parents, but they didn't react.

"None of you saw what happened to Toren?" Col asked.

"One minute he was beside me, and the next he was gone."

I wondered what he was up to. Although I trusted him more after he was so helpful in previous battles, none of us knew how much of his magical ability he still possessed or had regained. And no one ever knew what his personal motives were. But Oskar, the leader of the Stronghold, had insisted he accompany us on this journey.

"Do not, I repeat, do not try to find him," Col told her. "He can take care of himself, and if he wants to find you, he will."

"I understand," Ana said.

"Can you go on in the morning?" Madoc asked.

"I think so. Kerr should be recovered enough by then. Oh, one more thing. The quest for the Crimson Orb has become even more intense. We'll see what we can learn in Holden in the morning, and let you know what we hear."

"Thanks, Ana! Take care of yourself and your companions. We'll await your report in the morning."

The news was disconcerting. "We'll have to be on the lookout for attacks when we reach the woods," Holt said and everyone agreed.

"How dense are they?" Dreas asked.

So much had happened since I traveled through them, I wasn't certain.

"Rather thick and overgrown," Madoc said. "The road

disintegrates into a leaf-strewn path, and the trees are so tall that they block out the sun to some extent."

"But the road is wide enough for our wagons, isn't it?" Eva asked.

"Yes, just barely in spots. It will be slow going, indeed."

"Where do you think Toren went off to?" she wondered aloud, but no one had an answer, just speculation.

"He could be hiding in the woods," Dreas suggested.

"Or asleep in a warm bed at the tavern in Holden," Donal said.

"I can assure you, those beds aren't very comfortable!" I remembered the night Blane and I spent there.

"Speaking of which, I suggest we make it an early night and get some rest," Col said. "We have a long journey ahead of us, with many possible dangers along the way."

CHAPTER FIFTEEN

In the morning, we rose early. My head had been filled with frustrating and frightening dreams, a mixture of the worst I'd experienced and what I feared. In the light of day, they seemed silly, not even worth mentioning, only a sign of nerves. Still, it felt good to be up and dressed and doing something, rather than dwelling on what might happen.

Cook had gone all. We ate a wonderful breakfast as we waited for another report from Ana. It came as we were finishing.

"Everyone in Holden is determined to join those already in Meecham. The reports indicate that it's become a wild and lawless place, but none of the people here believe there's any danger to them specifically."

"Did you tell them anything of our mission?" Col asked her.

"No, nothing. We just wished them well as they left this morning."

"How is my brother?" Adair asked.

"Mending quickly. His injuries weren't severe. We'll continue east after another cup of tea."

Col smiled. "We'll leave the Manor soon and talk to you again at luncheon time, unless you run into more trouble."

"All right," Ana said.

"Has there been any sign of Toren?" he asked.

"No. The proprietor at the tavern hasn't seen him, so he

wasn't here last night."

"Well, I expect he'll show up eventually."

Ana seemed to speak to someone before adding, "Carys reminded me to tell you there's little in the forest to add to your food supplies, so be sure to take ample food."

Carys always worried about everyone having enough to eat.

"Safe journey," Col said.

"And you," Ana replied.

We drained our tea cups, and collected our packs. When we assembled at the stables, several people waited to see us off. Mother brought packets of herbs and salves for Helga and my father returned the swords he'd collected to resharpen. Glynis' and Adair's parents came to bid their children farewell, along with the rest of us.

"Safe travels!" the Duchess said. She'd accepted the fact her sons would be gone, but we hadn't told her that Kerr had been injured the day before.

We hung our packs on our horses and mounted. Col and Holt rode out first and the rest of us followed with the wagons in the middle of the procession.

Last time I left the Manor, we headed north. Now, Madoc and many others accompanied me, but it was Blane, Carys, Kerr and Ana we sought. At least we knew where they were earlier.

Morna rode alongside me. "What are you thinking?"

"About how different this journey is from others I've taken, and about what good friends we have sharing it with us."

"We can be grateful there are still decent, agreeable and admirable people in this world."

I laughed. "Not everyone is obsessed with the quest for the Orb."

Madoc rode up to join us. "The Orb and crystals like it are very powerful, but also a lure for the greedy, for those seeking fame and fortune. If we only wanted crystals, we could have gone to Padras." Crystals had been found there several years before, and it became a boomtown for those seeking them, mostly for jewelry and decoration.

"Any crystals there have already been found," Morna said.

We'd reached the hills and located the path Kerr said was the best way for us to take the wagons. After a short debate whether anyone should stick to the road while the rest went with the wagons, Col decided we should stay together. "Enough of our group are already separated from us. This way may be longer and slower, but we can bring the wagons through."

The path wound around the hills, and stayed almost flat with a gradual rise for more than a thousand gyrds before beginning a gentle descent on the other side of the hills. On foot that might take an hour but on horseback, even with the wagons, it took much less, and then the Dalton plain spread out before us. It looked larger than I remembered.

We stopped soon after we reached the plain for a brief lunch. Helga took out sliced meats and cheese, and bread baked that morning. She also had salads to eat while they were still fresh. Plenty of time for dried and smoked meat, and longer lasting foods over the days it would take to reach East Harbor. We washed our food down with water from our flasks.

Morna, Gita and Wim tended to the horses, feeding them carrots and apples. We'd look for a stream where they could drink as we crossed the plain.

Ana hadn't called since breakfast time, but we didn't want to wait for her call. The trees were in the distance and we needed to prepare for any attacks once we reached them. We arranged ourselves in a formidable formation, with defenders and those skilled in swordsmanship on the outside, but once we reached the tree line, we couldn't continue that way.

Instead, we rode between the trees, surrounding the wagons full of precious cargo, with Holt and Eva at the forefront, and Adair and Donal bringing up the rear, swords at the ready. I sensed Madoc reaching out his mind for anyone was nearby. I tried to do the same, but didn't sense anyone.

We kept a steady pace. The clomp of the horses hooves created a rhythm. As Ana described, the forest was fairly thick and the path through it was narrow. Our minds, ears and eyes were alert for any signs of others approaching, and still we never noticed them until they were there, in front and around us, about a dozen men on horseback.

They were no match for all of us. I expect they underestimated our fighting ability. We didn't have to resort to mind attacks. A few of us fought them off, causing injuries, and luckily sustaining very few ourselves. I crossed swords with one of them and surprised him with my quick feints and strong thrusts. My height and long reach certainly helped, and I was adept at using the energies around me to focus my arm and, by extension, my sword. I cut my opponent's arm, and maybe his shoulder as well. He didn't give up easily, lunging at me a few more times, but then he realized his companions were turning tail and leaving, so he took off as well.

Once they were all gone, we took stock. Gudrin had wrenched her arm trying to wrest an opponents sword from him. Holt had re-injured his leg.

"You should change your stance when you fight to prevent that from happening again." Gudrin told him.

Many others had minor cuts and scrapes, but we were all well enough to ride. We made sure the horses were fine before we mounted again.

As we started off, Ana's voice came through the receiver that Donal was securing in one of the wagons.

"We're stopping for a late lunch," she said.

"What was the delay?" Col asked.

"We encountered a group of soldiers and had to explain who we were and why we were on the road."

"Soldiers?"

"One said the merchants in East Harbor hired them, not only to protect their businesses, but to keep unwanted travelers from coming anywhere near the town. I guess you knew Carys was a princess."

I looked at the faces of those with us as they heard this. "That's right. She's Princess Carys of the East Islands."

"No wonder she thought her father would help us!" Eva said, then stared at Madoc. "So, I guess that means you're a prince, huh? Will wonders never cease!"

"What does Carys' royalty have to do with anything?" Col asked Ana.

"When the soldiers recognized her, they accepted she was returning home and bringing friends with her." Ana's voice held a hint of laughter.

"So they let you go on." Col sighed. "I suppose we'll have to do something similar. By the way, we ran into your friends in the woods."

"Oh! Well, I expect they were no match for you."

"Quite right!" he said. "So how far have you gotten?"

"It's dry and pretty barren here. Blane says it's a plateau and we're not far from a village where the Dorri live, whoever they are."

I smiled, remembering the small hairy people in that village, particularly Kif and his wife Lyra. They'd treated us with kindness and fed us as well. "Say 'hello' for me and tell them we'll be there before long."

"We'll stop for the night in another few hours," Col told Ana. "Please call when you've camped."

"Yes, we will."

"You're all well, I hope," Helga said.

"Oh, yes, we are."

Once we finished talking to her, everyone had questions about Carys and Madoc, too. Madoc shrugged. "We didn't think it important, just as Kerr being Duke Alec's son wasn't."

"But you're royalty!" Dreas said. "I mean, we should be addressing you differently, shouldn't we?"

"Dreas, if I haven't earned your respect by my actions and abilities, no title will change that. Besides, you all come from places where there is no royalty. It just happens to be the way people are governed in this part of the world. And even Duke Alec never treated me differently because my father is a king."

He was so matter-of-fact about it, everyone had to accept it. And I wasn't going to bring up the way everyone treated Carys at the Manor when they first met her, until they realized she wanted to be treated the same way as the other young women there.

CHAPTER SIXTEEN

We continued out of the woods and towards Holden with no idea what to say to the soldiers. We avoided the Oaken Bucket since the advance party had already collected any useful information there.

Instead we rode through the town without stopping, ignoring the curious eyes of the people. They obviously saw us. You couldn't miss an entourage of more than a dozen people, horses and wagons. But they made a point of ignoring us.

By the time we reached the far side of the town, it was almost dinnertime. Before traveling through the trees ahead, we stopped to eat. This time Madoc lit a fire by focusing energy and using broken branches we found at the edge of the trees.

Helga assembled a pot of root vegetables, potatoes and dried meat and set it above the fire. She didn't have Carys' flair, preferring to use well-known recipes than experiment. Morna and Gita helped her prepare our meal by cutting up vegetables. We also had individual breads. I brewed a large pot of tea, although some of our companions preferred ale. We finished our meal with our favorite cookies.

Well-fed, we rode through the line of trees and found ourselves on the plateau. We didn't know how far ahead the others were, but we decided to camp for the night.

The plateau was very dry with sparse vegetation, and therefore little in the way of food. Luckily we still had a large supply. We built another fire and set out our blankets for the night.

The guard rotation was set, with Donal, Dreas and Katya taking the first watch.

I should have been used to sleeping outdoors with only my blankets between me and the hard ground, but maybe it's something you never get used to. I tossed and turned for a while, trying to get comfortable wishing I could sleep even closer to Madoc. Having his arm around me would help. My exhaustion from the long day finally took over and I fell asleep. I almost didn't waken when it was our turn to guard the camp, but I'd developed a sensitivity to Madoc moving nearby.

I rubbed the sleep from my eyes and took a blanket with me. It wasn't very cold but it would be comfortable to sit on. Eva shared the watch with us. "Should I patrol the perimeter first?" she asked.

"That might be best," Madoc agreed.

I hadn't had a minute alone with Madoc all day, and welcomed the opportunity to talk to him.

"So, what are you worried about tonight?" His arm slipped around me.

"I'm not always worried about something," I protested, but nothing supported that claim. Every time we talked, I poured out my concerns to him. Then again, who else should I discuss them with? "I thought this part of the journey would be what Eva calls a piece of cake. Instead, it's been more dangerous than when Blane and I came this way four months ago."

He drew me closer. "The fever to find the Orb has spread north, along with the lawlessness in Meecham."

"That doesn't make me feel any better."

"No, I'm sorry but I don't have anything to say to dissipate your anxiety this time." His closeness helped more than his words. "There's more, isn't there?"

"Well, I wonder what Toren is up to. We'd begun to trust him, but now I don't know what to think."

"Toren has his own plans. He certainly hasn't shared them with me." Madoc paused. "If he's in trouble, however, I think he would contact one of us, and he hasn't."

I nodded. "That's true. But I can't seem to 'find' him."

"Nor I. He's being purposely elusive, our friend Toren." He sighed. "It's wasted effort worrying about him. Let's focus on our own immediate problems."

"Like what to tell the soldiers when we encounter them."

"Aye. It will have to be something that covers our large entourage, and especially the wagons."

"We can say we're bringing them to your father," I suggested. I know it was lame but it was all I could think of.

"Yes, definitely an option."

"Col hasn't suggested anything, has he?" I asked.

"No. He's preoccupied with keeping us all together and safe. He's good at logistical planning, but I'm afraid he hasn't the imagination for strategy."

We were silent for a few moments, then Madoc went on, "What do you think of Dreas?"

"Why do you ask?" The young man was skilled at hunting with a crossbow, big and strong, and very quiet. "I'm afraid I don't know him well."

"I think he has hidden talents, and is much more intelligent than he appears," Madoc replied.

Just then, the object of our discussion woke and joined us. Eva returned and sat down next to us.

"Anything?" Madoc prompted.

Eva shook her head. "All's quiet on the western front. And the eastern, northern and southern."

"Morna has explained to me how you can reach out with your minds to sense anyone nearby," Dreas said. "I...I tried, but there was nothing."

Madoc and I exchanged a look. It appeared he was right about Dreas. "We'll take a stroll and then try again in a little while," Madoc said. "If you would like me to work with you on focusing your mind, I'd be happy to."

Dreas blinked. "Would you really? I didn't want to ask."

Madoc smiled at him. "It can help us if we all develop any talents we have."

He nodded. His eyes shone in the firelight.

"Would either of you like something to eat or drink?" I asked, starting to rise.

"No, no," Eva said. "There's no need."

"We were discussing what story to tell the soldiers from East Harbor," Madoc said. "It's odd that the merchants there would employ them."

"They must feel threatened," Eva guessed.

He shook his head. "It's a port town, and all sorts of people arrive by road or ship, transients with unknown purpose. They've never felt danger before."

"Something's changed," Dreas said, finally sitting down.

"So it would seem."

"I wonder if any of your father's people are in East Harbor," I mused. "Or maybe Gareth's guards."

"Gareth's your brother, isn't he?" Eva asked. "Carys has mentioned him. What kind of guards?"

"He's the leader of the royal guard in Fairhaven," I said. "He and two of his men came with us to Meecham."

"We can speculate about this but I suppose we won't know until we arrive." Madoc sighed.

He and I took our circuit around the camp, stopping now and again to send out 'feelers' for the presence of others. A group of men, women and children, who'd passed us just before dinnertime were camped to the east, and all but one of the men were asleep. That was all, not even any wild animals.

When we returned to our fire we found Eva and Dreas talking about their swords and his crossbow. Soon after, the next group took our places, and we were free to go back to sleep. I dozed but kept waking with another thought of what could go wrong with our journey and mission. Each thought was more dire than the one before. There were just too many unknowns.

In the morning, we ate a quick breakfast, saw to the horses, then packed up and continued on. The plateau continued for a while, but then we saw the village of huts that I remembered. A few Dorri went about their business, but when they saw us, they hustled inside. They were a shy people.

Madoc and I rode ahead for a pace, since some knew both of us. Sure enough, Kif appeared in his doorway and, as we approached, a smile appeared on his hairy face.

"Master Madoc!" he exclaimed. "And Mistress Nissa, I believe!"

"Hello, Kif." I dismounted Gallin and walked to him. "It is good to see you again."

They had their own language, but Kif was fluent enough in

Learic. "You bring others."

"Yes, we and our friends are on our way from Holmdale to East Harbor." Madoc appeared at my shoulder.

"Four others were here before. Master Blane and three more."

"They are part of our party, but rode ahead to see what difficulties we might find."

"Many people ride through. The road is busy," Kif told us.

"Busier than usual?"

"Yes." He took a look at the size of our group. "May we help you and your friends?"

"We'll stop here for a while. We have our own food and do not wish to disturb you and the other Dorri." Madoc bowed.

"Of course," Kif said and walked back into little house.

"What...what are they?" Morna asked.

"I told you about the Dorri before," I reminded her.

"They are a shy but generous people who've lived here undisturbed for many years. We don't know where they come from, originally, for they speak an odd language, unlike any that are known."

"Oh!" Katya said. "I'd like to hear it." She was our linguist specialist, after all.

"I'm sure Kif will oblige when you tell him you study many languages, and you're not just treating him and his kind as an oddity."

We took the horses to a small stream north of the village to drink. Meanwhile, Helga prepared our lunch with help from Gita. When we assembled to eat, Kif returned with his wife, Lyra, bearing fruit, cut up on a large tray she could barely carry. A few of our people rushed to help her, while Katya made her request of Kif. He immediately switched to his language, and she laughed and told him to slow down while she tried to write what she heard. He offered to bring her a book, written in the Dorri language and she grinned.

I noticed Lyra was wearing the pins I gave her and complimented her on how well they looked. I think she understood what I said, because she blushed a deep scarlet.

In return for the fruit, we offered her Meecham cookies. Her eyes went wide and she smiled with pleasure, bowing and thanking us profusely.

Kif returned with his book and handed it to Katya, telling her to keep it until she saw him again. The other Dorri still hadn't come out, but we told Kif to share the cookies with them all. I wondered if we'd ever meet the others.

Regrettably, we had to finish our meal, mount our horses and leave. We bade Kif and Lyra farewell and continued eastward.

CHAPTER SEVENTEEN

We hadn't heard from Blane, Carys, Ana and Kerr for a while. A distance from the Dorri village but before we reached the River Tavy, we stopped to contact them.

There was no immediate answer, but just as we were about to give up, we heard Kerr's voice. "Where are you? We tried to call earlier."

"We didn't hear anything," Col told him. "We're in a valley east of the Dorri village. Madoc estimates we'll reach the river in less than an hour."

"Crossing is tricky, as you know. The upstream shallow place Blane remembered is now much deeper, with fast-flowing water."

"So how did you get across?" he asked.

Kerr replied, "We went downstream instead of up, and found a place where someone had constructed a make-shift bridge with massive rocks."

"Good, we'll look for that," Col said.

"We're just beyond the hills but won't go into East Harbor tonight, not with what we've heard about difficulties there lately."

"Okay, Kerr. We'll stop this side of the hills and meet you in East Harbor tomorrow."

"Blane said there's a restaurant where he, Carys and Nissa ate. We'll check the docks and meet you there for dinner."

"That would be Gillie's," I remembered. "We'll see you

there."

The way through the valley was relatively easy. We reached the river as the sun neared the horizon and rode downstream, looking for the crossover point Kerr described.

"There it is!" Baca pointed.

It wasn't very wide, but enough for the wagons to cross. Once all of us reached the other side, we rode upstream, and then searched for the road again. It wasn't obvious because it wasn't paved. Finally we found it.

Soon the hills rose in the distance. The road went between them. They weren't that high, but it would still take more care to make our way through, so we stopped for the night.

This time we used Col's cooking boxes to roast the last thick pieces of fresh meat and some potatoes. The boxes used cubes of coal instead of wood. We had four with us, large enough to prepare food for everyone at once.

"Dinner's ready!" Helga called. We all gathered around the tables with folding stools to sit on. It wasn't the dining hall at the Manor, nor the refectory at the Stronghold, but better than sitting on the hard ground.

Helga had sprinkled tasty herbs on the meat and potatoes. She even had a cake that she cut into pieces for each of us, with pieces of apple and lots of cinnamon in it.

"I'm afraid we've finished most of the fresh food, but we'll get more in East Harbor." Helga finally sat down to join us when she knew everyone had plenty to eat.

After dinner, we sat around talking until Baca took out his mandolin and played a rousing tune, one I'd heard a few times at the Stronghold.

"Do you know, 'The Happy Cow'?" Morna asked him. It was an old Arrandis folk song.

Baca shook his head. "Can you sing it, or at least hum it? I'll try."

My sister started and Donal and I joined in the round.

Baca listened for a minute or two and started to pluck out the tune. Others picked the song up right away. Glynis and Adair already knew it. A few clapped their hands in time with the music.

We were laughing when we finally stopped, but then went on to another tune. We should have thought to do that on previous nights. It was probably the last evening that we all had a good time together, and I still wish Blane, Carys, Ana and Kerr had been with us.

In the morning, we ate bread and cheese with an apple to top it off and washed it down with lots of tea, then made ready to depart.

It was slow going through the hills but we plodded along until we came to the other side. As we emerged, we came upon the soldiers we'd been warned about. They were much closer to the town than when the forward party met them.

They wore dark blue uniforms. The one in front had extra decorations on his chest. "He's the leader of this group," Madoc told me.

Sure enough, he spoke, holding up a hand to halt our procession. "Who are you and what business do you have in East Harbor?"

We hadn't devised another story to give him, so Col, as the leader of our group, replied, "We are coming from Holm Manor, in Holmdale, bringing the contents of our wagons to Fairhaven and hope to book passage there."

"What's in the wagons?" the man challenged.

Now, how were we going to explain that? We should have anticipated the question.

Clearly, Madoc had. "They are some curiosities that King Owen wished to see."

Without asking permission, the man pulled back the cloth covering one of the wagons. Luckily, it was the one holding the cooking boxes and a few small gadgets, which were easier to explain than the imaging and communication devices.

Donal and Col demonstrated how one of the cooking devices worked, satisfying the soldier's curiosity. But then he took a closer look at our party.

"You're not all from Holmdale," he said, staring at Col.

"I'm originally from Standia, and I've lived in Solwintor for several years. My wife as well." He indicated Gita.

The soldier nodded thoughtfully, shifting his gaze to Katya's black face, and Mai's with her slanted eyes. "What about them?"

"I'm from Rinaga," Katya said. "And my friend is from

Minis, of course. But we all came from the Manor in Holmdale."

"If you still have questions, I can refer you to the King of the East Islands and his son, Prince Gareth," Madoc said, staring intently at the man.

He was still suspicious, but there was nothing he could do. The story we'd told held up. "Be on your way," he finally said.

We continued on, even though the experience had been unnerving. As we approached East Harbor, we noticed the large number of people crowding the narrow streets, even more than the last times I was there. Holt asked, "How will we get the horses and wagons through to the harbor?"

Madoc had a solution. "I know of a stable not far from here, before we reach the main streets. We can leave our horses there, and the wagons too."

"Will they be safe?" Dreas asked.

"Aye. The stableman wouldn't cross me. He'll charge as much as he can get, but he's an honest businessman."

So he led the way, with the rest of us following. The stableman greeted him by name, and Madoc made his proposal. "Lim, the horses and wagons will only be here until we've secured passage to the islands."

"I don't have room for all of these!" Lim replied. "And the wagons, too? Sorry, Master Madoc. It's impossible."

"We'll pay you handsomely. You'll earn more for the next few hours than you have all week!"

Lim debated with himself but not for long. "Twenty copens each. Per hour."

That was a lot of money. Unfortunately, we didn't have much choice.

"Fifteen," Madoc haggled, and was able to get the price down to eighteen with another eighteen for both wagons, since they wouldn't be 'eating him out of house and home' like the horses.

Without the horses and wagons, we made our way into the town in threes and fours, approaching Gillie's by different routes. I entered with Madoc and Donal, and took a table, not far from where Blane, Carys, Kerr and Ana were already seated.

The waitress who brought us menus was the same one who'd waited on us when I was there the last time. Once she took our orders, I asked Madoc softly, "Why the secrecy?"

"While the soldier was questioning us, I tried to plant some thoughts in his head so he'd be less suspicious," he explained. "His mind was too strong, but I did sense some things. One was that the soldiers were hired by some of the shop owners in East Harbor, but there are some here who oppose them." He looked around to see whether anyone was paying exceptional attention to us, but they weren't, so he went on. "This restaurant is a place where my father's agents can exchange information. It is also one of the businesses the soldiers were hired to protect."

"But that still doesn't explain why we're eating in separate groups and pretending not to know one another," Donal said.

"Just a precaution."

"Like passing on information as fortunes in cupcakes?" I asked.

Madoc laughed. "Did they use that old one on you? I think Dita likes to make things more interesting."

"Who's that?" Donal asked.

Madoc indicated the woman at the bar with his chin. "She owns the place, and is an old friend of my family."

Our food came, as good as I remembered. No cupcakes this time, though. Instead, our dessert was a lemony flavored cake with a creamy topping. After dinner, we walked out into the street. The advance group stood just outside the restaurant. Blane said something to the others and walked away. We followed him, winding our way between the tall buildings and down a short alley, coming out not far from the harbor. When we reached the dock I saw a familiar vessel, the Flying Dragon.

"I don't know whether this is a good omen or a bad one," I said.

"You know this ship?" Donal asked.

"It's the one Blane and I took to Fairhaven."

"When you killed the ruda?" he asked excitedly. "That's great!"

We followed Blane aboard and I was greeted warmly by Captain Woryn and Lem. I introduced them to Donal but they seemed to know Madoc.

"Everyone here knows Prince Madoc."

Obviously that hadn't included the soldiers who met us on

the road, or any of the patrons at Gillie's.

"We told Blane we could carry part of your party to Fairhaven, but there's not enough room aboard for so many." The captain shook his head. "And the horses! Well, maybe a few."

"What about the wagons?" Madoc asked.

The captain shook his head. "We might find room for some of your cargo."

Blane spoke up. "We tried to find the Queen Bronwyn, but she's not here. The harbormaster said she's due in later today."

Carys came across the gangplank, followed by Helga. Not long after, Kerr arrived, and then Col, Gita, Wim, and Raj. And they were followed by Morna, Dreas and Baca. Finally, Ana showed up. And the rest of our group wasn't far behind.

CHAPTER EIGHTEEN

"Ya'll be glad ta know, we got ourselves a new cook." Lem grinned.

"Have you really?" Madoc tilted his head.

"Yup. Come aboard jes' this mornin'."

Col looked questioningly at Madoc. I suspected Madoc was wary of the cook because of the one on the Queen Bronwyn who'd sabotaged the engine before taking his own life.

"Nissa, be so good as to show me the way to the galley," Madoc said.

I nodded, and led him down to the room where I'd spent most of my time when last aboard the Flying Dragon. The door was only open a crack, letting off-key singing and clanging of pots and pans reach us.

Madoc pushed it open, and before us stood our errant mage. "Fancy meeting you here," Madoc greeted him.

One of Toren's stranger smiles crossed his face, but all he said was, "I knew you'd show up before long."

"But how did you know which ship we'd take?" I asked.

"Nissa, you've mentioned the Flying Dragon more times than I care to count. You know the captain and you're familiar with the ship. It was a logical assumption."

"Where have you been?" Madoc got right to the heart of the matter.

"Oh, here and there." Toren waved his left hand about. "I

thought it might be easier to move without an entire entourage, or even those four in the scouting party."

That didn't explain anything but it was the only answer we could get.

When we returned to the deck to let the others know what we found, they'd decided who would travel on this ship, and who would wait for the Queen Bronwyn, a much more luxurious ship that couldn't accommodate any more of our party, including the horses, than this one.

"We'll bring half of the horses and one wagon load," Blane said. "We can leave the wagon with Harbormaster Barwyn and take the contents on board."

Several people went with him while I showed the rest around the ship. The crew was loading cargo, but everywhere we went, they remembered me.

"Gonna teach the new cook to make them omelets we 'ad?" Rog asked.

"Hope we won't see any rudas this time, but at least you'll be aboard to fight 'em," Fel said.

It felt like I'd come home. I was as welcome here as at the Manor.

Morna was surprised by how small the ship was. "They make use of every space," she marveled. "Just like on the Great White."

"Do you think Madoc can construct an engine to power this faster than the sails?" Ana asked.

"With some help from Donal and Kerr, I bet he can," I replied.

By the time Blane and the others returned with the horses, the Queen Bronwyn approached the harbor. We helped stow the wagon's contents aboard the Flying Dragon. Lem showed us where we could take the horses so they'd be comfortable during the journey.

Col and Madoc talked to Captain Woryn, but it wasn't until later that I learned they'd told him our eventual destination, and asked if he would take us that far. He agreed to think about it. We'd work on him throughout this journey to Fairhaven, to convince him.

Madoc and Col left as soon as the Queen Bronwyn docked.

When they returned, Col said, "Captain Trahern has agreed to transport the rest of our party, including the horses and cargo, to Fairhaven. He seemed very pleased to see Madoc and Carys traveled with us."

Six of us retrieved the remaining horses and the second wagon. Now the more difficult and probably dangerous part of our journey would begin.

The Flying Dragon would sail that evening, while the Queen Bronwyn would berth at the dock overnight to allow the crew shore leave. But the royal ship was faster because of the engine Madoc constructed, so both would arrive in Fairhaven about the same time.

Captain Trahern insisted that Princess Carys sail aboard his ship, but Madoc convinced him he and I should sail on the merchant ship. Madoc likely wanted to keep an eye on Toren. He told Captain Trahern, "I need to build an engine for Captain Woryn similar to the one I constructed for you."

Trahern accepted the excuse, and so we sailed on the Flying Dragon, leaving Carys and Blane behind. Morna debated with us and herself which ship she'd prefer, but I pointed out, "If you sail with us, when we leave Fairhaven for Fartek, you can travel in comfort on the Queen Bronwyn." I assumed King Owen would insist Trahern take part of our group farther east.

We hadn't been out to sea for long before Lem found me on deck, looking back to shore. "Cap'n sez yer headin' east to Fartek."

"That's right. We've asked him to take us, but so far he hasn't agreed."

"That's cuz of them rumors, stories o' real dragons an' birds the size of horses." The awe in his voice showed he half believed what he'd heard. "We bin as far as the Scattered Isles, but never ventured beyond."

"Can you take us that far?" I asked. "Maybe someone there would take us farther."

"Ain't no one there. Deserted like, they are."

"Oh." I turned away from the distant shore and changed the subject. "Did you know Madoc will build an engine for the ship?"

"A engine?"

"Yes. It can power the ship, move it without wind or oars."

"You joshin' an ole sailor?"

"It's true. He built one for the Queen Bronwyn. That's why it can make the voyage between Fairhaven and East Harbor so much faster than the Flying Dragon."

"Well, I'll be!"

We were both silent for a bit, but my curiosity got the better of me. "Tell me some of the stories you've heard about Fartek." There had to be some truth in the tales just as there was in the legends about the Crimson Orb.

"There are them what thinks there's nothin' but wild animals left there. And the trees are taller than any you've ever seen! There's no harbors to dock, just rocks and steep cliffs, and a current what could blow the biggest ships off course."

"Then I can understand why the captain wants to stay away."

"Aye! No sense askin' fer troubles. Well, I best get back to the fo'sail." He pushed off the railing he leaned against and walked away.

I remained on deck for a while. I love the smell of the sea and, as long as the waves are calm, the gentle sway is pleasant. Morna and her two admirers were below deck, with many of my companions, but I saw Wim asking some of the sailors questions, and Raj was at his side.

Madoc, Donal and Kerr were still talking to the captain about the engine. Could they convince him to take their offer? All four, and the first mate, Karn, suddenly strode aft. Donal and Kerr went below but emerged soon after with bits and pieces of machines. I wandered over to see what they were doing.

I didn't know what half the parts were, but I recognized something that looked like the engine on the Queen Bronwyn. Only, instead of a box to burn fuel, there was a much smaller part containing one of our crystals.

"The crystal will focus the energy around us, and cause this gear to turn, and thence this wheel. These fins will push the water under or behind the ship and force the ship forward," Madoc explained. Donal and Kerr seemed to understand what he said and the captain, though still skeptical, was willing to give it a try.

I was fascinated watching them build this thing. They must have known it would work or else they wouldn't have tried. Unlike earlier experiments, where they tried to recreate something from a book and only then experimented to find what it could do, they knew exactly what they wanted to create.

Was this the kind of machine used to propel ships Before? Not just ships, but land vehicles as well? Would we find any when we reached Fartek? That would be so exciting! I wondered how fast those could go. Faster than a horse?

Meanwhile the wind did its job, propelling the Flying Dragon across the sea toward Fairhaven. The farther east we went the darker it became, until it was dinner time. I couldn't wait to see what Toren would prepare for the crew and passengers.

He appeared in the doorway to the stairs with an instrument in his hand like the one a man at the Stronghold played. Toren hit it with a small hammer and it resounded across the deck. "Dinner is ready," he announced.

I'd expected a stew, like the ones Carys often made, but instead he brought out a huge roast, and sliced it there on deck. As each of the crew men walked past with a metal plate held out, he placed a thick slice, a piece of bread and a roasted potato on it. I smelled the food, and my mouth watered.

The captain was the last member of the crew to get his food. It showed how much Captain Woryn cared about his men.

"There are plates for the passengers down in the galley," Toren said, so Morna and I went down to get them. Then he served all of us. I couldn't wait to taste what he'd made.

We all found a place on deck to sit and eat. The roast was good, moist rather than dry and very flavorful, but the real surprise was the potato. "Toren, how did you get the outside of these potatoes so crispy and salted?" I asked.

He raised his left eyebrow and said, "Do you really think I'd give away my secrets?"

"But why haven't you ever offered to cook for us before?" Morna asked.

Toren shrugged. "Carys was always around, or someone else. Did you really want me to take away their jobs?"

"I suppose you can also sew." I smirked, making him laugh.

"I might be able to. Wait until you taste my dessert."

Hearing that, I rushed to finish everything on my plate. When he brought out his cookies, I could see, without tasting one, he hadn't been boasting. The smell of cinnamon and chocolate were strong, and I loved both of those flavors. I bit into one, and closed my eyes with pleasure. They were even better than Meecham cookies! When I opened my eyes again, I looked around and saw smiles of pleasure on everyone else's faces.

"I hope you made a lot of these!" I told him. "And that you'll be willing to share the recipe with Carys." It was too bad she was back in East Harbor, waiting to sail on the other ship.

CHAPTER NINETEEN

After dinner, Madoc, Donal and Kerr went back to work on the engine. The rest of us went below. Toren refused our help with cleaning. I wondered if he was hiding something in the galley. Or someone.

I sat in the bunk room I shared with Morna, Helga, Gudrin and Katya. I told them the stories Lem related to me.

"Do you think there are real dragons in Fartek?" Morna eyes were saucers. She was still young enough to want to believe the unbelievable.

"Real dragons can fly through the air, and wouldn't have stayed in Fartek, but flown across the sea. We would have seen them by now," I reasoned.

"But there were so many things in Solwintor that we never imagined, why can't there be any in Fartek?" she argued.

"They'll certainly have different technology," Katya predicted.

"I want to know what it's like in Fairhaven, since that's where we're going next," Gudrin said. "Nissa, you're the only one of us who's been there. What's it really like?"

"It's a beautiful city. The buildings are as tall as in East Haven, but spaced more widely and they're made of a material that reflects the sun so the city shines."

"And the Citadel?" Morna asked.

"It's a castle, but unlike any you've ever seen." I pictured it in my mind.

"I've never seen a castle," Helga said.

"Set on a hill above the city. We walked to it from the dock in just a few hours," I told her. "You can see it from many parts of the city. There are many parks with flowers and trees, and walking paths. You'll see soon enough."

"And the king and queen? What are they like?" Katya asked.

"They're very nice and welcomed us warmly. They'll be so glad to see Carys and know she's well! And Gareth, well, you met him, Morna. He intimidated me at first, but I came to depend on him, his strength and his integrity."

"Isn't there another brother?" Gudrin's brow wrinkled.

"Elwyn. He's the eldest and will inherit the crown. He seemed...aloof. He wasn't concerned that Madoc was missing and frowned at Carys' and Gareth's determination to find him."

"You don't like him, do you?" Katya guessed.

"I...I don't really know him."

"But you weren't impressed by what you saw."

I shook my head.

Soon after, we went to sleep. I expected to think about the dangers awaiting us in Fartek, but instead, my mind recalled the time we'd spent with Madoc's parents at the Citadel and I fell asleep smiling, looking forward to seeing them again.

When we woke, we washed as best we could and changed our clothes. Before I went up on deck, someone knocked on our door. I opened it, expecting Madoc, or perhaps Gita, but instead Toren stood there with a frown on his face.

I stepped outside and closed the door as the others were still not dressed. "How can we help you?"

"You can tell me how you made the omelets the crew can't stop raving about!" He sounded almost angry, and I could understand that. After the wonderful meal he'd prepared the night before, all the crew could talk about were omelets I made them four months before.

"It's simple, really." I walked with him toward the galley. He hesitated, then opened the door for me. There was no one inside. In fact, it looked the same as it had when I'd been in charge of it.

"I used this huge skillet, setting it on the fire and cooked some bacon since I didn't see any butter or fat." I looked around for the big bowl I'd used to beat the eggs. Spotting it on a high shelf, I took it down. "I broke some eggs into this and stirred them with this wooden spoon, then added them to the pan."

He did what I described. The bacon sizzled in the pan and the eggs did too when he poured them in.

"While the bottom set, I chopped up whatever vegetables I saw, onions, those green things..."

"...they're peppers..."

I nodded. "...tomatoes, morels, um, oh, and after I turned the eggs, I added them and then topped it all with cheese that I sliced. Once the cheese started to melt, I turned one side of the eggs over on the other, then slipped the whole thing on a platter." I didn't see the platter but it had to be somewhere in the galley. "Then I cut that into three or four portions and sent them up to the crew with a slice of a bread from that shelf."

He nodded, getting the idea. "Thank you, Nissa." It seemed to be a dismissal.

"Well, good luck with making breakfast." I turned and walked out the door. When I climbed the steps to the deck, Morna was waiting for me. "What did Toren want?"

"He wanted my recipe for the omelets I served the crew."

"You should have demanded to learn how to make his cookies in return," she said.

I smiled at her. "I still might!"

Before long, Toren appeared with the first portions of omelet. Again, the crew were fed first, but I realized that he couldn't cook and bring the food up at the same time.

"Would you like help delivering breakfast?" I offered.

His face clouded over. "No, no, I can handle it myself."

I wished I could have discussed Toren's odd behavior with Madoc, but he was still busy building the engine. Instead, I sat down with Gudrin and Helga on the deck, out of the crew's way.

"I never took Toren for a gourmet cook," Helga said.

I wasn't sure what gourmet meant, but the statement opened up the topic I wanted to talk about. "He's acting very strangely. It's not just the cooking. He asked for my advice on preparing breakfast, and let me into the galley, but now he wants to do everything himself, even though we both know it would be easier if I delivered the food while he concentrated on cooking."

"What do you think he's hiding?" Gudrin asked. I knew she'd developed feelings for him and I'd seen them together at the party before we left the Stronghold.

"I don't know, but my curiosity is growing."

"Do you think he'll remain on the ship when we arrive in Fairhaven?" she asked.

"That's a good question. Has he really rejoined our group or not?"

"It looks like Madoc, Donal and Kerr have completed their machine." Helga pointed. "Let's go see." She stood and started forward, joining them as they carried it to the captain. Gudrin and I followed.

Toren delivered the captain's breakfast but the captain left the plate untouched while Madoc and the others explained what they'd done and how they wanted to try it out.

"Will we have to lower the sails for this to work?" Captain Woryn asked.

"If you want to see whether the engine can move the ship, it might be a good idea. That way, you'll know it wasn't a sudden gust," Kerr said.

So he ordered the sails lowered, took a few bites of his omelet and declared it delicious. Madoc had two of the crew help them install the engine in the ship's aft. Donal and Kerr turned a dial and pushed a button, and suddenly the ship was moving forward at twice the speed it had before.

"Would you like to have it go even faster?" Madoc asked. "We could be in Fairhaven by dinner time."

The captain hesitated only briefly before agreeing. Kerr turned the dial again, and the ship sped up even more.

Kerr and Donal grinned, and Madoc looked satisfied as well. We all congratulated them.

"The most amazing thing I've ever seen!" a crewman said.

Knowing that we'd be in Fairhaven by dinner time was also good. We'd have enough time to travel to the Citadel before nightfall. I wondered when the Queen Bronwyn would arrive. We hadn't seen the other ship yet. Were they far behind? They hadn't left East Harbor until this morning.

Toren finally brought us breakfast and we told him about the engine. He just nodded his head, so I asked Gudrin's question. "Will you disembark with us? Coming to the Citadel?"

"I haven't decided yet," he said. "I may stay on the waterfront for a while."

"What did you tell Captain Woryn?" Morna asked. "Will you continue on as his cook?"

"That depends," he replied guardedly. It was like peeling the skin off a burce.

But Madoc knew how to get him to open up. "What if we convince Woryn to take us to Fartek?"

"That would increase the odds that I'll continue on." He turned and walked away, making a big show of collecting empty plates and taking them to the galley.

Now that Madoc was finished with the engine, I talked to him about Toren. He agreed with me, that the mage was hiding something in the galley.

"But what can it be?" I asked. "There was no one else there when I showed him how to make omelets, and almost everything that had been there before was there still." I tried to picture the galley that morning and the time I spent in it three months before. "I couldn't find the serving platter I used, but it could have just been put somewhere else." I didn't know who cooked for the captain and his staff since I left the ship. "How are we going to find out what he's hiding?"

"We may have to be patient until he's ready to tell us."

"He takes great pleasure in being unfathomable."

"I think you're right."

I finished my eggs. They'd come out fairly well, considering this was Toren's first attempt at them. And I was glad I wasn't the one who had to do all the cooking. I collected Madoc's plate and those of some of my friends and started for the galley, but Toren returned for them, so I resumed my spot along the railing and stared out at the sea.

CHAPTER TWENTY

Madoc draped his arm around my shoulders. I leaned into him and sighed, still staring out at the rolling sea.

"I expect you're looking forward to going home," I said.

"It's always pleasant, and this time even more so, since you'll be with me."

"Will your parents give Blane and Carys their blessing while we're at the Citadel?" I turned to face him.

"I would imagine so." He smiled. "Gareth said they liked the two of you as much or maybe more than I expected."

"Liking us and agreeing to let their only daughter marry Blane are two different things," I pointed out.

"Don't worry about it. Gareth and I will give your brother our ringing endorsement, and that should be enough."

I swallowed. "I hope so, for Carys' and Blane's sakes."

"And what about us?" He took my hand.

I stared into his blazing eyes. "What about us?"

"Nissa, you know how I feel about you, and I believe you feel the same way." He tilted his head.

I sucked in a breath. "And? I don't think we need your parents approval, do we? You haven't asked them to sanction anything you've ever done in the past."

"But I have," he said.

"Well, we're not contemplating the same thing as Carys and Blane..."

"And why not?" He raised one eyebrow.

"Madoc, what are you saying?" Dared I hope?

"I'm saying that we love each other and should marry." His smile lit his face.

My eyes widened and mouth fell open. "But...but..." I sputtered, unable to put two real words together. "Oh!"

Madoc chuckled. "I didn't think it would come as such a surprise."

"Well, it did." I had to think about this, let it sink in. Of course my answer was yes. Then again, he hadn't asked a question, just made a statement. Well, you can agree with a statement, couldn't you? "Yes."

And then he put his hands on my arms and kissed me, squarely on the mouth, in front of all the crew and many of our friends.

When I could, I tried to sound casual, normal, although my heart raced in my chest. "I guess it's my parents who have to give their approval."

"Hmmm. I doubt they'll object. If they did they would have by now."

I nodded, but I don't remember if I said anything else.

My mind was in a fog for the next several hours. It wasn't only the surprise of what Madoc said or how he said it, but the entire concept, what my future would be.

I ate lunch, although I couldn't tell you what food we had. As the import finally penetrated, I began to smile, and then to grin. I was happy, happier than I'd ever been. Somehow it seemed I would always be happy now.

Morna noticed. She's my sister and she's known me her entire life. "You're in a good mood."

"Yes."

"Did it have something to do with that kiss earlier?" She flashed her cheekiest look.

***

By the time we finally saw land, my optimism that our mission would succeed had reached new highs.

The Flying Dragon docked at Fairhaven just before dinner

time. Madoc and Col debated whether to take the group from this ship to the Citadel, where we weren't expected, or to wait for the other ship to arrive. The third possibility was to find food at a harborside restaurant. At one Captain Trehern had found the cook who'd sabotaged the engine on the Queen Bronwen. It was owned by a nobleman who wasn't loyal to the king. But there were several other establishments to choose from.

Meanwhile, Captain Woryn waited patiently to speak with Madoc and Col. Finally, he cleared his throat loudly for their attention. "How long will you stay?"

"That will depend on how quickly we can make arrangements to continue east," Madoc replied. "Why? Have you made up your mind?"

The captain rubbed his chin. He'd probably pondered that same question all day, particularly after the engine was installed, and he saw the difference it made. "Could be."

"You know we can offer a good price for your help."

"Oh, it's not the recompense so much as the assurance that we can avoid any dangers out there."

"No one can guarantee that," Col said.

"And some would say we attract danger." Madoc leaned against a post.

"You're not helping," Col told Madoc with a grin.

"Why would you take up the seafaring life if you didn't want the possibility of a challenge?" Madoc ignored Col and addressed the captain.

Woryn laughed, a deep, hearty laugh. "Well said, Master Madoc!"

The rest of us stood around open-mouthed, watching the discussion. If I were a betting person, I would have said right then that Captain Woryn was sold on the idea, and we had ourselves a ship. They might have discussed it for hours, but one of the crew shouted for the captain's attention. He'd sighted the Queen Bronwyn, speeding toward the dock.

In the end, the captain didn't say aye or nay, just that he was still considering, and we moved down the dock to where the other ship pulled up so we could greet the rest of our group. All, that is, except for Madoc, who went with the crew to ready the horses and find wagons for us and our accouterments. He also looked for some of Gareth's guards, to send word to his family at the Citadel and let them know we were on our way.

To say I was happy to see Blane, Carys and the others again is an understatement. Yes, it had only been a day since we'd seen them last, but in some ways, it seemed much longer.

"We built an engine for Captain Woryn," Donal reported with a proud grin.

Blane clapped him on the back. "Well done!"

"And now the captain is considering whether to chance transporting us farther east," Kerr said.

"Trahern says he'd be honored to," Carys said.

"He'd never refuse you, Princess!" Ana said with a sly grin.

She and Eva had taken to calling Carys that every chance they got. She was likely ready to clobber them, but with her usual good humor, she refrained.

"Madoc is arranging transportation to the Citadel," Col said. "In the meantime, I think we should eat."

"There's a lovely restaurant one street over," Carys said.

As we walked to it, Morna and I told her about the Flying Dragon's new cook.

"That man never ceases to amaze me," Carys said. "What do you suppose he's planning now?"

"Only he knows," I said, and then went on to relate some of the stranger things he'd done. "But he's actually a good cook!"

"How would you know?" Morna teased. "You ate luncheon mechanically. I don't think you tasted a thing." She grinned. "Tell Carys what we had, I dare you!"

But I couldn't, because she was right. I hadn't been paying any attention.

I suppose someone told the others who'd been on the Queen Bronwyn about Toren's reappearance, because when we reached the restaurant and sat down inside, Eva asked, "So has Toren rejoined the group?"

"He won't say," I replied.

"Frankly, I don't care whether or not he does," Dreas said. "He's unpredictable and unreliable."

"But he cooks a wonderful roast!" Kerr said.

"As good as Carys?" Ana asked, forgetting to call my friend 'Princess'.

"No disrespect to you, Carys, but at least as good," Helga confirmed.

"We'll have to ask him about it," Carys said.

"He'll probably keep his recipe secret, just as he won't say how he made cookies as good as our favorite Meecham ones," Morna replied. "Maybe you can cajole it out of him, Helga. I think he fancies you."

"I wish!" she replied.

A waitress finally approached and we let Carys decide for us, since she'd been there before. Just as she finished ordering, Madoc arrived and joined us. Donal, who'd been sitting on one side of me, took an empty seat next to Katya, allowing Madoc to sit beside me.

"I've ordered for everyone," Carys told him.

"Did you make sure they'd bring some of their leak soup?"

"Absolutely," she replied. "So, will we be able to go to the Citadel after dinner?"

"Yes, I've secured horses for everyone and two wagons, and I've notified Mother and Father we'll be on our way as soon as we've eaten. They tried to convince me to bring everyone there for dinner, but you know what the cook is like."

Their cook wasn't very good. She could never handle food for so many at such short notice, either.

On the other hand, the food at this restaurant was quite good. The leak soup, in particular, was delicious.

"How did they sound?" Carys asked. "One of my fears is that, after so many months away, they might not allow me to continue on."

We told her we'd point out our need for her skills. But she wouldn't be convinced until her parents actually agreed. And, in a way, that was tied into getting their approval of Blane.

"They're looking forward to seeing us all," Madoc said. "But especially you."

"Did you mention the assistance we might need from them?" Col asked.

"I thought I'd wait until we arrive and they meet everyone. I think they'll be impressed with the devices we have, and that might convince them what we're doing is worthwhile."

Some of our party were happy to be ashore, even for only a day or two, while others looked on this stop as a halfway point for our eventual goal.

CHAPTER TWENTY-ONE

We rode through the city toward the hill surmounted by the Citadel.

"You were right about the beauty of Fairhaven!" Gudrin looked in every direction.

"It's the open spaces and all the parks," Helga decided.

"And the way the buildings reflect the setting sun," Ana added.

We reached the gate at the bottom of the hill. I recognized the guards in their braid-trimmed uniforms. One greeted Carys with a bow. "Welcome home, Your Highness!"

"Thank you, Derek." She smiled, as he allowed us all to pass and begin our ascent.

The king and queen awaited us at the intricately carved doors to their home. Four liveried men saw to our horses and Carys' and Madoc's parents urged us to enter. I remembered the entry hall as huge, but I realized how huge when all of us didn't come close to filling the space. My companions mouths hung open as they looked around at the marble floors and high ceilings

Ana faced Carys. "This is where you grew up? Why would you ever want to leave?"

"I wanted to see the world. When Nissa told me about her adventures coming here, it sounded difficult but also so wonderful!"

"We've made rooms ready for all of you," Queen Branna

said in her slightly husky voice. "Please take your time getting settled and freshening up. We'll see you in the blue drawing room anon." She smiled broadly. "If you need anything, all you need do is ask."

She didn't follow Carys to her room to speak to her daughter in private; perhaps she was waiting until later. I was assigned to the same room, and marveled again at the amenities. It felt good removing the traveling clothes I'd worn since that morning. After cleaning the dried saltwater and the dust from my body, I changed into the fresh blouse and skirt that were prettier than most of my clothes, a pale blue blouse with a bit of lace around the neck and a skirt in a soft fabric the color of the evening sky. I wanted the King and Queen to see me at my best.

Someone would launder the clothes I'd worn the past days if I left them outside my door, so I opened it to set them down and came face-to-face with Elwyn.

"You're back," he sneered.

"Yes," I replied. "And so are your brother and sister."

"But only for a day or two, I've heard. Then you'll be gallivanting off somewhere again, leaving Mother and Father worrying about Carys' health and safety."

"But not you?" I'm not usually so blunt, still, he annoyed me with his tone of voice, and the look on his face. "You don't care one iota about either Carys or Madoc, do you?"

"They don't care one iota about Fairhaven!" he retorted.

"I disagree. Everything we've done and plan to do will benefit everyone in all the lands. Or are you afraid things will change so much you'll never be king of the East Islands?" I challenged. He was much like Duke Alec in that respect, but at least Duke Alec tried to do what was best for his people.

"That's preposterous! What could change so much?"

I shook my head. "You really know nothing about life in other parts of Leara, let alone Solwintor, where the leaders are chosen, not because they come from a royal family, but because they evidently have a vision of what can be improved. No one knows what we'll find when we reach Fartek." Where had I gotten the nerve to stand up to him like that? Perhaps these ideas had been brewing in my head for days or even weeks, and this was the time to express them, to someone who didn't share my viewpoint.

Elwyn looked past me and said, "Your apprentice here has a mouth on her," he said with another sneer.

"I've found what she says is always right," Madoc said. "You should heed her words, whatever she said."

"I'm afraid I've been rude to your brother, Madoc," I said.

One eyebrow went up and down and he smiled. "I'm sure he deserved it."

"You've always had your head in the clouds," Elwyn told him. "But she does you one better, predicting an end to royal rule."

"I did no such thing!" My cheeks felt warm with embarrassment.

"I'm curious about what you did say, dearest."

The fact he called me that almost undid me completely, but I stood my ground. "I only said other forms of governing exist, and some are more helpful than others."

"Very true. Of course, that doesn't mean kings and queens can't rule just as successfully, if they embrace progress."

"You mean change," Elwyn said.

"Why, yes, but mainly change for the better."

"I hope you'll come and see what our friends have done, the machines they've constructed," I urged the would-be king.

"No thanks!" he bellowed. "You can dazzle Mother and Father with your trickery and your gimmicks, but not me!"

Madoc and I both shrugged. I'd tried, but I wasn't surprised Elwyn dismissed what they'd done at the Stronghold as frivolous. Still it didn't bode well for the future of the East Islands that a man like him was the heir to the throne.

"Are you ready to go to the drawing room?" Madoc asked me, dismissing Elwyn.

"Yes."

He took my arm and we walked down the corridor together. I realized his intention was for his parents to see us hand-in-hand, and my heart beat even faster. He squeezed my hand in encouragement. I took a deep breath and let it out just before we entered the room.

I needn't have worried. His parents were bent over a device Kerr was showing them, and they barely acknowledged our arrival.

"It's different from the communication system Madoc built here for Gareth, I believe, but it works over an even greater distance," Kerr told them.

"Like many of the devices, it's powered by crystals that concentrate and focus the energies around us," Donal explained.

"Amazing!" King Owen said. "You young people have been working hard, I see."

"Yes, but we're just beginning." Donal vibrated with enthusiasm. "We're hoping when we reach Fartek, we'll find some technology remaining from Before, and knowledge of the machines we haven't yet discovered."

"So the stories are true, about what happened a thousand years ago?" the queen said.

"Yes, Your Highness, they are. We've seen proof of it and descriptions in some of the old histories preserved for generations."

"And you're all determined to make this perilous journey?" the king asked.

"Yes, we are," Madoc spoke up.

"But you'll stay a few days before you do," his mother pleaded.

"We can't stay long. Winter is approaching, and we don't know what weather we'll encounter."

"Oh, come now. Father, you're not going to believe this fantasy Madoc and his friends are spinning out of whole cloth, are you?" Elwyn's voice boomed behind me. He'd followed us to the drawing room after all, and was continuing to voice his disbelief. "What claptrap! What utter nonsense! But then, I wouldn't expect anything else from my brother or these outsiders he's associating with."

"Now, Elwyn, you've seen how useful the system Madoc constructed for Gareth has turned out to be," the queen said as if she was reasoning with a child. "Come see this new one. It's quite remarkable and very real indeed."

He stared at her as if she'd betrayed him, turned on his heels and walked away.

The queen sighed, but said nothing more.

"What's wrong with Elwyn?" Carys asked, entering with Blane, Morna and Katya. "He wouldn't even acknowledge us as he went by."

"He's just being Elwyn," Madoc said. "A naysayer,

skeptical beyond belief, and utterly rigid."

"Now Madoc," the king began. "Don't sell your brother short. He has an understanding of politics and diplomacy you'll never have."

"And a good thing too," Madoc murmured with a smile.

His mother chuckled. "You never did care about any of that, did you?"

"No, I don't suppose I did."

"Well, enough about all of that," she said. "Why don't you introduce me to your friends. I think if I meet them in small groups I might be able to remember all the names."

I had no doubt she already knew many of them, but we complied with what she requested.

"You know Nissa and Blane, of course," Madoc began. "And our two young gadgeteers, Donal and Kerr."

"Yes. Donal is Nissa and Blane's brother, and Kerr is Duke Alec's son, if I'm not mistaken."

"Yes, that's right."

"And this must be Morna, the fourth Day child," she said, putting a hand on my sister's shoulder. "Madoc has described you well, my dear."

"He has?" Morna had a pleased smile on her pretty face.

"And this is Katya," Madoc said, indicated our friend with the distinctive black face and perpetual smile. "She's a language specialist, and the daughter of one of the other leaders at the Stronghold, where we've been living and working."

"That's in Solwintor, Donal told us," the king said.

"Yes, in a large cavern, north of the town of Osterbruk."

"What did you mean, 'one of the leaders'?" Queen Branna asked.

"There's a group of Leaders and Planners, including Katya's father, Niko. Two of them are with us on this journey, Col and Madoc."

"You're one of them?" Madoc's mother asked him with a proud smile.

"Yes," he admitted. "But we're no more important to the success of the efforts there than any of the scientists, engineers, translators, and others."

"Including the cooks and seamstresses," Morna said with

one of her more mischievous grins.

"I'm sure there's a story in that statement," King Owen said.

"I think Morna means I've learned to cook," Carys announced. "And Nissa is not only a seamstress, but also alters clothes better than anyone at the Stronghold."

"And what do you do there, Morna?"

"I help Gita with the baby animals," she replied.

"You raise animals? In a cave?"

"And grow food and plants. There are chimney holes in places and they let in lots of sunlight. There are also underground streams that flow through the caverns."

"And we use some of the devices we've perfected to provide lights in the darker places and at night," Donal added.

"It sounds like a wondrous place," the queen said.

"It is," we all agreed.

CHAPTER TWENTY-TWO

"So the people at the Stronghold came from many lands?" The Queen stared at Katya.

"Oh, yes. Which makes it more interesting because we learn about the food and culture, the languages and customs, even the songs and dances of the different lands."

"And now you intend to travel to Fartek to learn even more." Queen Branna said.

"If we can secure transport," Kerr looked at the king.

"Captain Trahern seems willing," Madoc told his father. "But he needs your permission."

"The Queen Bronwyn won't be large enough for all of us, but the captain of the Flying Dragon is convinced," Donal added. "So between the two, there'd be room for all."

"I'll need time to decide whether to risk my ship," the King tapped his chin.

"Carys, can we convince you not to go?" her mother said.

"No." Carys hugged her mother.

"I was afraid of that, probably ever since you left with Nissa and Blane three months ago."

"Mother, please understand."

Queen Branna nodded. "I was young once, too, you know. I'll have to content myself with knowing Blane and Madoc would never let anything happen to you."

I wasn't surprised she'd noticed the attachment between her

daughter and my brother.

"I will guard her life with my own!" Blane pledged.

The queen chuckled. "I'm sure you will."

Carys glanced around the room. "Mother, Father may we speak to you in private at some time?"

"Of course, my dear," the king replied.

The elegant room became crowded with our friends. The remainder of the introductions filled the next hour. Madoc told his parents the names of each of our companions, and a little about what they did, while servants brought in platters of food.

"You're all eager and ready for this task ahead," the king said at one point. "I'm glad our son and daughter have found such wonderful people to work and travel with."

After dinner, everyone retired for the evening. Madoc pulled me to the side before I went to my room. "Let Carys and Blane make their case before my parents tonight. We'll have time to talk to them tomorrow. As you pointed out, it is your parents we need to convince."

I nodded. How would the king and queen react to Carys and Blane? They already appeared to accept their feelings for each other. And if they agreed to their betrothal, they wouldn't object to Madoc and mine.

I couldn't believe what I was thinking. The idea of marrying Madoc had always seemed so completely out of the realm of possibility. And now... I didn't want it to distract me from our mission, even though it consumed me. Listening to Glynis go on and on about being married, I'd smiled at her indulgently. I wondered what she'd say when I told her.

"You're back in that foggy state again." Morna broke into my reverie. "I've asked you a question three times and all you've done is nod. It's not a 'yes-or-no' kind of question, you know."

"I'm sorry. I guess I'm tired and distracted."

"A-ha. I buy the distracted part."

"What was the question?"

"Is Blane going to ask for Carys' hand in marriage tonight?"

"I believe so. And that is, too, a 'yes-or-no' kind of question."

"Well, technically."

Madoc had gone off with Donal and Kerr somewhere just after the king and queen left with Blane and Carys.

"I really am tired," I told Morna. "I'm going to bed. I'll see you in the morning."

"Suit yourself. I'm going to explore."

"What, alone?"

"I suppose Dreas and Baca will come with me," she said.

"Morna, playing them off each other is a dangerous game," I warned. "Neither one deserves to be hurt."

"Oh, don't worry about them. They both know exactly what's going on."

I frowned. "You're taking advantage, and that isn't very ladylike."

She frowned, too, confirming she knew I was right. "But I don't know what to do. I like them both, and...and I never had one boy who liked me, but now there are two."

"First of all, they're not boys, but full-grown men. You should make up your mind which you really want, and make sure they both know."

"That won't be easy." She looked at the floor.

"No, of course it won't. But until you do, at least be fair to them both, okay?"

She nodded, but she wasn't smiling. "How did you know Madoc was the one you wanted?"

"I guess...I guess he always knew, and the more I've learned about him and about myself, the more convinced I've become."

"Nissa, are you going to marry him?"

It seemed somehow right she was the first one I told. "Yes, Morna. If Mother and Father approve, I'm going to marry him."

She smiled, and I could see in her eyes she approved whether or not anyone else did.

"C'mon, let's go to bed. You can explore with Dreas and Baca in the morning." I linked my arm in hers and she came willingly.

"Which would you pick if you were me?" she asked.

I shook my head. "You have to decide. They're both very likable. They're good looking. I guess some would say Dreas is handsome, but Baca's appealing in his own way. They each have talents and abilities. How do you feel when you're with each of them?" I hoped that would help her clarify her choice.

"I feel beautiful, and smart, clever but also intelligent, you know? I enjoy talking to each of them about different things, and I miss them when I haven't seen them for a while, each in a slightly different way."

I wasn't certain what to say. I'd never been in that situation, so there was nothing else I could advise.

We'd reached the room assigned to her. "Good-night." I hugged her. "I know you will make the right decision."

"I'm glad you have so much faith in me." She hugged me back. "Good-night Nissa. You're the best sister anyone could ever have!"

I entered my own room two doors away and found my clothes had already been laundered. I undressed, washed again, and pulled on my nightgown, then slid between the sheets on the comfortable bed.

For the first time, I allowed myself to think about what it would be like to be married to Madoc. Would we live in his rooms back at the Manor? But we'd both agreed we were going back to the Stronghold after this mission was over. His rooms there, then.

In the morning I woke with a smile on my face. I quickly made myself ready for the day, unsure what we'd be doing. The sooner I found out, the better I'd feel.

I walked down the corridor and listened for voices so I'd know where to go for breakfast. A room on the other side of the entryway from the drawing room was the dining room, but the table there couldn't hold all of us. Still, that's the room where everyone was congregating.

The table was filled with food. I didn't expect it to be very good, since I'd tasted the cook's food before. At least there was plenty. But I was surprised. I opened one covered dish and found toasted cheese sandwiches and big fat sausages that exuded a delicious odor. Another held eggs, cooked with chopped onions and other vegetables, almost like the omelets Toren made after my instructions, but not quite. And there were pastries of various kinds and crusty rolls with butter.

I filled a plate with everything that looked good, then saw Glynis and Katya sitting in chairs along one wall and joined them.

"I wonder if the king and queen have a new cook," I said.

"Yes, they do. Carys!" Katya said.

"I knew we couldn't keep her away from the stove!"

"I'm a little surprised her parents would let her do that," Glynis said.

"If it makes their daughter happy, I think they'd indulge her. But where's Blane? And Adair for that matter? I haven't seen you away from Adair's side for days."

"They both went to meet Gareth and his men," Glynis explained. "Along with our other defenders."

"They've returned?" We'd been told Gareth and a few of his guards had gone to the west shore where the men on a foreign ship had attacked a farm.

"They arrived last night and I gather they were pleased Carys and Madoc had returned, and you and Blane as well, although they seemed rather surprised at the size of our party," Katya said.

"I'll be glad to see him again. But why are our defenders meeting with them?"

Glynis shrugged. "I suppose we'll find out soon." Her eyes had gone to the doorway and a smile appeared. Her husband, Blane and the others entered with Gareth, Rees and two others in guard uniforms.

"We leave for a few days and come back to a full castle!" Gareth walked toward me. "Welcome back, Nissa!"

"Hello Gareth!" I said. "It's good to see you again. And you, too, Rees!"

"I hear you've been off having adventures without us." Rees was a slightly older man, maybe Col's age, an exceptional guard and quite the ladies man, but I didn't hold that against him.

Gareth looked more like the eldest, Elwyn, than Madoc, the youngest son, but you could tell they were all brothers by their coloring and the shape of their features. Gareth was more like Madoc in personality.

"I gather my sister and your brother are about to become engaged," Gareth said.

So the king and queen had approved. I wasn't really surprised.

"Welcome to the family." Gareth grinned at me.

"I think we could all see that happening when we traveled together," I told him. "I'm glad your parents approve."

"They were predisposed to like your brother, and you, too, of course, from all Madoc told them. Once they met you for themselves, they were quite impressed, and I must say I've given them glowing reports about how well you did during Madoc's rescue."

"So what did my brother and the others want to discuss with you?" I asked.

"They wanted advice about tactics to use in battles, although, I must say, they need little instruction."

"Gareth told them rather than give advice, he'd be willing to travel with them and show them in person," Rees said. He had more ribbons on his uniform than in the past, and I guessed he'd been promoted.

"You're coming with us?" I asked Gareth. I grinned, not all that surprised. But I wondered whether the king and queen would feel the same way. Three of their children would leave on this perilous journey.

"If the leaders of this expedition will have us."

I smiled at him. "I don't think Madoc will object. You'll also need to speak with Col. But won't this delay your marriage even further?" He'd been betrothed when I'd met him, although I'd never met his fiancée.

He laughed but without any humor in it. "My former fiancée has decided there were bigger fish to fry and has set her cap on my brother."

"Elwyn?"

"Certainly not Madoc. I think she shares Elwyn's views on magic and our younger brother. Besides, we all know where his heart lies."

I could feel my cheeks redden when he said that, and looked around the room for a diversion. I saw Col talking to his wife and Mai. "Let me introduce you to the leader of our expedition." I led Gareth over to them. And that was how our group grew again.

CHAPTER TWENTY-THREE

Col welcomed Gareth as an addition to our party. The only debate was over how many of his men would be coming with us. Rees would, of course. He'd been promoted to second in command. With the number of defenders we already had, Col decided Gareth and Rees would be the only two.

Gareth reported on his trip to the east coast of the island. "The seamen who attacked seemed to be a splinter group from the Legion you told us about. We learned they'd ventured south after they took the entire east coast of Solwintor. But we fought them off, so it may be a while until they try to attack the East Islands again."

"We left a cadre of guards to patrol the coast," Rees said. "And we've also sent word to East Harbor and points along the Learan coast to be on the lookout."

"It's times like this that make me wonder whether we were too quick to dismiss Brun's push to build new weapons." Col told Gareth and Rees about the faction that wanted to use our crystals and the facilities and talent at the Stronghold to build weapons instead of other machines.

Col, Gareth and Madoc decided we would depart in two days. The king gave permission for us to use the Queen Bronwyn and her crew. Col returned to the dock with a few others, including Gareth, to talk to Captain Woryn again.

Meanwhile, Carys had taken over the kitchen at the Citadel,

and prepared some food for us to take with us. She attempted to retrain the royal cook, but wasn't encouraged by her progress.

After luncheon, I found myself alone with the queen.

She smiled. "Hello, my dear. It seems all is going well."

"Yes, I think so."

I didn't know what to say to her about Carys, but she saved me deciding by telling me, "I very much appreciate the way you've helped my daughter these past three months. You've encouraged her to do what she never has before."

"So, you're pleased she's taken up cooking." I grinned.

"After I tasted her food, I realized it was a good choice for her."

"She has many talents going unused." I didn't know whether she was aware of Carys' abilities to use her mind and follow Madoc's teachings.

"With three older brothers, she needed a sister and she's found one in you."

I nodded. "I do love her as a sister and a friend."

"You're aware, of course, that she hopes to become your sister-by-marriage."

"And you've given her and Blane your permission, I hope."

She nodded. "Nissa, may I ask you a personal question?"

I had a feeling I knew what, but wasn't quite prepared. Still, this was a queen asking me. How could I refuse? "Of course."

She smiled. "Your feelings for my son, and his for you, are as strong as those between Blane and Carys. Am I right?"

I nodded and said, "Yes," in a faint voice.

"Madoc could not have picked any better." She smiled again.

"Oh!" The meaning of what she said struck me immediately. "You really think I'm worthy of him?"

"Why, of course!"

"I'm very pleased to hear that." I returned her smile.

"The two of you suit each other very well."

"We think so!" I blurted, then laughed, my nervousness beginning to fade.

"I have every confidence you and the others will succeed in this mission, and afterward, who knows, perhaps we will witness a double wedding."

I had never thought of that, but it seemed like a splendid idea! "Perhaps. Madoc will want to speak with my parents, of course."

"That can be arranged."

I didn't know what she had in mind, but so much else had to happen first. There would be time for that in the future.

"You know Gareth will be joining our party," I said, rather than dwell on what we'd been discussing.

"So he's informed us. His father and I won't try to stop him, especially since his presence with you will ease our worries about Carys and the rest of your party, too. I wouldn't want Carys to work too hard, but I hoped we could have a small celebration tonight for both couples."

"I...I really think it would be best if we would just celebrate Carys and Blane. Perhaps Helga and your cook could do the cooking needed and I can distract Carys in some way."

"Oh, would you? But of course you would, or you wouldn't have offered."

Unfortunately, nothing came to mind at that moment. "I'll think of something," I promised.

"I'm certain you will, my dear."

As I walked away, I wondered whether anyone else would have any ideas. I found Ana and Eva out in the garden Carys showed me the first time I was at the Citadel. "Queen Branna would like to have a party for Carys and Blane this evening, but she doesn't want Carys to have to cook for it. How can we tear her away from the kitchens?"

"We could ask her to show us the arbor up there," Ana suggested.

"Or maybe have her help us explore the Citadel."

"That might not take very much time," I responded thoughtfully. "But I'll keep both of those in mind."

I continued on. Gudrin was showing Adair, Glynis and Donal a plant she'd never seen either at the Stronghold or at the Manor. I repeated my dilemma, and Glynis immediately said, "We should take her into the city to show us where the best shopping is."

That would take much more time than the previous ideas, but still, there had to be something even better.

Donal came up with it, based on Glynis' idea. "Why don't you ask her what she's going to give her groom-to-be?"

"Yes," Adair immediately agreed. "Glynis gave me this timepiece when we became engaged. Perhaps you can suggest that to her. She'd have to go into Fairhaven to find something of the sort, wouldn't she?"

"Yes. And once we're there, we can find ways to delay her return so the cook can prepare everything that's needed."

"I'll go tell the queen and Helga, while you talk to Carys," Gudrin offered.

"I guess the king and queen have given their approval to Carys and Blane," Glynis said as we walked inside to find Carys.

"Yes."

"Does that mean there'll be a wedding when we return from Fartek?" Adair asked. "What about your parents?"

"The queen says she'll make the arrangements while we're gone."

"You both sound like we're sailing off for a pleasure cruise," Donal said. "A lot can happen between now and when we return."

That sobered us all quickly. "We'll make sure we all return safely," I said.

Carys and Blane were walking toward us. I wasn't sure how to tell her what we planned with Blane there, but Donal took charge by asking Blane to go with him to see whether we needed anything for the horses. Once they left, Glynis asked Carys whether she wanted to buy something for Blane to commemorate their engagement.

"Oh, what a great idea!" she said.

"I found a timepiece for Adair when we were betrothed. But, of course, you can decide what is most appropriate for Blane."

"Let's go shopping in Fairhaven," Carys said. "I'm sure I'll find something."

Our plan was working perfectly! We went to the stables where Blane and Donal were still going over the equipment.

"We're going shopping," Carys told them, kissing Blane's cheek. "Is there anything we need for the horses?"

"I think we need new straps for this pack," Donal said. "But perhaps the groom has some for us."

We checked, and sure enough there were plenty. So there wasn't anything else we needed. A small group of us saddled and mounted our horses and rode back into the town. Carys knew exactly where she was going.

Carys was very pleased with the worked metal box she bought Blane for his razor and shaving brush. We all agreed he would like it.

Next we bought traveling clothes for everyone.

"I can't wait to see the expressions on all the women's faces when we show up with these!" Carys said.

Our shopping had taken enough time and delayed our return long enough that we agreed we should return to the Citadel. We mounted our horses and set out. As we rode through the town, Carys was hailed frequently by people who recognized the princess. They all seemed happy to see her, evidence she was a popular figure in Fairhaven.

CHAPTER TWENTY-FOUR

Carys and I returned to the Citadel with Glynis and Adair in the midst of bustling activity. In addition to the aromas of cooking, every room was filled with streamers and flowers.

"What's all this?" Carys looked around as we walked from room to room.

"A celebration for you and Blane." I smiled at how festive it looked.

We entered the large dining room, transformed for a party. Baca was building a small platform in the middle, just big enough for a table and two chairs. Morna stood by, handing him tools. Gudrin sat on the floor cross-legged, making garlands of late summer flowers from the Citadel gardens. The queen directed Dreas and Rees to move tables and chairs.

"Where's Blane?" Carys asked. "Did he know anything about this?"

Donal shrugged. "Gareth took him to see some ancient armor or something."

"Just as Nissa took me to town, I suppose." Carys frowned, but she wasn't really angry. A twinkle lit her eyes. "Let's go dress for dinner." Carys linked her arm in mine.

"Oh! I wonder if we have clothes elegant enough!"

"Don't worry. I can loan most of the women something, and I'm sure Gareth has clothes the men can wear." Carys tugged my arm. "Come with me."

As we walked to her room we collected a few other women, and at the same time told them about the trousers we'd gotten them in town.

I'd been in Carys' room before, huge befitting a princess, and furnished with delicate pieces with flower-patterned walls and matching draperies and bedding.

"What a beautiful room!" Morna said, not that our quarters at the Manor were dingy and ugly, only smaller.

Carys had lots of beautiful clothing. She pulled out gowns, each more magnificent than the previous one. Every color of the rainbow, some with lace trim, others with embroidery and even some with both. The dress she'd borrowed for the party at the Stronghold had been lovely, especially on her, but not in this class.

"They may be a little short on some of you," Carys apologized. "But they'll fit well enough." She started going through them and pulled out a soft blue with intricate stitching on the bodice, but no other ornamentation. "This will be wonderful on you, Nissa."

I was afraid to touch the delicate fabric, let alone try the dress on. I studied it and finally reached out. It felt like silk. My finger traced the lines of stitching.

"There's a woman in Fairhaven who does the most exquisite embroidery," Carys said. "Mother won't have anyone else do our clothes."

She picked out dresses for each of us, including a lavender one for my sister. We went off to change. By the time I was ready for dinner, the rest of the preparations were done.

Besides the table for Carys and Blane, there were several set for four, six or eight people. We filled them all. I noticed Elwyn was missing, but the king and queen were there, along with all of our party including the latest additions, Gareth and Rees. I sat with Madoc, Morna and Donal.

Once everyone was seated, King Owen rose and lifted his glass of wine. "I'd like to propose the first toast to our daughter, Carys, and the fine young man she is going to marry, Blane Day."

"To Carys and Blane!" Gareth echoed, rising to his feet.

Then it was Donal's turn. "As my parents are not here tonight, I'd like to represent them in congratulating my brother, Blane, and his beautiful fiancée, Princess Carys. Welcome to our family, Princess."

"How long have you been practicing that?" Blane asked with a chuckle.

"Weeks, months maybe."

Everyone laughed. It was true, we had anticipated this day.

Helga had done an excellent job on the food. Two kinds of roasts, salads, cooked and raw vegetables, and crusty bread and rolls. Everything tasted as good as it smelled. Queen Branna watched Helga as if she was considering asking her to stay on to take her cook's place.

As the meal went on, several others proposed toasts to the couple.

With our leave scheduled for the next day, we wanted to make it an early night. Still we remained in the dining room for a while after the food was gone. Eventually everyone drifted off to bed.

Just before I left, Madoc requested a private word with me. "My mother told me you insisted this party should be just for Blane and Carys," he said. "I quite agree. They deserve their own celebration. We can have ours some day."

"That's what I thought," I agreed. "Your mother also wondered whether we'd want a double wedding." Just saying it gave me tingles.

Madoc smiled. "My mother's a romantic, but it's not that bad an idea."

"She said she'd arrange for my parents to be here by the time we return from Fartek."

"She's assuming a lot."

"They're good assumptions."

"Oh, aye, and I hope they turn out to be valid." He put an arm around me and squeezed. "But now, off to bed, dearest. We've much to do tomorrow."

"Aye," I agreed and pecked his cheek. "Good-night Madoc."

He pulled me closer still and kissed me soundly.

In the morning, I woke early, dressed in my new trousers and joined everyone in the dining room. Helga provided hot and filling eggs, sausage, even some porridge.

"It'll stick to your bones," she said. I wondered if she might return to the Citadel in the future, but she said, "We'll make a good cook out of Mattie yet. She did all I asked for last night and this morning, and very well at that."

Mattie was the mediocre cook who'd fed the royal family for some time. I guess Helga thought with a bit more instruction, her skills in the kitchen would improve.

The grooms and stableman had our horses ready. Gallin looked not only well-fed and -brushed, but pampered by their ministrations.

"Don't get used to that kind of service," I told him as I mounted, but he just snorted in the way that indicates he's laughing at me.

The king and queen saw us off. They hugged their children, but also every one of us.

"I told you they were great," I reminded Morna when she seemed surprised.

We rode through the town to the docks. People along the route stopped and stared at our procession, and Gareth and Carys waved to them all.

Both ships stood ready to leave. Donal and Kerr had devised a version of the communication system for each ship so we could maintain contact. It took almost an hour to load all of us, our horses and the rest of our machines, and to set up the system. We could use our minds to talk to each other, but we refrained from doing so unless we absolutely had to because it drained our energy reserves.

We'd divided the group the same way as for the journey from East Harbor. Gareth joined the group on the Queen Bronwyn and Rees joined ours on the Flying Dragon, but they were both introduced to Captain Woryn and to Toren, who, surprisingly, asked no questions concerning our sojourn at the Citadel.

I hoped this journey would reveal what he'd been hiding.

The two captains had the most recent maps of the sea we planned to traverse. "No one's approached the coastline of Fartek or Sudark in years, so all we have to go on are rumors and legends," Captain Woryn told us.

"There are barrier islands before we reach the mainland, but we've been told they're overgrown and the few people there are hostile," Captain Trahern added. "So we'll avoid them if possible.

We'll sail due east, use the engines to travel as far as we can in as little time as possible."

"With all you've brought, we have provisions for five or six days, and can always supplement them with any fish we catch."

The ships pulled away from the dock, one after the other, and sailed around the largest East Island. I stood on the deck, watching the shore, since I'd never seen the east side of the island. It wasn't as populated as the capital city, Fairhaven. One of the two smaller islands that made up the group was so rocky no one ever went there and the other was pretty and peaceful. It wasn't long before we cleared all of the East Islands and entered the open sea.

All that water as far as the eyes could see was mesmerizing. Madoc put an arm around my shoulders. "This will be the greatest adventure of our lives."

CHAPTER TWENTY-FIVE

At sea we worked on our knowledge of Fartekana and the Ministic languages. Katya held lessons on the Flying Dragon, while Mai did the same on the Queen Bronwyn.

Neither of them had any idea whether they were saying the Fartekana words correctly. Twice each day we assembled in a bunk room and practiced, building our vocabularies.

I struggled with some words. "What do they speak in Sudark?" No one, not even Katya, seemed to know.

Toren still acted mysteriously. His meals were delicious and varied. One luncheon we had stew, another meat pies, and the next, hot sandwiches. But he still wouldn't let anyone help him in the galley.

That meant he washed the clothes, too, with water heated on the stove. But twice he requested I mend some garments he'd washed.

After three days at sea, we still didn't see land. How much longer would it take? The Flying Dragon felt smaller and smaller. There were few places to go and only limited things to do: our language lessons, eating and occasionally fishing. The days passed slower and slower.

There weren't even pirates, the Legion or sea creatures to deal with.

Madoc and I found occasional moments of privacy but there weren't many places aboard where we could be alone for any length of time.

The fifth day dawned gray and overcast. We'd been through storms at sea, and knew what damage they could do. My boredom combined with anxious anticipation. At least we weren't dependent on sails to propel us, so there wasn't any danger of damage to them.

The seas quickly became much rougher, and the headwinds made it more difficult to go directly forwards. Captain Woryn tried tacking to avoid going straight into the wind, and Captain Trahern called to say he was doing the same.

The captains ordered all passengers below deck as a precaution. We were happy to comply, but crowded around the portholes watching the storm build and the waves intensify. We heard the captain and his first officer calling orders to the crew since they had to shout to be heard above the wind and waves. Footsteps overhead seemed to run in all directions at once.

Donal paced nervously. We'd been bored for so long, but now something was happening, we had no control over our situation. The crew had only limited control over the ship.

With no land visible anywhere nearby, no sheltered harbor or cove to sail into, the ship hewed to the right and then the left, threatening to tip over, but we knew that was highly improbable. Occasionally we each had to reach out to hold onto something so we wouldn't fall. Gita kept a tight hold on Wim, who didn't object. Raj curled himself into a ball on the floor and I wished I could do the same. Luckily, no one became seasick.

Minutes went by, and then an hour, before rain lashed the sides of the ship, rocking it back and forth. We felt and heard a crash, but had no way of knowing what had happened. I squeezed Madoc's hand, and he squeezed right back. Then another crash, and a third. Then all motion stopped so suddenly, we fell where we stood. We could no longer hear the captain or the crew. Anything could be happening on deck and all we could do was hope it would end soon.

An hour later the pounding ceased. We strained to hear the engine. It was silent. We heard the captain and crew moving about above us. A few of us ventured up to the deck to offer assistance. That's when we realized what had happened. The ship had run aground on a reef. There was no sign of the Queen Bronwyn.

The deck was awash, and a few of the crew were hurt. Morna and I rushed to find our supplies to tend to them. None of the injuries were severe, so we bandaged them, and soothed abrasions with salves.

"I've tried hailing the other ship," Captain Woryn said. "I'm afraid there's no answer."

"Where do you think we are?" Col looked around. The reef didn't appear large and no other land was visible nearby. The waves were still higher than normal, but not enough to free the ship.

"Hard to tell," Captain Woryn replied. "Once it's dark, the stars and the moon can help us know which way we want to go."

Madoc hadn't said anything, but I'd sensed him trying to touch his sister's mind or Blane's. I'd added my efforts and we received a faint reply. That, at least was encouraging. We'd continue trying.

Toren appeared on the stairs. He looked ashen and was frowning. When he saw Morna and I were caring for the injured on the deck, he walked toward us. "I need your help."

I raised an eyebrow in question, but he didn't go on. We'd finished with the crew, so I gathered our bandages and salves and followed him down to the galley. When he opened the door, I saw a young woman, not more than a girl, sitting on the cot. Blood streamed from a cut on her forehead. I frowned at Toren, but went to work immediately to staunch the blood.

"I would expect you'd know how to do this yourself, even if you don't have the magical power to heal the cut," I challenged.

Rather than answer me, he said, "She hit her head on the griddle."

"No, it hit me when it came flying through the air!" she shouted. She spoke Learic without any accent.

"I'll need a wet cloth. Clean," I told Toren.

He looked worried when he handed it to me.

"We'll clean this up and see how bad it is before I apply any salves," I told the woman. "And once I'm done, I want to hear what you're doing here." I gave Toren an annoyed glance. "And who you are."

Fortunately, the cut wasn't deep, but it was very close to her left eye. She was lucky the skillet hadn't hit slightly lower. I applied one of Mother's salves that healed facial cuts quickly with no lingering marks.

"Okay. Now talk."

"She's..." Toren began.

"I wasn't asking you." I scowled at him. "You've kept her hidden all this time. I wouldn't trust anything you said."

The woman smiled at me. "I'm Berel. I...I'm from Holden but I had to get away. Master Toren agreed to help me if I would help him."

"Help him how? No, you don't have to answer that. You were the one who cooked those wonderful meals he took credit for."

"He did?"

"Didn't you know he hadn't told anyone about you? How else would he explain the food if he didn't lie and say he'd made it?"

"Oh!" She frowned at Toren.

"What I still don't understand is why he helped you."

"It's simple, really," Toren said. "I'm surprised you didn't guess that too."

"You're not still thinking lying with a young virgin will restore your powers, are you?" I rolled my eyes. "Toren, every time I think we can trust you to be decent, you do something like this!"

"Nissa, I thank you for your help with Berel, but could you please refrain from telling the others?" Toren asked, no, begged.

"And how would I explain what you wanted of me?" I asked. "That is, if I agree."

"Maybe that I needed your help with dinner?" he suggested, but he obviously knew I wouldn't do it.

I poked his chest with a finger. "You're going to have to tell Col, Madoc and Captain Woryn about Berel. Yourself."

He frowned again, but nodded. Sighing, he led the way up the stairs to the deck. I encouraged Berel to come with us. The sooner she was introduced to everyone, the better. Knowing she was the one who'd cooked for us would make her more welcome.

When we reached the deck, I noticed several of the crew, as well as Donal, Kerr, Holt, Dreas and Baca, had left the ship and were working to free it from the reef. It was more than the lack of water underneath that was holding it in place.

Col and Madoc studied Toren's face as he emerged on deck and then glanced at Berel and me. "What's going on?" Col asked.

"I'll come clean," Toren said. "I haven't been cooking for you all. It was this girl all along."

"And this girl is?" Madoc prompted.

"What, did you pick up a stray on your way to East Harbor?" Col asked.

"She had to escape from home," Toren explained. "I won't go into details, since there are young ladies present, but I thought she'd be safest with us if no one knew she was here."

"That doesn't explain much." Col continued his acrimonious exchange with Toren.

"No, I don't suppose it does. But she's here and you'll have to admit she's a good cook."

"So you took her out of one dangerous situation and put her in another."

"It would seem so."

"Her name is Berel," I said. "She was hurt when the ship ran aground, and some of the galley equipment was tossed about."

"Are you all right now?" Morna asked her.

"Yes, thanks to Nissa." Berel smiled at me.

"Are those the only clothes you have?" Gita wanted to know.

"I have one other skirt and blouse," the young woman said.

"We should be able to find other clothing for you," Morna told her. "Come down with me and we can see what will fit."

They were about the same height and shape, and probably the same age as well. Once Morna took her under her wing, I was sure Berel would be alright, so I turned my attention to what was happening off the ship.

"Will they be able to free us?" I asked Madoc.

"It may take a lot of effort, but eventually they will. Meanwhile, the captain is still trying to reach the other ship, and to decide which way to head once we're free."

"Have you received any more response from Blane and Carys?" I took his hand.

He nodded. "But it seems even fainter. I can't make out what they're saying. Perhaps if we worked together..."

I joined my mind with his and we focused on what Carys mind was like, gentler than Blane's but with a firm core. We'd found we each had very distinctive minds. If we concentrated on just one, it reinforced any thoughts we sent. Madoc's face held the same anxiety I felt. Would it work?

CHAPTER TWENTY-SIX

Carys and Blane's response was almost immediate, but came from a great distance. They weren't aground as we were, but their ship was damaged, and they'd lost two crewmen, with several severely injured. Helga was working hard to care for them with help from Gudrin and Katya.

Like us, they had no idea where they were. Among the casualties of the storm was the communication device. Ana was trying to fix it, since all of the other gadgeteers were on the Flying Dragon.

We reported what we'd learned to Captain Woryn. He didn't question how we knew. After all, Madoc was a wizard. "I'm glad you've established some contact with the other ship."

"We've managed to release the port side," Donal called to us as he and the others moved around to the other side of the ship. It had taken them over an hour to free the starboard side.

As the clouds broke, the setting sun glinted off the water. "Now we know which way is west." The captain shaded his eyes to look at the sun. "But the stars will be a better guide to where we have to go."

Berel reappeared on deck in Morna's wide-legged pants and a clean blouse. "I'll make dinner now."

"Would you like some help?" I wanted to get her alone. Perhaps she would tell me more.

"If you'd like," she said. "Morna has already offered."

My sister and I crowded into the galley with her. I cut vegetables for a stew while Morna sliced more for a salad. Berel roasted meat on a spit that turned over the fire. That hadn't been there before. "Did you construct that?"

"No. That was Master Toren's doing. It works quite well."

I raised an eyebrow. "So he did help you with the cooking."

"Somewhat. Mostly he perused the recipe books and picked out what I was to make."

"Berel, was it really so terrible where you came from that you would run away with a strange man?" Morna tended to push people to reveal what they kept hidden. "You don't have to answer or give details if you don't want to."

"I don't like to talk about it, but you've been so kind to me. Nothing could be as bad as some of the things my father had me do for his patrons. And Master Toren has been a perfect gentleman, despite what you said earlier, Nissa."

"He has?" Morna couldn't hide her surprise. "The man is so full of contradictions. I don't think we'll ever figure him out!"

"He took pity on me, and told me how to get away and where to meet him. He said he had friends who'd be sailing on this ship, and if we could join the crew, we could travel with you."

"Did he explain the possible dangers?" I asked. "We're going to the land of Fartek. No one has heard from the people there for a thousand years, and we don't know what we'll find when we arrive."

Berel swallowed hard. "I'm willing to face any danger."

"Berel, do you know how to defend yourself, to use a knife at least?" Morna asked.

"I never have, but I think so."

"We'll show you," Morna promised. "And maybe also to use a bow and arrow, and a sword."

"You can use those?" Berel's eyes widened.

"Our father is swordmaster at the Manor in Holmdalc."

We continued to prepare dinner. Berel worked with confidence. It was probably one of the things she did for her father. I didn't want to think about what the others might be.

We were ready to serve when we heard excited shouts from above. "I hope that means we've been unstuck finally, and can continue eastward."

"Master Toren said there was another ship. Couldn't they rescue us?" Berel asked.

"They need rescuing themselves. They suffered even worse damage during the storm and we're not quite certain where they are." I didn't feel comfortable telling her how we'd tried to contact them. "But we'll find them. Our brother is on that ship with many of our friends."

"Will I have to cook for them all?"

"Actually, there's a cook aboard the Queen Bronwyn, the other ship," Morna explained. "Our friend Carys. And Helga, she's been helping."

"But why isn't there one on this ship?"

"Because Captain Woryn told us he had a cook," I replied. "We didn't know at the time it was Toren, or you were doing the cooking for him."

"You'll like them both, Carys and Helga. You can trade recipes," Morna told Berel.

We brought food up to the crew and the men from our party who'd helped to extricate the ship, then returned to the galley for dinner for everyone else. As we ate, the captain explained his plans. "We might be able to locate the other ship. If we continue east, we can keep a lookout in the crow's nest for them. There's still enough light to go on for a while."

After dinner, while we cleaned up, the crew made ready. The engine started again with just a bit of fiddling, and we were on our way.

Periodically, Madoc and I sent out thoughts to first Carys and then Blane. When Morna and Donal realized what we were doing, they joined their minds with ours. Madoc was reluctant to ask Toren for help reinforcing our endeavor, but he must have sensed it, and joined in anyway. His mind was very strong and focused.

I smiled when we finally received another response from both of them, and then they suddenly stopped again. That was more troubling than if we hadn't gotten any at all.

"We'll try again later," Madoc said, but I knew he was as worried as I.

The sunlight was soon gone, but the moonlight on the sea was bright enough for us to continue. We voyaged on through the night, taking turns trying to sleep. We were too worried to doze for long or very restfully.

By the light of dawn, we still hadn't seen the other ship. There hadn't been any further contact with Blane or Carys, either. I remembered what it had been like when we were trying to find Madoc. At times, I couldn't touch his mind with my own because he didn't want those who'd abducted him knowing what he was thinking. But that couldn't be the case now.

"Are you still here on deck?" Madoc asked as he came up behind me.

I was looking eastward, straining my eyes, willing them to see the Queen Bronwyn. "I guess I won't be able to sleep until I know what's happened to them."

He nodded. His sister and brother were both on the other ship, along with many friends.

"Land Ho!" the man in the crow's nest called. "Off the starboard bow."

We both looked up and then out again. From where we stood we couldn't see it, but obviously he did. Still, he'd said 'land', not 'ship'.

We veered slightly starboard, plowing through the water now we had a near destination. It wasn't long before we could see the island, and then just off it, the Queen Bronwyn, with few people on the deck.

We pulled in next to the other ship and called to them. The damage from the storm was obvious.

We dropped anchor. A few of the crew went ashore with Donal, Kerr and Adair. Col and Madoc followed. They boarded the Queen Bronwyn, and spoke to those on deck then returned to the shore and called to us.

"They say everyone else is searching the island," Col reported.

The island was highly wooded. There was no sense searching in the thick, tall trees. We set up camp on the shore.

Crew from the Flying Dragon helped those from the Queen Bronwyn. We'd been there an hour when everyone else emerged from the woods. I'd never been so happy to see anyone in my life.

CHAPTER TWENTY-SEVEN

Donal ran to the few of us standing on shore. "The engine on the Flying Dragon and the communication devices are working again."

"We could stay here tonight," Captain Woryn said.

We set up camp on the sand near where the two ships were anchored. Our party and the crewmen from both ships built a huge bonfire. After Berel was introduced to Helga and Carys, she helped them prepare a meal for everyone.

The short trees near the beach had strange fruits on them but one of the Flying Dragon's crew said they'd eaten similar ones before on previous trips. They were oblong with a soft but thick skin.

"Some eat the skin, but it's bitter," Lem said. "Now the inside, that's mushy but sweet."

Once you peeled off the skin, the fruit was a pale yellow and very soft, but just as sweet as he said.

"If you wrap the leaves from the tree around any kind of food and put it in the fire, the food comes out tasting better than ever," he added.

There were also nut trees, so we gathered some.

We decided to sleep aboard our vessels where we'd be protected from the elements. But before we retired for the night, both the passengers and crew, sat around the fire and talked about what we should have done the previous night and that day to improve the situation.

"I know you were trying to communicate with the passengers on the Queen Bronwyn at times." Captain Woryn looked at Madoc. "Is it some wizard's trick?"

"Actually, it's something many people can do," he explained. It was time to reveal what we did. "I've taught several of the young people at the Manor how to use the energies around us. It involves a great deal of concentration. One result is the ability to focus our minds on each other, and send messages of sorts. The more we use this ability, the better our control and skill."

"So you were trying to reach those you trained?"

"Aye. But there's more. Those who can do this must also learn how to block their thoughts from others with lesser abilities who might use knowledge of what they're thinking in battle against them."

The captain looked at those assembled around the fire. "Which of you can already use this ability?" He was surprised at the number of us who admitted to it.

"That will be useful." Captain Trahern eyes widened in awe. "Very useful indeed."

"We also use that energy to improve the accuracy of our sword thrusts," Donal added.

"I've been wondering whether the energies are a remnant from the Fall, whether they're emanations from the satellites that fell and the crystals deposited all over the world," Toren said.

It was unusual for him to share his thoughts, but he had a reason this time.

"We're carrying crystals with us as part of the devices. Do you suppose they're reinforcing the energies we use?" I asked.

My question was greeted with a mixture of smiles, nods, and quizzical expressions.

Madoc nodded. "I've thought for a long time something like that was the case."

"Should we try to use the crystals to increase our abilities?" Kerr asked.

"We need them for the devices."

"Only certain kinds of crystals have that power, isn't that true?" Trahern asked.

"All crystals can focus energy." Donal spread his hands wide. "But some also amplify it."

"Like the ones my husband is growing at the Stronghold," Mai said.

Donal nodded. "There are also natural crystals. A few are unpredictable in what they can do. But the ones Kwan is growing are of a uniform composition and size and intended solely to power machines."

"And crystals were used that way Before?" Captain Woryn asked.

"That's right. There were machines then, beyond your imagining." Madoc pointed to the Queen Bronwyn. "Ships that sailed the skies, and ways to travel on land without the use of horses or other animals, communication systems much more advanced than those we've reconstructed, machines for the home, and factories building many more."

"Madoc's books and others have pictures of many marvels but we've only been able to build a small number of them," Donal said. "And we don't have the crystals to run many more."

Helga smiled. "The way your minds focus energies is similar to the way crystals do. Ever since I've learned about some of this, I've wondered about the connection, whether it works in the same way. Our minds might be the ultimate crystal."

She had a way of thinking about things and expressing her thoughts that always caused me to shift my views of the world, just as learning about the catastrophe had. We could do things with our minds we hadn't revealed to everyone, but they fit with her theory. Although all this talk made me wonder about Toren, what he could or couldn't do, and what else he was keeping from us.

"Well, we can talk about this all night, but I propose we all get some sleep so we can depart at first light." Col rose from the circle around the bonfire.

We said goodnights and went off to our ships. A group of passengers and crew would stay ashore and patrol the beach, and a few others would walk the decks, watching for attacks from the sea, while the rest of us slept. Others would take their place in a few hours.

It had been a long, eventful day and I hadn't slept much the night before, so I fell asleep quickly, but in the very early morning hours I was visited by the dream I'd had before, a dream about being pursued down a corridor by people trying to remove the brooch I wore 'round my neck, the one Madoc bought me at the market in Arris with the blue stone in it.

When I woke, although the dream had receded to a dim blur, I immediately felt for the necklace under my nightgown, even though it was cool against the skin of my chest. Relieved, I rose and dressed. When I went up on deck, I saw Donal and Kerr fishing at the rail.

"You won't catch much this close to shore," I warned.

But my brother smiled and proved me wrong by pulling in his line with a good sized fish on it. He added it to a growing number in a pail at his feet.

The fire on the beach still burned, and Carys and Berel were already cooking breakfast. I walked through the sand. "Looks like we'll all have fish for luncheon today, but what's for breakfast?"

"We're toasting sandwiches with cheese and meat in them." Carys pointed to the stack she'd made.

"And we're also making breakfast cakes." Berel flipped one.

I grinned, because I loved both of those. "Do we have syrup for the cakes?"

"I saw some down in the galley of the Flying Dragon," Berel said. "Can you go to look for it?"

I nodded and returned to the ship. Now everyone knew about Berel, Toren had joined other men in a bunk room. There was no one in the galley when I arrived. Supplies and utensils had been moved since I'd worked in it, but after a short while, I found the syrup she meant in a crockery bottle with a stopper. I opened it to check how full and fresh the syrup was. A crust of sugar on top showed it hadn't been used for a while, but there was plenty, so I took it up to where the two women were preparing breakfast.

As we ate, we confirmed the plans. We weren't sure how far north or south of our original route we'd strayed, but Col, Madoc and Toren agreed, if we continued east, we would eventually land in Fartek. Madoc said, "The two ships can keep in eye contact, but we also have the option of using the communication system, and as a last resort, our mental abilities."

After breakfast we doused the fire with seawater, and packed everything we'd brought ashore. We boarded the boats, and weighed anchor, using the engines to move the ships from the shallow water out to the deeper sea.

We voyaged into the rising sun, ready to face whatever the day brought. The sea was calm, and the wind almost nonexistent, so it was fortunate we had the engines to move us.

The crew had their assigned tasks, but the rest of us had chores as well, including the language lessons. Berel's main job was to cook meals. A few of us helped her with both cooking and delivering the fish stew she made for luncheon, full of the meat of various kinds of fish, as well as some vegetables and potatoes. She had a nice touch with seasoning.

There were no more islands or reefs. The sea stretched in every direction, and reflected the sun.

By dinnertime it was obvious we'd be spending another night at sea, and probably another day.

CHAPTER TWENTY-EIGHT

We finally saw land on our fourth day at sea, but it wasn't what we expected. The entire coast consisted of a sheer cliff, rising from the sea without any docks to pull into.

A flock of huge white birds with wide wing spans and a piercing cry circled us for several hours. We sailed south along the coast seeking an inlet or cove or someplace to anchor.

But the cliff continued for several dulnos. Just as we were about to turn back and try going north, a break appeared in that impenetrable wall of stone. As we drew closer, we could see it was wide enough for the ships to pass through. The Queen Bronwyn went first and our ship followed not too far behind. As we moved between the massive walls of stone we could see a sheltered bay. The water was shallower and there was a thin strip of beach, although it didn't appear to be sand. Black as night, it rimmed the entire bay. Beyond the beach, the cliff walls rose to incredible heights with no obvious way through or over them.

Both ships dropped anchor a little ways from the beach. The water was so shallow the captains were afraid they would run aground any closer, but they could lower a gangplank for us to walk off and slosh the rest of the way onto the beach.

Except for more birds, the place was as desolate as any I'd ever seen. No vegetation except for some hanging from the cliff walls. As we neared them, though, we realized they weren't natural vines, but braided and sturdy enough to support the weight of a man.

Captain Woryn pointed. "We can use those to climb to the top."

"But we don't know what's up there." Col squinted in the sunlight.

Toren scooped black sand and let it run through his fingers. "We can send five or six people up while the rest of us remain here."

"The people who made those are probably up there and use them to come down to this beach," Madoc said.

"But there aren't any boats." Donal looked back out to the sea. "And there aren't many fish in the water here. Why would they even try?"

None of us had any answers, so we agreed to do as Toren suggested. A party comprising Holt, Eva, and two crew members, one from each ship, was selected. We watched as Holt tested the lowest vine to make sure it could support him, and then began to climb, using it to pull himself up the face of the cliff and his feet to walk practically vertically. He looked like he'd done this all his life.

Ollie, a crewman from the Flying Dragon, followed once Holt switched to a higher vine. One by one, all four made their way to the top. We could barely see them, but we heard Eva's voice shout down. "It's beautiful up here!"

"We should have given them communicators." Kerr belatedly slapped his forehead.

"I'll take one up to them, and I'll use my mind to communicate, too," Donal volunteered.

His arm and leg had now completely healed from the fall off his horse in the spring and I knew he was agile enough to do it.

"All right. Just be careful." Col didn't have to say that.

Balancing a small pack of food and supplies on one side and another containing the device on the other, he started up the way the others had gone. I watched him with trepidation and breathed a sigh of relief when he gained the top. Soon he called over the communication system. "Eva was right! You have to see this for yourselves!"

We all looked at each other. What had gotten him so excited?

"Can you describe it?" Col asked.

"Well, there are trees, not too tall, but with enormous leaves, and some kind of spiny fruits hanging down. And flowers. Gudrin, you'd love this place! Every color in the rainbow! A few small animals. They don't seem afraid. They're just standing there, looking up at us. We can hear water, but haven't found the source yet."

Many were ready to climb to the top to see for themselves.

"If you're certain it's safe, we'll send more people to join you," Col told Donal.

The ships' captains insisted most of their crew stay on the beach or the ships to guard them, but the rest of us were free to join those at the top of the cliff.

We left part of the communication system with the crewmen, took quite a bit of food, our swords and bows and arrows, some salves and bandages, and a blanket each in case we decided to spend the night up there.

Col carried Raj, although Wim could climb by himself. Some of our group were more nimble than others, but with great effort, an hour later we'd all reached the summit.

Eva and Donal hadn't been exaggerating. It resembled the way paradise was described in some old books, so much more alive with animals and birds and plants than the beach below. And colorful. Donal was right about that. The flowers were not only brilliantly hued but huge.

"They must get lots of rain up here." Gudrin lifted a flower to her nose. "Look at the size of this peony!"

"The climate must be more temperate than in Leara and Solwintor." Helga walked from plant to plant. "The flowers back there have already faded for the season."

We spent the next hour or so exploring the wonders of this place. Gudrin was thrilled with the plants she found, and Gita and Morna made friends with some of the small creatures who inhabited the land.

We set up a makeshift camp in a grassy meadow, and had our luncheon there, cold meats and cheese, bread and fruit. We supplemented our stores with some of the fruits growing here. We found some root vegetables, too. None of us could kill any of the small animals for food, but perhaps we'd find some wild deer or sheep to give us more meat for dinner.

Wim and Raj had a great time running around the meadow. But it was the boy who first saw the three men, hidden in a copse of trees, watching us. "Gita, Morna, come look!"

Once the men realized they'd been discovered, they came forward. They addressed us in a language quite unlike the Fartekana we'd been practicing, or any other language any of us knew, even Katya. Their skin was almost as dark as Col and Gita's and they wore animal skin vests and a kind of short britches, but nothing else. They didn't appear threatening, and I suppose we didn't to them, either.

Katya spoke to them first in Fartekana, but they didn't seem to understand.

Then Mai tried some of the Ministic tongues. Still no sign they comprehended.

We tried Learic and Solwinish. Toren said a few words in a language that sounded very strange with lots of gutteral sounds, and Baca spoke in a sibilant one.

That seemed to get a response. One of the men smiled at us and motioned for us to follow him through the trees. We left Eva, Gareth, Helga and Holt to guard our camp, while the rest of us strode after him.

As we walked, the trees grew thicker and taller. The birdsong in the background became more pronounced and shriller. There were big insects here. "Are there any snakes?" Morna asked and Baca and Dreas immediately took one of her hands.

Soon we saw huts ahead. They were similar to those of the Dorri, but larger. I counted about fifteen. Unlike the Dorri, the people stood outside and watched our approach, not frightened at all by strangers. They weren't particularly welcoming until the leader of the men who brought us to them said something.

Another man stepped forward and held out a hand in greeting. He spoke a kind of Fartekana and we were able to understand him. "Welcome to our village. I am Karf, the elder."

I didn't know whether he meant he was the oldest of the village, the oldest Karf, or whether elder was a position in their society.

Mai addressed him in Fartekana, explaining we'd traveled across the sea seeking Fartek, but went off course. She finished by asking where we were.

"You are in the village of Teyab. A humble place in the greater country of Hiyab in Sudark."

"Can you tell us the way to Fartek?" Mai asked him.

"It is a long journey north, over many mountains and across great rivers."

"Can we travel by water up the coast?" Katya stepped closer.

Karf frowned. "You do not want to go to Fartek. There is much violence there. They do not trade with peoples from Sudark, only fight with them."

"What else can you tell us about them?" she asked. "Do they have machines?"

"All machines, destroyed in the Downfall."

We looked at each other. That was what we expected and yet had still hoped to find some remaining.

"But they have weapons," Mai guessed.

Karf nodded. "Many weapons. Weapons of great force. We have nothing to defend."

"Are there other villages in Hiyab?"

"Few, but there were many more one time. Long time past, before two moons roamed the skies." He waved his hand upward.

"Do you have commerce with the other villages?"

"We trade our harvest for clothing and blankets. Some villages friendly, others..." He shook his head.

"Ask them whether any satellites landed near here," Col urged in Solwinish.

Mai repeated what he said in Fartekana. At first, Karf didn't seem to understand, but at last his head went up and down. "Great pieces rain on our land, then men come from Fartek, take away. Take our people, too."

"Didn't you go after them?" I asked.

"The ones who go, never return," Karf replied. "We stay on our land, try to protect it."

"Were you the ones who made the ropes to the beach?"

"From the vines that grow on those trees." He pointed to a cluster of tall trees on the right.

"But where are the boats?" Baca asked, trying out his Fartekana.

"They are hidden so no one takes," Karf said.

As we talked more and more of his people had come out of the huts, including several children. They seemed mesmerized by the boy with us, with his blond hair and blue eyes, so unlike their darker ones. Or maybe it was his dog. Wim said a few words of greeting in Fartekana, but none of them understood. Karf interpreted for him and the other children smiled and said something that sounded like, "Konee."

Karf told Wim, "They say 'hello'."

The boy tried to repeat what they'd said, "Konee." The children began to laugh, then motioned for him to join them in a game with sticks and a ball.

Then Karf had questions for us: why did we look so different from his people and from each other, how long had we traveled, and why were we looking for Fartek?

We answered as best we could but he didn't understand too many things. When he was satisfied he'd gotten enough answers, he introduced us to his people, and we each said our names, but both groups were so large, I knew none of us would remember everyone. By then it was getting late in the day. We told the villagers we had our own food, but they insisted we join them for a feast.

"It is not often outsiders find us," Karf said.

I was surprised they weren't more suspicious about us. I soon found out why.

CHAPTER TWENTY-NINE

The women from the village brought out bowls of food, mostly cooked vegetables. Lots of vegetables, some I'd never seen before and some I'd only eaten raw. There were cooked fruits, too.

"You live off this land, don't you?" Mai asked Karf, and he nodded.

"That looks delicious." Carys examined a pot of carrots, beans and a kind of grain. "Smells good, too! I wonder how they make it."

Leave it to her to add more recipes to her repertoire from every experience. But she wasn't the only one. Helga and Berel were also analyzing the contents of each dish.

"You are very kind to share your bounty with us." Helga pointed to her plate.

"And you are very gracious. It is so difficult for outsiders to reach us, but when they do, they ridicule us about the little we have. They leave and then don't come back." Karf's lips curled.

"What is beyond this village and the woods around it?"

"The land is barren, save for some poisonous plants. We do not go that way often. It is two days walk to the next village."

"Don't you have any animals of burden?" Mai asked. Our horses were still in the hold, so they hadn't seen them. "Do you have any domestic animals?" She'd seen how the children had reacted to Raj and the blank looks Karf was giving us. "Animals like Raj." She indicated the small dog, "Or larger ones that can carry a man or packs?"

He shook his head. The entire concept seemed alien to him.

"Raj is a dog," Katya explained, and a light flickered in his eyes.

"There were such, many years ago, but not any longer."

"Not even wild ones?" Even in Leara and Solwintor there were wild dogs and related animals.

He shook his head again. "These small creatures you see here are the only ones in the dale."

"And in the other villages?" I took a bite of an orange vegetable. It tasted like potato.

"The same."

"But there are birds." Katya waved a hand toward the sky.

"Oh, them." He looked up at the sky with a frown. "They eat our crops, and much of the fish in the sea below."

"Do you ever eat any fish?" Typical Donal question.

"Oh, yes. There is an abundance far from shore. But bringing our catch up to our village can be difficult."

"How far does the cliff extend to the north?"

"Many lomers." We didn't know how far a lomer was. "And beyond the cliff there are dangerous shoals, where the water swirls, and many ships are lost."

"How long have your people lived here?"

"Since before the Downfall." He had to mean the Fall after the Night of the Two Moons.

"And you don't want more than what you have?"

"If we had more, someone would come and take it from us."

I could understand his resignation, but it wasn't a way I could live.

Wim came running back from where he'd been playing with Raj and the other children. "They have a waterfall!" he exclaimed in Solwinish.

I thought of the one near near Dulno Lake. It was the Pelbens' source of fresh water. Perhaps we'd be able to bathe or at least replenish our water supply. I didn't know what plans Col, Madoc, and Toren had to continue on to Fartek, but we could always use water.

"Is the waterfall your water source?" Katya asked.

"Ah! It is where we wash. But the water is cold."

"And for drinking or cooking?" Mai motioned.

"There is a spring, near those trees. The water from there has miraculous powers."

Several pairs of eyebrows went up, and then some more when Mai translated what he said into Learic and Solwinish. I searched for the source of that power with my mind. He'd said the Fartekana had taken all of the crystals that fell in this area after the Fall, but perhaps they missed some. I sensed something, but it didn't feel like other crystals I'd seen. Perhaps it was a different kind of energy. I touched Madoc's mind and asked whether he felt it too. He seemed to think there might be crystal dust buried near the trees, fine enough that it didn't have the same power as the crystals we used in our machines, but still possessing the ability to give the water the powers Karf described.

After our dinner, we left the villagers and withdrew to sleep where they'd found us. They accepted that and we promised to talk to them more in the morning.

Back at our campsite, we used the communication device to let the captains and crew know what we'd learned. They didn't seem surprised, but took our word.

Karf told us we could build a fire if we tended it with care, and didn't let it spread to the trees or plants. We used fallen timbers and kindling to build one, even though we didn't need it for heat, and Madoc got it started.

We sat around it discussing what we would do the next day, and how we might resume our search for Fartek. It would be even more difficult than we presumed, and the people there would most likely be hostile. But, despite Karf's claims they didn't have machines, they'd stolen the crystals in the area, and they had to have a reason.

"We should learn more from Karf and his people before left to journey north," Col suggested. We debated asking some of them to come with us, but decided that would depend on what else Karf said.

The day hadn't gone badly and I went to sleep with a heightened curiosity about the peoples of Sudark and Fartek, rather than my usual worries. It was warm enough, and the ground soft enough, that one blanket sufficed.

When I woke in the morning, the fire that had been banked when we went to sleep, had been built up again, and our cooks were preparing coffee and tea, and the toasted sandwiches we all liked.

Once everyone was more or less awake and had eaten, we walked back through the trees to the village. Karf immediately asked if we wanted to use the waterfall to wash ourselves or our clothes. He led us to it, although we probably could have found it ourselves. The water falling over the rocks made a pleasant sound that could be heard from a distance. But the most wondrous thing about this waterfall was the colors. The water reflected the sun in a myriad of shades, almost like a rainbow. That alone was magical.

Cries of delight arouse around me. "We can take turns bathing in it!" Gudrin suggested, and everyone agreed.

When it was my turn, I found the water warmer than I expected, and soft on my skin. I could have stayed under the waterfall all day, but I knew others waited their turn.

Then we talked further with Karf. He said some of the younger men and women of the village might be willing to accompany us farther. He'd leave it to them, warning of the dangers as he'd warned us. There were two men and a woman who were best suited, since they were among those who set out in their fishing boats every few days. We didn't have the heart to explain we had experienced sailors on our ships or they were powered by machines he wouldn't understand. Frankly, I didn't either. I just knew they worked.

Before we left the Stronghold, I was concerned our traveling party would be too large and cumbersome. Slowly but surely, we added to that number, first Glynis and Adair, then Gareth and Rees, and most recently, Berel. And that didn't even count the crew of both ships. They'd all shown their worth, so I didn't complain.

Karf introduced the three to Col, as the leader of our group, and to Katya and Mai, the two who'd done most of the talking with him. But the three didn't know Fartekana, let alone Learic or any other languages anyone in our group could speak. It reminded me of trying to learn Solwinish. It had taken a while, but now I could speak and understand it pretty well, and was making progress in learning a mixture of Fartekana and Ministic languages.

In the end Karf agreed to come, too, if only to act as translator.

Was it a surprise Wim had already picked up some of the language of the village? I supposed playing with the other children, he'd heard certain words whose meaning was obvious. The other children seemed to enjoy playing with him, but more than that, they worshiped Raj. I knew he'd be sad to leave his new friends.

We spent the day learning about life in the village. The people had adapted native plants to produce the food they needed, and used the resources available to develop a way of life that didn't differ all that much from my life at the Manor. I supposed there were small communities like this throughout the world, that over the years had done the best they could with what they had, and not ventured forth to search for something bigger or better. Would I have been content to remain at the Manor if I'd never seen what life was like beyond Arrandis? I know I'd always felt some need for more, but beyond wanting to do what I was not expected to, I'd had no idea what I was missing.

Once Karf and the three young people left the village with us, they might not want to ever return, at least not to stay. Or maybe what was out there would frighten them so much they'd come back as quickly as they could, and hide in the village as they'd been doing for hundreds of years.

It was a pleasant place. Gudrin spent time with Karf and the planters and gatherers learning all she could about the flowers and vegetation. She hoped to grow some of them in the Stronghold. She collected seeds and shoots of the plants she thought would be best adapted to the conditions there.

Carys, Helga and Berel watched the cooks as they prepared luncheon to see how they made such delicious dishes from their simple plants. Our menu choices would be expanding yet again.

The three young villagers had readily agreed to go with us, and spent their day preparing for the journey and saying farewell to their families. Two of them were brother and sister, and their mother was beside herself when she learned they would both be going. It reminded me of my mother's reaction to our insistence we all continue on with our friends.

CHAPTER THIRTY

Since the villagers provided luncheon, we insisted they join us for dinner. We built up our fire and our cooks prepared a spread to show our appreciation for the help they were giving us.

For dessert, we had Meecham cookies. The children all loved them, and Carys tried to explain how they were made, but realized too late that the flour and sugar needed weren't readily available to the villagers.

"Do they make any cakes or cookies?" Helga wondered aloud.

"They haven't given us any," Katya said. "And I didn't see any ingredients or pans for them when they made luncheon."

Gudrin nodded. "They don't grow any grains. But they have plants that could be used to replace sugar as a sweetener."

"We could give them ingredients and pans," Morna suggested.

"But once those are gone, what would they do?" I shook my head.

My sister frowned but seemed to understand.

"Instead, we can give them seeds to plant grains that grow in warm, wet climates." Gudrin went down to the beach and brought them back, giving them to a couple of the women with instructions, aided by Karf.

The next morning, we all descended to the beach. We'd communicated with the ships' captains, letting them know we'd returning and bring four others with us.

I anticipated Karf's reaction to the ships and what was on them, akin to our reaction to the vale and the village.

Morna had only one concern. "How are the horses?"

Captain Woryn chuckled "We've let them out each day, as you instructed."

"Which way do we go?" Captain Trahern eyed the villagers who'd accompany us.

"North, along the coast." Col pointed. "We'll have to go quite a distance until the cliffs end. The people who live beyond that aren't as friendly as these folks."

Karf and the three young people weren't very impressed with the ships, but hadn't seen either the bunk rooms on the Flying Dragon or the accommodations on the Queen Bronwyn yet, let alone the horses we had aboard, the engines that moved the ships, or some of our cargo.

"Three masts." Karf pointed. "But the sails will not do much when you are sailing against the wind."

"Don't worry about that," Mai told him.

Since the royal ship Carys and Blane were on had more room, we assigned him and his friends to it. Once everyone was aboard and settled, the crews weighed anchor and we were off. The hum of the engines had become a part of my seagoing experience.

The day passed slowly. The shoreline remained unchanged, a wall of stone. And to the north, west and south, nothing but water. We had another language lesson. It made me wonder how the peoples of different countries conversed Before, when they used the satellites to communicate over long distances.

Later that afternoon, as Madoc and I stood at the railing looking toward the unending cliffs, I asked. "Did they have a way of understanding each other built into their communication devices?"

"More likely there was one language all educated people knew, so they could talk with others."

"Educated?"

He nodded. "There were many who continued their schooling beyond what is taught today, so t they would have a greater understanding of science and history, medicine and the laws of all the lands. They also learned more than one language because travel and communication between nations was quite free to all. I've always wanted to learn as much as many of them did."

"But it would take a long time to learn all of that."

"Yes, it did."

"And still, with all they knew, they created a catastrophe we're still living with today."

"Aye."

We stood side-by-side in silence for a short time, then he said, "Along with technology and other artifacts of civilization, I think we lost our desire for knowledge."

"You didn't, and neither did anyone at the Stronghold. All of the people who sequestered books through the years and then brought them there and other places like it didn't lose that hunger."

He nodded. "That's true, isn't it? A deep hunger to know the unknown, to seek out learning. You have it too."

"We've been feeding that hunger with this trip, and still it's not satisfied. Will it ever be?"

"Not until we die, which I hope is a long time from now." He wrapped his arm around my shoulders and pulled me closer. "Even after this journey, whatever we learn, we will continue to seek knowledge and truth and ways to better our world."

"That's a rather lofty goal." Toren's voice floated to us from behind.

Madoc turned toward him. "But you have the same hunger even as you mock ours."

"Only because knowledge is power, even more power than the crystals we seek."

"You would not have rescued Berel if your only goal in life is to be powerful," I guessed.

"Who's to say." Toren shrugged. "Perhaps I had something else in mind beyond rescue of a fair damsel."

"Don't tell us that ridiculous story about young virgins. No one believes you believe it any longer."

Toren laughed. "Nissa, Nissa. You're one of a kind! Madoc, I'd keep my eyes on her if I was you."

Madoc just smiled. I hoped he'd keep more than his eyes on me. "Toren, I'd meant to ask you before this. What do you think gave the waterfall it's energy?"

"Probably the dust from the satellites and crystals that fell here. There didn't seem to be anything unusual about the water itself, and the rocks it fell over were just common stone. I did sense something, though. Is that what you mean?"

"Yes. We've speculated about it and came to a similar conclusion."

"The dust could have given it the ability to reflect the sunlight," I offered.

Toren nodded. "It's too bad the people of the village are so content to be isolated from the world."

"Who knows what happened when the Fartekana invaded and took so much," Madoc said. "But it certainly made them quite insular."

"But not wary of all strangers. They accepted us without much question."

"Maybe we look honest and reliable." Toren sounded so matter-of-fact we laughed.

The cliff walls were changing. Breaks showed in those we passed, promising they might be ending finally. We'd been at sea for almost eight hours.

Karf had said it would take much longer to reach any navigable harbors, but he had never traveled these waters in ships like ours. Crewmen climbed to the crows nest of each ship for a better view of the coast nearby, and then the two captains and Col deliberated about the possible landing sites they saw. They finally settled on one of the larger bays that looked like a natural harbor.

As we approached, the bay seemed free of people or any sailing vessels, but that didn't mean anything as we learned from Karf and his people. A small landing party left each of the ships, meeting on the sand before setting out to explore, equipped with one of our communication devices, and a few other gadgets that might prove useful. The group included Baca and Dreas from the Flying Dragon, and Katya and Ana from the Queen Bronwyn.

The rest of us remained on the ships to wait for their return or for word from them. We hoped they'd make contact with peaceful people from this area, who could help us reach a main Fartek town.

An hour passed, and then another, with no word from the landing party.

"What's taking them so long?" Morna asked. But no one

had an answer.

Col called the other ship to ask whether they'd heard anything we hadn't. They were as anxious as we were and Carys insisted we try to call them. Col finally agreed. Donal made the call for us. There was no reply.

Ana had demonstrated some ability to use her mind to communicate in the past so Madoc, Blane, Carys and I worked together to try to touch her mind, wherever she was, but to no avail.

"I told you these people are ruthless," Karf said. "They'll capture anyone you send, maybe kill them."

"But we can't just sit here and wait!" Donal cried.

Col and Madoc devised a plan to give us the best possibility of success without endangering anyone else.

"We'll need eight volunteers to search for our friends," Col said, and that was relayed to the other ship. "And we'll need eight more to form a line from the shore to the searchers."

For once it was good we had so many people with us. Donal, Morna, Glynis, Adair, and I volunteered from our ship, but it was felt Donal should stay aboard, manning the communication device. We rowed ashore, and Glynis and Adair set out to join those from the other ship. The rest of us formed a line between them and the shore.

As the searchers moved out in the same direction as the first landing party, we strung out behind them, keeping each other in sight at first, but as they moved farther away, spreading out a little more. The search party soon sent word they saw signs of which way the landing group had gone. There was an obvious pathway and as they walked it they marked their progress, attaching twine to the trees.

Then came word they couldn't go any farther. "It looks like there used to be a bridge across a chasm up ahead, but it's gone now," Glynis reported. "There's no obvious way across."

"Then where did the landing party go?"

"They didn't fall into the chasm, did they?"

"There's no sign of them," Adair replied. "And there's no way to get across."

CHAPTER THIRTY-ONE

We frowned as we returned to the ships. While we were gone, Donal and Kerr unloaded the devices to ensure they still worked. We'd only used the imaging device and the communication system since we left the Stronghold.

Captain Woryn allowed Karf and his companions to take one of the row boats to return to their village.

The sand here was almost white and my shoes sunk into it. It went a distance to the tree line and provided quite an area to set up camp. With the ships nearby, we didn't remove everything. Many people worked on the site and very quickly we had a large sleeping area, a cooking table and fire, and a tent constructed of heavy fabric over a wooden frame to protect several of the devices we carried.

Periodically, Donal and Kerr tried to contact the group lost in the woods. There was still no sign of anyone else in the area, either. But as we discussed the best approach to crossing the chasm, another ship sailed into view from the north.

It was larger than the sailing ships we knew and had five masts with huge square sails. We prepared for any eventuality, not knowing whether those aboard would be friendly or hostile. A man hailed us, "Woo nee?" We took that to mean "Who are you?"

Mai replied for us in her best approximation of Fartekana, telling him we came on the two ships anchored offshore and were looking for the way to reach Fartek.

The ship sailed alongside, confirming how much larger it was than our ship. The man who'd spoken earlier and two others, a man and a woman, came ashore. He seemed to ask why we were seeking Fartek and where we'd come from. I was surprised I could follow as much of the conversation as I could, but it was Mai who spoke most since Katya was missing along with the rest of the landing party.

Mai related they'd been driven from their fishing village by the Panshee, and forced to live aboard their ship. They didn't say more about the Panshee, except they were evil and wanted to rule all of Fartek and Sudark.

The Fartekana they spoke was very close to her native Ministic language so she could talk with them fluently, after a while switching to her own language. She didn't tell them everything, only that a small group of our people had ventured into the woods and never returned. Their reaction made me think the Panshee probably captured them.

"Ask if they know this wood or a way across the chasm," Col told Mai.

She nodded and translated the questions. Each of the three had something to say, and they said it so fast I wasn't sure I understood.

"They've never landed here before," she said. "That chasm runs for many dagims, maybe thirty. That's a measure of distance, although there's no knowing how far it is."

"Yes there is," Madoc said with a smile. "Ask them how many days it would take to walk that many dagims."

She smiled in understanding and repeated his question in Ministic. Only the spokesman answered, and she nodded. "From sunrise to sunset."

"Close to half a day. So it's about a hundred and seventy-five dulnos, or close to four thousand gyrds." Madoc always did the math faster than anyone else.

"That's far!" Donal exclaimed.

"So we need to find a way to cross near here," I concluded.

"Why do we have to cross it?" Dreas asked. "There's no telling whether the landing party is on this side or the other."

"Are there bridges anywhere along the chasm?" Col had Mai relay the question.

They didn't know of any. Next, we asked about the Panshee again. The spokesman went into a long and somewhat complicated discourse, which Mai summarized. "There are several factions in Fartek. They believe the Panshee want to control all of the land. There are small groups of fishermen, like themselves, and farmers, all of whom call themselves Min, or The People. And there's still another group who keep themselves hidden deep in the continent. They are called Yin, or Secret Ones."

"Which do you think took the crystals from Karf and his people?" Carys asked.

"And which may have captured our friends?" Blane added. I noticed they stood close to each other and held hands.

"I'm sure they'd blame the Panshee for anything bad that happened," Col said.

Sure enough, the three fishermen said only the Panshee would do anything to harm anyone else. But that did nothing to help us find our friends or get them back.

"Where would they take any captives?" Madoc asked.

Mai relayed that. They seemed to argue among themselves before responding. "There are two camps not too far from here where they might have our friends," Mai interpreted. "The closer one is on this side of the chasm."

"Can they take us there?"

"They can tell us how to get to it, but won't go themselves."

"These Panshee may be militant, so we should be prepared to fight," Col said. "But we have no idea what weapons they have. They may be some left from Before, weapons we have no defense against."

Without waiting for our questions, Mai asked the three. "They only know about the swords and sticks the Panshee use. The sticks breath fire."

"Some kind of flame thrower," Madoc guessed.

"The texts the translators deciphered showed some," Kerr said.

"How can we protect ourselves from those things?" Donal asked.

No one had an answer. I knew he'd think about it and maybe even devise a solution if he could.

But we weren't going to wait for the Panshee to attack us,

especially if they'd captured our friends. The fishermen told us where they probably were before returning to their ship.

"We'll use the approach we tried before to search the woods, send a small group with a relay line of people." Col said.

The same people volunteered again. Col insisted on slight modifications. Both Kerr and Donal would remain behind, attempting to devise a defense using their memories of what was in the books they'd seen. The forward group was Glynis, Adair and Gareth from our ship and Blane, Gudrin, and one of the crewmen from the Queen Bronwyn. They carried communication devices with them, as well as weapons. As they moved north, the direction the fishermen said they should go, we formed a chain trailing back toward the camp to maintain visual contact for as long as possible. I was one of those closest to the forward group, walking with them for a while as they moved off. If Kerr and Donal came up with anything, we'd pass it to the forward team for their protection.

The heavy canopy of trees obscured the sun, making the woods darker than the beach. Even without real paths, everyone found the going easy. The ground was flat and covered with fallen leaves, all gold and brown. The forward group passed out of sight of those of us near the front of the line, but we still heard them moving through the trees. We took a chance and spread out a little more even though we knew the forward team would be moving further and further away.

And then we waited. For a while I stood in my position, second in the line, near a very tall tree. It was quiet except for the birds and insects, some high up in the tree. Eventually, I sat down and leaned against the trunk, wondering how long it would take the team to reach the Panshees' camp. Then I heard voices. Someone was talking to Gareth who was first in the line. I didn't know who it was until they started to walk back toward me. It was Glynis.

"We found signs of the Panshee," she said. "We can't tell how far it is to their camp, but they've been back this way recently."

"Probably looking for any companions of the people they captured," Gareth speculated.

"Could you tell how many there were?" I asked. We could deal with a small force, but if they had weapons like the flame throwers, we'd have a hard time fighting off a large group of them.

"It looked like just a few. The lower branches of trees were broken in places and the underbrush was trampled, with few footprints," Glynis reported.

"How much further have you gone?" I asked.

"Maybe twenty-five gyrds, not that far."

"We need a longer line," I said. "We'll stay here while you return to the camp to report."

She nodded and continued back in that direction. I knew Gareth had experience fighting off attacks on the East Islands, but wondered whether he'd ever faced anything like this.

As if reading my mind he said, "We need to plan our strategy for the coming battle."

I nodded. I wasn't a stranger to battle myself. The expeditionary force to Dulno Lake withstood attacks from Brun who wanted the Stronghold to develop weapons rather than other machines.

"We need both a defensive and offensive strategy," Gareth said. "Is my brother the next one in line after you?"

I nodded, wondering if he was planning on leaving me to seek Madoc.

"Tell him to come here so we can discuss this. Then he can relay the information to the others."

It was a good suggestion. I focused my mind on Madoc's. It was easy; I'd communicated with him that way many times before. I told him what Gareth suggested and he agreed. He wasn't that far from where we stood, and soon joined us.

"We need to find the best way to defend all of us from the Panshee," Gareth said. "But we also have to rescue our colleagues."

"What do you suggest?" Madoc asked. "As far as I know, Donal and Kerr haven't come up with anything yet."

"How did you fight the marauders in Solwintor?"

Madoc and I described the battle, as well as our clashes with Klaus Brun and his men.

"So, those tricks with your minds are good for something other than talking to each other and fighting ice bears," Gareth said.

"We learned we can focus a scream with our minds that hurts our opponents heads so much they can't concentrate on fighting," I told him. "Unfortunately, if they know the attack is coming, and are strong enough, they can block the effect."

"How many of you can do this?"

"At least seven. We've shown others, too, and they've had limited success. Ana was able to do it, but she's one of those who were captured."

"But you never faced flamethrowers or other weapons, only swords and knives, right?" Gareth asked.

"That's true," his brother confirmed. "But if we can disconcert the enemy, their ability to fight us will be diminished."

"We can't count on that," I cautioned.

"So what can we count on?" Madoc asked. "Nissa, we have to rely on our strengths and abilities."

I nodded. I just hoped they'd be enough this time.

CHAPTER THIRTY-TWO

Glynis returned from spreading the word about the possible nearness of the Panshee and brought news that Donal and Kerr had made progress in devising shields against flamethrowers. She brought one of their inventions with her. It looked like the chest armor used against swords, only a bit larger, and made of a solid piece of metal.

She tapped on it. "This material can deflect fire, even reflect it at the person shooting. I think I know how it works. I'll need a burning stick to demonstrate."

Madoc found a long twig under a tree, and used his mind to focus enough energy to ignite it. Glynis pressed a button on the back of the shield, and it began to shimmer a green color. When Madoc held the burning twig to it, the fire went out. I felt like clapping.

"Let's try that again," Glynis said. This time when she pressed, the shield glowed blue and when Madoc held out the newly lit branch, the entire thing burst into flames. He had to drop it to avoid being burnt.

"Oh, well done!" he exclaimed, stamping on the branch to put out the fire.

Gareth examined the shield and nodded. "This should work, but how many can they make ready?"

"They're attempting to make eight or ten, but don't have enough material for more. Everything they used came off the ships."

"It's a start," Gareth said. "Combined with your abilities it might be sufficient."

"Abilities?" Glynis questioned. "You mean you can do more than use your minds to talk to each other and start fires?"

I nodded, realizing I'd never told her about how far we'd gone in developing those skills. Just as we had for Gareth, I explained how we'd been able to fight off the marauders and Brun's people.

"We should rethink who will take the lead here." Gareth surveyed the group. "Our first line of defense should be our best, although we have to keep some in reserve."

"You should talk to Col," Madoc said. "But I agree. Blane, Toren, Nissa and I should be at the forefront."

"What about Carys?" I asked. He was reluctant to expose his sister to danger, but she was quite capable.

"She, Donal and Morna should be next."

Gareth nodded. "And you should have one or two others who are well-trained in combat."

"Like yourself, I suppose?" Madoc had a twinkle in his dark eyes.

We called those ahead of us and everyone returned to the beach to consult with Col and collect the shields Donal and Kerr devised.

Madoc presented the plan. Col stroked his chin. "Are you sure you want Nissa at the front?"

"I can handle myself." I faced him with defiance in my eyes.

"Oh, I know that. But perhaps we should put our Defenders first, followed by our wizards."

"You mean Madoc and Toren."

"I mean all of you who have mastered the use of your minds."

In the end, we compromised. Gareth would be first, followed by Toren, Madoc and Blane. Next my sister and me, Carys and Eva, and finally Donal.

"But then we'll need nine shields," Kerr said. "We'll be hard-pressed to make eight."

"If the Panshee can get through the first eight with shields, having one more won't help me much," Donal pointed out.

While we waited for them to finish, we ate bread, cheese, and a fruit that grew on the trees at the edge of the forest. It looked like a deep red apple and had the same kind of skin, but inside it was softer in texture and the taste was sweeter than most apples.

We put food in our packs and slung them on our backs, and then set out again into the forest.

It was dark in the woods. The canopy of trees blocked what little sunlight was left, and I doubted we could see the Evening Moon when it rose. The sound of our footfalls on the recently fallen leaves competed with birdsong and the chittering of insects. The brightly-colored birds were huge, like the trees they lived in. The saucer-sized leaves decorating the trees were still green, but those that already changed color carpeted the ground in golden red hues like a dying sunset.

"Nissa, this shield is heavy!" Morna held hers low, as if she couldn't lift it.

"Would you rather have no protection against the Panshee's flamethrowers? They're heavier because of the crystals that power them. Donal said they'll absorb the energy of the fire, magnify it and send it straight back where it came from."

"But couldn't he and Kerr have made them lighter somehow?" Her face was already covered in a sheen of perspiration and she'd tied her red curls back like I always tied my brown tresses. She swatted at the tiny insects that came and went in swarms.

"What are you complaining about now?" Blane stopped to wait for us to catch up.

Rather than answer, Morna asked, "How much farther do you think it is to the Panshee's camp?" The whine was gone from her voice, replaced by a determination she'd been showing more and more as our travels continued. I realized she'd been complaining only as something to say during the long walk from the beach.

"Madoc and Toren just reported they've seen fresh tracks they think were made by Panshee," Blane replied. We were using the communication devices to keep in touch since not everyone could communicate with their minds. Although the Sudark village we'd recently visited had a strong power source, there didn't seem to be as much energy here in Fartek. We also didn't want to alert any nearby Panshee that any of us could use our minds like that.

"But that doesn't mean their camp is nearby." I strained my ears for sounds besides the birds and animals.

"They won't wander far from their camp."

"Unlike us." Morna tried to be sarcastic, but she didn't have it in her.

Carys and Eva had caught up with us by then. "What are the three of you dawdling for?" Eva asked. "This isn't a Sunday stroll in the park."

I still had problems at times interpreting her words or Ana's. Madoc called it jargon. I took her to mean we should walk faster. Blane took Carys' hand and the two of them led the way. As we followed, Morna asked Eva, "What kind of park do they have where you come from?"

But she never had a chance to answer. We were suddenly surrounded by ten men, as if they had dropped from the trees. They were shorter than Eva and me, about Morna's height, with long black hair in braids, and their chests were bare except for some markings made with blue dyes. I was certain we'd met the Panshee.

Two of the men grabbed Blane's arms, but didn't touch any of the rest of us. I wondered if it was because we were women.

One of the men began speaking rapidly to us. It sounded like the Fartekana Mai and Katya had taught us. Was he asking where we were going? I made a stab at replying, hoping I didn't say something offensive. "We are looking for friends."

They laughed, either at my feeble attempt to speak their language or what I said, didn't matter.

"What are they going to do to us?" Morna's voice was low, not that we expected them to understand Learic.

They motioned for us to come with them. I hoped they'd go in the direction of the rest of our party, but instead they led us at an angle toward the chasm we hadn't been able to cross.

The Panshee carried long and thin sticks, made of a kind of metal with a wooden end like a handle, their flamethrowers. I wondered what made the fire in them, whether crystals were used, and how the fire was propelled any distance, but concluded we'd have to take one apart to learn how it worked. And first we'd have to get one.

Tentatively, I reached out to the mind of the man who'd addressed us. He seemed to be the leader. But all I encountered was a shield preventing anyone from touching his mind. Did he know some of us were capable of doing that? Had any of their captives tried? Ana was the only one among them who could. And what abilities did the Panshee have? But more than anything else, I wondered where they were taking us and whether we'd be able to get away.

Hoping the Panshee leader's mental shield would also prevent him from hearing me, I focused the little energy there was and sent a message to Madoc, just a visual of the Panshee herding us ever closer to the chasm. But there was no response. I couldn't tell whether he heard my call or not.

The rim appeared in the distance. Was the Panshee camp at the bottom of the chasm? If so, how would we get to it?

CHAPTER THIRTY-THREE

No stairs were visible in the sheer stone on the other side of the chasm, or even vines like the ones we used to climb the cliff in Sudark. I didn't dare go close enough to the edge to search for any on our side.

The Panshee leader reached into the bole of a tree near the chasm rim and, wonder of wonders, a mechanical whir accompanied the extension of a metal platform over the abyss towards the other side.

"There IS a bridge!" Morna exclaimed. The end met the opposite edge with a decided click, and the whir ceased.

Waving his flamethrower, the leader herded us onto the narrow span. We had to walk single file over the narrow band. I avoided looking down at the snaking blue line of a river way below us. Instead, I looked toward the trees ahead. The bridge wasn't as solid as it looked. It flexed with our combined weight. No hand rails, nothing to steady me as I stepped forward on legs that felt like melting wax. The end of the bridge appeared far away, but I wasn't really anxious to reach its apparent safety. Once we reached the Panshee camp, we'd face new perils.

Blane walked ahead of me, and I concentrated on his back. I knew Morna followed me, but I couldn't do anything to help her except move steadily forward, or as steadily as my limp legs could take me.

We reached the end and stepped onto the far rim of the chasm. I'd half expected a greeting party, but no one was in sight. Once we stood on solid ground again, the leader turned down a path to the left and his men urged us to follow. There was nothing else we could do.

The forest on this side wasn't as dense. Before long we reached a clearing, and in the center of it, a camp of sorts. Two tents, close together. Most of the people clustered around a fire. Ana and Katya sat on the ground with two Panshee standing over them. They looked up towards us, and Ana frowned. We obviously weren't there to rescue her and the others of our party. Still, perhaps we could work together to escape our captors.

I thought back to how Carys and I managed to get away from Galen Evans and his men in Meecham by putting thoughts in the heads of the weakest. It would be difficult to do the same thing, especially since I didn't know much of the Panshee's language. I'd have to keep my eyes and ears open for opportunities, and my companions would do the same. I had a lot of faith in my brothers and sister, in Carys and Eva, and even in Ana, Katya, Baca and Dreas.

I counted the Panshee. There were at least twenty of them and only ten of us. We'd have to do something surprising, something they wouldn't expect and hope that would give us the edge. The Panshee were all men. Did they allow their women to be warriors, or expect the females among us to have any fighting skills?

Reaching out my mind to Blane, Carys, Morna, and Ana, I told them what I thought. Amazingly, the strongest response came from Morna. I bet they'll ignore us if Blane, Donal, Baca and Dreas keep them occupied.

Good idea! Blane agreed immediately. I'll pass the word on to the others as unobtrusively as possible. You girls be ready to take off.

Of course, escaping would be just the start. We'd have to find our way back, find the mechanism on this side of the chasm to extend the bridge. And what would happen to Blane and the others if we got away? I must have projected my doubts, because Carys added, We'll only do that if we're sure the rest of you can get away, too.

Eva walked past me, whispering, "What are you planning?"

Ana explained to her out of the side of her mouth as she continued on, and added that the Panshee didn't seem to understand Learic or Solwinish, meaning we were free to speak without them knowing what we said.

That was the first good piece of news I'd heard in a while. But we still had the same problems with our plan, to ensure the men could escape, too.

Meanwhile, the Panshee leader addressed Blane. From his tone, and the few words of Fartekana I knew, it sounded like he said we were their prisoners, as if we didn't know, and they were going to find out why we were there.

The man walked off when he finished, entering a tent. He returned with a young man, slim with dark hair and piercing blue eyes. The man said a few words to the newcomer, who then turned to us and said, in fairly decent Solwinish, "Tell me why you're here." So much for them not knowing our language.

I looked at Ana, silently asking her whether this person questioned them before, but she shook her head almost imperceptibly. *I've never seen him. He must have just arrived*, she mind-sent to me.

The young man had addressed Blane. Did he think my brother was in charge of us? Blane replied, "We come from over the sea, seeking any remnants of the civilizations that existed in Fartek before the Night of the Two Moons."

The man looked puzzled, but then his face cleared. "You mean when the Second Moon was launched, and all the devastation followed. What makes you think any of that ancient civilization remains?"

"We didn't know for certain, but thought it worth finding out. We've found some vestiges of machines, of technology, and of science in our own lands, and are trying to rebuild."

That was true, but there was a lot Blane wasn't saying.

"My name is Fong-Wei. And you are?"

"My name is Blane Day." My brother essayed a half bow.

Fong-Wei led us to the largest tent in the complex, red and green striped with an awning in front of the flap door. A piece of tent material covered the ground under the awning and he wiped his shoes on it before holding the flap open for us.

It was cooler inside and free of those nasty little bugs that had plagued us since we entered the jungle on the other side of the chasm.

Fong-Wei offered blue and red striped cushions to Blane and Dreas. The rest of us had to sit on the dirt floor, but that was what we'd done outside. It was crowded with all of us inside, but at least we weren't separated.

"Tell me more about your voyage here." Fong-Wei sat on a third pile of brightly colored pillows.

Blane took the lead he was offered. "We began seeking the source of two books we believed were in the language of this country. We hoped people here had kept technologies alive that had perished in other parts of the world."

Fong-Wei inclined his head. "We have some of that knowledge, but those who possess more of it guard it closely and refuse to share it." He seemed to provide information freely, and acted friendly enough, but I instinctively didn't trust a cold edge to his voice.

"And who are the ones with that knowledge?" Ana asked.

He ignored her, but Dreas said, "My friend asked you a question."

He took a deep breath. "We are not accustomed to having our women participate in important discussions."

"Well, no offense, but we are." My brother smiled to soften his words.

"Very well. We call them Tektek. You may call them something else. They horde the machines. The ones we have, we stole from them at some cost to our tribe." He frowned. The sadness in his eyes made me believe he'd lost at least one person dear to him. "It isn't much to show for the lives of eight of our own."

"Where do the Tektek live?" Blane asked.

"Two days walk inland. Their buildings are covered by a protective field. You can see inside, but we could never penetrate it, even with our weapons."

"Then how did you steal what you did?" I blurted.

Fong-Wei turned to me. "I can see I must abide by your customs and allow your women to talk."

"Sorry." I ducked my head.

"No. You are right. We should not impose our ways on you. Men and women are equal in your society." He looked around at all of us. "Are you all even from the same society? You seem so different."

Blane waved a hand to encompass us all. "We are originally from different lands, but have banded together to redevelop the civilization that once was."

"I wouldn't be so eager to do that. Look at what happened to that civilization."

Blane nodded. "That is true, but we learned from the mistakes they made."

"And yet, we still have two moons that appear every night, the Real Moon, and the Moon of Destruction."

CHAPTER THIRTY-FOUR

"Is that what you call the moons?" Morna asked. "The real moon and the moon of destruction?"

Fong-Wei nodded. "And you call them, little one?"

She'd been called worse things. "We call them the Evening Moon and the Second Moon. Not very imaginative, of course. But we didn't know the history until recently."

"We did." Ana shrugged. "And yet, that's what we call them as well."

Fong-Wei studied her, then again looked at the rest of us. He pointed at Katya. "You must come from one of those lands where the sun baked the people."

She laughed, flashing her white teeth. "Are there those who still believe that? The world has changed, yet some things remain. Some don't even know where their ancestors came from. I was actually born in Rinaga in the far west, but grew up in Solwintor."

"And the rest of you?"

Blane indicated Morna and me. "My sisters and I are from a village in Arrandis, a part of Leara."

Our host shook his head. "You don't look related."

I laughed. "I can assure you, we are."

"Carys and I come from the East Islands off of Leara." Rees didn't call her Princess Carys, I noticed.

The others added their birthplaces. By then I think Fong-Wei was totally confused. He blinked his eyes several times. We didn't dare add to that confusion by adding all of our names.

"And you? We know you are called Fong-Wei, but who are your people? And how do you know Solwinish?" Holt asked.

"You know we are called the Panshee." At our nods, he went on. "That was the name of the part of Fartek where our ancestors lived. Far to the north, but the floods drove us to these forests. Others with better weapons than we had completed what the floods started, and we hid here for decades. You asked how I knew Solwinish when most of my people only speak a dialect of Fartakana." He nodded. "My forefathers were teachers. They tried to keep knowledge alive in our people, but couldn't, only with our family."

"So you're more educated than the others?" Blane asked.

"Educated, yes, but education is not valued here, you understand." He sighed. "And our family is dying off. If I do not choose a mate soon, and provide children to her, our line will end with me."

"Your parents had no other children?" Morna frowned.

"Parents. You mean mother and father, right?"

She nodded.

"My father was one who perished during the raid on the Tektek. He was there to convince the party there was another way, that the Tektek might be open to negotiation. Instead, he was killed along with a few others, and the raid was a failure."

"Where did you get the flamethrowers?" Rees asked.

He looked at the weapon still in his hands. "We've had those many years, obtained from a party crossing through the forest on the way to Sudark."

Blane's eyes narrowed. "A party from where?"

Fong-Wei shrugged. "They did not stop for us to ask."

"You said you hoped to choose a mate. Where are your women?" I hadn't seen any. "Is your mother with them?"

He swallowed hard. "We keep our women hidden. My mother is among them. She teaches the women some of our traditions."

I groaned. I knew what it was like to have someone decide what women should learn. But it wasn't my place to tell him. The women of our party might show by our examples how much we could contribute to our group.

Holt asked, "Have you picked a mate among the females?"

Fong-Wei frowned. "I thought I had, but she would not have me. She went with Do-wer instead, claiming he was a fiercer warrior. I realized she was not the kind of woman I would want for a mate."

"What kind is that?" Carys asked.

"One who would appreciate what I have up here," he pointed to his head, "and here," he thumped his hand over his heart, "are more important than how many animals I have killed."

I smiled, beginning to appreciate him more. Morna caught my eye and smiled as well. There were still many things I didn't like about him or his people, but he might be more open than anyone else in this village.

"I will take your females to meet ours, but you men must stay here. You will be safe and so will they. You have my word of surety."

I sent my brother a reassuring thought. He knew we could handle ourselves better than Fong-Wei might suspect.

"We'll wait here," Blane said.

"It could take some time. It is not close and the way is difficult. My people will bring you food. We'll take a trusted few to protect your women on the trek."

Blane and Rees nodded.

While Fong-Wei was gone we talked amongst ourselves in our mixture of Solwinish and Learic. We had no reason yet to try to escape, but Blane proposed that while we were gone, he would try to reach out to Madoc and Donal with his mind to let them know what was happening with us.

"We'll do the same, Morna, Carys, Ana and I. All four of us working together should be able to reach them wherever they are." I shouldered my packs and prepared to leave.

Carys put her arms around Blane's neck and kissed his quickly. We were ready when Fong-Wei returned with three other Panshee, each carrying a flame thrower.

"These are our guards." He made no other introductions. "They will see us safely to the women's compound. I have packs of food for our journey."

The six of us women followed him and the guards out of the tent and back into the woods towards the chasm. I hoped we wouldn't have to cross the bridge again. More important, I wondered what dangers Fong-Wei thought we'd face that we needed guards along.

I breathed a sigh of relief when we veered away from the end of the bridge. Instead of having to brave it, Fong-Wei led us to a series of stone steps cut into the side of the cliff. They were narrow but not too steep, and the going was easy at first. Then the stairway curved to the right and grew steeper. After about fifteen steps, a level section appeared. We stopped to catch our breaths and then continued on. Another section of stones brought us to another even wider level section.

Two men sat cross-legged on the ground, but stood when they saw Fong-Wei and the rest of us. "All is quiet," the taller said.

He nodded at them. "Sit. We will join you and share our food."

There was barely enough room for us all. Fong-Wei distributed the bread and cheese he had wrapped in a piece of red cloth, then passed around water skins for us to drink.

The two men stared at us, but didn't ask questions.

Still, Fong-Wei told them, "I am taking them to our women," it sounded like to me. A suspicion sneaked into my mind. Did he want us to become part of the group of women the Panshee kept secluded somewhere on this cliff, perhaps close to the bottom? I glanced at Katya. She knew his language much better than I did, but she wasn't adept at mind-thought. I caught her eyes and tilted my head. She smiled. I hoped it was to reassure me.

It reminded me we'd planned to contact Madoc and Donal on our way. I reached for my sister's hand and squeezed it. She took my meaning, as I could feel her mind combine with mine, that youthful 'voice' her mind had was unmistakable. Carys quickly joined us, followed by Ana, but we hit a wall of some sort, as if something was reflecting our call back at us.

Once we finished our food, Fong-Wei shook hands with the two men and he led us farther down the stone stairway. As we descended, the sound of rushing water confirmed we were nearing the river at the bottom of the chasm. The smells of water and plants were different from the piney ones up higher, more mint and herbs. But there were more insects, the kinds you feel but never see. I waved my hands about to keep them off my face without much success.

"Rub some of this mint on your skin. It'll ward them off."
My sister must have learned that from Mother or from Gudrin.

Without the insects to deal with, I could concentrate on the
increasing feeling of great power I had as we neared the bottom.
Something shiny glittered on the sides of the stone steps. I bent to
pick a piece up. Could it be a crystal? It was irregular in shape, but
it seemed to focus energy. I showed it to Carys and she nodded.

Soon we heard voices, high-pitched, but not women.
Children. I smiled. Of course. Where the women were, there were
bound to be children.

We were closer still to the water. The stairway continued to
wind down the hill. As we came around still another bend we saw
them, a cluster of seven or eight children of both genders, chasing
each other, laughing, and tossing bits of the crystals to each other.
They stopped when they saw us and stared.

CHAPTER THIRTY-FIVE

Fong-Wei strode toward the children and ruffled the course black hair of one of the older ones. "How many times have we told you not to play with those, Eng?" The more I heard his language, the more I understood. But we couldn't let on we knew what they were saying. We needed every advantage until we knew what they wanted with us.

"Sorry." The boy looked down and dropped the piece he held. Then he stared at us through half-lidded eyes.

"These are visitors from Solwintor. Remember what my mother told you about that, and why you should learn their language?"

He nodded.

"Well, now you can practice. Say 'hello' to our new friends."

Eng swallowed. "Hallo," he said carefully, and smiled at us. "Welcome to the Pin Shing camp." He looked up at Fong-Wei for approval.

Fong-Wei grinned at him. "Very good." He tousled the boys head again.

Taking their cue from them, the other children imitated Eng's attempts at Solwinish. We all smiled at them and murmured our approval.

A short woman approached. Like the rest of her people, she had narrow, slanted eyes and dark hair, even darker than Carys', but hers was tinged with gray, long and braided down her straight back. Although her skin was unwrinkled, it was clear she was older than most of those we'd met, perhaps my parents' age. She wore a robe in one of the multicolored fabrics that brightened the village at the top of the cliff.

In very precise Solwinish she said, "Welcome to our enclave. I am Ying, mother to Fong-Wei."

"You're the teacher." Morna smiled back. "I'm called Morna and this is my sister, Nissa, and our friends, Carys, Ana, Katya and Eva."

"You have come a long way. What brings you on this journey?"

We hadn't told Fong-Wei the precise reason for our quest, so I kept it simple. "We are seeking any vestiges of civilizations that existed before the launching of the Second Moon, the one you call the Moon of Destruction, and rightly so."

In rapid-fire Fartekana she spoke to her son. I caught the words 'alone' and 'men', also 'how many.' Katya likely understood more of what they said, but Ying was obviously curious how six females made such a journey.

"Come, sit. I will tell you about our people, and how we came to be in this place." She sounded more willing to talk than Fong-Wei had been. "When the floods came." She stopped. "You know about the floods that washed so much away after the Moon was launched?"

We all nodded.

"Good, then I won't have to explain. Many here no longer believe it happened, but we have records."

"You do?" Katya couldn't hide her excitement. In all our books, reports of the devastation were sketchy. Perhaps we'd learn more than we thought from these people.

"Yes, but only what happened near our land, you understand." She spoke like a teacher, clearly, concisely, waiting periodically for an indication we comprehended what she meant. "We lived far to the northeast. The floods covered our land and we fled to the mountains, losing contact with everyone all over the world. There was much communication before that, exchange of information between nations, trade as well. You know what that is?"

Again, we nodded.

Ying smiled. "We took what we could and climbed as high as possible to avoid the invading waters. Many years we stayed there until the seas receded again, but never to the old boundaries."

"The seas cover more than three times as much land as they did Before." I emphasized the word Before as the people of Solwintor did.

"So we also believe. We left the heights after that, seeking a place for our people. Up high in the mountains the land was not rich enough to grow crops." Her command of Solwinish was astonishing. She never had to think long for a word. "We found a pleasant valley to the east of here but were driven out before long by men who didn't want us there, men of the Far-Teka race."

"So you are not Far-Teka?" I tried to pronounce it the way she did.

"We call ourselves Pin Shing, but others call us Panshee. Pronunciations have changed over time. It has been a millennium, has it not, since the many nations could talk freely with each other?"

"Yes. We know of the artificial satellites used for communication." Should I tell her about the one we retrieved? That it seemed to have been made in Fartek, or as she said, Far-Teka?

But Ana beat me to it, using her sometimes incomprehensible jargon. "The label on the one we hoisted from the bottom of a lake said, 'Made in Fartekana'. Unmistakable, even if we couldn't decipher much else."

Ying stared at her, then blinked and nodded. "Yes, many were made there, or at least parts. Their technicians and scientists were known world-wide for their splendid devices."

"Powered by crystals, no doubt." Ana pointed to the shiny flecks at our feet.

Ying raised an eyebrow. "My mate believed so. He thought we could negotiate with the Teks, offer them crystals in exchange for devices we could use."

"And it got him killed. Your son told us. He called them Tekteks."

"Technicians from Far-Teka. They've cut themselves off from contact with anyone else using a plastic dome."

"Plastic?" Morna asked. She seemed to be struggling to understand everything Ana and Ying said.

"A material made by men in factories years ago, long before the catastrophe that ruined our world. It can be very strong but flexible and yet you can see through it. The amount of sunlight, or moonlight, that can penetrate is adjustable."

I'd have to remember to mention this to our scientists. If I ever saw any of them again.

"You say you were able to retrieve a satellite?" Ying addressed Ana again.

Ana glanced my way, then Eva's, looking for guidance, I thought.

"We came here to find out if any other satellites had been found. Ours wasn't complete, but our people are working on determining how it worked and whether any of it is still salvageable after all this time. You understand, it sat under a lot of water for a thousand years, and--," I turned to the others and asked, "What was the word they used? About the metals and crystals that were absorbed by the water?"

"Leached." Ana smiled at me. I'd told just enough without revealing how many people were working on all aspects of the Stronghold.

"How did that affect the water?" Ying was astute enough to ask.

"It changed the color, especially deep down, and it also had surprising effects on the plants and animals. Deer who drink from the lake are very strong."

"And there are some very big fish." Everyone laughed at the way Morna held her hands far apart to indicated how big.

"We warn our children not to play with the crystals. The ones here are natural, but I would imagine any used in the satellites were refined, with powerful focusing power."

I remembered how the Yashii used the Crimson Orb to focus power and heal Carys' broken foot. But who recently speculated our minds were even greater at focusing?

"My son says your men are still at the top."

I nodded. "He insisted they couldn't come here, but we should meet you and the other women."

"Then come, I will introduce you. It shouldn't take long,

and then we shall have tea and tell each other more about our lands and peoples." She beckoned with a slim finger, and we followed her to a group of women sitting on the ground around a low table. One had a loom in front of her. I'd seen one before during a trip to Arrandis. Strands of several colors fed back and forth through it as she worked a wooden shuttle. Another woman wound very fine red thread. Still others were embroidering like I learned at the Manor. I pointed and looked at my sister and Carys. They both knew how much I hated that kind of sewing.

I'd come to appreciate practical sewing at the Stronghold, but decorative work held no thrill for me.

I tried to remember the names Ying said for each of the five women, but they looked so much alike, and the only thing that seemed to differentiate them was the work they did. I thought the weaver was Sen and the embroiderer was called Pen. Even the names were similar. I understood why Fong-Wei wasn't interested in picking any of them, but wondered which was the one he wanted who selected someone else.

A sixth woman joined them. She appeared taller, although it was hard to tell when the others were sitting. Her long black hair flowed down her back in a cascade. She was very graceful as she sat and then she looked at us. Somehow the combination of slanted dark eyes, small nose and mouth, and slim face came together into a lovely picture none of the others had. Part of it was the light shining in her eyes.

"And this is Chin." Ying continued her introductions.

"We wondered why the women live here, while the men stay on the top." Ana smiled.

"They must hunt for food to supplement what we can grow here."

"And raid other peoples?" Katya crossed her arms.

Ying looked down. "To our regret. It is not the right way, but the others have so much more than we do. Our numbers are dwindling, we have a harder and harder time to support our people."

"Perhaps if you let the women have a say. We come from very different nations, but in all of them the women are a part of the society, shaping what happens."

I nodded at Katya. She was right. "My sister and I grew up

in a place where women had defined roles and men had others, but that didn't mean we were shut away, kept isolated to protect us."

"How did you come to travel here together, then?"

Again I chose my words, picking something she would understand. "A friend of ours had two books in a language we didn't know. One had star charts, very different from the way we see the formations at night. The other had pictures of devices none of us knew. We traveled north from our home on the continent of Leara and crossed the sea to Solwintor. By chance, we met a man who worked with the others here." I waved my hand to encompass Ana, Katya and Eva. I stopped and waited for her to nod.

"We're looking for the source of those books and concluded the language was Fartekana."

"How many?"

"What?

"How many of you are here in Far-Teka? You women, and the men with you. How many more are on the other side of the chasm? How many near the beach?" She sighed. "You've told us much, but it is only part of the truth."

"And you've been completely upfront with us!" Ana glared.

"Upfront?" It was the first time Ying questioned her words. I learned a while back that sometimes Ana uses her vocabulary as a weapon, as a way to make others uncomfortable. They spend time trying to understand what she said and forget what they asked. It seemed to work, at least for now.

"Mother, what are you talking about?" Fong-Wei appeared.

She laughed. "Don't let them fool you. They understand the language of this place well enough to know what you are saying. You might as well speak their language." So she knew. I suppose we gave ourselves away somehow. I chuckled. I was picking up some of Ana's expressions. Not long ago I would never say 'gave ourselves away', I wouldn't even know what it meant. "Our tall friend finds this amusing."

I shrugged. "I was thinking about something else. Neither of us trusts the other completely yet, and why should we? Your men captured us. They hold us prisoner. We know you are not above raiding other groups to get what they have. We're strangers. You only know what we've told you about why we're here."

Ana nodded. "So how do we convince you to trust us, or you make us trust you?"

"What can we tell you that will reassure you we are not here to harm you?" Carys asked.

"You have seen how many are in our enclave down here, and how many men above. Tell us how many of your people are here." Ying crossed her thin arms around her body.

CHAPTER THIRTY-SIX

Should I include the ships' crews in the numbers I gave Ying? The last count of those from Solwintor was eighteen. Then there were Glynis and Adair, Gareth and Rees, and Toren's friend. "Another fourteen plus the members of the crew that sailed us here."

"And they are probably looking for you." The woman cupped her chin and tapped her cheek with a finger, as if she was contemplating my answer.

"I would think so." Madoc and Donal would, at least.

"Do they have the two books you spoke of?"

Was she going to demand that we hand over the books? Madoc would never do that, not without surety he'd get them back.

"They do," Eva said. "They might even allow you a look at them if you release us."

"You aren't prisoners, you know."

"Coulda fooled me," Ana muttered under her breath.

"You are free to go any time you like."

"Of course, first we'd have to climb all the way up to the top to the men, then find the mechanism that works the bridge across the chasm and brave it again, and finally find our friends on the other side." Ana shook her head. "I don't think so."

"We will take you. The bridge is not the only way. And there is a hoist to lift us up a few at a time to avoid the stone steps."

"Were they here when you arrived or did you construct

them?" Leave it to my sister in a tense situation to ask questions only to satisfy her curiosity.

"The stairway? There was one, but it was in disrepair. Our forefathers spent many years repairing the steps, making them safer, but we needed a way to bring food to the top when the men began to explore the area." She motioned to two of the women. "Now we will have some refreshments before we take you to your companions."

The two women brought out woven mats and spread them on the ground. We sat around them and watched as they covered the mats with many vegetables and some dried fish. I've eaten so many strange foods in recent times, I didn't hesitate to eat each of them. The spread reminded me of the Yashii, the strange swamp race that guarded the Crimson Orb. I don't think the swamp people cooked any food, but some of this had been baked. I watched Carys examine everything she ate before she took a bite. She'd analyze how each item was prepared.

"You seem to have an interest in our food," Ying said.

"I do some of the cooking for our group."

"Carys likes to experiment. What she makes is quite delicious." Morna plopped some kind of root vegetable wrapped in a leafy one into her mouth and chewed thoughtfully. "This is too. What herbs do you use?"

"You are interested in botany?"

"Our mother is a herbalist and healer," I answered. "We noticed the mint and some other plants growing here. Some we know, but others are strange to us."

Ying smiled. "You have much knowledge about many things. It has been difficult convincing our people to keep what knowledge we have, and few are interested in learning more."

"Curiosity killed the cat, but first he became very wise and knowledgeable," Ana said, much to everyone's confusion.

"Tell me, what skills were you taught?" Ying asked me.

"Mostly embroidery, like your women do." I pointed to their work. "But I much prefer constructing practical clothing."

"Nissa made the suits divers wore to bring up the satellite from the bottom of Dulno Lake." Morna smiled at me proudly.

"They needed pockets and pouches to hold – everything they carried." She didn't have to know how advanced some of those devices were. "And the fabric seams had to be made water-tight."

She nodded. "Interesting."

"The water changed the color of the fabric, too," Eva remembered.

I smiled. "It was a good learning experience for everyone."

"Did you all go?" Ying looked at each of us.

"Yes, and some of the men up at the top of your cliff." I pointed. "It was a large expedition."

"And the equipment you used? The devices? Who made those?" She'd gotten to it much sooner than I'd expected.

"Our people built them from the few books we have, but Before there were so many more that could be used to make people's lives easier."

"As opposed to weapons?"

I nodded. "What's the sense of weapons if there is nothing to defend with them?"

"What about the lives of the people? If they are struggling to live, fighting off others, nothing that makes it pleasant is important."

"That's an argument we've had before."

"And?"

"We used the weapons we've always had, and managed." I couldn't tell her those weapons included our mind control abilities, and the way they could enhance our skill with basic weapons. I pointed to the stick in Fong-Wei's hand. "Nothing like that, of course!"

"Where did you get that?" Ana asked. "Did you cop it from some other group of people?"

"We brought something like it from our home, but it took effort to get it to work again. We now have a few we can use, and I must admit, more only for show." He smiled. "But I won't tell you which is which."

We chuckled. Most of the food was now gone. Fong-Wei ate with us, but the women hadn't joined in. I still found that disconcerting.

"Come, we will ascend to the cliff top and collect your men." He rose and shouldered his weapon. "Mother, thank you for providing our guests with so much information. I hope it helps them trust us so they will work with us in the future."

None of the women had said much, but we waved to them. "Goodbye, we hope to see you again."

Fong-Wei took us around boulders to an almost hidden large box like a cage for some huge animals. The door latched simply. "I'll take three of you up and then return for the other three."

While I waited with Ana and Eva, he entered with Morna, Katya and Carys. The cage rose slowly, jerkily. Once it made its way past the first few trees, though, we lost sight of them and could only hope they were alright.

Finally we saw him descending, but he wasn't smiling.

"Was there a problem?" Ana asked.

"Not really, but your men are still not ready to accept our help, even though the three young women tried to convince them."

"They're skeptical. Give them a chance."

He opened the door and we entered. The ride up was even shakier than it looked. More than once I worried we wouldn't make it past a jagged bit of rock outcropping or some huge trees, but finally we were at the top.

Blane and Holt rushed to help us tumble out of the box.

"Did they tell you Fong-Wei will take us back across to the rest of our party?" I asked my brother.

He frowned. "Morna said you told them a lot about us."

"And they told us more about them. Some of those things I still don't like or agree with." I put a hand on his arm. "I think we should trust them, at least tentatively."

He nodded slightly. Meanwhile, Fong-Wei called over two men. The three faced us.

"We go this way." Without another word, he walked again toward the cliff. We followed with the other two Panshee bringing up the rear. This time when we reached the cliff and Fong-Wei worked the mechanism to extend the bridge, he pushed another button that created rails along the sides and solidified the platform.

That made it easier to cross. We marched single-file across, reaching the other side in no time. I almost expected to find some of our party waiting, but the woods seemed deserted.

"Call your friends," Fong told my brother. "I'm sure they're not far."

Blane hesitated, then called, "Madoc. Donal. We're here and all right. The Panshee want to meet you."

One by one, Donal, then Madoc, and finally Toren and Gareth appeared. I couldn't help myself. I rushed to Madoc and threw my arms around him, burying my head in his chest. He nuzzled my hair and then held me away to look into my eyes. I felt the light touch of his mind on mine. I replied with, *We tried to contact you but something prevented it.*

"Are you really okay?"

"As my brother said." I smiled at him. "We learned things about these people and told them about us." In my mind I added, but not everything.

"And you think we can trust them?"

"Not completely, just as they don't have complete faith in us, but we can work together." I turned toward Fong. "This is Fong-Wei. He understands Solwinish so we could communicate. They have different ideas, beliefs than we do. And different goals."

"They know about the two books," his sister added. "Fong-Wei and his mother would like to see them. There are several sects, maybe even races of people here. The Panshee, or as they call themselves, Pin-Shing, have had some conflicts." She went on about their history.

"How many are there?"

"We saw perhaps twenty or twenty-five, but I expect there are more," Ana said. "Fong, there are, aren't there? I mean the men at the top and women and children down in the gorge aren't the only members of your group remaining, are they?"

"There is another group of men out hunting, and two women ready to birth. Also a few other children, but we are only thirty left."

Madoc sighed and Donal frowned.

"And the other groups on this continent?" Gareth asked.

"There is the group we call the Tektek."

"Those are the scientists and technicians, who protect themselves under a plastic dome. Plastic, right?" Carys turned to Fong for confirmation. "They refuse to share any technology with anyone else. Sound like some people you know?" She smiled.

Toren laughed. "I guess those are the people we're really here to see." He turned to Fong-Wei. "Take us to them."

"Not until after we examine the books Nee-Sa told us about."

The two mages exchanged looks, then Madoc withdrew one of the books from inside his vest. "Tell me what language this is."

It was the star maps. Fong smiled. "These are maps of the sky as we see it here at night. The words are an ancient form of Far-Teka. Hmm, possibly ancient Ministic. You know the language in this part of the world is derived from that tongue?"

"Yes."

"And a few of your people can speak it. So why is it they cannot read it?"

"Only one comes from a land that also speaks a Ministic language. Katya is a specialist in languages, as well, and she learned some of the words from Mai."

"Where is this Mai?"

Donal replied, "Back at the beach where we landed. Unless some other tribe of unfriendlies has taken her."

"Unfriendlies?"

"You threaten us with your flamethrower." Madoc pointed. "Do you call that friendly?"

"Lin, give this Ma-Doc your stick," Fong told one of the other Panshee in their version of Fartekana.

"Only some of their weapons work," I said. "That's probably one of the ones that doesn't."

Fong chuckled. "She is clever, Nee-Sa. I wish our women were so."

"If you let them, they would be." Morna crossed her arms and glared at him. "But you keep them from taking part in making decisions for your people. Perhaps if you had, you wouldn't be down to only thirty members."

"Perhaps."

CHAPTER THIRTY-SEVEN

"Will you take us to the Tektek dome?" Ana asked.

Fong scratched the back of his head. "It is far. We will need provisions, and perhaps two more of our men who know the way. When the hunters return, we will be free to go."

"So we have to cross the chasm again?" Morna groaned, but there wasn't the dismay there might have been after we crossed the bridge the first time without the extra support.

"I'd like to see what's on the other side," Toren said. "And to meet the rest of your people."

Fong looked at him. He seemed uncertain who was in charge of our group. And those who hadn't been with us before didn't know Fong's place with his people.

I pulled Madoc aside to tell him about the dealings the Pan-Shing had with the Tektek in the past, and about the crystals at the bottom of the chasm.

"I expected there was bad blood between them, but your friend Fong has a personal grudge against the more advanced Tektek."

I nodded. "He also resists the approach his father proposed to use the natural crystals as bargaining tools."

He stroked his chin. "Those crystals might be what prevented us from communicating previously."

I frowned. "But crystals should have amplified the energies around us, focused them better."

He shook his head. "Perhaps, because they are natural and not faceted like the man-made ones, they only absorb the energy and don't reflect it back."

"So maybe they aren't such a good thing to offer the Tekteks."

"If the Tektek are good at what they do, they might be able to convert the bits and pieces into focusing crystals that would work well." He looked toward the edge. "You say the chasm floor is littered with them?"

"They're shiny and they have to warn the children about playing with them."

"Before we go with them, what about the people on the beach?" I asked.

"We told them we'd likely proceed farther when we found you, to wait a month. If we don't return, they're to return west."

"What are you two talking about?" Fong appeared at my shoulder. He was slightly shorter than I am.

Madoc put an arm around my shoulders. "We haven't seen each other for several hours. We missed each other." He pulled me closer and kissed my forehead.

I looked into his eyes and smiled.

Fong seemed to accept that.

Everyone had collected their belongings, and we marched back to the edge of the cliff where Fong extended the bridge. Madoc and Toren's gaze followed the process, and so did Donal's.

Once more we crossed the narrow gap. Fong made sure we spread out enough that there weren't too many on the bridge at once.

I knew the way from the end to the settlement. I entwined my fingers with Madoc's as we walked through the jungle. As always, he took everything in with a glance, looking for advantages for us if needed, examining the terrain. His mind reached out, looking for energy changes.

We were quickly surrounded by Pin-Shing men. Fong addressed them, explaining what was planned, and asking, no, begging them to cooperate with us all.

Before long another five men appeared from the deep woods, two carrying a large, dead animal, and the others brandishing more flamethrowers. At least they used their weapons for a good cause.

Fong smiled. "We will have a feast before we leave."

"Will the women and children join us?" I asked in my best Fartekana.

The other men frowned at me, but Fong-Wei seemed to consider my suggestion. "Certainly, why not? I'm sure they will enjoy it, too." He turned to the two men who'd accompanied us to the other side of the gorge. "Go. Retrieve my mother and the others. You can use the lift."

They nodded and left to do his bidding. At least we knew those two were loyal to Fong.

"We can help you build a fire to roast that animal," Donal offered.

"It is a boar, a kind that lives in this part of the world. Very tasty. It will take a while to cook, though."

"Do you use the skins for anything? What about this matted hair?" Eva examined the animal, and Katya joined her.

"We use everything we can." Fong pointed to the hooves of the animal. "Even those. Resources are scarce. The meat of the animals are food, of course, and the hair can be used for clothing and bedding. Also the hides. They make good boots and foot coverings."

"We do the same," Gareth agreed. "But our animals are quite different from this one. We have horses which take us from place to place, and cows for food and milk."

"Do you have those?" Morna asked.

"Many hundreds of years ago we had horses. But when other animals became scarce we were forced to eat them and have had no beasts of burden since. We travel on our feet." He pointed to the tops of his boots.

I couldn't imagine covering the large distances we had on foot, but expected we would find out. "How far is it to the Tektek community?"

"We will walk for almost two days to reach it."

Morna's sigh was the loudest.

"And we will take some of the meat from this boar, along with bread and many water skins. There are shrubs and trees along the way that will provide berries and fruits."

I nodded. "We've foraged for food as we travel, but I don't

think any of us are used to walking such great distances."

"We can stop as often as you wish."

Toren made a guttural sound. "We want to reach the Tektek as soon as possible."

"Why are you in a hurry? It's been so many years, a few days shouldn't make a difference." Fong's eyes narrowed as he waited for a reply.

"There are many forces in Solwintor and other places that plan to destroy the world with the weapons they've developed. There are others who want to enslave the rest of the peoples of the world. They all want energy, as well as power over everyone else." Toren replied for us all.

I'd suspected for a while the stakes were higher than I'd been told.

"Is that true?" Katya's eyes swiveled between Toren and Madoc.

Toren nodded. "I'm sorry I haven't told any of you what a few of us believe. There were reasons. We couldn't even tell Madoc or Col. But now we're here, it is imperative we have cooperation from everyone. And I've made a unilateral decision. The best way would be to tell you more about what we know for sure."

"Who are these factions? I guess one is the people we've fought before, who were with Klaus." Madoc sounded more curious than angry.

Toren nodded. "In addition, the Legion."

"The one that's terrorized the towns in the eastern part of Solwintor, including the people who fled and became scavengers." Eva rubbed her mouth. "What about the marauders?"

"They're probably too scattered to be a real threat to anyone, and yet they'd be an annoyance if we were spread thin fighting our other enemies."

Fong raised an eyebrow. "It would seem you have more enemies than we do, people who are stronger and more aggressive than those throughout Far-Teka."

"If we can join forces with the technologically advanced peoples here, we would have better means to defend ourselves." Toren surveyed those around him. "Not to be aggressors, but to protect our people and our ability to rediscover all the world lost during the Fall."

That reminded me of something Fong said. "They call it something else, and they call the Second Moon, the Moon of Destruction."

"Interesting. Yes, that is apt." Toren turned to Fong. "I know this is not your fight, but ultimately it could become a fight for the sanity of this world, of rebuilding vs. even greater destruction."

"I think I understand." Fong stopped to explain some of what we talked about to his own people just as the first of the women arrived. "When my father was killed by the Tektek, I vowed I would not do as he did. It seems it is to be my fate."

When Ying came over, I introduced her to the men in our party. "Ying is one of the few people here keeping knowledge and learning alive. She's very fluent in Solwinish and told us much about the history of her people."

Madoc nodded. "We're well aware how important it is to pass on what our ancestors knew. It could be the only way to avoid the errors of our past."

"Perhaps." She smiled at him "If we can convince everyone, but it hasn't been easy. People all have their own beliefs, no?"

The tiny woman with her long black braid commanded respect, but I realized some people would find it easy to dismiss her and her message.

"We heard your husband was unable to convince others."

"Husband? You mean mate. We do not take husbands and wives, but pick a mate for life."

Madoc nodded. "We do that as well. Some of our societies insist on making it official with ceremony and documentation, but with or without those, the commitment is the most important thing." He smiled at me and I felt color and heat rush to my cheeks.

It took a while for the men to bring the rest of the women and children. The roast was almost done by then. The women looked around as they arrived, and I wondered when they'd last been allowed to come to the top.

The children ran around. Their interaction with the men was a joy to see.

"Can we help?" the eldest two asked the men tending the fire. "Is that really a boar?"

Three of the little girls shyly hid behind the women, peeking out at us. None of the children brought crystals with them.

When the food was ready, including vegetables the women brought from below, we sat around the fire in the clearing and ate it. The meat was tough, but tasty and moist. The only talk was about the food. Ying asked what foods we ate back in Solwintor which brought the conversation to some of Carys experiments in cooking.

"She added berries to a stew that gave it a sweet taste and tenderized the meat." I smiled at the memory.

"I've tried different fruits and herbs for that," she added. "Some work better than others."

"And then there are the Meecham cookies." Morna grinned. She explain what those were and how they were made.

The concept of baking sweets was new to these people. Bread they knew, but not cakes or cookies. We didn't explain where we first ate our favorite dessert, though.

"We eat fresh fruit from the trees at the end of each meal," Fong said. "Sometimes we cook them in the fire, but they are also wonderful directly from the trees."

I looked up at the tall, straight trunks. We'd only had one or two fruits in this land, but there was an abundance of a variety of them. I noticed the yellow-skinned ones we'd eaten a few days earlier. "I like that fruit." I pointed to a bunch hanging from a low branch.

A few of the children gathered some and gave them to anyone who wanted a taste.

"We have many nuts, too." Fong indicated a few low-growing bushes. "And berries, of course. We grind the nuts to a paste and wrap it around the sweetest berries for a special treat."

"Do you have any cookbooks?" Carys asked.

Ying shook her head. "Only one or two. Most recipes were passed down by word of mouth, like so much else. It is a pity."

Carys nodded her agreement.

When we finished eating, the women and some of the men of our party offered to help clean up. We'd eaten off of the huge leaves from the trees that held a kind of fruit or nut I hadn't tasted yet, and these leaves were tossed into the fire, creating a pungent but not unpleasant smell. The women refused any help with the rest of the clean-up, so the rest of us began preparing for the trek across the land to wherever the Tektek camp was.

Since our own party was already so large, Fong-Wei asked only three others of the Panshee men to accompany us. He gave flamethrowers to four of our men and showed them how to use them. It looked easy, but I didn't have a chance then to find out how heavy and unwieldy they were.

CHAPTER THIRTY-EIGHT

We set off across the top of the cliff in a southeast direction. At first, the land was flat, extending for many dulnos to the horizon, but before long the way ahead rose to rolling hills covered with low shrubs and plants. Fewer trees blocked our view of a mountain range several hours away.

"We'll reach those before sunset and camp in the foothills to eat and rest, but should start again before daylight tomorrow," Fong explained in Solwinish and then repeated in Fartekana for his men.

So far, they seemed to agree with his plan to take us to the scientists and technicians, even though many of his people had been opposed to any contact with them.

My feet tired from all of the walking, although thankfully I wore my boots. Some of our party were not as well prepared for the terrain which became rougher the closer we came to the mountains.

I'd ridden through mountain passes before, and even walked part of the way when the trails were narrow and it was easier on us and the horses to walk more slowly. The rest who hadn't made the trip from the factory to the Stronghold had traveled to the coast and then across Leara, so they were experienced with covering long distances and varying terrain, but perhaps they hadn't expected they would do so much walking on this part of the trip. I looked at Katya's flimsy shoes and hoped she wouldn't have blisters before we reached our goal.

The hard-packed soil strewn with rocks and stones made the ground uneven. We slowed until the ground was smoother again, and then the rise became more noticeable. Going uphill tired our legs more quickly. By the time we reached the mountain we were all ready to rest.

"This is the best place to make our camp," Fong said. "It's defensible and relatively flat. There isn't much protection from the wind, though. Be prepared. Some nights out here the winds whip around in every direction."

Gareth, Madoc and Toren nodded in acknowledgment.

We had our blankets and packs containing our supplies, as well as food from the Panshee camp.

"We usually set up watches of three or four people for each time period," Madoc told Fong.

"The women too?" he asked.

Madoc smiled. "Absolutely. I know that is not your way, but everyone must help to ensure we arrive safely."

My brothers built a fire to heat water for tea, while others cleared the ground of rocks and twigs. Groups gravitated toward each other. My family, Madoc and Carys formed one, Fong and the other Panshee another. I thought Gareth and Rees would join us, but instead they sat with Toren, speaking in low tones. I wondered why.

"They still don't trust Fong and his men." Madoc followed my eyes to his brother.

"They have little reason to trust him. But we'll have to, won't we?"

Eva and Ana distributed food. The boar meat wasn't as good cold. Even Carys commented, "Perhaps tomorrow they'll let me make a stew from it so it will be hot and more tender."

Holt came to sit next to my sister. I knew he'd been attracted to her in the past but I thought he'd given up. Guess not.

We washed our food down with tea. Katya and Eva examined bushes nearby for edible berries to add to our stores. It seemed an infinite number grew in different parts of the world. We never knew whether they'd be sweet or tart without tasting them.

Fong finished his food and spoke. "Tomorrow we will go through the mountains over there." He pointed to a narrow crevice in a nearby formation. "It will take us a good way through without climbing too high at first, but I'm afraid we will have to go over that one." He waved at one of the highest in the area. The jagged edges promised it would be difficult to climb. "I hope you are all sure-footed. It can be dangerous."

Madoc sniffed the air. "I hope the rain holds off until we're on the other side."

"You smell it too?"

"There's a definite shift in the weather coming soon." Madoc pointed to the gathering clouds.

Fong nodded. "That's why we must get an early start tomorrow."

We cleaned up the campsite and spread our blankets. With many of the rocks and branches out of the way it wasn't as unpleasant to sleep on the ground than it might have been.

The Evening Moon had almost set when I sensed Madoc rise from his place near me. I wrapped myself in a blanket and walked to where he spoke with Fong and Toren.

"You will be able to watch our camp until the Moon of Destruction is high in the sky?" Fong asked.

"Easily."

"It was quiet through the last watch," Toren said. "I'm going to rest now. See you in the morning." He walked off. I wondered if he was worried about the woman he'd rescued. Who knew whether the rest of our party had any idea where we were, or what we were doing.

For the first part of our watch, it was quiet. The usual night noises of small animals and birds, and the smells of those flowers that bloomed at night filled the air. The sky held strange star formations only familiar to me because of Madoc's book.

He slipped an arm around me and I leaned toward him, comforted by the familiar scent and feel of him. "These are very strange people."

I looked at him in the firelight. "No stranger than others we've met in our travels."

"True."

"What do you make of Fong-Wei?"

"Underneath he's a good man but he's been influenced by what happened to his father." He laced his fingers with mine. "Did they say how long ago that happened?"

I shook my head. "It had to be at least five years, though. Fong was still a lad at the time, not old enough to go with his father and the others."

"And another of their leaders was killed at the time?"

"So they said. But there are details they've never revealed. Even Ying withheld some of what she knows."

He smiled. "I bet their treatment of women makes you realize you didn't have it so bad at the Manor."

"Oh, I realized a long time ago my life was quite good, just not what I would have selected."

"And your life now?"

"You know if I'm with you, nothing else is as important. Besides, I still enjoy having new experiences, meeting new people, and especially learning more and more about our world."

He nodded and put a hand on my shoulder

The rest of our watch was uneventful. When the next group took our place, including Eva, Rees, another of the Panshee, and Holt, I stretched out again in my blankets, but I couldn't sleep. My mind was too occupied in speculating what the next day would bring. I felt the touch of Madoc's mind and willingly told him my fears.

All will be well, dearest.

I hope you're right. So much depends on our being able to get the cooperation of the Tektek. I think we can talk to them better than the Panshee because of our experience trying to rebuild so many devices and machines, but I wonder if they will listen to us or guard their secrets or consider us invaders or worse.

Speculating about it will only make you more nervous. Instead, concentrate on what we should be telling them. I think you were judicious in what you shared with Fong and his mother. We will continue with that approach.

What about the things Toren said today? Did you have any idea that was our true mission?

We've all known there are threats to the Stronghold. We know so little about the Legion or any of the other groups. What do they want? We may never know, only that they're enemies of what we want for the people remaining on this world.

In the morning, as the sun sent its first rays from behind the mountain, we woke and collected our belongings, ate bread and drank tea, then set out for the rest of our hike through the mountains. It wasn't too difficult at first. The path was narrow but the rise was gentle.

Fong and one of his men led the way. When he held up a hand, we stopped. He turned to us. "The gap narrows beyond here, and when it widens, we'll begin the real assent. It is the only way to get to the other side of this range."

I took a deep breath and went on. It took a long time for all of us to get through the narrow defile. Once we did, we could see he was right. The way forward went almost straight up. Although the ground was uncluttered for a while, we kicked up so much dust it interfered with breathing.

Then we arrived at a section where the path began to wind upward, almost like the stone stairway we'd used to go down to the women in the chasm. Only this time, there were no steps, only loose soil and the occasional boulder to avoid. Round and around we climbed. Was it my imagination or was the air thinner here? Breathing became more labored, whether from the climb or the lack of air.

At one point, Fong and the other man in front disturbed a flock of birds. They looked like the red birds we sometimes saw at the manor, robins some called them, but they were quite a bit larger.

Before the sun was straight up, Fong called a halt again. "We will eat here before going on."

The land wasn't flat at all. We tried to find rocks and boulders to sit on. Without any grass to soften the ground, it was rough even through our clothes. It was cooler here than it had been on the cliff plateau and much drier than down in the gorge.

"We can't make a fire here, so I can't make any stew," Carys complained.

"No matter," Fong replied. He took out some dried meat and vegetables and handed them around. Both were chewy but flavorful. We needed lots of water to wash them down. There was little waste or trash after we were done, but we wrapped what there was in a piece of colorful Panshee cloth for later disposal.

The ground higher up was rockier still and the path we'd been following seemed to disappear. I didn't know how Fong knew which way to go.

CHAPTER THIRTY-NINE

Our guide took us higher into the mountain. Definitely cooler up here. As steady as we were on our feet, a number of times one person had to reach out to grab the arm of another to prevent them from falling.

Morna glanced up to the top. "How much longer? My legs are beginning to feel like rubber. Burning rubber."

We were on a relatively flat section. "Let's stop for a short while and drink some water," Fong said. "It's especially important to prevent dehydration up here."

"Dehydration?" Donal asked.

Fong nodded. "You're body reacts to a lack of water. Especially here in the mountains. Don't be afraid to drink a lot. There's a clear stream on the other side, a short way back down the mountain."

We each took out our skins and drank deeply. Maybe it was my imagination but I thought I felt better immediately.

"How often have you been up here?" Toren asked Fong. "You seem to know the way well."

"We used to come up more often, especially in the hot times. Then people were attacked by animals, like very large cats with striped white coats, similar to the ancient tigers. We didn't stop altogether but kept our expeditions to a minimum. Our women use plants that only grow here and so we continue."

"What do they use the plants for?" Carys probably expected

a food source.

"Some are medicinal herbs, but most are used in making the cloth they weave for our shirts, trousers, even our cushions."

Clothing construction interested me. "Do they get dyes for the gorgeous colors from these plants?"

He nodded. "Some. There's one that gives a bright blue color, and another that's a deep yellow. Your clothing is not as bright as ours."

"We use colors sometimes, too. But when we're traveling, we tend to wear subdued clothes that blend with the surroundings."

"Tell him about the ghastly color of the overalls we wear..." Morna slapped a hand over her mouth, but she'd already said so much, I had to explain.

"A work uniform many of us wear is green as my sister said, and the fabric is scratchy if we don't treat it. But it's strong and serviceable."

Morna beamed at me. "Nissa is a seamstress."

Fong listened to what we said. "Yes, she told us. Practical items rather than embroidery, right?"

I nodded. "Oh, there are times we wear more decorative things and use cloth items that are ornamental. But we also want to be comfortable."

"And the diving clothes you made, were they also of the green material?" Fong sounded genuinely interested.

"No, that was yellow, specially treated to be waterproof."

He nodded. "Of course. For use in the water that makes sense."

Morna chuckled. "It turned orange in the water because of the leached crystals."

"Or maybe something else." Katya frowned.

"No. We proved that was what happened." Toren knew from his experiments.

Our conversation convinced me there was a great deal we could all learn from each other, not only about our different cultures and ways of life, but also the knowledge each group had. I hoped the Tektek were as free to share what they knew, although from Fong's descriptions, I doubted it.

Finally, we moved on, wanting to reach the pinnacle before full dark so we could be over to the other side before we stopped for the night. The apex was in sight, and we pushed towards it, overtopping it as the sun was halfway to the horizon to our backs. We made our way downward slowly at first, stopping at a wide flat area for another meal. We built a fire, and Carys cooked meat and vegetables, although not for as long as usual. Still, it was more tender than it had been and tastier, too.

During our travels mealtimes loomed large in our minds. They were times when we could stop moving, fill our stomachs, and talk. But the Panshee men were less talkative than most, even with each other in their native tongue.

We always had a lot to discuss, thoughts we'd had as we went along, observations, even plans for the next day. Nothing seemed to get Fong's men to open up, though. Morna usually could get anyone to speak. She had that knack. But she failed with all but Fong, who, while not loquacious, at least was willing to converse with us.

We finished our meal and were descending the mountain, when an eerie sound pierced the relative quiet. It seemed to come from in front of us, either farther down the mountain or nearby in the forest at the base. Soon after, the sound came again. This time it clearly came from a short distance below us.

"Is that an animal or a person?" Morna asked. Either way she'd be concerned.

"It sounds like a woman or child." Toren rushed downward. "And not that far away."

We scrambled down the irregular path that snaked ahead of us from the clearing where we ate, narrow and treacherous. Still, it was better than trying to make our way between boulders and outcrops.

The cry came once more. "She sounds hurt." Morna's face was twisted with worry.

"It could be a trap," Holt told her. "Someone who wants to lure us into danger."

She shook her red curls. "I don't think so. There's a quality to the voice. Whoever it is, is clearly in danger. We have to help."

Making our way in ones and twos, we came to the spot the sound seemed to emanate from. There was no one there, but as we looked around and behind the jumble of stones, there was another sound to our left, like a scraping.

Morna, Holt and Donal took off in that direction. The terrain prevented more of us from following right away. When they returned, Donal carried a young woman. Her clothes were torn and the exposed skin of her arms and legs was scratched. She moaned as he placed her on the flattest spot.

She looked like the Panshee women, except her closed eyes appeared larger. The long black hair straggled over her shoulders.

The blouse and skirt she wore were a pale blue rather than the colorful fabrics of the Panshee women's clothing.

"Who is she and what is she doing out here on the mountain alone?" Blane asked.

"Give her some water." Ana unhooked her skin from her belt. "When she's able to speak, she might answer your questions."

Donal cradled her head, holding it so Morna could drip water onto her lips and then into her mouth. She opened her eyes slowly, then wide with a start.

She gasped and looked around with frightened eyes.

Fong knelt beside her and told her in Fartekana, "It's alright. We're friends. We want to help you."

She relaxed slightly, but continued to stare at all of us.

"Can you tell us what happened?" Toren asked. "Were you being chased?"

She looked at him uncomprehendingly, since he'd spoken in Solwinish.

I repeated what he'd said in my best approximation of Fartekana.

Her eyes narrowed again as if she was trying to remember. "Tiger."

"Were you being chased by a tiger?" Fong asked. "We can protect you."

"Who – who are you?"

"Some of us are Pin-Shing, what you might call Panshee."

Her lower lip began to tremble, and she muttered, "Enemy."

"But the rest of us are from Solwintor." Morna put a hand on the girl's. "We aren't enemies of anyone, and we hope we can be your friend." Her Fartekana was improving by leaps and bounds.

No one could look into my sister's eyes and think she would hurt them. The girl seemed to take her at her word. "My companions fell."

We automatically looked down. It was a long way to the bottom of the mountain. I swallowed hard, hoping they were only injured.

"How many were you?"

She held up three fingers. "We were trying to reach the top to find the flower that blooms this time of year and makes good tea."

I'd seen the blossoms. I think we called it hibiscus, and the tea was definitely good.

"Was there only one tiger?" Blane had Fong ask.

She nodded. "It was so big and it chased us. Kon tried to protect me but she was forced over the mountain. Ook attacked the beast with her spear but it leaped at her and she fell too. I ran."

"But where do you run on a mountain." Toren looked around. "Where is the animal now?"

"I don't know." She rubbed her forehead. "I hid after it attacked me and I got away. It ran off, but it can't be far." She waved a hand.

"What's your name?" Eva asked her.

"I am called Kem." She stared at Fong. "My people are the Mora. We live in the valley below."

"Are there other dangerous animals?" Morna's eyes were wide.

"Some. Also dangerous bands of people."

"But not the Panshee. We don't come to this side of the mountain, we are not your enemies," Fong insisted.

"For so long we have thought you were a constant threat. We have protected our settlement from everyone else. It was the only way."

"How many are you?" Morna gently brushed Kem's long dark hair off her face.

She hesitated. "There are fifty Mora. We used to be a larger clan, but over the years, attacks from people and animals, illness, and famine, our numbers decreased."

Fong translated for us before turning to the woman. "So have ours. Our band is even smaller. We are forced to stay in a small area, forced to keep our women and children hidden deep in a chasm while our men hunt for food to survive."

"Perhaps your two bands can join forces." Holt looked from Fong to Kem.

"I will take you to my people. We will talk about it." Kem stood clumsily. Donal helped her to steady herself.

"We'll continue down the mountain. How far is your village?" Toren asked.

"It's near the base of the mountain on the shores of the river."

It was dark before we reached the bottom. The Evening Moon was rising and the strange star clusters of this part of the world appeared in the sky.

Four people came running when they saw us. "Kem, you're alright!" A woman with her right arm in a sling was the first to reach us.

Kem swept her arm to indicate us all. "These people saved me." She touched her hand. "You broke your arm."

"It could have been much worse."

"Ook, what about Kon?"

She shook her head. "She perished. I'm sorry."

Kem swiped at her eyes and nodded, but a sob escaped.

A short woman addressed us. "We welcome you to our village. Thank you for helping Kem."

"It was all we could do." Gareth had Fong tell her.

"Many of you are not from here, is that not true?"

"We are from Solwintor," Katya told her. "We came to establish contact with the peoples of this land."

"Why?" Her face held a mixture of curiosity and contention.

CHAPTER FORTY

The Mora woman's question was simple but there was a lot behind it. Why, indeed, had we come here? We weren't going to share what Toren said was our real goal, not until we knew more. But we could mention a few acceptable motivations.

Gareth took the lead, using Fong to translate. "A thousand years ago the peoples of this world could communicate easily with each other. Since then, each group, each village has taken a different path. Some people of Solwintor hope that can change, that the different peoples can share what they know about the past, and prevent repetition of the disasters that occurred. Our expedition comprises people from a few lands across the sea to the west. We have accumulated books and other knowledge from the past."

She nodded. "Our people come from the south. We could only bring a few cultural items and documents from our ancestral home. We have tried to keep our tradition and language alive, but after so many years, our memories about what happened to our people have been clouded by folklore and legend."

"The Solwinish and other peoples have suffered the same loss of knowledge."

I chimed in. "The land we come from had no memory of the launching of the Second Moon. Is that what you call it?"

At the shake of her head, Fong supplied, "The Moon of Destruction?"

The woman looked up. "Bad Moon."

We nodded.

A large bonfire burned in the middle of the clearing. The surrounding huts were made of the leaves and twigs from trees growing along the river bank and held together by a kind of mud.

The woman who'd spoken to us seemed to be a leader. She ordered several others to bring food, tea and a wine made of berries that also grew nearby.

I watched Fong's reaction to the Mora, especially to the older woman who was not much taller than his mother. Women were in charge here. They did the fighting and hunting. Few of the men had weapons, either spears or knives with long blades, but all of the women did.

A man and woman together carried out a cauldron filled with water. They placed it on the fire and several other Mora threw vegetables into the pot.

The men and women were all short but muscular. They wore plain clothes like Kem's and moved with grace, almost gliding across the valley floor.

A white meat was added to the vegetables, probably fish from the river gurgling nearby.

I sensed little energy in this valley, and no crystals shone on the ground. I pointed to our guide. "Fong is taking us to the Tektek to talk to them about the devices they have."

"Those are the people under the glass." Kem frowned.

"Yes, the dome protects them, isolates them from the rest of the peoples."

I tried to remember the names of the Mora as they introduced themselves. The older woman was called Reet, and we knew Kem and her friend Ook. There was one man about my father's age who I think was named Fol. But my head was so full of names of the different people we met over the past few days that adding more was difficult.

"Why do you want to talk to the Tektek?" Reet asked. "They will not tell you anything about the machines they have, nor share them with anyone. We avoid them. As long as they do not threaten us with weapons."

"Do they have weapons?" Gareth asked.

She shrugged. "We do not know all they have. All we can

see are the strange carts with wheels they ride in. Our stories talk about such vehicles, but none of us has been in one for a thousand years."

Toren puffed up his lips. "Many such conveyances took people great distances in the past. Some for a few people and others for many."

"But we haven't found any books that tell us how to build them." Donal sighed. "We think they would need many crystals to operate."

"Crystals. Yes, our stories call them fairy dust. They are magic." Reet smiled for the first time.

"Not really magic," Madoc told her. "They focus energy to power devices. Fong and his people have some but haven't been able to use them."

The food was finally ready and bowls of the fish stew were passed around. I looked at Carys as I ate, wondering how she would have made it tastier. The fish and vegetables had little flavor, and the Mora hadn't added any herbs.

"We put garlic in our fish stew," Carys told Reet. "Does that grow here?"

She shook her head. "We have many vegetables, but I do not know this gar-lic."

Carys described it. I knew she was eager to look around the valley to see what did grow there.

We spent the night in the Mora camp without need for a guard system. We trusted these people after their gracious hospitality, and besides, we wanted them to believe we weren't fearful of them.

In the morning the large size of the village was more apparent. Several of their curious houses formed a semicircle facing the river. Past that, tall poles with points at the top formed a barrier between the buildings and the mountain. There was space between the posts for a thin person to get through, but not any large animals.

The fire still burned when we woke. Several Mora prepared breakfast, laughing and singing as they did.

"We will have a service for our fallen member later today. Perhaps you wish to stay before leaving for the Tektek city." Reet looked fresh but subdued.

"We must move on. It is still a distance to the dome." Fong studied her in the morning light. "Perhaps when we return I will take you to meet my mother. I think the two of you would have much to talk about."

"She is up on the plateau where the Panshee make their home?"

He shook his head. "Our women stay deep in the gorge. There is a river there like this one, and better land for growing."

Toren smirked. "The Panshee have a different attitude toward their women than you do."

"Their numbers are dwindling like ours," Kem said.

"Perhaps, as you suggested, we can find mutual cause in the future so both groups will be strong." A hopeful gleam made Fong's eyes shine.

She shrugged. "Perhaps."

We ate a gruel made of a grain I didn't know, and sweetened with honey. The Mora didn't have cows or goats, either, and so no butter or cheese, but they had a spread made of a berry that was good on their coarse bread. The tea to wash it all down was excellent.

The Mora also didn't have horses or other animals to carry us, and so we continued on foot. At least we wouldn't have any more mountains to cross. The paths were fairly clear of obstacles and ran almost straight eastward.

"Were the Mora in this valley the last time your people tried to approach the Tektek?" I walked beside Fong as we left the Mora encampment.

"No. I suppose they hadn't arrived yet from the south."

"How long ago was it?" Donal asked. "I thought only a few years ago."

"It was fifteen cycles."

"Then you must have been but a boy." Morna's eyes were round with concern.

"I was fourteen summers. They would not let me accompany them."

Her lower lip quivered. "You couldn't have done anything to change the outcome."

"No?" He frowned. "Perhaps I could have convinced my father not to push so hard with his theories."

"But if he was right--" Eva began.

"Being right is no compensation for being dead." He sounded bitter, even after all these years.

"So you don't think he was right to propose cooperation between the Panshee and the Tektek? Then, why are you helping us?" The look on my sister's face was familiar too, along with her determined stance, but Fong couldn't have known what it meant.

We trudged on for hours. It wasn't until we'd stopped for lunch and then continued on for a while that we caught our first sight of the dome. From Fong's descriptions I had no idea how large it was, how tall and extensive. The village inside was almost as big as East Harbor or Fairhaven. The buildings varied in size, some being multiple stories and made of assorted materials, including brick and glass, stone and wood.

The dome looked like clear glass, but Fong told us it was called plastic. I wondered if the people inside were watching us the way we were watching them. If they wanted to leave, how did they get out? No door or gate anywhere.

Trees and other plants grew inside. I even saw some animals, horses and cows. So it wasn't only technology they weren't sharing.

The closer we got, the more details we saw. Gardens were planted next to a glass-walled house.

"That's a greenhouse." Eva pointed, and Katya nodded.

A tall storage building stood not far from what looked like a barn.

Toren identified it. "That's a silo for storing grain."

The people walking through the city wore simple shirts and trousers, both men and women. Some of the vehicles we'd discussed earlier traveled through the streets. One large one stopped and five people exited before it moved on, its wheels turning quickly. No animal pulled it. It moved on its own power.

"How do we get word to the people inside?" Donal studied the dome. "They don't appear to be paying any attention to us."

"They don't have to. We pose no threat to them." Fong stood perfectly still.

"Fong, how did your father and your other people die?" I'd never asked before, but now we were here, it seemed unlikely the Tektek were aggressive.

"They touched the dome, then were dead. Min says they shivered first."

"Shivered?" Morna asked.

"He probably means their bodies shook. The dome shocked them." Toren stared at it.

"What does that mean?"

Madoc took a breath and let it out. "It means it's made of a material that focuses energy so strongly it killed them."

"So we can't even touch it?" Carys asked.

"No, but we can communicate in other ways across that barrier." Madoc walked a few steps closer, studying the material. I reached out with my mind to it and was completely stopped as if it were a solid wall.

I moved closer to Madoc and took his hand. "I can't penetrate it with my mind."

"No. It's acting a shield. We can only get through, physically or mentally, if the Tektek allow it."

"How do we get their attention?" Gareth asked.

Several ideas were proposed. In the end we decided to build a large fire.

"In the distant past, peoples used flashes of fire or puffs of smoke to communicate over large distances because those could be seen from far away." Rees occasionally stated something none of us knew about.

We tried the firelight first, building the flames high, then screening them, then letting them show again. Eyes on the other side of the dome turned our way. We tried it again. The people nearest us watched for a while, then turned back to whatever they were doing before.

"What language do the Tektek speak? Does anyone know?" Ana watched them turn away.

"A version of Fartekana, I guess. Why?" Toren asked her.

"Do we have anything to write on? Or with?" Ana looked around, checking her own packs and but finding nothing.

"You think we should hold up a message?" Holt scoffed.

"Sure. Why not?"

"Why not indeed." Toren seemed to have an idea. "Fong, do you have a piece of that cloth your women weave?"

"Besides what I'm wearing?"

Toren nodded.

Fong pulled out a large piece.

"Perfect." Toren took it. "You don't mind, do you?" But he'd already started working on the fabric, using use a piece of coal to write. The message read:

SPEAK TO US. WE HAVE CRYSTALS.

CHAPTER FORTY-ONE

The message displayed to the Tektek was simple and to the point. We waited, hoping they'd bite.

The first person who looked our way tapped another on the shoulder and pointed. Soon several stared either at us or our sign. A man and woman turned away, got into one of the vehicles, and sped off.

We waited for them to return. It wasn't long before they did. They got out of their vehicle. The man held up a large board so we could read it:

GO AWAY.

I frowned, and so did my companions.

The Tektek who'd been watching us turned and strode away. No one else came to see us.

"We can't give up so easily." Toren sat down on the ground.

Slowly we all joined him. We had enough food to hold us for a while. It wasn't a bad place to spend the night; flat ground with few rocks. Perhaps if we remained, eventually the Tektek would bring us in.

It was warm, not hot. After a while in the bright sun, I longed for shade. The few shrubs nearby offered no protection from the sun. I pulled my hair back and tied it up with a ribbon from my pack.

Morna took out a small book she'd been writing in over the past week or so, recording everything that happened. She wrote feverishly. No use asking her what she was writing. She'd show it to me when she wanted to, or not.

Few birds flew around, but the many pretty insects were a kind I never saw before. "What are those?" I asked Fong.

"Butterflies. So many beautiful colors. Our women cannot weave like the patterns." He pointed to one. "See how the colors are reflected from one side to the other. How no two are alike." He narrowed his eyes at me. "You've never seen one of these before? Aren't there butterflies where you come from?"

"No."

"Actually, there used to be." Katya sometimes came out with interesting facts. "You can see them in many pictures from the past. The butterfly was a recurring theme, representing beauty and fragility."

"Like some of the birds we no longer see." Fong waved a hand. "A few are still common but there used to be red ones that came every year as the flowers first bloomed, and blue ones that sang only at night."

"Has anyone tried to catalog the animals and birds that are still here?" Morna asked.

"Catalog?"

I explained, "She means make lists of them with descriptions so there's a record of what's here now."

"What a good idea." He smiled.

Morna chuckled. "One you never thought of."

"I suppose your people have done this?"

"Only in some places," Ana admitted. "But it's a start. We don't know what happened to those plants and animals that have disappeared, whether it was due to the Fall or might have happened anyway, and we've also seen some new species."

A roaring sound from the direction we came from made us all turn our heads. A second roar joined the first. They came at us in twos and threes, huge cats, five to ten times the size of the black ones at the Manor, but white with faint striped markings.

Those of us with bows nocked an arrow and let it fly to no avail. Swords were drawn, but there was no opportunity to use those, either. They moved too fast. We did what we could to defend ourselves.

"I've never seen such large cats!" Gareth exclaimed.

Six of them ran around our party until a high-pitched sound filled the air. The animals ran off again, and we breathed a united sigh.

Eva had scraped her arm when she fell, and Holt twisted an ankle. Morna and I tended to them both.

"I suppose the tigers here haven't always been so large." Gareth rubbed his chin.

"No, of course not. We never see any on our side of the mountain, but you heard Kem's story about the one that chased her and her friends."

We'd all relaxed enough to prepare our dinner, and then they came again. This time, they weren't to be turned away. Our weapons were no match for them. I looked quickly at Madoc and Blane as our minds found each other. With others joining in, we attempted to use mental means to fight off the big cats. Unlike the Ice Bear, they weren't to be deterred.

One directly attacked Rees. He fought with it as it stood on its hind feet.

There were more of us than of them, but they were so large and strong, with long teeth and powerful paws. We drew our swords and counterattacked, but our efforts couldn't hold them off.

Suddenly, a loud horn sounded, deafening us as well as them. The higher pitched one joined it. Where were the sounds coming from?

The tigers attacked once more but finally ran off.

This time Eva was badly hurt, and so were two of Fong's men. He himself had suffered several deep scratches to his head. As we tended to the larger number of injuries than earlier, the sound of the horns changed again.

A section of the Tektek's dome slid open. One of their larger vehicles approached. I watched it warily. It stopped not far from us and five people descended a set of steps on one side. They walked toward the injured and those of us tending to them.

"Is anyone badly hurt?" a woman asked slowly, as if we might not understand her.

"The worst is Eva," I said in my best Fartekana. I cradled

my friend's arm, the one I was attempting to bandage. "She was scratched by the claws and bitten."

"You have medicines?" She looked surprised.

"Some, but possibly yours are better." I sat back on my heels. "Would you care to do what you can for her?"

The five people conferred in private, then the woman returned to me and Eva. "We'll take her to our hospital." She looked around. "It might be best if you all came with us. The Bengos might be back."

"Is that what you call those tigers?" Morna asked, but no one answered.

The woman and a man carried Eva into the vehicle, along with the other three injured. The other Tektek herded the rest of us toward the dome. Once we were on the other side, the opening closed. We could no longer see where it had been.

The vehicle went in one direction and we were taken in another, toward a large building. The doors opened before we got to it. We marched inside. The vast hall with a high ceiling was lit by some sort of device. I pointed to the round bright light and narrowed my eyes.

"Don't you remember that picture in my book?" Madoc asked.

It did resemble it, a series of globes over a light-emitting device.

The Tektek who'd brought us to the hall didn't enter with us. We were left on our own again. Blane and Gareth walked around the room, examining the walls, while a few of us sat on the benches drawn up to a long table.

"Okay, we're in. Now what?" Rees asked.

"That's up to the Tektek," Toren replied. "But we have to all tell them the same thing. We're here to exchange technology, find out how advanced theirs is, and establish communications between them and the people back at the Stronghold."

"And to show them Madoc's books," Morna added.

Not to be outdone, Donal said, "And tell them about the crystals back in the Panshee chasm. Find out if they can use them so the Panshee can trade for Tektek technology."

"Say that three times," Ana muttered.

I put a hand to my mouth to suppress a giggle.

It seemed like hours that we remained in that room. There were no windows, so we didn't know what was happening outside. Blane and Gareth finished their examination of the place and joined us at the table.

"These walls seem to be made of a kind of metal. And that box up there is curious." Blane pointed to a small one high up in one corner of the room.

"It's possible they're watching us." Toren narrowed his eyes at it. "That might be like the devices we used to see what the divers were doing at the bottom of Dulno Lake."

"A camera. Isn't that what it's called?" Katya asked.

"So we have to be careful about what we do."

"And say. They could be listening to us, too."

We'd been conversing in Solwinish so everyone except the remaining Panshee could understand. But it was possible the Tektek knew our language. We'd have to be cautious what we said.

"Do you think they'll feed us? I'm getting hungry. We never did have dinner." Morna certainly knew how to talk about mundane issues.

Holt smiled at her. "I doubt they'll starve us."

"Why do you suppose they put us here, in this room?" Carys asked.

"I expect they aren't sure what to do about us. Perhaps they need to decide in committee." Madoc voiced what I'd been thinking. He took out the two books he'd been carrying since we left the Manor. "Has anyone noticed these star charts still aren't quite right compared to the night sky here?"

"They could be from nearby, though." I found one and pointed to a cluster. "I saw these last night, only they were off to the right horizon."

He nodded. "So we're close. The Tektek might know where the stars are like the ones in the book."

"Certainly they have devices at least as advanced as in your other book." His brother opened the second one and found a picture similar to the vehicle they'd used to take our friends away.

"Or any of the ones we have back at the Stronghold." Donal was so proud of those.

"What did they mean by hospital?" Morna asked. "They said they were taking Eva and the others to it."

"It has to be a place they heal people," I guessed.

"But are they going to keep us apart? It would give them an excuse to do that, and then ask Eva, Fong and his people why we're here. What would they say?" Morna again had a point worth considering.

But before we did, the door we'd walked through earlier opened. Three people entered, including the woman who'd spoken to us before. I hadn't thought about it, but the Tektek were as much a mix of races as the people at the Stronghold. The woman looked more like the Solwinish I knew than anyone we'd met so far since we arrived in Fartek. And then she spoke to us in that language. "You are from Solwintor?"

"Yes," Madoc said. "Or rather some of us are. I'm from an island east of Leara, and a few are from Leara but have spent time in Solwintor."

"And what you said about why you are here, are those the real reasons?"

"Yes, again." He pushed the two books toward her. "I obtained these books and have been trying to find the source. My journey took me to Solwintor, and then here."

Toren had been watching him as he spoke. "Master Madoc found the place where many of us are working to rebuild technology lost or forgotten after the Second Moon was launched. We've made tremendous progress, but when we retrieved a fallen artificial satellite, we found it had been built in the same place as the source of Madoc's books."

The woman picked up one of the books and opened it, fanning the pages. I watched her face to see what she would make of it. "This is from Morata, a land to the south."

"Where the Mora came from!" I blurted.

"Who?"

"There's a group of people who call themselves the Mora" Carys explained. "They live in a valley half a days' walk west of here. They're from the south, but have been living there for a while."

"No one's seen anyone from Morata since the floods."

"Many people scattered then. These men," Toren indicated Fong's people. "They live on the other side of the mountains to the west, but they came from somewhere to the northeast. They call themselves Pin-Shing, but others along the coast call them Panshee."

"And what do they call us?" She was smiling.

I smirked at her. "Tektek. I guess that comes from the name many call this land, Fartek, and from the thought you have so much technology the others don't."

"You are being quite honest with me. I like that." She sat at the table. "I think it's time for introductions."

We each gave our name, and even told her how some of us were related. In turn, she said, "I'm Terry Olson, and my two companions are Cai Moon and Pim Boa." The two men looked more like Fong's people, dark hair and eyes, somewhat slanted.

"What about our friends? Is Eva all right?" Morna asked.

"She and the others are being treated."

"In your hospital. What's that?"

"Don't you have medical facilities where you come from?"

"That varies from place to place." Morna took out what was left of the salves we'd gotten from our mother. "Where my sister, brothers and I come from, all we have are remedies like these. Our mother concocted them."

"But where we come from in Solwintor, there are other kinds of medicines," Ana added. "Unfortunately, although we know about people called doctors, we don't have anyone with that training."

"We will take you to see them later." Terry turned to Cai and Pim. "I think our new friends need some supper. Have someone bring it."

"Sure, Terry," Cai stood and left to arrange it.

"I don't know how much of our technology we'll be allowed to show you, but I've thought for a while it was time to establish relationships with the other people here in Fartek. I think we may have more in common with you than with them. There are others, though, who want us to remain isolated."

"Ah, politics. It's the same everywhere," Ana said.

"So true." Terry smiled at her.

CHAPTER FORTY-TWO

Two women and a man returned with Cai. They carried platters of food, plates and utensils. "I'm afraid this is the best we can do at short notice," Cai said. "I didn't know what you ate, so we brought a selection. The fruits and vegetables are all grown in our gardens here, and the meats come from our animals."

"You raise animals, too? Oh, I'd like to see them!" Morna jumped out of her seat, then sat back down to eat.

I chuckled. "My sister is wonderful with animals."

"Mainly we raise them for food, you understand," Terry said.

"I realize that. We do back at the Manor, too. Except for the cats. They're small cats, black and very unlike the ones that attacked us today." Morna babbled on, saving the rest of us from talking. Instead, we concentrated on tasting the foods in front of us. Many were familiar. I noticed a fruit like burce and vegetables we ate for the first time at the Stronghold. My sister stopped talking only when Terry asked her about flowers after she mentioned the roses from Glynis and Adair's wedding. Before she answered, Morna helped herself to a piece of white meat that might have been chicken. "As her attendants, Carys, Nissa and I carried some. Larena, too, but she's not here." Morna took a bite and chewed slowly. "They grow in the Manor's gardens."

I ate some of the meat too; it was tender and seasoned with a spice like nutmeg. I filled the gap by asking, "Do people marry here? We've met peoples who don't and many who do, but the tradition seems to vary from place to place."

"We believe in family units, although we do allow variations." She stopped, probably because of the puzzled looks on our faces. "The ancient idea of a family was a father, mother and children. In this part of the world, that often extended to grandparents or aunts and uncles living with a couple and their kids. Old people were revered."

I could understand that part.

"In time it became apparent a single parent and a child could also be a unit, especially after wars or other disasters that killed large numbers of people." She took a breath before going on. "Another form of family also developed over time. Two women or two men who raised children together."

They didn't talk about it at the Manor, but I knew there were some people who were attracted to the same sex. And I think there were such couples at the Stronghold. But they never had children. I looked at the others in our party as they processed what Terry said.

"So there are two men or two women here with children? But how is that possible?" Carys asked.

"It's part of the technology you've lost, along with other medical advances. We still have most of them, although not all. I can tell you more about it, but I don't think you're prepared to understand."

There was so much more to what they knew and we didn't than I ever imagined. The more we learned, the more we found we didn't know, although she didn't have to put it so bluntly. The width and breadth and depth of knowledge lost to most of civilization was staggering. How could we ever hope to reestablish it all?

"If you're finished here, I can take you to see your friends. At the same time, you'll see some of our medical technology."

I prepared myself for surprises, but I'd been so shocked by the revelations in Solwintor, I didn't think I could be as floored again. We followed Terry, Cai and Bao out of the building and through the city streets. I looked more carefully at the ground. Similar to the pavement still existing in places in Leara and Solwintor, but in much better repair.

Everything in this city looked new or at least well cared for. I remembered my first glimpse of Fairhaven, the way the sun was reflected by the sides of the graceful buildings. I was also impressed by the factory in Solwintor. This was another experience entirely. Sets of buildings were separated by a slightly lower level of paving the vehicles moved on. It was very orderly, even though the buildings differed from each other in height and building materials: stone and the plastic dome material, metal and small, regular rectangles that were stone-like but appeared to be man-made.

We walked for a short while, then Terry turned where one set of buildings ended. We followed her along another side of those buildings, then crossed one of the lower paved sections.

Some of the people we passed stopped to look at us, but most ignored our group. Finally, we came to a large white building. It was cool inside the metal doors, but the slightly pungent smell was strange. A low hum vibrated through the floor. Terry led us down a long hallway that reminded me of the ones in the Stronghold because of the light green color, but the floors were even and signs attached to the walls displayed numbers and arrows.

Each door we passed had a number on it, too. Moans emanated from a few. The people we passed all wore long white coats over shirts and pants. Pinned to the coats was a card with a name and words like OR Nurse, Orderly, and Pediatrics.

Terry stopped in front of a door with 134 on it. She pushed it open and we all entered. Eva lay on a high bed with very white sheets. Her head was bandaged but she was awake and reclining against the pillows.

She smiled as we came near. "Hi, everyone. I hoped they bring you to see me."

"Are you alright? How are they treating you?" My sister asked question after question. "What did they do? Where are Fong and the others?"

Eva chuckled. "The things they did are amazing. I can't begin to describe their instruments. Would you believe how this bed works?" She grabbed a small box next to her and pushed a button, and the bed moved. The part under her head tilted up, then down. Then the entire thing moved up and down.

I couldn't keep my eyes from widening.

"And look at the monitors. We thought ours were advanced." She meant the ones we used at the lake.

My gaze swiveled to the screens above her head. They showed numbers that must have meant something to the people treating Eva.

"They show my temperature and something called blood pressure, even how much oxygen is in my blood." Eva grinned.

I didn't know what to say. This was beyond anything I could imagine. I touched Madoc's mind to gauge his reaction. He was as awed as I was.

Terry showed us a few other things, but then two of the white-coated people came in and shooed us out so they could tend to Eva. "I'll take you to a leader now. He'll want you to repeat everything you told me and will have some questions for you."

"Toren and I will speak for everyone," Madoc said. No one objected.

We left the white hospital building and retraced our steps for a short while, then turned toward another large building, this one covered with stone. Four wide steps led up to the massive wooden doors. A sign over them read: CITY HALL.

Inside, as in all of the buildings in this city, it was cooler than out in the sun, and the same type of hum vibrated. Our feet made a tapping sound as we walked across a wide entryway floor covered in large blocks of white and black stone. Doors led into a room with a table at one end and several rows of chairs facing it.

"Please take seats. Chou will be here momentarily." Terry sat at the end of the front row and we filled that one and two behind it.

A middle-aged man of medium height entered with two other people following. They sat at the table facing us.

"I am Chou Caw," he said. "I speak for the leaders of this community. My two companions are also members of the committee that governs. Who will speak for you?"

Madoc and Toren stood. "We'll represent our group," Madoc said. "I want to thank you for tending to our injured and for feeding us earlier, but most importantly, for saving us from the tigers."

"We couldn't ignore your plight. Know this, though. We do

not welcome strangers to our city. Once your companions are well again, you will leave us."

Madoc and Toren exchanged looks.

"Now, as we understand, many of you are from the land of Solwintor and a few from Leara. Also there are Panshee among you."

Toren nodded. "That's correct."

"And you're on a mission with several purposes?"

Toren repeated the reason for our journey as we told it to Terry. "I believe we now know where the two books came from, and we've seen marvels of technology you were able to salvage. The Panshee are with us because their gorge is filled with natural crystals. They, and we, hoped to trade those for some of the more basic devices you have. It has taken us more than a decade in Solwintor to build just a few. It would be a tremendous help to us if you shared at least some of your knowledge."

Madoc took over. "I don't know what else we can barter that you would want, but know this. We aren't here to hurt you or your people in any way, only to establish some kind of contact, communication with peoples of other lands."

"Why?"

"Because it's time. Because the longer we are isolated from each other, the harder it will be for reintegration into a larger society. Isn't a part of being civilized, working together to promote advancements?"

"There were many efforts to promote that kind of international cooperation in the past. A few worked. Many didn't. People are too different, their goals often mutually exclusive. I don't mean ethnically different." He waved a hand to include his two companions. "Here we have many different races and we work together well, but only because we have a mutual goal. We can't be sure yours is the same, and certainly most of the groups here in Fartekana have one goal only, to survive."

"If you continue to withhold means to improve their lives, they will always have to fight to survive." Madoc's jaw tightened.

"It's not our fault, and we can do little to help them."

"You've lost sight of the struggle they have, the difficulties that could be eliminated easily. We're not suggesting you give them your motorized vehicles, or even your most advanced medical devices. How about means to keep food cold? Or to light the insides of their homes? Simple things."

Chou shook his head. "We give them those, and they'll want more. We can't feed, clothe, and protect so many."

Madoc scowled. "Their numbers are dwindling."

"They called that survival of the fittest."

"The fittest or the smartest? Or maybe the luckiest? How did you come by all of this?" Toren waved an arm vaguely. "Where were you and your people when it happened?"

"We're the descendants of a group of scientists and technologists at an institute of learning not far from here. As events occurred, they were able to find protection in bunkers built for a war that occurred fifty years earlier. They took all they could, and remained there for two centuries, continuing their work as well as they could with limited sources of power."

"Crystals?"

"Yes, crystals, and some other sources used back then. These men and women came from every corner of the globe to this institute. The work that was done there wasn't all that advanced, not like some of the lost technology." He stopped and stared at Madoc and Toren. "You said you've spent long years trying to recreate a fraction of that. How is that possible?"

Toren nodded. "We, too, work with people from all over. They gathered in one place in Solwintor, bringing what knowledge, devices and books they had."

"And someone mentioned one of the satellites?"

Madoc hesitated. "We retrieved one from the bottom of a lake that formed when it fell."

"Intact?"

"Not completely." Toren pressed his lips together. "Some parts must have burned up as it fell, but many of the devices remaining were in good enough condition for us to determine how they worked."

"And they had markings and even an instruction book in the language of my books." Madoc smiled at Terry. "Your friend here confirmed the books are probably from Morata. When we leave you, we'll go that way, but the implication is that the parts of the satellite were made there, and that the science there was very advanced. I don't think anyone still there has that knowledge. We met some Mora on our way here. They have no technology whatsoever."

"And yet, you still want to go south?" Chou asked.

"Without communication, there's no way to know what's left there. I would think you would want to find any technology out there. Are you content with what you have?"

Chou conferred with the other two. Their voices were low, but our hearing had been sharpened along with our other abilities. It seemed they'd never considered there might be other pockets of knowledge remaining in the world, or that they could learn anything from anyone else. We'd opened their eyes after all.

He cleared his throat. "We will send some of you south, along with a half dozen of our own scientists. The rest will remain here."

"As hostages?" Gareth spoke up for the first time.

"As our guests. They can learn more from us."

"We're not all scientists." Madoc stopped before he told him what our skills and knowledge were.

Some of our people were back on the beach near the ship. One was in the hospital along with some of the Panshee. I wasn't sure whether it was such a good idea for us to split up even more, but Chou was in charge. Still, I was determined to stay with Madoc and hoped to keep Morna close. My brothers had shown they could take care of themselves, but as much as my sister thought she could, she was still a sixteen-year-old.

"How many of us would go on this expedition south?" Toren asked Chou.

"Six of yours and six of ours. We'd provide all you need to make the journey. Food, clothing, even medicines." He lifted his chin toward our swords and bows. "Even additional weapons so you can protect yourselves."

"I suppose this means it's decided we have no say." Toren glared at him.

"Pick those who go and those who stay. We will do the same." Chou stood. "The expedition will leave tomorrow. For now, Terry will see you to quarters for the night." He walked out with the other two who hadn't said a word.

CHAPTER FORTY-THREE

We looked at Terry, waiting for directions. She tapped her ear. I'd seen her do that a few times before and realized there was a tiny communication device just inside.

"Rooms have been prepared for you. If you'll follow me. The women will have to share one room, I'm afraid."

"That's not a problem," Morna said. "We share a dormitory with several others back in Solwintor."

Terry's eyebrows rose. "I see. And there are two rooms for the men. You can divide as you like." She led us out and down the stairs. "The building is nearby. It is mostly used to house our university students."

Morna turned a puzzled look at me. I mind-spoke 'I think university is a kind of school to prepare young people for the work they will do.'

Our rooms were on the second of three levels. We climbed the stairs inside to a long hallway with many doors off of it.

"The women will be in here." Terry opened a door on the left. Six narrow beds occupied the room, not unlike the beds back at the Stronghold. The room also held a few plastic chairs and small wooden cabinets. The light in the ceiling operated by pushing a button near the door. "The women's washroom is down the hall."

The thought of a washroom made me smile. It had been a while since we'd had one to use.

Before Terry led the men away, she told us, "I'll be back at six hours to take you to dinner."

She was gone when Carys asked, "How will we know the time?"

Ana pointed to a device on one of the tables. It showed the numbers 05 12 20, but the last one was counting up. "That probably means it's after five hours. I'm not sure how they count time here, though."

We each selected a bed and put our packs down.

"Who do you think should go south on the expedition?" Katya asked.

"I guess either Madoc or Toren will go," Ana replied. "Most likely Madoc, since the books are his. Which means you'll go too, Nissa."

I nodded. "Morna, you should come with me."

Carys shook her head. "She'll be safer here. Blane and I will stay. But Katya, since you're the most fluent in their language, you should go."

"I want to go," Morna said.

"Carys is right. Stay here with her and Blane."

"So that's three going." Ana held up three fingers. "Who else?"

"Donal," Morna said. "He'll want to see what devices they have."

"Making four." Ana's eyebrows came together. "What about any of the Panshee?"

"Probably not. They're already out of their element here. If Fong had recovered, perhaps he could go, but I think it should be Gareth or Rees to protect you all." Katya had a point.

I smirked. "I'm sure the men have their own ideas of who should go."

My sister nodded. "And they'll tell us."

I chuckled. "In that way, they're not unlike the Panshee."

We all laughed.

"Well, I'm finding that washroom Terry mentioned." I took out a clean blouse, my soap and wash cloth, and a towel.

"Good idea." Carys did the same.

"We'll go after you." Katya was rummaging in her packs for something.

Carys and I walked down the hallway. The door to the washroom was clearly marked with the Fartekana word for woman. Inside, everything was gleaming white, the floor, the walls, the sink, even the washing stalls, similar to the one back at the dorm in the Stronghold.

I glanced at it and smiled. "I guess I'll use that after dinner. There isn't enough time right now."

Carys nodded. "Just having a sink to wash in is a pleasure." She took off her blouse and washed her arms and upper body before drying them and putting on another blouse.

I started with my face, then moved down. Once I was finished, I undid my hair and brushed it. "I wouldn't be surprised if these people had machines to wash our clothes."

"I hope so." Carys sniffed the blouse she'd removed. "Most of what I have needs a good scrubbing."

We returned to the room and sent the others off to wash. They returned just before the device read 06 00 00, and Terry came for us.

"You all look refreshed."

"It's been a while since we've been able to wash in a sink," Ana told her. "I think we're all looking forward to using the washing stalls later."

"The showers?"

"Is that what you call them? We have something similar back at the – back in Solwintor." I don't know why we were still reluctant to use the word Stronghold, since we told them what we did there.

She stared at me a brief time. "We'll collect the men on the way to the cafeteria."

"I guess that's like our refectory." Carys smiled. "I'm interested in seeing how they prepare their food, and what they had besides all the cold meats, fruits and vegetables we ate earlier."

The two men's rooms were on the other side of the washrooms across from each other. They were ready to join us, and had cleaned up, too.

Madoc took my hand when he saw me and smiled.

"We've decided which of us will go south," Toren said and was surprised when the five of us women laughed. "What's so funny?"

I squeezed Madoc's hand. "We knew you'd pick who was going without asking us. But then, so did we. Let's see how close we came to your choices."

"I'll stay here, and Madoc will lead our half of the group."

I nodded.

"You guessed that?"

"We reasoned Madoc would want to go with his books, but both of you shouldn't go." I smiled.

"Hmm. Okay, who else? You I guess."

I grinned at him. "Of course. Initially I wanted to take Morna but Carys convinced me she'd be happier here. She still hasn't seen their farm or animals."

At that my sister's face brightened.

"Katya, because she's the best at their language, either Rees or Gareth, and Donal. That was as far as we got for certain."

He snickered. "Not bad. At least it means you agree with us. We also thought Ana should go."

"Me?" She pointed her thumb at her chest. "Why me?"

"If Eva were well, we'd definitely send her, but since she's still recovering, you're the next best with certain skills, shall we say?" Toren meant her ability with a knife and in hand-to-hand combat. "And Gareth decided he should stay here so he's sending Rees."

With that settled, we were ready to face what they called a cafeteria. It was a huge room, smelling of food, and filled with people. It resembled the refectory in that groups sat around tables eating, and the food was set out to collect on tables along one wall of the room. But here, there were people behind the food to hand it to us. Cold foods were kept over ice, while hot ones were kept warm by something underneath the containers that produced steam.

The people we'd seen in the streets all wore blue trousers and light colored shirts, but here they were dressed in a greater assortment of clothing. Perhaps what we'd seen before were uniforms, like our green coveralls. Now, in the evening, they were free to wear what they wanted. That was only speculation and would have to be confirmed at another time.

Some of the foods available were familiar: meat pies like the ones Col introduced us to and roasts like the ones we had back at the Manor. Others, though, were quite strange. Long sticks with pieces of meat and vegetables on them, chunks of meat crusted, then coated with an orange sauce, stew-like concoctions containing meats or fish and vegetables spooned over small white grains. The most surprising was at the end of the long display where a man sliced meat and vegetables and then cooked them directly on the table top. How did they get it hot enough to cook on? I had to taste it, so I waited for the cook to finish and let him deposit the result on my half-filled plate.

Terry indicated we could sit at a table that had just been vacated. It wasn't quite large enough for us all, so the rest spilled over to the next one.

I liked the food cooked on the tabletop, but the rest not as much. The stuff with the orange sauce was too sweet, and everything on the long sticks was dry. Still, we had plenty to eat. No shortage of food here.

We talked about nothing more substantial than the food. Carys tried to analyze the flavors of those she liked.

"I bet while you're here they'll let you talk to the cooks," Ana told her. "It's not something they'd keep secret." She grinned. "Maybe you should offer the recipe for Meecham cookies in exchange."

"Are you implying there are things they'd keep secret?"

"I'm sure there are." Toren nodded. "These people have taken us in and will cooperate with us up to a point but they already know our knowledge of technology is nowhere near as advanced as theirs, and they're not about to give away their edge."

Donal shrugged. "Then why are they going with us to the south?"

"Oh, just in case we stumble on some piece of the puzzle they don't already have."

"Because that would give us the edge?" Morna asked. "Is there any way we can imply we know more than we do?"

Madoc shook his head. "That time came and went. And I don't think we should have in any case. We'd have nothing to back it up."

"Is there anything we should do while the rest of you go south?" his brother asked.

"Just keep your eyes and ears open. Ask questions, but not

so many they stop answering."

Morna's eyes went wide. "Are you going in one of their cars?"

"Cars?" Donal asked.

"That's what Terry calls the vehicles, the small ones." Morna held her hands a short distance apart.

Toren shrugged. "I don't know. Chou didn't say, did he?"

"He also hasn't told us yet who's going with us." Madoc's eyes scanned the room.

I couldn't see him. "How far will we go?"

"As far as we have to. I expect from what the Mora said it's quite a distance. It took them years to move this far north and establish a community in the valley where we saw them."

Before we finished our meal, Chou showed up. "I expect you've selected the six who will travel with our people."

Madoc nodded and pointed to each of us as he said, "Donal, Nissa, Rees, Ana, Katya and myself. I hope that's agreeable."

"What skills do each of them have?"

Donal replied for himself. "I test the devices recreated from the documents we have and I know quite a bit about the science of how crystals can power them. I'm also good with a sword and bow."

"Master Madoc, why do they call you Master?" Chou asked.

"I'm a teacher. At the Manor where these four grew up, I taught science, or at least all of the science I knew. That meant I was always learning and seeking new knowledge to pass on to them."

Chou raised an eyebrow and tilted his head. "I understand now. And the ladies?"

Katya spoke up. "I suppose I am the most proficient in the language of this land. That is my job, to learn the languages of the books we accumulate and translate them for the technicians and engineers who build the devices." She turned to Ana. "My friend here is one of those engineers. We're both quite handy with a knife, and other weapons."

"And you?" Chou stared at me in such a way that I felt small even though I was taller than he was.

My mouth twisted into a smirk. "I'm a seamstress. I make

and alter clothing."

"Don't let my sister fool you." Donal rolled his eyes. "She designs clothing that is functional, practical. But she's also a swordswoman and archer, maybe even better at it than I am."

Rees had been silent. I wondered how the big man would describe himself. "I'm trained to protect. Guess I'm going along to make sure everyone gets where they're going in one piece."

A few of us chuckled at that.

"But we haven't met our traveling companions," Madoc said.

CHAPTER FORTY-FOUR

Chou beckoned three men from a nearby table. "Lin is what you call an engineer." He indicated a slim young man with a thin mustache and the narrow eyes of the Fartekana. "He improves our technology through experiments in one of our labs." Chou put a hand on a taller, broader man with a round face and muscular arms. "I suppose Tak will help Rees protect the party."

Finally, a handsome man with the blond hair and features common to the Solwinish, spoke. "I'm Dens. I will chronicle the journey and everything we find along the way."

Two women had come forward as the men were introduced to us. Chou smiled at them. "Bin and Vee also work in the laboratory with Lin."

"And the sixth?"

"We've decided Terry should accompany you, since she knows your language, just as Katya knows ours," Chou replied.

I tried to remember their names and what each of them did.

Chou sighed. "You will leave after morning meal."

"Will we travel in one of your vehicles?" Donal asked.

"No, that wouldn't be prudent." Although Chou didn't say more, that implied either the vehicles never left their city, they didn't want people living outside the dome to know about them or, possibly, they wanted us to be inconspicuous and not give away the fact we came from the city.

"Please join us for dessert." The woman named Vee smiled

at us.

We looked at the companions we were leaving behind. I shrugged and went with Vee and Bin to a recently vacated table. The twelve of us talked for a while to get to know each other, although most of us didn't know a lot of the language spoken by the others. When we finished, everyone else had left the cafeteria, the food cleared away and the lights dimmed.

"We will see you in the morning." Vee and the others parted from us outside the doors. We found our way back to our rooms.

Carys and Morna were already in bed. I smelled their soap. I grabbed mine and a clean nightgown and headed to the wash room with Ana and Katya trailing behind.

There were enough stalls for us to shower at the same time. Feeling much fresher and cleaner, I put on my night clothes and pinned up my hair. We were ready for bed, knowing we should get some sleep before we left in the morning. Our past experiences told us opportunities to wash, sleep and eat were chancy when traveling.

But sleep didn't come right away. I reached out tentatively with my mind and found Madoc was awake, too. My first question for him was, should we trust them?

The Tektek? To a point. I don't think they wish us ill.

No of course not, but they seem very cautious. How deep does that run?

You remember what I said earlier. Chou doesn't want anyone to have technology they don't. But are they willing to share whatever we find?

I guess that means we'll protect each other until we reach the source of your books and whatever technology still exists there. Then, as Ana would say, all bets are off.

I sensed his agreement. Get some sleep. I'll see you in the morning. He broke the connection.

I drifted off to sleep speculating about what we would find when we went south. Light filled the room when I woke, but not from the window. The overhead lights were very bright. Ava and Katya bustled about, filling their packs.

"Here, take this." Carys handed Ava a packet of herbs.

Katya smiled at me. "You're up at last. Hurry. We should

be ready to go before we eat breakfast."

I nodded and rose. They were already dressed, so I went to the washroom and put on my wide-legged pants that were relatively clean and the last of my clean blouses. I packed some of the soiled ones, hoping we'd find some stream where I could wash them.

"Here, Nissa, take this in exchange for one of your dirty ones." Morna handed me one of her blouses.

It might fit me, even if the sleeves were too short. I took it and gave her the dirtiest of mine. "One of your tasks will be to locate where these people wash their clothing."

"Gladly." She grinned at me, then threw her arms around me. "I'll miss you Nissa. Please, take care of yourself."

"Don't I always?" I cupped her chin and looked into her blue eyes. "And you do the same. The people here seem friendly and welcoming, but we don't know what they want from us. Obviously, crystals aren't what they're after."

She nodded and hugged me. "Yeah, like Madoc keeps saying, we'll keep our eyes and ears open, and you do the same. Between us, we'll learn what we can. Will you try to 'talk' to me while you're gone? Because I really want to be reassured you're all right."

"Sure. When we can, and when we're sure no one else is 'listening in'." I tapped her pert nose.

"Yeah, like Toren did back at the Stronghold before he became a friend."

"Exactly." I closed my pack and turned to the others. "Okay, I'm ready."

The three of us hoisted our belongings and headed for the cafeteria with Carys and Morna. The men were just ahead of us.

"Wait up!" Ana called to them.

Madoc, Gareth and Blane stopped and turned.

"All ready for the trek south?" Gareth asked.

I pointed to my pack. "Ready as I'll ever be. Except I'm starving."

We all laughed.

When we reached the cafeteria, I didn't know whether to sit with our friends or with our traveling companions. Chou solved my dilemma by summoning the twelve who were going to sit with him and one of the people who'd been with him the day before.

Bin eyed my wide-legged pants. "Do women in your part of the world wear those?"

Ana shook her head. "Nissa and Carys came up with the design a while back."

I smiled. "The women where I grew up wear long skirts most of the time, but not trousers. We thought these would be more practical for riding and even walking long distances."

"I like them," Vee said.

I pointed to hers. "We like the trousers the women here wear."

"Chou, do you think we have any we can give Nissa, Ana and Katya for the trip?" Terry asked.

"I hadn't realized they didn't have appropriate clothing for the journey. Of course we can provide them with some."

So we replaced more of our dirty clothing with that provided by the Tektek. The men did, too. The fabrics were comfortable, soft and pliable. The colors boring but that didn't bother me. At least they weren't a ghastly green.

I selected the foods that looked most like ones I enjoy for breakfast, including sausages and something the Solwinish called egg toast, especially good with sugar or honey on it, potatoes fried with onions and peppers, even some apples cooked in sugary water. I had two huge cups of tea and a smaller one of fruit juice.

When I finished and wiped my mouth of the last crumbs, Vee stopped staring at me. "Where do you put it all? You're so slim."

"I'm also tall. And we probably won't have many meals like this for a while. Have you ever left here?"

"Never. I'm not sure what it'll be like out there."

"My advice is to eat as much as you can this morning. We can't always stop when it's mealtime, or build a fire to cook food. Many meals will be bread, cheese and water."

She smiled. "They packed dried meat and fruit for us."

I nodded. "As long as those last, we can have those, too. We might find berry bushes or fruit trees, maybe some nuts. Vee, It won't be easy. You're used to an even cozier life than we had back in Solwintor. Did you ever sleep outdoors? On the ground?"

"We'll have sleep bags and blankets, even tents."

"Really?" I wasn't sure what a sleeping bag was. "Those will help."

"Of course they will." She patted my hand. "Don't worry. It will be fine."

Chou took us to the section of the dome where they'd brought us through. I was surprised more people weren't there to see us off, only our friends and a few of the Tektek we'd met. I thought about our departure from the Stronghold when almost the entire population turned out, or even when we left the Manor on our way here. Why wasn't this expedition more important to these people?

Chou made a speech to send the twelve of us on our way. Something about keeping sight of our goal and staying safe.

Finally, someone, probably Chou, did something that opened a door in the dome. We walked out onto the plain that surrounded it. At the last minute I turned and waved to Morna, Blane and Carys.

At a steady pace, we walked south, keeping the sun to our left. Vee walked next to me. Every once in a while she would ask a question, mostly about what I did in Solwintor.

"Do you really do all that work by hand?" She was fishing for information about the extent of our technology.

It couldn't hurt to be truthful about some of it. "The engineers are trying to construct a machine that sews, but so far they haven't been successful. Do you have machines that do?" I could fish too.

"Of course." She was silent for a while before asking, "Are your washrooms like ours?"

"Similar, except all the women share a washroom with only one washing stall. It's nice to have so many here." That brought up the question we had, the one I asked my sister to explore. "How do you wash your clothing?"

"In washing machines." Her narrow eyes became slits. "Don't you have those either?"

I bit my lip. "That's another thing they're working on." I hoped that was true. Donal would know. "Many parts of Solwintor and Leara do not have the water distribution systems it would require."

"But you do? At the facility where you live and work?"

"Yes." I smiled at her. That was one of the things that had impressed me at the Stronghold. She'd probably think the place primitive.

When the sun was overhead, we stopped near a grove of low-growing nut trees. Katya and Bin collected some while Terry took out food for our lunch. Much of it was similar to the food they served us when we first arrive inside the dome.

I sat next to Madoc as we ate our cheese, sliced meats, and raw vegetables. I touched his mind and told him the questions Vee had asked.

Lin asked me similar questions. Perhaps we should tell them the Stronghold is as isolated from the rest of Solwintor as the facility under the dome is from Fartekana.

I think they may have guessed that by now, but it could make them view us more as allies if we do. I took a bite of cheese and chewed slowly.

I'll let Rees know. He looked at the big man, sitting nearby and talking to Terry.

And I'll tell Ana and Katya. What about Donal?

I already talked to your brother about it. He's been getting more specific questions from Dens.

Oh? What did he ask?

About the satellite and what we learned from it mostly.

Our mind conversation was interrupted when Lin came over to sit on the other side of Madoc. "You too are very quiet."

"Nissa and I don't have to talk, do we my dear?"

"No. As long as we're near each other, we both feel more relaxed." I lifted a hand to touch the brooch with the blue crystal under my shirt.

He nodded but there were still questions in his eyes. When we started again Lin made sure to walk beside me instead of Madoc. His questions were more personal than Vee's had been.

"Madoc said he was a teacher in Leara. Were you one of his students?"

There was no reason to deny it. "Yes. We learned a lot from him."

"About science."

I nodded. "Well, as much as he knew at the time."

"He's learned more since?"

"We all have. There were legends about what happened all those years ago, but we knew nothing about the Second Moon except it shone every night."

"I'd be interested in hearing about those legends," he said. "Dens is the one you should tell them to." He indicated the man walking just ahead of us with Ana.

"In our travels we've heard many legends. Over time, the stories have grown." I chuckled. "People want explanations for everything, don't they? And when they don't have any, they create them."

"Yes, that's true. What about the stars? Do you have legends about those?"

"A few. We did study the patterns they make. What intrigued us about Madoc's books was that the patterns shown were so different from what we saw." I thought a bit before I went on. "The patterns we've seen here are closer to those in the book, but still not the same."

One eyebrow went up. "Yes, I gather that's why we're going south to Morata rather than any place else."

"The version of Fartekana in the second book also pointed to Morata being the source."

"Where did your friend Madoc get those books?" he asked.

I chuckled. "He got them a while back from a traveler from Solwintor, in exchange for a blanket and some provisions."

"And your relationship with him is no longer teacher and pupil?"

"My relationship with Madoc is none of your business. Just know we do have one." I walked away from him, tired of his ongoing questions. Instead, I joined Katya and Bin.

CHAPTER FORTY-FIVE

Time to ask my questions. "I guess you've all been inside the dome all your lives."

"We don't usually accept anyone new." Bin studied me. "You and your friends are the first in a very long time."

Katya narrowed her eyes. "Has anyone ever tried to attack you?"

"Early on. But they stopped after we turned them away."

"What about the Panshee?" I asked. "We heard they tried to contact you about a decade ago, but were refused, and some were killed."

She was taken aback. "Where'd you hear that?"

I shrugged. "From the Panshee. They sent a group, and one of the leaders and Fong's father didn't return. They were reported killed."

She shook her head violently. "Not by us."

"Maybe they were attacked by the tigers," Katya speculated.

It suddenly made more sense. "Or maybe a few of them killed the two men, and the others blamed it on the Tektek."

Bin laughed. "I'm sorry, I know that's not funny. Whenever you call us that, I have to laugh."

"What do you call yourselves?"

"Our compound was originally called the Institute for Science and Technology, and we still call ourselves the Isties. I guess that sounds even funnier than Tektek."

"I don't know. I think it suits you better." If they were willing to share, we could too. I looked at Katya before I revealed, "The place we come from is called the Stronghold. It's housed in a huge cave in Solwintor, and most people outside don't even know it's there or what goes on inside."

Katya quickly got over her surprise at my revelation. "We don't call ourselves anything. We're not all Solwinish, and we all have different jobs. I guess you can call us the Westerners."

"Or Strongholders." I giggled.

"Or simply Holders."

"I like that." It could mean anything, but after a while, everyone would know it referred to those from the Stronghold.

We continued to walk across the plain. The only features were the low-growing fruit trees, even lower bushes, and a sparse weedy grass. We gathered the little fruit that wasn't spoiled. No animals, and few birds. I was glad we hadn't encountered any more tigers, but it would have been nice to see something else alive out here.

In the distance, taller trees lined the horizon. We walked for a long time and they didn't seem any closer. "What kind of trees are those?" I asked Bin.

She shielded her eyes with her hand and shook her head. "From here they look like palms, but they couldn't be, could they? I mean, those grow in tropical climes where there's plenty of water. In the pictures I've seen, they were growing near the sea."

As the sun crossed the sky, it became quite hot, but there was no sign of water, certainly not an ocean.

She tapped Lin's shoulder. He was walking in front of us, talking to Donal. "Lin, do you know what kind of trees those are?"

"I'm no tree expert, but I'd say they were coconut palms."

She raised her shoulders in a shrug. "Then I guess they are after all."

"Maybe there's water on the other side of them." I didn't really believe it. The shore we landed on was many dulnos to the west, more than two days journey on foot. Unless we were walking more west than south, the Great Sea was no where nearby.

"Does anyone have a map of Fartekana? From Before?" Donal asked.

Lin pointed over his shoulder. "There are a few back at the compound but they are suspect. No one knows for sure how the continent changed during the flood."

I'd forgotten about that. They told us in Solwintor that only about a third of the land that was above water Before still was. The seas receded, but not before greatly altering the coastline of every land mass in the world.

"What did the Mora you met tell you?" Lin asked us.

"They were driven north by the floods, but didn't seem to have any concept of time, how long ago that was, and how much they wandered since." I realized how vague that sounded.

Donal grinned. "So there could be seas that never existed before, maybe even one south of those trees."

That spurred us to walk faster to see what we'd find when we finally reached the palms.

We stopped again for an evening meal before the sun reached the western horizon. This time Rees and Lin built a fire and we cooked meat and vegetables in water for a soupy stew.

"Too bad we don't have any berries," I lamented.

"Berries? You put those in stew?" Vee seemed astonished.

"Carys did it with great results, so it's become a variation we use sometimes. The fruit adds sweetness. She always experiments like that. I bet by the time we get back, she'll have taught your cooks a thing or two." I grinned at the idea.

"I hope so," Lin said. "Their repertoire could use some expansion."

Donal's eyes narrowed at him. "I thought the food was pretty good."

"Don't mind Lin. He likes to find things to complain about. If it's not the food, it's our clothing or his schedule." Bin smirked at him.

Lin shrugged. "It passes the time and gives me something to talk about."

The best you could say for the stew was that it was hot. We ate it anyway.

After we ate, we cleaned up, leaving no trace we'd been there. We continued toward the trees, hoping to reach them before we stopped for the night.

CHAPTER FORTY-SIX

Rees didn't reveal how we knew when it was our time to guard our camp to Dens or any of the Isty.

I spread my blankets near Madoc's, knowing it would be hard to fall asleep, no matter how physically tired I was. I must have drifted off for a while because I woke with a start when Madoc's mind touched mine, telling me it was our turn.

The evening moon was halfway across the clear sky but the air was still warm. The strange pattern of stars shone brightly. We sent Tak, Lin and Vee to their blankets as Katya joined us near the fire.

"It's been quiet," Lin said as he walked away.

They came without warning, without a sound, two huge beasts that walked upright like a man. They may have been men once, but the lack of any real intelligence in their faces made it hard to believe.

Perhaps they didn't see the others asleep away from the fire. They attacked the three of us like wild animals, fiercer than the tigers. Our shouts woke the others. Rees must have slept with his gun at the ready, because he shot at them first. His aim was true, hitting one in the head and the chest. As he fell, the other became even more enraged, clawing at me since I was nearest. I raised my hands in defense, trying to fight him off. He wasn't much taller than me, but infinitely stronger with claws at the ends of his long arms. They raked my face and I screamed in pain but continued to fight back, hoping one of my companions could take a shot at him to stop his onslaught.

It felt like I fought him off forever, even though it was only a few minutes. Then he crumbled in front of me.

I'm not the type to cry, but between the pain and the effort it had taken me, I let out one sob after another. Arms encircled me and Madoc's calming mind touched mine, joined soon after by my brother's. I leaned against Madoc and slowly my sobs ebbed.

Once I was breathing normally again, Vee came over with salves and bandages. "Let me see how bad those cuts are." She cleaned my face with a liquid that smelled like the hospital back inside the dome, then applied the salve and one tiny bandage. "You may have a small scar from the deepest cut."

Madoc cupped my chin. "You're still beautiful." He'd never said anything like that to me before. It made me feel like jelly inside.

Meanwhile, Lin and Donal were examining the things that attacked us. "They're humanoid." At our questioning looks Lin added. "Man-like. But they regressed to a time when men were little more than beasts."

Their bodies were hairier than men and they wore only strips of cloth.

"We've heard there were creatures like that out here. Never saw any until now." Bin took a small box from her pack. Similar to the device we had from the Stronghold, the one that took a person's image and then recreated a picture of them on paper. "There's not much light but I think I'll take a few photos now and more in the morning."

When we didn't question what she was doing, Lin asked, "Do you have cameras where you're from?" There was surprise in his voice.

"It was one of the devices we recreated. On our way here, we demonstrated it to people with mixed results." I sat on the ground, occasionally touching my damaged face. "Some thought it was magic, others thought the work of the devil."

"I could understand that. People who'd never seen any such devices before would be suspicious." She continued using her camera while she spoke. I didn't understand why she didn't wait until morning when there would be more light, but she explained she didn't need it.

"Nissa, why don't you try to get some sleep." My brother put a hand on my shoulder.

I looked up at him and tried to smile. "I don't think I can, but thanks, Donal."

"Well, at least lie down."

"Donal's right, my dearest." Madoc took my hand. "There are enough people to guard our camp, and somehow I don't think there will be any more incidents tonight." He led me to my blanket. I was afraid he'd tuck me in like a child, but all he did was help me lie down.

As I suspected, there was no way I could sleep. I watched as many of the others examined the monsters that had attacked us. I could still feel those claws on my face, and reached up to touch it once more. It was tender, especially where Vee bandaged it. I could imagine what I looked like, despite what Madoc said.

After a while, most of the others went back to their blankets. The third trio of guards took over the watch, but Madoc was right. There were no more incidents that night.

In the morning, my face felt stiff and sore, but it didn't stop me from eating breakfast. This time, Bin took out a different cheese, darker orange and sharper tasting, very good. After I'd eaten that and some bread, washed down with some hot tea, I went to look at what had attacked the night before.

They were uglier than I thought, with heavy lower jaws and deep set eyes. Their long brown hair was dirty and tangled in leaves, and their teeth were sharp. Bin took more photographs of them. "No one back inside the dome will believe our descriptions of these without pictures."

We packed everything up, and set out once again for the palm trees to the south.

We finally reached the trees as the sun reached it's highest point. They were palms as we thought, coconut palms, with fruits hanging heavy from the branches. We picked a few.

The trees continued for quite a while and in some places grew so thickly we had to fight our way through. Eventually we heard the sound of rushing water.

"Are those waves?" Bin asked.

"Sounds like it," I replied.

Her eyes and mouth opened wide, and Vee said, "We've never heard real waves before, only recordings of them."

"You should get out more often," Donal teased.

We smelled it, too, the salty aroma of the open sea. The soil became sandier before we made it to the open beach. As far as we could see, an ocean stretched out in front of us.

"How are we ever going to get across that?" Dens asked.

I grinned. "In a boat, of course." Again it was something we'd experienced before but they never had. Now who had the advantage?

"Do you mean you think we should build a boat? One that's seaworthy enough to cross that water?" Tak pointed to the waves that lapped the shore.

"It's our only choice. Unless you brought some kind of air ship with you." Madoc was already gathering branches with help from Donal and Rees. Ana, Katya and I joined them. Finally, the Isty did too.

"Do you know how to build a boat?" Bin dropped an armful of wood on the sand.

"We never have, but we have some idea of how to build a raft, and I guess we'll go from there," Ana replied.

I looked at the materials we'd accumulated. "We'll need a mast and a sail, too."

Rees pointed to a couple of long straight logs. "Those would work, but what about the sail?"

I could see some sewing in my near future. "Blankets would be too heavy. I'll need a few shirts."

"Nissa's going to make us the perfect sails." Katya smirked at me.

I shrugged. "Sewing's my fate." I laughed, and she joined me. I took out my needles and thread as a few of the men brought me shirts. They were mostly white and light gray. I ripped off the sleeves and began to spread them out with an eye to creating two large squares.

The fabric was easy to work with, but I was more concerned with the shape. After a while, Vee stopped what she was doing to watch me. I used the energy on the beach and a needle and thread from the medical supplies to sew the pieces together without being obvious about it. Time was of the essence. By the time I had the first sail done, some of the others had lashed twenty or twenty-five logs together and were examining the rest of the wood for the best additional ones.

"Collect some of the coconuts," Lin said. "They provide a liquid we can drink, and food, too."

"What about the fronds?" Dens asked. "Those broad leaves must be useful for something."

Shouts to our left drew our attention. A group of eight men and women came running toward us. Their skin was brown but they had the narrow, slanted eyes of other Fartekana. They wore simple clothing and two carried staffs made of wood from palms. The man in front shouted something, but none of us understood.

"I think they're asking who we are, what we're doing on their beach," Katya said. "It's not the Fartekana we know, but closer to ancient Ministic." That language was the basis for Fartekana as well as the language Mai's people spoke. She said something to the man.

He stopped shouting and came closer, but the others held back.

"I'm telling him we come from the north and we're heading south once we have a boat that will hold us all." Katya spoke to him again and gestured as she did.

Another man and a women came forward. They conferred for a short time, and the first man spoke again. Now that I knew that their language was related to Fartekana, I could pick out the words "stranger" and "walk".

Haltingly, Katya continued to tell them something. It sounded like she was reassuring them we meant no harm.

"Ask him if they can help us build this boat," Madoc said.

Terry said something to them. She was as much of a linguist as Katya.

The man turned to the rest of his people and motioned to them to help those building our raft. Two of them went back to the trees but returned soon with something that looked like small boats they use on the rivers in Leara.

"A row boat?" Terry asked. She said it again in the language of these people.

It was small, too small to hold all of us, but perhaps we could arrange to use it with the raft. Or possibly the sticks that were used to propel it.

"I wonder if they have any more." Lin went to examine it.

Meanwhile, three of the people came to see the sails I was making. They jabbered to each other about it. Katya joined me to translate, although I understood a few of their words.

Working together we finished the raft soon after mid-day. It was in two parts with the rowboats attached to the rear for use when the winds were calm. I hadn't noticed a few of the women leave and return with food wrapped in the large palm fronds. We built a fire from the scraps of wood left from the construction and they cooked the food in the leaves for a short time, then distributed it to our party and theirs.

As we sat around the fire eating, with Katya and Terry as translators, we told them about the two people we'd found the previous day, and the beasts we killed during the night. That caused a considerably agitated conversation among them.

The food cooked in palm leaves was particularly tasty. I'd have to tell Carys about it when we got back. If we got back.

Lin presented the first man who'd approached us with a gun and ammunition, and had Terry show him how to use it. It was our thanks for their help.

The man smiled and bowed slightly to Lin, and then to each of the rest of us.

We packed up again, and loaded the rafts, then pushed them out into the water. We waded out to them and climbed on as the people on the beach waved goodbye.

The wind drove the raft south by southeast. If we went too far east we could correct with the oars, or turn the sails slightly.

As we sailed onto the open sea, I remembered past boat trips. The Flying Dragon wasn't large, but it was certainly more of a ship than this, with quarters below deck, three masts, and a railed deck. In fact, I'd never been on a sea vessel this small. But this was all we had to cross the sea if we wanted to go farther south.

CHAPTER FORTY-SEVEN

The water stretched as far as we could see. No one knew how far we'd have to go. What would happen if we were still on the raft when night fell? We couldn't go to bunks somewhere to sleep. But when I realized there was no galley either and therefore I wouldn't be cooking for everyone, I had to laugh.

"Should we be fishing to add to our food supplies?" Donal asked. I guessed he wasn't used to being idle.

"Sure, why not?" Madoc smiled at him. "Dens, I saw you fashioning some fishing rods from branches. Where did you put them?"

"They're right here." He picked up the poles next to him. "There are only four." He looked around to see who wanted to use them besides my brother.

"I'll take one." Ana reached out a hand, then shifted her position so she was closer to the edge of the raft. Donal sat on the other side. Vee took the fore position, and Dens himself moved aft. Each pole was equipped with a piece of thick thread I'd provided and a stone as a sinker. The only bait they could tie on was ripped pieces of cloth.

But when the sun was half way to the horizon, none of them caught anything.

"Maybe there aren't any fish in this sea."

"There have to be," Bin scoffed. "Maybe you're not dropping your lines deep enough."

"Here, you try then." Vee handed the pole to her friend.

Bin examined it. "Is there any more of this?" She held up the line. Dens used what we had, which wasn't as thin as fishing line.

"You want to lengthen it?" Lin dug into his pack. "I think I have some string in here that we didn't use to tie the logs together for the raft." He pulled some out and handed it to her.

She replaced the heavier line with a longer length of it with a hook on the end and tossed it over the side. It took a while longer, but the tug was visible. And then she didn't know what to do. Donal moved quickly to her side. He's always loved fishing, and is the most expert of any of us at it. He helped her pull the fish up from the depths.

It wasn't the largest sea creature I'd ever seen. That would be either the ruda Blane and I killed or the monster fish at the bottom of Dulno Lake. But it was quite large. In fact, the weight of it threatened to be too much for the raft. In the end, we shifted some things to the canoe, including two of our party, Katya and Vee.

I hoped we'd find land soon, because the sun approached the western horizon. But there wasn't any in sight yet. So we ate cold sandwiches for our evening meal as we sailed ever southward.

The sun had set and the evening moon begun to rise when the first tiny island appeared. Using the oars and tacking the sails, we made for it. It was no more than a hill rising out of the sea, but it would have to do as a mooring place for the night.

We pulled the raft and row boats half-way up on shore and anchored them by tying them to the poles pushed as deep as we could into the ground. If we moved them up more, there'd be no room for any of us to spread our blankets. We didn't dare light a fire. Instead, we huddled close for warmth as the daytime heat disappeared. Even without any sign of other people or animals, we posted guards over the raft and boat, and took turns sleeping.

I slept better than I had for a couple of days with Madoc nearby. The guard shifted just before dawn. By that time, my body was rested.

I sat next to Madoc not far from the raft, hugging my knees. "How much farther do you think we'll have to sail?"

He shook his head. "There's no telling. Dens says the land

on this part of the continent was very low Before, and could have all been flooded. The nearest mountainous region is another day's sail at the rate we were traveling yesterday."

"Is this an arm of the Great Sea now?" I asked.

"That's likely."

"So, if we sailed west, we'd reach it?"

Madoc looked at me. "You're thinking after we accomplish our goal, we could sail around to where we left the rest of our party on the beach?"

"Only then we'd have to journey back east again to the dome."

"Yes. Across the chasm and the mountains." He'd been drawing something in the sand. I realized it was Fartek as we now knew it. "It might be better to go back the way we've just come."

"I suppose we'll have to wait and see what we find in Morata."

"If there's something there to find."

"You think there might not be?"

He shrugged. "The Mora went north. The question is whether they left anyone or anything behind."

But they had to have left something. They couldn't have taken much with them, and the current Mora didn't have the technology their ancestral land had. "Another question is whether the devices that existed in Morata before were kept someplace where they weren't destroyed since."

"You've been thinking about this." He smiled at me.

"Yes. Haven't you?"

"Of course. But we won't know anything for certain unless we go and see for ourselves."

We sat in silence through the rest of our watch. As the sun rose, the rest of the group woke. We ate another cold meal for breakfast and then pushed the raft out to the water before climbing aboard.

"We should do something with this fish if we can't cook it today."

"We could eat it raw." I remembered how the swamp people prepared and served their seafood. "Slice it very thin and salt it."

Terry took out a slim knife and set to work cutting the fish into chunks, removing the scales and skin, deboning the flesh and slicing it.

After a time, Ana joined her. They packed the thin pieces in coconut leaves. "I guess we know what we're having for lunch."

Lunchtime came and we ate the fish with bread and fruit. Lin cracked open two of the coconuts and we all tasted the milk.

"I understand people used to cook fish in this." Vee sipped hers, then took a bite of raw fish. "I would imagine that would be better than this."

"Oh, I don't know. I like it," Katya said.

The wind was still moving us mostly southward at a good rate, and there was still no sign of land, not even another island like the one we'd stopped at the night before.

Bin and Donal were preparing to fish again, more to pass the time than anything else, when Dens pointed off in the distance. "Is that a tree?"

We all looked in the direction he indicated. I saw what looked like one massive tree. We sailed closer and it resolved itself into a grove. They weren't palms but more like the oaks we had back at the Manor. Lower growing shrubs grew on one side of them. I hoped they were berry bushes or something else that would provide us with additional food.

It took longer than I expected to reach the wide shore. The soil was sandy but gray instead of white. Small birds flying between the trees made the only sound besides the waves that washed the shore with a low foam.

We pulled the raft completely onto the beach this time. Lin, Tak and Rees trekked across the sand and into the trees to explore while the rest of us unloaded the raft and row boats. We set up a camp and waited for the three men to come back. By the time we were done, they returned, walking slowly toward us. They were alone.

"No signs of anyone anywhere nearby." Rees gestured back the way they went. "These trees go on for a distance. In fact they get thicker the farther you go."

Tak nodded. "There are other varieties as well."

"Any sources of food?" Katya asked. "We found some berries on the shrubs near the beach and we're trying to decide if they're safe to eat."

Lin looked at the round red spheres in her hand. "They look like red gooseberries."

"That's what we thought," Ana said.

"We didn't find any fruit trees, but there are maples. We can tap them for their syrup," Rees suggested.

"We're cooking some of the fish for dinner." I'd fashioned a holder and filled it with the fish in its coconut leaves. It was already giving off a delicious aroma. Who said Carys was the only one to improvise?

"Sounds good." Rees came over to warm his hands over the fire, even though it was hot here as it had been out on the sea.

Once the sun set, though, it would probably become colder. We'd be happy to have the fire and hot food. There was enough room over the flames to heat some water for tea.

The Isty men had brought some other drink with them. The only alcoholic beverage I'd ever had was wine, but it seemed the Isty were used to other drinks.

The dinner was delicious, not only the fish, but also the vegetables that cooked with it. The berries finished off the meal. Maybe we were hungry after two days at sea, but there was nothing left after we ate.

Ana went through our supplies and reported we had enough to eat for three more days. If we didn't find any other food before then. "I guess one of our priorities is finding more food."

"We can catch some more fish." Donal was always ready to do that.

"And pick some more berries."

"What kind of staples do we have?" I asked Ana. "Can we bake more bread?"

"There's flour. We can do bread or maybe some kind of fruit muffins for a change."

A few of us set to work making those while others went in search of more berries or other edibles.

Madoc and Rees brought more logs toward the camp.

"Are we building another raft?" Donal asked.

"No, a shelter, using the extra blankets. It'll be a cold night."

Dens and Ana came back carrying armloads. "Look what we found. There are a few old apple trees. They're not in great shape but they do have quite a bit of fruit on them." Ana held one so we could see.

"And there are mushrooms on the ground near the apple trees, but we need someone to identify whether they're poisonous or not."

"I'll go look." Vee took off sprinting into the trees.

By the time everyone finished searching the nearby area, and Donal had done a bit more fishing, we had almost doubled our supplies, and the bread and muffins were almost finished baking. Too bad I couldn't make Meecham cookies, but that would have to wait until we had the right ingredients.

With the usual rotation of guards, we made it through a peaceful night. Breakfast was so much better than the previous day. We reheated the muffins, and had some apples, cheese, and lots of tea. It was a pleasant meal, even though we all knew we'd have to move on before long, continue our trek south.

We redistributed our supplies, demolished the shelter that had been helpful against the wind, and packed up all we could carry before setting out again, through the trees, hoping we'd find more sources of food and shelter as we continued on.

After two days at sea, sitting most of the time on the raft, we weren't used to all the walking. We stopped often to drink, to rest our legs or to eat. The trees seemed to go on for a long time. Some of them were taller than near the beach. There were still no signs of people, or even animals, very few birds and those too small to provide much meat.

We trudged through a carpet of fallen leaves under the trees. With the canopy, it was hard to follow the sun's progress across the sky. But eventually it became quite a bit darker and we knew night was close. There weren't any clearings that would accommodate all of us. We found the largest in the area. A few of us would have to sleep between the trees.

We were afraid to start a fire, afraid the trees would catch, so we feasted on the fruits and berries, and the bread we'd baked the night before.

After another uneventful night, we moved on. Now the trees were mostly like the fir trees at home. It was hard to tell, but we were climbing. The needles on the ground gave off a pleasant smell and reminded me of winter solstice, that cold time of year when the sun shone for the shortest length of time. But it wasn't that cold. Some of the chill was because the trees prevented sunlight from reaching us.

That day we found what Lin called cabins. There were three of them, built of logs, in a clearing among the tall fir trees. But like the forest itself, they were empty, save for a few pieces of furniture. Although it was midday when we found them, they were the first real shelter we'd come across in days, so we decided to spend the night.

Outside the largest cabin was a well, the only source of water. And next to one of the other buildings was a much smaller cabin. I opened it to explore. It was like the privy behind the tavern where Blane and I stayed at during our journey to find Madoc.

The largest cabin had a hearth. It was cold with few ashes remaining from the last time it was used. We lit a fire in it and cooked meat and fish. A table of rough-hewn wood sat in the middle of the single room with benches on opposite sides and a chair at either end. It was almost civilized.

CHAPTER FORTY-EIGHT

"I wonder who built these." Dens helped himself to meat from the platters we'd set on the table in the middle of the largest cabin. "And lived here."

"They've been gone a while, but how long?" Donal sat next to him with Ana on his other side. "Why did they leave and what happened to them?"

She shook her head. "Something drove them out, something they feared enough to keep them from returning."

"Look what I found!" Katya had been rummaging in the single cupboard next to the hearth. She brought over a small book and sat down on the other side of the table. "It looks like the same language as in Madoc's books."

Madoc looked over her shoulder. "It is. What does it say?"

"It appears to be a religious work, perhaps a prayer book." She squinted at the page she was reading.

"Why would they leave something like that behind?" Donal asked.

The cabin wasn't the kind of place someone would live in who could build the devices in Madoc's books. There was no sign of any machines.

With no beds in any of the cabins, we'd have to sleep on the floors. We split into three groups of four, each taking a buildings. The largest, with the hearth, would be the warmest, but being inside was enough to protect us from the wind and cold, especially wrapped in our blankets.

In the morning, we all assembled back in the largest building. Breakfast was a duplicate of our dinner the night before.

"I suppose we're continuing on today." Bin sounded exasperated.

"We still haven't found any people or signs of the machines that must have been developed in this part of the continent," Lin reminded her.

"But we found that book!" She pointed to the small volume sitting on the table.

"It only indicates the people who lived here spoke and read the same language as those who developed the technology described in my book." Madoc took out his own book. "We'll continue south as long as it takes to find what we can of that technology. Whoever wants to stay here or turn back, is welcome to do so, but we're going on."

"Absolutely," Ana agreed. "So, who's coming with us?"

All of our faction raised their hands, and so did Lin and Dens. Slowly but surely, Terry, then Vee joined us.

Bin's shoulders slumped. "Okay. I'm not staying here with Tak." She looked at the big man. "No offense." She sighed. "I guess we're all going."

We finished our meal and cleaned up. We left the cabins like we found them. The only thing we took was the small religious book.

Grabbing our packs, we headed out. The sky was filled with clouds, hiding the sun. It was colder than it had been. I took out my cloak and wrapped myself in it. The Itsies had outer clothing that looked like the skin of animals.

"Is that warm?" I asked Vee.

She nodded. "Very. See, it's lined. That cloak looks warm, too."

"Warm enough." It was made from woven wool from the sheep at the Manor and had served me well for some time.

The trees thinned out after a while, but it was still gloomy without the sun. We had set off again after the midday meal when the first drops fell.

"Do you have raincoats?" Vee asked me.

I shook my head. "What are those?"

She pulled something clear out of her pack. It had sleeves and a piece that went over the head. "It's made of plastic and keeps the rain off."

I could see the water running off it without penetrating to her clothing underneath.

"I think some people have extras. Perhaps they'll give you one." She tapped Terry's shoulder that was also covered by the see-through clothing. "Terry, do you have a raincoat for Nissa?"

Terry wasn't the only one. Soon we all had borrowed coverings to protect us from the rain.

It kept up all afternoon, making the ground muddy and sometimes slippery where there were many leaves. There was nothing to huddle under. I thought of the way Col created a shelter using a piece of something like this plastic over a few trees and suggested we do the same, but Madoc and Lin wanted to keep walking.

The rain became colder later in the day. I couldn't feel the wetness, but the temperature came through all my layers of clothing. It wasn't as bad as the Frozen Tundra of Sorn, but came close.

By the time we stopped for the evening meal, we were ready for a fire. Unfortunately, all of the wood around us was wet.

"We should have stayed in the cabin," Bin complained through chattering teeth.

"But we're much closer to our goal now." Lin pulled her close. I'd never seen him do that before with anyone. "It's okay, Bin, you can survive a little rain and cold."

Donal and Madoc finally used my idea and formed a partial shelter for us all using some of the raincoats hung over trees that were close together. We crowded together under them, fumbling with wet fingers to open the packets of food. Anything would have tasted good at that point.

"How much farther will we go today?" Terry asked.

"The rain's not going to stop soon, so I suggest we go on until the Evening Moon begins its ascent." Madoc used our term for it, although the Isty just called it the moon. They considered the Second Moon an interloper, but didn't call it the Moon of Destruction like the Panshee. Instead they called it Luna Two. I vowed to ask why.

We finished our meal, but no one was eager to walk on. Finally Madoc pulled down the makeshift shelter and redistributed the coats he'd used. We shouldered our packs and were on our way.

The Evening Moon was faint behind the clouds. As it started its climb we passed through a relatively clear area with sparser trees. There was evidence of a forest fire but it could have been the day before or a hundred years. The charred remains of trees were all we could see, especially through the raindrops, so it couldn't have been long.

"This is as good a place as any to stop." Lin looked around for trees tall enough to construct another shelter and found some at the edge of the clearing.

We removed our coats and handed them to him, hoping we wouldn't be soaked through before we could get underneath it. The ground was wet and no one wanted to sit down without something under them, but all the protective cloth was being used overhead. Then I had an idea. I searched through my pack and found the piece of yellow fabric I carried with me. Why hadn't I thought of it before?

"We used this to make the divers' suits. It's waterproof." Ana helped me spread it out. It wasn't very large but we could take turns sitting on it. Too bad we didn't have a fire to warm and dry ourselves. I did change my foot coverings. That felt a little better, but the boots were hopeless.

We ate cold fruit and vegetables with some cheese and bread, wishing it was hot soup or stew. We drank water, wishing it was tea. And then we prepared for bed.

Everything we had was wet. We couldn't protect it all from the rain. We could only hope the sun would shine the next day and dry everything.

I slept in the driest of my clothes, hoping the moisture in my blankets wouldn't seep through. But it was the cold that made my muscles tense. When it was our turn to guard the camp, I stood stiffly, pulled on my damp boots and joined Madoc.

The rat-tat-tat of the rain on our shelter had let up a bit. "Do you think it'll stop by morning?"

"I hope so. You look cold."

"I'm not sure I'll ever be dry and warm again. Oh, I know I will. I warmed up after the Tundra and this is nothing like that, but it's as if the chill has penetrated my bones."

He slipped an arm around me and pulled me close. "I'm afraid the cold will increase as we go south. We should have realized this time of year the weather would be like our cold months here."

"Would that have stopped you?" I smirked at him.

"Of course not, but I might have brought warmer clothes and some that were waterproof."

"And a way to keep everything else dry." I looked at my boots. "Do you think there are resistant footwear?"

"I'm certain there are, and I'm surprised our friends from the dome don't have any."

Ana had gone out from under the covering to check around our campsite. She returned soaking wet and shaking her head. "Aside from the rain, it's quiet out there." She shook her wet hair spraying us with water. "Sorry." She hit her mouth with a hand, but was giggling behind it.

She sat near us in silence for a while, then asked, "What do we do if this rain keeps up?"

"I'm more worried it will turn to snow," he said.

She nodded. "Yes, it could, the way the temperature has plummeted."

"We're not equipped to walk in heavy snow." I looked at my boots.

Madoc sighed. "We'll worry about that if we encounter any. Meanwhile, we still have to deal with the rain and the dampness."

"But we're going on, no matter what, right?" I tilted my head and looked at him.

"Right."

Ana ran her fingers through her wet hair. "It's good the Isty had raincoats and you have some of the waterproof fabric."

"Madoc, what happens if we go as far south as we can and still can't find evidence of the people or technology that existed so long ago?" I knew he'd be disappointed, but I was curious about what he thought we should do next.

"There has to be something, some vestige of the civilization. Even if the people we find know nothing about it, the way we didn't, there'll be clues, fables they've created to explain the past, and things that don't fit."

"Like the ruins in Dunswell or even the Crimson Orb."

He nodded. "Exactly."

"What if they've hidden what they have? If they have means of communication or transportation, they'd use them, unless they don't want anyone anywhere to know about it." Ana squeezed some of the wetness from her sleeve.

"Perhaps they've built their own version of the dome, or have sequestered their knowledge and experimentation the way we did in the Stronghold." It seemed likely we and the Isty weren't the only ones. "What if they won't talk to us? When we approached the Isty, it was with the promise of crystals. They didn't want them, but it made them curious."

Madoc didn't get a chance to answer. Lin and Vee came to tell us our turn was up, and they were taking over. Dens had already gone out from under the protective shelter to check around our camp as Ana had done.

We went back to our blankets. They weren't any drier. In fact, they were colder than before without our body heat to warm them. Still, I wrapped myself in mine in hopes I could sleep a little more and be ready for whatever we'd have to face in the morning.

When I woke, the patter of rain had stopped. I crawled out of my blankets and stood, looking around. The others were waking too.

We took down the cover. I shook the raindrops off it before folding it, but I didn't put it away because it was still wet.

Dens and Rees built a smoky fire with damp logs and leaves so we were able to make tea, but we'd have to wait for a hot meal until we found a drier site. Content with bread, cheese, dried meat and fruit, we packed up all of our belongings and set off again.

I wore my cloak to ward off the cold. As we went farther south, though, it became colder still. I draped one of my blankets around me and I wasn't the only one.

The trees grew more dense again. The piney scent increased, more from the needles beneath our feet than the trees. It had rained here, too. The limbs dripped on us. But it wasn't only rain. There were deposits of snow, too.

Madoc was ahead of me, but slowed his pace so he soon walked beside me. "I've been thinking about what you said during our watch. That was always a strong possibility. I've always known whoever we found might not be willing to share their knowledge or even talk to us."

I nodded. "They could even be hiding in something equivalent to the Stronghold."

"If so, I'm not sure we'd even know they were there, but you and I and a few of the others would be able to sense the change in energy."

"I hadn't thought about that." I smiled at him. "You're right, especially since the energy levels here have been quite low."

"You noticed that, too. I'm not surprised. You're very sensitive to how much there is around you."

I laughed. "I think that's your fault. You made me pay attention."

He laughed with me. "I suppose I did."

"What's so funny?" Donal joined us.

"We were talking about the low level of energy in this area."

He nodded. "It's true. I wondered why. What drained it?"

Madoc blinked. "Good question."

"Madoc, when we channel the energy around us, we don't 'use' it in the sense of depleting it, do we? Could the energy here have been used up in some way?"

"Not to my knowledge. I've never noticed any decrease no matter how many of us are focusing what's there."

"The Isty don't know about what we do, so we can't ask what they might know about it." I frowned.

Madoc shrugged. "I suppose we'll have to wait and see what we find in the next day or two, and act accordingly."

CHAPTER FORTY-NINE

I frowned at Madoc. "If we're going to find anyone, will it be soon?"

"We can't push the Isty much longer. Bin's complained all day about how far we've come and how tired she is. It won't be long before the others join her." He sighed. "No, two more days maximum and then we'll turn back north."

Sure enough, when we stopped for lunch, Tak joined Bin's whining. "Give it two more days," Madoc told them. "By then we'll be so far south that chances of finding anything still farther will be slim."

Lin smiled and patted Madoc on the back. "I'm glad you set a finite time for this journey. I was beginning to worry we'd soon have a mutiny on our hands."

"It seemed prudent to give them an end point. I only hope I'm right."

We built a fire and cooked the remaining fish with some vegetables before it went bad. If we had the time I might have made a soup. I'd keep that in mind for the evening meal.

As we cleaned up, though, it began to snow. No one seemed surprised, but Bin had a new complaint. "What's next? Locusts? Frogs? Flies?"

Ana explained the religious reference. "But snow wasn't one of the plagues."

"Snow's not so bad," Katya said. "It's pure and soft."

"And wet. I'm tired of being wet." Bin wouldn't stop.

The rest of us ignored her. We were wet, too, but complaining wouldn't help.

The snow piled up, and soon we were walking in the footprints of the person in front of us. Ana began to sing:

Snow falls softly, covering the ground
The earth is covered in a mantel of white
Snow falls gently on my little town
The tree limbs bow low with the weight of the snow
Snow falls lightly on my little town

Katya joined her. I'd never heard the song before or I would have, too. Their voices were sweet.

Hush! The sound is as faint as a whisper
Hush! And listen to snow as it falls
Hush! Each snowflake kisses the others
Snow falls lightly on my little town

Vee hummed along, smiling. When they finished, she said, "We sing a similar song, even though there's never snow inside the dome."

"And now I'm glad there isn't. Snow, nor rain for that matter." Bin hadn't stopped. The song hadn't soothed her the way it did me.

"Bin, give it up!" Ana threw up her hands. "There's no pleasing you. I'm surprised you didn't complain about the hot sun before the rain, or about how long the trip on the raft took. Come to think of it, you did."

Bin looked daggers at her and walked as far ahead of us as she could.

"Just ignore her. I'm sure she won't even join in building a snowman later." Katya exchanged a mischievous smile with Ana.

"Great idea!" Donal was all for it. "I'd love to see how you do that."

I'd heard about snowmen, but it snowed so rarely and so little at the Manor, even in the cold months, we didn't have enough to build one. "Sounds like fun."

So we were in a jolly mood when it happened. One minute we were tramping through the snow at a pace that kept us warm, and the next men with sticks and bows and arrows were swarming all over us. Wearing animal skins, there seemed to be fifty, although we learned later it was only twenty. They certainly made enough noise for fifty, whooping and shouting, jumping and running.

We were strung out in a long line but were able to regroup quickly after Madoc called Terry and Lin's names. The primitive weapons were no match for our guns. Rather than fire at them, those who had them shot into the air, and the snow covered ground. They didn't seem to know what to make of our response. At least half ran off and those who stayed, continued to think their sticks and shouting could frighten us.

Katya tried to speak to them with a few of the words she picked up from the people we'd met on the other side of the new sea. Either they didn't hear her in the din, or they didn't understand. They didn't stop until another man appeared. He held up a hand for silence, then addressed us in a form of Fartekana similar to that spoken by those others.

Terry and Katya interpreted. He asked why we came to enslave them, as others tried to do. Katya reassured him we were there to find any people still living in that part of what used to be Fartek.

"Really?" he asked, his eyes examining each of us in turn.

"Truly." Terry nodded and smiled.

"We are the only peoples left." The man indicated those with him. "Before Sion made the moons and set them to keep the sky bright all night, many peoples lived here and that way." He pointed north.

"I've never heard the word Sion before, but I think that's what he said," Katya explained to us in Solwinish, and then again in the version of Fartekana the Isty spoke. "He says his name is Mogo."

The man eyed her with a frown. "You come." He motioned with his hand.

I didn't need Katya to translate that one. I looked at Madoc. He shrugged.

We followed the man through the snow with the other

remaining men surrounding us and casting furtive looks.

I was surprised no one commented on how different Katya looked, but then she was the one who spoke their language. And the rest of us didn't look alike either. Most of the Isty had narrow slanted eyes. Only Donal had red hair and Ana was blond.

These people looked a little like the Isty, but their skin was darker and their eyes rounder.

A group of log houses stood in a clearing not far away. The few people outside them stared at us as we approached.

The man who had spoken to us faced them and held up his hands. He made a long speech, most of which I didn't understand.

In a low voice, Terry said, "Mogo's telling them to be kind to these visitors from the north."

My shoulders relaxed.

Mogo motioned for us to follow him to a long, low building near the center of the village. Inside, three wooden tables took up most of the room. There were benches on either side. At the end of the building, opposite the door, was a raised platform with a pedestal in the center. There was something on it, something that seemed out of place in this simple log structure.

I stepped closer to look at it. So did most of our party. Yes, it was what I thought, a crystal almost as large as the Crimson Orb and roughly the same color.

Mogo said something in a tone indicating his surprise, but we needed Katya or Terry to translate.

"He asked if we, too, worshiped the source," Katya said.

Terry shook her head. "He said we should revere it."

Katya tilted her head toward her shoulder. "In any case, it's definitely a crystal, one of the large ones used in bigger machines."

"Like the satellites that fell."

"Or vehicles used on the ground." The closer I got to the crystal, the stronger the energy. I turned to Terry. "Is that what they use to power your cars?"

She nodded. "They're also used in many other systems." But she didn't elaborate. The Isty instinct to keep everything secret from outsiders was very strong.

Madoc questioned the man with Katya's help. "Where did you find the source?"

His eyes narrowed as he answered.

"He says there is only one source. There isn't another. It came from the sky, many cycles ago, so many he can't count, and it belongs to us, to the Borogo. The Sion can't have it, and neither can we." Katya swallowed.

"How do we find the Sion?" Rees was more interested in that than any crystals or what they could do.

"No one can find them. Or maybe he said 'No one can discover them'. Terry, what do you think?"

"The word could mean either."

Rees scowled. "So how do they know they're there, or want the crystal?"

"And where do we go next?" Bin crossed her arms. "That is, if Mogo and the rest of the Borogo let us continue on."

"I'll tell him we don't care about the crystal, but need to find the Sion before they do something dreadful." Katya turned to Mogo and slowly told him that. He stared at her for a while. Then his mouth started to twitch and his lips went in and out of his mouth. Finally, he sighed. He waved an arm as he spoke. The only words I understood were 'south' and 'water'. The latter could have been lake or sea.

Katya nodded solemnly at him before turning back to us and saying, "We must continue south but go east when we see the blue lake. And he wished us good fortune."

"So we can go? I thought they'd at least feed us." Tak sounded like Bin.

"Tak, they can barely feed themselves." Lin pulled his pack onto his shoulders. "Let's go. We have enough food for dinner."

As we left the building, though, three women came forward, each with a bundle they handed to three of us, including me.

Mogo spouted some more words, including the Fartekana word for 'food'.

We smiled and bowed and thanked the women as best we could. Hopefully it would be food we could eat. I added the bundle to my back and we were on our way. I turned and waved before entering another wood south of their village.

"I think they were happy to be rid of us," Dens said.

The snow wasn't too deep among the trees. The air around us warmed through the rest of the day and much of the snow melted away. When we stopped for our evening meal on the other side of the wood, we'd reached dry ground. In front of us spread a huge lake. It wasn't the size of the sea, but it was formidable.

We built a fire and took the time to cook some stew. I opened the bundle the Borogo woman gave me to find something that resembled carrots. I sniffed them. They even smelled like carrots. I cut a few up, then added them to the stew, thinking all the while how much Gallin liked carrots and other root vegetables.

The stew took a while to cook, and meanwhile everyone seemed to be content chewing on fruit and nuts. We drank tea, too.

When I dished out the stew, I expected everyone to thank me because they were at a point when they'd eat anything. Instead, they genuinely enjoyed it.

"What are these carrot things? They taste slightly different than usual," Donal said.

"The Borogo gave them to me. Guess they grow them here."

"Isn't it too cold?" He chewed on more.

"Not all year."

"That was very good, Nissa." Ana handed me her empty bowl. "May I have some more?"

By the time we finished eating, it was growing dark. We put out the fire with nearby mounds of snow and packed everything up again. "We won't go much farther tonight," Lin said. He looked up at the clear sky. "I hope it won't rain or snow tonight. "

CHAPTER FIFTY

The Evening Moon guided us east along the lake. Madoc walked beside me again. "I hope the Borogo's directions will take us to the Sion."

"If the Sion exist and will let us find them."

"Still worried they may be hiding in a cave or inside a dome?" He slipped his hand in mine.

I looked at his face in the moonlight, the chiseled jaw and high cheek bones, the dark eyes. "If I had the only technology in a land where everyone else lived under primitive conditions, I'd share it. But some might not, and if they didn't, they'd probably stay as hidden as possible."

"The conditions the Borogo live in aren't much more primitive than ours back at the Manor."

"At least we had indoor water pumps and cold boxes, and methods to light and heat our rooms. Most of the houses and shops in Holmdale had those amenities."

He squeezed my hand. "I was teasing you, you know. The truth is, without communication and motorized transportation, Leara, and Solwintor, too, were divided into pockets possessing more or less mechanization. When we left the Stronghold, part of our mission was to spread technology redeveloped there to everyone. We're so focused on finding the source of my books, and any remaining technology now, we haven't been doing that."

"You think we should have shown the Borogo some of our

devices? We don't even have many with us. They're back on the beach, or with Morna, Blane and Carys inside the dome."

"That's true, but the Isty have devices with them they aren't sharing even with us."

I hadn't noticed them using any, but Madoc must have. "What kind of devices?"

He looked around, then said softly, "I believe they have some kind of communicator and are in contact with those back inside the dome."

"What? Really?" It made sense. "I shouldn't be so surprised."

"They're also taking measurements. Dens isn't only recording what's happened but also the conditions, the geography, all sorts of data."

I shrugged. "He probably should. The Isty know little about what's happened to this part of their land. They're the only ones we know of who are maintaining any records."

"Yes, but that's a lot of information. How are they keeping it?"

"I overheard him say something to Lin about a database, whatever that is."

"When was that?" Madoc asked.

"The other day when we were on the raft. We were so crammed together I couldn't help hearing them."

"Did you hear anything else?"

I shook my head. "But I'm sure there's more back in their city they're keeping from us including devices that might be useful for everyone. How do they cool the air in their buildings, for instance?"

"I asked. They use a machine installed in every building in their city. It not only cools the air, but also filters out dust and other harmful particles."

"Really? Wow! So I was right. Who knows what else they have, what the civilization had Before that the Isty preserved?" I sighed.

"Perhaps after this journey the Isty will share more with us."

"I hope so. I'm sure Blane, Carys and Morna are investigating as much as they can."

"And Gareth, as well."

"I can't even imagine what they have. Except for the pictures in this book, of course." I tapped the book he was holding.

He flipped through it, stopping periodically to look at the oddest devices depicted. "I understand more of what the directions say, and how these things are constructed and work."

"And what they're for? That's good. So, if we don't find the Sion or any of their devices, and if the Isty don't share with us, we'll still be able to build these."

"Still it would be better if we met the Sion. I'm very curious about them."

"Then let's keep walking."

Tak, who headed the column with Lin, suddenly shouted. "There's a building ahead. It looks like a castle or fortress or something."

"The Sion!" Lin's smile was fleeting. "Definitely a fortress to keep everyone else out."

"So how do we get in?" Tak asked.

"Not easily." Madoc studied the structure.

"There may be a weak spot in the stone, one we can use to penetrate their defenses." Tak looked high and low. But nothing showed.

"We can scout around the other side," Rees said. "They wouldn't expect an attack from the south, would they?"

"Probably not, but that wouldn't stop them from protecting it." Madoc slipped his book inside his tunic.

"So you think it's impregnable." Ana walked a little closer.

Madoc nodded. "Very likely."

"Why don't we just find a door and knock?"

We all stared at Ana.

She shrugged. "It's worth a try, isn't it? Why are we assuming they won't let us in? Or talk to us?"

We approached the fortress and found the door. There was no one outside to guard it.

"It was my idea, so I'll knock." Ana strode forward. Tak and Rees followed closely behind her.

There was no knocker, so she rapped on the metal door with her knuckles. Nothing happened at first. She knocked again, more insistently. A small panel high up in the door slid open.

"We would like to speak to you," Ana said.

Katya moved to her shoulder and repeated in Fartekana.

The panel shut. Nothing else happened.

We didn't move, but stood waiting. A smaller door opened halfway down the wall from the main one, a door we hadn't seen before. Three people bundled in furs came out and closed the door behind them. They walked slowly to where we stood.

"What do you want to talk about?" the middle one asked in both languages. The voice was female, high-pitched and squeaky, but there was no other sign of the gender of each of the three.

"We've come from the north seeking the source of two books. We believe they're in your language." Madoc took out the two books again.

The person who spoke stepped forward and took the top book. She looked at the cover then opened it. "Where did you get this?" Her eyes narrowed at Madoc.

"Far away from here. In Leara."

"That's on the other side of the world. Are there still people there?"

"Yes. And in Solwintor. North of the new lake here in Fartek, too. There are people all over, some living under primitive conditions, and others with bits and pieces of the old technology." That all he said.

We were so focused on the three people, we never heard the main door open or the men troop out behind us carrying long guns like the ones the Isty called rifles.

The woman's eyes flicked up to the people behind us and she smiled. "You will come with us."

There were twenty-five to our twelve, so we didn't object. Besides, this was our chance to enter the fortress.

They took us to a room not unlike the one we waited in when we first entered the dome. A long table filled the center with benches down each side. But this time no one brought us food. The guards stayed with us while the woman and her two companions went off somewhere.

The guards were silent, holding their guns at the ready. They didn't demand we give up our own weapons, though.

Before long, five people entered. Although she'd removed her outer clothes, I recognized the woman who'd spoken to us by her cold black eyes, long nose and firm mouth. If I hadn't, the moment she began to speak I would have known it was the same woman.

"My name is Worgu Fami. That is all you need to know about me, the people here or this place. You asked to talk to us, so we've brought you into our reception chamber. You will speak your piece, and then return north, swearing you will not speak a word of our existence. Is that clear?"

Madoc had spoken the most before, but now Lin addressed Worgu. "I am called Lin. I come from the northern part of Fartek, from a compound of scientists and technologists. Six of us have accompanied the travelers from the west, but like you, we work in seclusion and do not welcome visits from outsiders. Still, we have learned from our Learic and Solwinish friends, and expect your people and ours have much we can share." It was a different approach than the one Madoc took.

"If this is so, did you not know about the machines in the book they brought?"

"Oh, we have many such machines, but our people were not the source of those books and Master Madoc here was determined to find the peoples who produced them." Lin pointed to the second book. "And we were curious about where the constellations were like those in the second book. The stars aren't quite the same where we are, and very different in Leara and Solwintor."

"And now you've satisfied your curiosity. I hope that's enough." The note of finality in her voice implied we'd learn no more.

Lin shook his head. "As I said, it is important we share our knowledge. We have come to believe it is time for civilization to be restored to all of Fartek, in fact, to all of Lorsik."

She sneered. "And you expect us to go along with that? You haven't proven you have any technology at all. What would we get from it anyway?"

"We know where there are natural crystals," Katya said.

"We have all the crystals we need." She frowned.

"Is that why you wanted the one the Borogo have?" I crossed my arms and stared her in her eyes.

Her brows came together. "How did you know about that?"

"They told us."

"You saw it? You know where they keep it?"

I looked at Lin and Madoc. Madoc tilted his chin. I licked my lips. "We saw it. It's theirs and should remain so. They consider it a religious item, something to worship even."

"They have no idea of the power in one of those," she scoffed.

"I think they do." I grinned. "They know they can focus energy, and can heal in that way. That's all they need to know."

"And what do any of you know about crystals?" she demanded.

Lin chuckled. "We use them to power some of our devices. We can be just as secretive as you, so pardon us if we don't share what those are. Suffice to say, we live very comfortably."

"Where did your devices come from?"

"Some we were able to save when the floods began, others we've recreated, as the people from Solwintor have done. Once you start and have the diagrams and crystals to do it, it's not hard to build, say a communications system."

That was a cue for Madoc to add, "And that's what we'd like to see. More communication between the more advanced groups. Eventually, we can distribute some of that knowledge to others, but we found a gradual approach works best. Bombard people with too many machines at once and they think you're the devil."

"Did that really happen to you?" A hint of interest.

"On our way to Fartek, we stopped in small villages and demonstrated a camera." He shook his head. "They didn't understand how it worked, so they were convinced it was magic or worse."

"I suppose if you've never seen one, you might be leery of it." She frowned again.

We were having such a calm and agreeable conversation with her that when she gave her order, we were all surprised.

CHAPTER FIFTY-ONE

"I'm afraid you won't be able to leave here, after all. Guards, take them to the cells." The woman surprised us by her order.

They divided us into four groups of three. I was taken by guards with Ana and Bin to a room smaller than the bedroom I shared with Morna back at the Manor. Once we were inside, the door closed, and the lock clicked.

Before Bin could complain, Ana said, "The good news is we're inside the fortress and can observe these people and the devices they use."

It didn't stop Bin. "But the bad news is we're locked in this¬this shoebox of a room."

"It's indoors." I counted the advantages of the room on my fingers. "There are three real beds and a real sink. And it's warm and dry in here."

Ana started to strip off her jacket and every layer underneath. "Well, I for one, am going to take the opportunity to wash out a few of my clothes. Even I can't stand the smell of what I'm wearing."

Bin looked aghast. "You're getting undressed in front of us?"

Ana stared at her, then rolled her eyes. "I'm not ashamed of my body. Are you?"

I needed to distract Bin, but what could I say? "Bin, what makes the floor vibrate?"

"How should I know?" Her shoulders went up.

"I felt the same thing back inside the dome."

She thought for a short time before replying. "I guess it was the generator there. Perhaps they have one, too."

"The generator?" Ana's eyes narrowed at Bin.

"The one that creates the power to run everything."

I remembered a word I heard in the Stronghold. "Like a reactor."

Bin shrugged. "I have no idea. It's always been there. I guess we don't even notice."

"So you don't know how it works?"

She rolled her eyes. "Why should I? I'm not an engineer." She turned away from us and sat on the bed she picked, the one nearest the door.

I frowned at her back. Ana took off her top and pants. I thought she'd be cold in her underthings, but she didn't rush to put on fresh clothes. Instead, she sorted through what was in her pack. Finally, she picked a pair of gray pants and a white shirt.

I decided to do the same thing. "What do you think they want with us?" I removed my shirt and shivered, so I grabbed the first one I found in my pack.

"They probably think we know too much about them and might spill the beans."

"Might what?" I stopped removing my wide-legged pants.

She smiled. "Tell the rest of the world about them."

"Even if we promised not to?" I let the pants drop to the floor and stepped out of them.

"They don't know us well enough to trust we'll keep our word."

I pulled on a long skirt and hoped it would be warm enough. "We don't know that much."

"Just knowing they're here..." She didn't get any further before the door opened.

A woman stood in the doorway. She was younger than Worgu Fami. "You will come with me." She turned and started down the hallway.

Ana and I shared a shrug and followed her. Bin trailed behind.

As we walked, I murmured, "What now?"

Ana sighed. "We're about to find out."

The woman opened each door along the way and our traveling companions joined us. My heart lifted when I saw Madoc. He, too, had changed his clothes, as had almost everyone.

We were taken to a large hall with rows of seats, all facing a platform similar to the place where Chou addressed us when we first arrived inside the dome.

There were five chairs on the platform, four occupied. Once we sat down facing them, Worgu Fami came in from a side door and joined the four. The man sitting in the center rose and cleared his throat.

"I could say we welcome you to the Enclave, but you must be aware you are not welcome here. On the other hand, we cannot let you leave." His scowl sent a chill through me. "We've evaded prying eyes for centuries. Most would never come this far south. But now you're here, you will stay. And you will be useful to us, much more useful than the Borogo could be. They are so primitive in their life and beliefs, but you, you have knowledge that will fill in gaps. No one here at the Enclave is idle, everyone contributes to our goals. Each of you will be questioned by an engineer. We will examine every device you have. And these books you brought us..." He lifted them and smiled but there was no warmth in it. "These contain plans we have been lacking. However you obtained them, they belong to us. I suppose we should thank you for returning them."

Madoc stood next to me. He grabbed my hand and squeezed it, but didn't touch my mind with his. Still, I sensed he was unhappy with events, and with the response of these people.

The man took in a breath and let it out through clenched teeth. "I am Riman Saw. My comrades here and I are the ruling committee here at the Enclave. Our laws are simple and will be explained to you by those assigned to question you." He emphasized the word 'question' as if he had another word in mind, perhaps 'interrogate'. "As you leave here, you will be given a paper with the name of your contact. What they say, you must obey."

These people made those from the dome seem warm and friendly.

"You are dismissed." Riman Saw rose and left the platform through the side door, then the other four left as well.

We filed out of the hall through the main door. A woman sitting there, the one who'd led us from our rooms, handed each of us a small piece of white paper. On mine was printed a name, Henza Kel. I wondered when I'd meet my interrogator, and whether he or she was as unfriendly as Riman Saw and Worgu Fami.

The young woman took us back to our rooms and locked us in again. Ana, Bin and I talked about our 'contacts' and what we'd tell them. Bin looked around the room. "I hope no one's listening to us."

"Listening? Oh, you think they can monitor our conversation?" I hadn't thought about the possibility.

"I'm sure if they can, they will."

"They want to find out what we know, how advanced our technology is, which would imply theirs isn't that advanced." But Ana joined Bin examining the beds and walls for something that might be able to transmit what we were saying.

"They were also quite interested in Madoc's books. That, too, would imply they didn't have diagrams or instructions."

"I wonder when we'll meet our 'contacts'." At least Bin was no longer complaining.

"From the name I can't tell whether mine is a man or woman." I read it again. "Henza Kel."

"All the names are strange." Bin waved here piece of paper. "Mine's Resto Eng."

"Our names probably sound strange to them." Ana smirked at her. "To me a bin is like a container."

Bin laughed. "I know an Ana, but never met a Nissa."

"I wonder whether they'll feed us. And I can definitely use a toilet." I laughed, too.

Before long the young woman opened our door again. "I'm Nata Wend."

"Then you're my contact," Ana said. She held out a hand. "I'm Ana."

Nata looked at it with a puzzled expression.

"Where we come from, people touch or shake hands when they first meet. I suppose we met before, but technically, since we didn't exchange names, this is our official meeting." Ana's hand was still outstretched.

Nata didn't take it. Instead she said, "I'm here to take you to evening meal. You two will meet your contacts in the dining hall." Once more she didn't stop to be certain we understood or followed her. She did stop outside a door she hadn't opened before. "You may use the toilet before your meal."

Inside was one toilet, nothing else. She let us in, one at a time, then proceeded down the hall. This time she didn't collect our companions. I hoped someone else had and we'd see them in the dining hall. But when we got there, the only ones there were Worgu Fami and two other women. The two were introduced as our contacts. Were we to be kept separate from our friends? Had they already eaten? I would have asked, but was convinced no one would answer.

Two lads appeared carrying trays of food. Mostly bread and cheese, but also slices of raw vegetables and apples.

"We didn't know what food any of you ate. We hope this is to your liking. Our diet is simple but nourishing."

Objecting wouldn't have done any good. We all nodded our thanks, even Bin.

I tried to start a conversation but Worgu Fami glared at me. "We do not speak during meals."

That forced me to eat faster in the hopes that after we finished we'd get some answers. Instead, we were each led off by our contacts. Henza Kel was a short woman with long, dark hair. The wrists extending from her tan shirt were thin and her shoulders were narrow. She took me into yet another tiny room, this one with a table and two chairs. Two candles in a holder on the table cast strange shadows on the walls and a sweet scent.

"Where you from?" Henza asked in oddly accented Fartekana.

"Originally, from Leara. Recently, I lived in Solwintor." That was true enough, and all I was willing to share.

"That is not to north."

"No, we sailed across the Great Sea from the west."

"Sailed?"

My eyes automatically looked up while I counted to ten. "In a boat with a sail." No need to say the ships also had engines. "The wind moved it this way."

"You know Fartek here?"

What language was her native tongue? "Our books and maps showed Fartek, but we didn't know for certain until we arrived."

"How you come from north?"

"We walked. And then we built a raft to cross the water."

Her brows came together in puzzlement.

"Do you have paper and something to write with?" I asked.

"You wait." She rose and left, locking the door behind her, but she wasn't gone long. When she returned, she put a piece of rough paper in front of me and handed me a stubby pencil. Even at the Manor we had better ones.

I drew a map as well as I could showing the general outlines of Leara and Solwintor, then the parts of Solwintor I knew, without any details of the different communities. Next to the body of water we crossed two days earlier, I drew a picture of the raft. There wasn't much energy nearby, especially inside the fortress, but I used what I could to draw as faithful a picture as possible.

I watched her face when she took the paper back and looked at my drawing. Was it surprise or disbelief that clouded her eyes? I reached out my mind tentatively, something I'd never done with the Isty, and found hers might be easy to manipulate if necessary.

She put the paper aside. "What devices you bring from north?" I no longer thought the questions were her own. Each of the interrogators were probably given the same list to ask. They should have been better trained, though, in hiding their own physical responses to our answers.

"We brought very little." We didn't have any communication devices that connected us to the dome and the Isty back there. Lin might have such a gadget, kept secret even from us.

"What are they?"

"A few lights we can hold in our hands." I stared at the flickering candles. "Why aren't there any lights in this room like there are in our bedroom or the dining hall?"

"I ask questions." Her mouth formed a straight line, and she glared at me.

"Sorry." But her response told me a lot. With every passing minute, my impression of how advanced these people were diminished. They saw us as a source of technology they themselves didn't have. I smiled.

"What else? Do you have weapons?"

I should tread carefully here. "Yes." I pointed to the sword at my side, and wondered if I'd have to use it. They hadn't taken away any of our visible weapons or searched us for hidden ones.

"Do you know how to use?" From the awe in her voice, I could tell this was not a question she was told to ask.

"Sure." I thought back to my longing to learn to use it. It seemed so long ago. So much had happened since. "My father is swordmaster back home."

She blinked, then cleared her throat. "Why did you come south?"

"We were searching for the source of two books and for any remnants of the civilization here before the Second Moon was launched. I don't know what you call it, but that's our name for it."

"The Second Moon. I like that. Because it rises after Luna." A faint smile passed over her mouth before it resumed its passive straight line.

"Is that what you call the Evening Moon? I like it." My smile remained.

She cleared her throat. I was becoming too friendly. "What you plan to do when you find what you look for?"

"We'll return to the north, satisfied with the knowledge. We hoped the people who printed the books would share some of what they know, but now we wonder if that will happen." Something had been bothering me. Were these the people we sought? "What do you call yourselves?"

"Call ourselves? I am Henza."

"I meant what do you call your people?" Perhaps if I gave her examples. "The people from Solwintor are Solwinish, and our friends from northern Fartek are the Isty."

"Oh, we are the Dedi."

"Have you ever heard of the Sion?"

Her face went white.

CHAPTER FIFTY-TWO

"Henza? Are you all right?" I moved close and put a hand on her shoulder, but she flinched.

"I think it's time to take you back to your room. We can continue tomorrow." She hurried to the door and opened it. Her downcast eyes never looked at me as she showed me the way back.

Ana and Bin were already there and dressed for bed. I found my nightclothes and returned to the small toilet to change so Bin wouldn't object.

When I stretched out on my bed, my feet dangled over the end.

Ana giggled. "Who told you to be so tall."

I hadn't noticed before, but the Dedi were all much shorter than I am. Most people are and I was used to looking down on everyone except my brothers and Madoc. Many Solwinish were my height or taller, but not Ana. She fit comfortably on her bed. Bin was small like most of her people.

"So how did your questioning go?" Bin asked.

"I think I learned almost as much as I told her based on her reactions." I was still putting it all together in my mind.

"Like what?" Ana sat up in bed.

"These aren't the Sion and, in fact, Henza froze when I mentioned them."

"Mine knew nothing about the satellites that fell." Ana laughed. "I didn't enlighten her beyond the large number before they fell. It took her some time to process even that tidbit. I had lots of fun with her after that, telling her the most absurd facts about the satellite we found."

Bin licked her lips. "I only learned they know less than we do."

"And want any tech we have." I touched the knife in the pocket of the skirt I took off, shifting it to under my pillow just in case. "Mine asked about what devices we brought with us, and what weapons. I showed her my sword and that satisfied her for the moment."

"I wonder what the others found out." Bin frowned. "And if we will ever see them again."

I couldn't tell her I could find out another way. We were still keeping almost as many secrets from the Isty as from the Dedi. "I doubt they learned any more than we did. If there was anything important, I'm sure they'd find a way to get word to us. Doesn't Lin have a way to contact someone back inside the dome?"

Ana smiled at me, and nodded slightly to indicate she approved my approach to Bin.

"I don't know. He hasn't shared much with us. We have communication means, of course, but whether any of them would work this far is questionable." Bin's gaze sharpened. "Do you have a way to communicate with the friends you left?"

I shook my head. I hadn't tried since the second night when the connection was weak, but I doubted I could talk to my sister from this far away. I fell asleep thinking about my sister, but when I woke it was Ana's face looking down at me.

"Hurry and get dressed. We've been summoned."

"Probably for breakfast, followed by more questioning." I covered my eyes with my pillow, a tiny job that didn't come close to cradling my head. I rubbed the ache out of my neck as I forced myself up. "Alright, I'll get dressed." That's when I noticed someone was missing. "Where's our third?"

"Bin left already. Her interrogator came for her for another session before breakfast. When Worgu arrived she didn't seem surprised she was gone."

"They know she's from the north and we're from the east."

"Well, yeah, but I don't think that's why. I figure she said something yesterday that indicated she might talk sooner than we would."

"I wouldn't be surprised." I took the skirt I'd worn the evening before, the only clean shirt I had.

"I won't mind if you change here." Ana winked at me.

"I wanted to use the restroom anyway. Besides, you've seen me in next to nothing." I took my clothing and left. The room was already in use. I waited, then smiled when Katya came out. "How did it go yesterday?"

"Okay, I think." She looked around, but there was no one there. "Listen, Nissa, I don't think these are the people we've been looking for."

"We don't think so, either. They're called the Dedi. The name Sion frightens them."

"Maybe we'll see you later. Keep your eyes and ears open."

"You, too." Once she walked off, I entered the bathroom and changed. As I walked back to Ana, I wondered why we were summoned this morning.

Ana wasn't alone. Worgu, Henza and Ana's contact, Nata stood waiting for me. Worgu glared at me when I walked in. The face of Jannet, my sewing teacher back at the Manor, flashed through my mind. She used to look at me that way before I learned to use the energy around me to improve my stitching.

"I apologize for taking so long. There was someone else in the toilet." I tried to look contrite, not sure it worked.

"We'll go now. Follow me." Worgu and Nata went first, then Ana and I with Henza last. We walked toward the dining hall. I smiled when we entered and saw the rest of our party. Even though we sat at different tables, at least we could see they were alright. Bin and her contact walked in right after us and joined us at our table. Worgu left us to move to the front of the room. She sat and ate, then waited for everyone else to finish.

"Each of you have now been interviewed by your contacts. We have concluded you may not be of use to our efforts here. Therefore, we will send you back north." She held up two books I knew well. "We will keep these, as you'll have to agree, they belong to us, not you. Do not come back, and do not tell anyone about our enclave." She turned to the two people who were with her when we first arrived. "Make sure they have enough food for two or three days, and then see them to the door." She walked off, clutching the books and didn't look back.

I sat there, stunned. The looks on my companions faces ranged from surprise to despair. As we were herded out to get our packs, everyone was murmuring their disbelief.

"I think they realized they'd never get anything from us," Rees said. "Unless one or another of you said something."

We all denied it.

Back in our room, Ana asked Bin, "What did your interrogator want?"

"Oh, you know. She went over the same things as yesterday. I think she wanted to be sure my answers were the same this morning."

We met the others by the main door to the fortress. Three of the contacts handed us packages of food. I hoped it was better than what we had the evening before, or the stale bread at breakfast that morning.

We walked north for a while, through trees and fields, then stopped.

"They're not the Sion," I repeated.

Madoc shook his head. "No, they're not."

"They don't have much technology, and they were trying to get as much information as they could about ours." Rees confirmed my impression. "I played dumb, but couldn't get much out of my contact."

"Well, we have to continue south." Lin looked in each direction, scratching the back of his head.

"But we don't have Madoc's books any longer."

"I only wish I'd thought to copy everything in them," Lin said.

"Ah, but I did." Madoc took sheets of paper from his pack. "I don't have all of them, or most of the star charts, but I did the best I could to draw many of the devices and write out the directions."

"We'll have to avoid the fortress." Lin pointed back the way we'd just come.

"Of course."

My eyes strayed to Bin. "Are you okay with continuing south?"

"Why not?"

"Because you haven't stopped complaining about the snow and cold and everything else." I frowned at her.

She shrugged. "I guess I've gotten used to being cold all the time. I certainly don't relish going back alone."

I didn't believe she'd resigned herself to anything. What was she up to, and why? I decided to watch her.

We walked east for a while before turning south again, sharing our individual interrogations by the Dedi, and comparing the questions we were asked. As I had expected, the contacts had a set of questions to pose. If they were led off track they had to get back to the core ones, as Henza did with me. We also compared our answers, which were largely consistent. We left the impression our technology wasn't any more advanced than theirs.

"I wonder if they think they can build the devices in my books." Madoc grinned. "I don't think they have the ability."

Lin's eyebrows went up. "But you did, from what I understand, and you couldn't even read the descriptions."

"That's true, but remember, I'm a wizard." Madoc cackled, held his hands up and wiggled his fingers.

We all laughed, although Lin didn't seem satisfied. He'd come back to the subject again some time.

Shortly after we turned south, we stopped for lunch. As we expected, the food the Dedi gave us consisted of their bread and some vegetables. I wondered if they lived on that diet. They certainly didn't look underfed. Maybe it was what they gave visitors so they'd leave quickly.

We had our own food, enough for a meal. But we'd need to supplement our stores before long. It would have been nice if we found a cow or goat to milk so we could have some to drink and even cheese before long. A lake or stream with fish in it would also be helpful. Unfortunately, none of that appeared. We found mushrooms Ana deemed edible and a fruit tree with a few pieces of fruit left.

A flock of birds flew by, but were too quick for us to shoot down. We contented ourselves with what we had, finished our meal and walked on.

It grew colder again. Signs of a recent snow didn't promise easy going ahead, but snow melt provided additional water.

There were no signs of any people living nearby. The

Dedi's reactions to the word Sion, as opposed to the more primitive peoples we met before them, was troubling. "Why would the Borogo practically worship the Sion while the Dedi fear them?" I asked, even though I didn't think I'd get an answer.

"Perhaps because the Borogo are amazed by everything the Sion have and do, while the Dedi fear what the Sion might do to them. That would make sense if the Dedi stole something from the Sion."

Madoc nodded. "Yes, that's what I've been thinking."

"But then how did the Borogo get their crystal if they didn't steal it?"

"I think the Sion gave it to them for being so loyal."

"Do the Borogo even know about the Dedi? Their directions to the Sion led us directly to the fortress." I plucked some berries from a bush we were passing. Some of the others did, too.

A hissing sound distracted us. We stopped to see where it was coming from.

"There!" Rees walked toward the left, looking down. "There's three of them." He point to a tree trunk where a snake was winding it's way up the trunk.

Tak reached out and grabbed it, while Rees trapped one of the two on the ground. A third headed away from us until Terry stepped on its tail end and then picked it up.

I held back until the three were dead. We only had small snakes at the Manor, but these were big, long and thick, with patterned skin. I wasn't afraid of them or even what they could do, but I also wasn't used to handling them. Clearly, Rees, Tak and Terry were.

"We get some near the dome and watch for them when we go out." Terry held out the one she caught so I could touch. The skin was drier than I expected. "Our cooks have developed great recipes for snake meat. It's almost as good as chicken."

I'd heard that before and wondered whether it was true. Now I was going to get to try it.

CHAPTER FIFTY-THREE

We stopped in a fairly large clearing and Tak showed me how to skin the snakes and collect the meat. I treated it like chicken, roasting it over the fire we dared to set, trying not to char it. I also cooked some vegetables on sticks to go with the meat. After our meager meals, it was a feast. As I ate, I wondered if the Isty cooks were sharing their recipes for snake meat with Carys.

With full stomachs, we moved on as far as we could before we stopped for the night. The Sion couldn't be much farther. As we put out our fire and repacked the remaining food, a sound came from the surrounding woods.

"Now what?" Dens groaned.

A face appeared through the trees. It was a man in a shirt and pants, carrying a basket. He didn't seem threatening. Katya called to him in Fartekana, and he came toward us.

"You are not Dedi." He studied us, then addressed Katya since she was the one who spoke to him. "Who are you and where do you come from?"

She gave him the same story we first told the Dedi, then added, "We were 'guests' of the Dedi for a day, but they decided we had nothing to offer them save two books."

"Books?"

"Two books in your language, one with diagrams and instructions for building machines like those that existed before the launch of the second moon and its consequences. Unfortunately, they took those books."

One brow went up. "And the other book?"

"Charts of the stars as they appear in the sky here." Lin pointed up.

"Why did you have them?" He was curious.

"I didn't." Lin put a hand on Madoc's shoulder. "Madoc here got them from a traveler. The Borogo said you gave them their crystal."

"We gave it to them because they admired it so much. It wasn't useful for our work."

"Doesn't it focus energy?" Vee asked.

The man looked at each of us again. "You all seem well-informed about how machines work. I'm surprised the Dedi didn't want to pump you all for information."

"We didn't let them know how much we knew." I grinned at him.

"But you're telling me. Why?" The brow now met his other one. "I'm Klar, by the way."

We gave our names, and Madoc smiled before answering him. "Because we believe you and your people are the ones we've been looking for."

"My people." He sighed. "Yes. All sixteen of us."

"There are only sixteen?" I slapped my hand over my mouth. That was an insensitive thing to say.

"There used to be more. No children born in years. Cycles, that is. As the oldest die off, our numbers dwindle."

I nodded. "We've seen that among other groups here in Fartek."

"Have you?" His eyes shifted to the embers of our fire. "Have you eaten?"

"We killed a couple of snakes earlier today, cooked them for our evening meal."

"Good. We have food, but it isn't much."

"And if you share it with us, you won't have as much for yourselves." I nodded. "We can give you the packets of food the Dedi gave us."

"No thank you. I know what they eat. That awful bread that's made with insects as their only source of protein. I'd rather eat small animals or birds we're able to trap."

"Do you grow any food?" Ana asked.

"Not much because of the weather here."

"Why don't you come north?" Lin offered.

"When our facility was formed, we didn't want anyone to know what we were doing."

"Hiding the remaining devices and building new ones." I knew what that was like.

"Not only devices. We collected books and information in other forms until the time when it would be safe to rebuild civilization."

We exchanged looks. That sounded so familiar. It was what the Stronghold and Isty were doing.

"How do you expect to go on?" Madoc shook his head. "You're a young man, but someday you'll grow old and so will the remaining Sion. What will happen to everything you've preserved and built here?"

"We've debated that for quite some time. The Dedi aren't the answer. They are greedy and would use the technology for ill rather than good. The Borogo wouldn't know how to use it, but still we considered trying to teach them. Considered, never decided."

"Will you share what you know with us?" Lin asked.

"That isn't my decision to make. It will depend on all of the Sion." He sighed. "It's too bad the Dedi have your books."

Madoc grinned. "I still have copies of many of the pages. I drew the diagrams and hand copied the directions, even though I couldn't read the language."

His eyes scanned the twelve of us. "I gather you each have different knowledge and machines."

"People who preserved books and devices in different parts of the world on the western side of the Great Sea came together in Solwintor in an effort similar to yours."

Lin picked up the story. "And many of the scientists and technologists working at a facility in central Fartek created their own sanctuary from that facility. That's where we're from."

"Yet you found each other and traveled here together." The man shook his head "Amazing."

I nodded. "Yes, we've been traveling for a few days, mostly on foot."

"Our compound is not far." Klar turned and started to walk.

"Come, we will at least provide you with a comfortable place for the night."

"Is it always so cold here?" Katya asked.

Klar chuckled. "Sometimes it's even colder. But inside, we keep it very comfortable."

We walked for a short time. I didn't see it at first, built to blend into the forest around it, with growing trees included in the construction.

"I should go in first, let them know you are friends." Klar opened a door and entered the strange building.

"Should we trust him and his people?" Bin said once he was gone.

"Why not? We needn't tell him everything, but we have to be fairly honest with him." Vee leaned against a tree and waited for Klar's return. "I like his reaction to what we've already said."

When he returned, he wasn't alone. A younger man and an older woman were with him. Both had short, dark hair and slightly slanted but large dark eyes. "These are Chan and Madi. They will take you to your rooms so you can freshen up."

Madi led us women to a large dorm-like room. "This is where the women who are not united live. Or did when we were a larger community." The dorm held eight beds and several chairs pulled up to work tables. "The room for washing is here." She opened a door on a large washroom with two stalls for washing and four sinks. The toilets were inside private cubicles. "Please take the time to clean yourselves and change your clothing if you wish."

I didn't have anything to change into that was fresher than what I wore. "We've been traveling for many days. Is there somewhere we can wash our clothing other than the sinks in there?"

"Oh! I will show you our washers and driers. I'm sorry. I should have realized. And I can bring you all some clothing to wear in the meantime." She looked us over. "I don't think we have anything long enough for you," she told me. "Perhaps from one of the men."

The two Sion men I'd seen so far weren't much taller than she was, about my sister's height, but I'd worn clothes that were too short in the past.

Madi returned with a stack of clothes in her arms. She dropped them on one of the beds we hadn't claimed. "I'll leave you to sort out what each of you needs. An hour from now, I'll return to take you to the meeting room."

The clothes were similar to what she and the two men wore: dark pants in a heavy fabric and white or light blue shirts, also heavier than what we wore. "These are warmer than our things."

"They need warm clothes if they're living here." Ana selected almost black trousers. "I think there's wool in these." She said it with awe. "I wonder where they get the wool if they don't have animals."

"They must have spinning machines." Terry sorted through the clothing for a while before she picked what she wanted. "Maybe even sewing machines."

Back at the Stronghold they were working on ones like that, but I'd never seen them. "Do you have any of those inside the dome?"

"Spinning, yes, but they can't seem to get the sewing machines to work better than hand sewing."

I nodded. That was one of the problems they were having at the Stronghold.

"Do you still sew by hand?" Vee asked me.

"You should see the fine seams Nissa sews!" Ana said, and I felt my cheeks warm. But, of course, it was because I used the energy around me to guide my needle.

Once we each selected clothing, we invaded the washroom. The trousers I picked were the longest in the pile, but still only came to my calves. I'd found some foot coverings that went all the way to the knee, so together my legs were covered. The shirt, a light blue one with buttons down the front, was almost long enough, but the sleeves only went partway between my elbows and my hands.

When Madi came for us, we were dressed. She took us first to the laundry. It contained three machines that washed clothing and three that dried it. "Since we can't very well hang it out to dry," she said. "You'll have plenty of time this evening to launder your clothes."

I couldn't wait to see how the machines worked, but first

we joined the men in the meeting room. It was large with row after row of seats facing a platform, not like the one the Dedi had because each row was higher than the one in front of it so the people behind could see.

"We have auditoriums like this," Vee told me. "I guess you didn't have a chance to see them before we left the dome."

Klar sat on the stage and so did Madi. Three others were with them. I think one was the man who took the men to their dorm.

We all took seats near the front. Once we were all settled, Klar stood.

"We welcome you to our compound." His friendly voice sounded like he meant it. "We don't often have visitors."

"How about never?" Madi commented with a grin.

"We never have visitors and we're all happy to see new faces." He grinned too. "I must say we get tired of seeing the same fifteen other people day in and day out."

The entire attitude was light and joking.

"We have serious matters to discuss, but tonight we celebrate your safe arrival and promise that we are willing to talk about anything you want. I'll introduce all of the members of our compound. Listen carefully. You'll be tested later."

Several of us groaned, but he laughed. "No, of course you won't. I hope you're here long enough to get to know us all, but we expect you'll remember only a few of the names."

He introduced Madi again, as well as the three others. Then others came in two and three at a time. Each gave their names. After the last had joined them on the platform, Klar asked us each to stand and give our names.

"We invite you to join us for dinner." Klar left and the rest of the Sion did too.

We'd already eaten but followed them down the hall to a huge dining hall. "Please share our tables with us." He indicated three long tables. A few Sion sat at each. There were many empty ones, a reminder of how many people lived here at one point.

CHAPTER FIFTY-FOUR

A few of us sat with Klar and three other Sion as they ate.

I expected the same kind of interrogation as in the Dedi fortress, even if it wasn't going to be one-on-one. Instead, the Sion talked about the difficulties they had feeding even their meager numbers.

"We tried to grow vegetables, but the growing season here is much too short. We have a few animals," Klar admitted. "Chickens provide us with eggs, and cows and goats with milk and milk products, but we try not to slaughter them because then we wouldn't have any of those things. There used to be more wildlife here, but even that's dwindled through the years."

"We noticed. There were snakes, though." I wrinkled my nose.

"Yes, for some reason their populations have increased while those of other animals decreased," Madi said. "We've managed to grow grains and vegetables indoors."

Katya nodded. "Yes, we do the same in Solwintor."

"You do?" Bin sounded suddenly curious.

"Don't you?" Katya countered rather than explain.

"In greenhouses, yes, but we've never even tried to grow anything inside." Bin looked at Lin for confirmation.

He nodded. "We have lots of fertile land and seeds that were kept for generations."

All of the talk made me realize how much we had at the

Manor. "Back in Leara, we had many gardens. Fruit trees, flowers, and vegetables." I hadn't seen much in the way of cultivated flowers since we left there, although there were some in Fairhaven.

Bin's eyes widened. "Flowers? You really have flowers?"

I nodded. "Roses and bulbs like daffodils, annuals and perennials." I'd heard Glynis' mother talk about them so often I could name them all, but it seemed none of these people had ever seen a flower. "My best friend's mother oversees the flower gardens. You should have seen what she did for Glynis' wedding."

"What's a wedding?" The young man whose name was Cru, I think, looked totally lost.

"When a man and woman marry," I explained.

"It's like the ceremony when two people pledge their futures together," Madi told him.

"We grow flowers, but many were lost," Vee said. "It seems there are many things in addition to technology our peoples can share."

"People enjoyed a quality of life Before that they don't have anywhere now." Madoc sighed. "There are pockets of technology at various levels, like ours, and some advancements in other sciences like horticulture, agriculture, even animal husbandry, but nowhere comes close to what was achieved then."

"Perhaps if we work together we can make faster progress but that would mean being able to communicate." Lin took out a device I hadn't seen before, probably the one he used to talk to his people back inside the dome.

I stared at it as he tossed it on the table. "I was supposed to be able to contact my colleagues with that, but it only worked within a short distance of the dome. I don't know what kind of communication systems you have." He looked directly at Klar. "But perhaps there is a way to amplify the signal this sends so we can get word back to them."

"Let me see that." Madoc reached for it. He'd built devices for Gareth at the Citadel in Fairhaven, and worked with the one developed at the Stronghold. So had my brother. "Donal, what do you make of this?" Madoc tossed it over.

Donal looked at it carefully. "Well, first of all, if you put the crystals here instead of here, it would focus the energy to the receiver." He handed it back to Lin.

"Thank you." He smiled. "I'm surprised you aren't scolding me for keeping this from you, but since it didn't work anyway, it wasn't worth revealing."

Madoc shrugged. "None of us are surprised you've kept things from us. However, you've learned you can trust us, and also that we can help you as Donal has."

Klar had been watching and listening. "We can provide whatever tools you need to make the change to your device."

"Thank you," Lin said. "This shows how we can cooperate. I do want to contact our people." He turned to Donal. "But do you have a device to communicate with yours?"

Donal shook his head. "Unfortunately, whatever we had was left on the beach where we landed with the rest of our party. The group that reached your city was less than half of it."

"What about the others who were with you?" Lin asked.

"The Panshee? They're one of two groups of people that live between the western seashore and your city. The other group lives in a valley at the base of a mountain. Neither group has any technology."

"Like the Dedi." Klar bit his lip.

"Yes, very much like them. They each have their own superstitions and their knowledge of other people living not far away is nonexistent." Ana smirked. "Bringing all of them up to speed will take some doing."

"But that doesn't mean we can't try." Madoc sat up straighter. "We can start with the Dedi, and then seek out other settlements and villages. How many communities can there be?"

Klar sighed. "Too many, but we have to try."

"So, it's agreed we'll share what we know and then introduce some of it to every community in Fartek?"

"Agreed."

"Agreed." Klar stood and rapped on the table before speaking in a loud voice. "We have decided our group and our friends from the north and the west will share what we know about technology. Once we've established a common ground, we will tell the Dedi and the other less advanced communities in Fartek what we know. I hope there are no objections."

There were murmurs among the Sion. A man stood, taller and fatter than the other Sion. "How can we trust these people?"

Madi stood and rapped the table in front of her. "I think we can trust these people. They have been perfectly open with us. There is much we know they don't, but also they've accomplished much we haven't been able to."

The discussion among the Sion went on for some time. It was fascinating to watch. No one said anything derogatory about the person who spoke before them. They kept their arguments to whether or not it would benefit them to work with us. Finally, they agreed with Madi and Klar.

Klar took the floor once more. "Tomorrow, I will meet with our head scientists and representatives of our visitors and begin the process. All agreed?"

Shouts of 'aye' filled the room, so it sounded like there were more than sixteen Sion.

There was no question as to who our representatives would be: Madoc and Lin.

"I'd like Dens to accompany us," Lin said.

Madoc nodded his agreement. "And I want Nissa."

"Me?" I couldn't hide my surprise.

"Nissa, you bring an insight we'll all need as we decide what the communities would understand and be comfortable with, how to start."

"I agree." Lin smiled at me. "Nissa, you are the perfect person to represent our people and yours. It seems much besides technology was lost and must be found again and shared. You are very aware of what those are."

I felt warm all over from their praise. "Of course I'll do what I can."

Dinner and the discussion were over. I asked Madoc and my brother if I could wash their dirty clothing then returned to the laundry. They each brought me several items to add to my own. It would be good to have clean clothes. Much as I appreciated what the Sion brought us, I was more comfortable in my clothing.

The washers worked in a fascinating, magical way. The clothes spun as water entered and mixed with them and a special soap the Sion supplied. After some time, the water, dirty by then, drained out and fresh water flowed in. Finally the clothing spun without water being added, I suppose to remove some of the water still soaking the fabric. And then the machine stopped.

We transferred the clothing to a drying machine, which was no less miraculous. "Warm air is blown in to absorb more moisture from the clothing as it is heated. Doing that for enough time completely dries the clothing," Madi said.

When I pulled my skirts and shirts, and my brother's and Madoc's trousers from it, they were still warm, but perfectly dry. "This would make wash day so much easier!"

"In the past, it did just that for billions of people."

I brought the men their clothing. "Next time, you can do the laundering." I couldn't wait to see the looks on their faces when they saw the machines in action.

Taking my own pile of dry clothing back to my bed, I relished the clean, fresh smell. Stains I'd have a hard time getting out by hand scrubbing were gone. I filled my pack with the garments except for my nightdress and underthings. It wasn't time yet to go to bed, but I wanted to wash my hair. It had been many days since it been able to do that.

Standing under the almost too hot water, I felt my muscles relaxing and some of the aches I hadn't noticed go away. And my scalp! It felt as if my hair hadn't been completely clean in much longer than days.

I dried my body with a large towel and slipped on my night clothes. The Sion gave us all soft shoes to wear from the bathing room to the bedroom. They kept my feet warm and dry.

I stretched out, pulling the sheet and blanket over me. The bed was more comfortable than it looked. I fell asleep immediately.

When I woke, I felt better than I had since we left the dome.

"Madi says breakfast is a big deal here." Ana was already dressed and ready to go.

I took clean clothing and returned to the washroom. Bin was the only one there. I realized she hadn't said anything since we'd arrived at the Sion house. "This is so much better than with the Dedi, isn't it?"

She looked at me with a scowl. "I wouldn't say that."

"Oh, come on. Did you like being locked up in our room, unable to go anywhere unless they said so? The incessant questions and hostility?"

"The Dedi cared much more about us, about our comfort and whether we were doing the right thing." Her scowl changed to a determined straight line.

"The right thing? Did they even know what that was?" I blinked a few times. What a strange attitude she had. I shrugged, dressed, and forgot about Bin and what she said.

When I exited the bathroom, everyone was headed for breakfast. The familiar smell of oatmeal greeted us. I smiled. It had been a long time since I'd had any. I took a bowl and some tea, some bread and cheese and sat at a table where Madoc and Lin were already talking to Klar.

"Did I miss anything?" I took a spoonful of oatmeal as I waited for someone to answer.

Madoc aimed his chin at their host. "Klar was just telling us their ancestors were able to collect equipment used to monitor the satellites when they still circled Larena before the stations were destroyed by floods."

Klar nodded. "They watched as the lands to the north were covered with water as the sea moved across the continent cutting them off from the rest of the land mass."

"What about the satellites? Did any fall near here?" I asked.

"Unfortunately, no. They would have told us so much about how the crystals could be used to power such complex systems, even so far from the surface of Larena."

I looked at Madoc.

He smiled at me. "We retrieved one from a lake. Many parts were made here, based on the writing in the instruction books with them."

"A satellite? You have one?" Klar's eyes were like those of someone who'd just received a tremendous present.

He nodded. "It's still being examined, deconstructed and the components tested. It took quite an effort to bring it up from the bottom of the lake that formed after it fell."

"Where is this satellite now?"

"In our facility in Solwintor."

"And you say people are disassembling it?"

Madoc nodded. "Our best engineers and scientists, people who've been able to create machines from nothing more than partial plans and diagrams, and parts fabricated from whatever materials we had, which weren't many. Donal is one of the people who tested the new machines, but the ones who built them have been working for cycles, that is, years to build very different machines. We used a few in the mission to retrieve the satellite: monitors, cameras, oxygen generators, and others."

"Did he tell you about this?" Klar asked Lin.

"Yes. Remarkable achievements."

"And you believe him?"

"He has proof." Lin smiled. "Show him."

"One moment." Madoc stood and strode from the Cafeteria. We were silent until he returned. He held out the photographs from the expedition and others of the pieces of the satellite.

Klar studied them, his smile growing into a grin. "Oh, well done! Well done, indeed."

Madoc took them back. "It seems you've also been able to perfect mechanical devices, including very advanced ones. Nissa told us about the wash and dry machines. I gather Lin and his people also have such machines."

"Yes, we do," Lin said. "And many more things you didn't see before we left on this journey."

"I'm sure the rest of our party are learning about them." Madoc turned to Klar. "They have mechanized vehicles, for small groups of people and for larger groups."

"But we still haven't perfected any flying machines." Lin frowned. "I understand those took long times to develop originally."

"Yes that's what I've heard," Klar said.

"We knew nothing about them, except for the satellites, but it would make sense."

"The civilization that existed back then took hundreds of cycles to develop everything. It has been only one thousand years since the moon was launched, bringing about all of this." Klar waved an arm around. "All we have left, the remnants of that civilization, is in tatters and scattered across the remaining continents."

"We will do our best here in Fartek, both parts of it, even farther north than our city," Lin said.

"We can only try in Leara and Solwintor, but we've already seen some resistance and downright opposition," Madoc added.

"And we can't forget the Legion." I frowned, thinking about them although we never saw them, only the results.

"Who are the Legion?" Lin asked.

"A group in the far east of Solwintor. We've heard they are an organized military group menacing the cities and towns, driving people from them into the countryside. At some point we'll have to face them and force them to relinquish their hold."

"This Legion, what kind of weapons do they have?" Lin asked.

Madoc frowned. "From the reports we've heard, they have automated weapons, much like the guns your people have." Madoc waved at Lin, whose hand went immediately to the place he usually carried his. He hadn't told Klar about it, and Madoc had been careful to avoid mentioning he had them.

But Klar wasn't stupid. "Do you have any with you?"

Lin could have been annoyed with Madoc. Instead, he pulled out his gun. "We don't have many. The truth is, we hadn't hidden more than fifteen or twenty, and not all of them worked, but it wasn't a priority for us to manufacture any more."

"Anything else you want to tell me?" Klar sighed.

"There are the scavengers, but they're little kids who take food from travelers at night. The marauders are more of a problem. They don't have guns, only swords, bows, and knives." I ran out of air and stopped talking.

"What do the marauders do?"

"Since the people in the villages have little to defend themselves, they prey on them. They've taken over a few towns in the middle of Solwintor. We fought a band with our own swords and knives, but they're still a threat."

"We didn't see any signs of similar groups in our travels through Fartek," Madoc added.

"And that in itself is strange. I suppose everyone here is part of a community, no renegades or outlaws or whatever you want to call them."

"The Legion are too organized to be called that." Donal frowned. "We don't know who commands their activities, whether it's someone in the east in Solwintor or elsewhere, but they're much more formidable than the marauders."

Klar threw up his hands. "So many groups!"

"We'll have to find them all."

"Some have skills to offer," I said. "The Panshee, for example, make colorful cloth and clothing. The women weave the dyed fibers."

"And don't forget about the bridge across the chasm," my brother said.

"Oh! I had actually. They have a mechanism that propels a bridge across the chasm, but if you don't know it's there, well, you'd think there was no way across. It extends for dulnos." I spread my arms as wide as they'd go. "And it's very deep. But that seemed to be the only mechanization known to them."

Klar took a deep breath and let it out. "Then, we have our work cut out for us."

CHAPTER FIFTY-FIVE

Klar grinned at us. "Together, we can do it. There may be groups that will be reluctant to abandon their old ways."

"We shouldn't force them," Madoc advised.

"No, of course not."

Madi came over and whispered something in Klar's ear. He looked down and frowned. Then he lifted his head. "A group of Dedi approaches."

Madoc nodded. "We could start with them. They're eager to have the technology you possess."

Klar shook his head. "I'm afraid if we give them any, they will use it unwisely."

"Can we dictate how anyone uses what we offer them?" I asked.

Donal rubbed the back of his head. "Do we have to give them anything we believe can be used to harm anyone else?"

"We should decide before they arrive." Klar started for the door. "They've left us alone for some time. There must be a reason they come to us now."

Madoc frowned. "I'm afraid we may have caused this."

"Not all of us." I finally put it together. "Bin, one of our group. She's been acting strangely, and this morning she defended the Dedi's actions. I think she is providing them with information about our activities. How, I don't know. I didn't see any communications devices."

"Nissa, are you sure about this?" Madoc asked.

"Almost certain." My eyes sought her out. She sat with Vee and Ana not far from us. "I think one of you should ask her."

"Why would she help them?"

"The morning before we left their fortress, she met with her contact before breakfast. None of the rest of us were asked to do so. She's been very quiet ever since."

Donal laughed. "I did notice she stopped complaining."

"Exactly."

"That's her, isn't it?" Klar pointed to her table.

"Yes."

"I assume you have reasons for not approaching her."

"Well...when I talked to her this morning, she was evasive."

"She might not talk to me, either." Madoc had already risen.

"I think you impress her for some reason." I couldn't hide my smile.

He walked to the table just as Katya joined the three women. Madoc said something softly, and Bin looked around as if she sought help, but she came with him without an argument.

Lin looked into her eyes. "Bin, have you been hiding something from us?"

"No! What would I hide?" She crossed her arms in front of her.

"Did you know the Dedi were coming this way?" Klar stared at her.

She looked around at all the eyes watching her. "I...I didn't do anything. They deserve to know what the Sion are doing, don't they?"

"Yes, and we planned to tell them, along with everything your people have and the group from Solwintor."

"You...you did?"

Madoc stood next to my chair. "We've been talking about sharing everything with everyone in Fartek and everywhere else, at least those who are interested in bettering their living conditions."

"What about...what about weapons?" She practically whispered it.

"Those would come last, of course, after we see how each community uses everything else we give them."

She bit her upper lip, and her brow furrowed. "None of us knew."

"Because we've been meeting this morning to discuss it and have just decided it's the right thing to do. Now, tell us how you're getting information to the Dedi."

She seemed to deflate like one of those rubber toys they have at the Stronghold for children, that blow up until they're very large, and when you let the air out, they return to their normal size.

"Bin, I'll repeat the question, how are you getting information to the Dedi?" Madoc crossed his arms.

She reached inside her shirt and held up a small device on a chain that hung around hr neck. "This."

Lin didn't take it off her, but examined it closely. Then Madoc took a turn and said, "This looks like the communication devices our divers had when they examined the bottom of Lake Dulno."

Even from my seat I could see he was right. "It's even smaller. I had to make large pouches in the diving suits to hold them."

"Could you really hear the divers from a distance away?" Lin asked.

"They dived to almost a thousand dulnos. I don't know what that is in your distance measurements but it's quite far."

"Where did the Dedi get such a device?"

"Not from us," Madoc said. "I hope this will switch it off." He pushed on an indentation.

"They didn't steal it from us, either." Klar looked at the small box. "Could they have had it since Before?"

I laughed. "Now you're calling it that, too. Before."

He shrugged. "Whatever we call that time. The Dedi must have hidden some items. The three of us are the only pockets of technology left."

"Probably not." Madoc examined the box again.

"So how do we deal with them?" Donal asked.

"We don't." Klar set his mouth in a line.

"But they're on their way. Your house is out in the open for them to see."

A smile spread across his face. "Is it?"

Madoc, Lin and I exchanged looks. "Do you have a way of

making it disappear?" Lin voiced what we all wondered.

"Another piece of our technology. It would seem none of you do, right?"

I shook my head. "Klar, that might be very useful."

"Oh, it is." His smile lit up his eyes. "It is based on a masking system, but goes beyond what it was originally." He seemed very proud of that.

"So, what do they see?" Madoc scratched the back of his head.

"Nothing. They can look straight at us and there's nothing here."

"But it's solid, large. If they walk into it, won't they be aware it's here?"

"Partly, it convinces them they shouldn't come close to this area." His smile widened.

"How does it work?" Lin's narrow eyes became slits.

Klar hesitated. "You know about the energy between all things, living and not?"

Madoc and I nodded, and Lin's focus shifted to us. "The what?"

Klar explained it to him, so we didn't have to. It also told us how much Klar understood. "There's energy out there, ready to tap. The crystals focus it to power machines and smaller devices, but it can also be focused by our minds." He tapped his forehead.

Madoc reached for my hand.

"Focus it how exactly? And what can it do?" Lin was completely lost.

"If you concentrate, you can sense the energy. It's actually not very strong here, but there's enough to do simple things." Madoc explained as he had the first time he taught me about it. "You can focus the energy you sense to increase the precision of everything you do."

"For instance, sewing." I smiled and made a sewing motion with my fingers. "Or drawing, or even using a knife, sword or bow."

"You may be surrounded by so many devices and machines you haven't had to develop this skill as we have in Leara." Madoc winked at me.

We'd all forgotten Bin was still with us. She sat there, her mouth and eyes wide open. I turned to her. "Now whose side do you want to be on?"

"There are no sides, of course. However, Bin, I hope you've learned something from this." Lin removed the chain from around her neck. "Whatever the Dedi told you about the Sion, or whatever motivated you to turn against us, I think I'll be taking this now."

Her eyes filled with tears.

"For some reason she was annoyed with us, or possibly with me." I stood and took her hands. "Is that right, Bin?"

"We should have been superior to you," she spit out. "Yet you were the one who received praise for your cooking and for your ideas."

I couldn't refute what she said, but her resentment was strong, stronger than it should have been. There was nothing I could say, no way to make up for what had happened, no way to soothe her hurt feelings. There was only one thing I could say. "I'm sorry, Bin."

"None of that was Nissa's fault. Maybe you should be angry with the rest of us, but she only did what was asked of her. And now you have some idea why she was so good at what she did."

"It doesn't explain why she had solutions for so many of our problems."

I squeezed her hands. "Bin, I've been traveling for quite some time. When you do, you learn to improvise. That's all I do, look at a situation and find a way to make things better, or at least more comfortable. Instead of complaining, if you spent time thinking about what else we can do to improve conditions, you'd be able to come up with suggestions everyone would praise."

"How do you know?" Her lower lip pushed out.

"That's also something I've learned from experience."

She folded her arms tighter. "So, smarty, what do you think we should do about the Dedi? Even if they can't see this house, they know it's here from my transmissions."

"Why don't you start using your own brain finding a solution to this." I took my hands out of hers and folded my arms, staring at her.

Her eyes narrowed, then she looked at each of the men. Their expressions ranged from challenging to encouraging. She licked her lips and swallowed hard. Her eyes blinked a few times. I wondered if she was trying to sense the energy here.

Slowly a smile spread. "We could use the transmitter to send them false information."

"That might send them away, but we've decided to see what would happen if we shared a few things with them."

She lifted her hands and rubbed her head. "Then the false information should take them somewhere you can do that, not here, but someplace where you can control the situation."

We all slowly nodded at her. Now that was a suggestion we could embrace.

Her smile broadened when she saw our reactions.

Klar's eyes lit up. "I know just the place."

"Take me there." Bin fingered the chain. "I'll turn this back on and act surprised the device was off, as if I didn't know how it happened."

"I'm liking it better and better," Lin said.

"You'll all come with me? Including Nissa?"

"Sure. We'll want to negotiate with the Dedi when they arrive."

"The place I'm thinking of is deep in the woods, abandoned for quite some time, but it still looks inhabited." Klar announced to everyone what we were planning. There were few objections. "Het, actuate the cloaking device."

"How will we find our way back afterward?" I asked.

"That's the easy part. As long as I'm with you."

It wasn't far to the place Klar described. The house was much smaller than the Sion place. Bin took up a position near the door and turned on her device, then went through the pretense she'd described.

The rest of us went to other rooms where we could watch for the Dedi approach through windows.

In less than an hour, four Dedi approached the door. Bin opened it for them.

"I've convinced the Sion to share more technology with you," she said. Could we trust her? We'd have to.

CHAPTER FIFTY-SIX

Klar and Bin entered the front room, as we watched through a one-way glass.

"Where are the rest of your people?" Riman Saw who I remembered from our short time with the Dedi led their party.

"They're all someplace safe." Klar faced him with arms folded.

At a nod from him, we joined them. Were the Dedi really surprised to see us? They'd expected Bin to be there so why not the rest of us?

"Why have you agreed to meet with us?" Saw asked.

"After much discussion with our friends from the north," Klar waved a hand to include all of us, "we've all decided it's time to share what we know with all groups living in Fartek."

"And why have you kept this knowledge to yourselves for so long?" Saw demanded.

"For the same reason you never told us about the device you gave Bin." Klar held it up. "Trust. Or a lack of trust."

"And now?"

"There is much we can gain from cooperation among the many peoples of this continent and all of the world." Klar pointed to Madoc and me. "The people from Solwintor have pieces of knowledge, as do those from northern Fartek." He used his other hand to point to Lin and Bin. "We each have something to contribute, why, even the Borogo do. If we all work together it will benefit everyone."

Saw clapped his small hands. "A fine speech. But we all know what happened in the past when groups and nations worked together. There were advances, yes, but there was also disaster. What else brought about the destruction of our world? Is that what we look forward to repeating?"

"I hope we've learned from the mistakes of the past." Madoc's voice was clear and strong. "But the only way we can, is for everyone to know what was tried and done Before, and what actions to avoid."

"You're the one called Madoc, correct?" Saw studied him.

"Yes."

"Bin told one of our people you're regarded as a wizard back in your land."

"Some would call it that. I know more about the science of this world than most. They think it's magic, but it's only what can be done with knowledge of the world around us. That's the point. If everyone understood, scientists and engineers, leaders and policy makers, we would be much better off."

Saw shook his head. "Most wouldn't understand."

"How do you know if you don't try? Sure, many who don't know better think it's magic or witchcraft. Some are superstitious or not open to learning new things. But that doesn't mean we shouldn't try to teach them."

"We found starting that education with simple devices can gain acceptance and an open view." I pointed to Bin's communicator. "Items like communication devices or ones that can capture someone's image worked."

"What used to be called ice breakers." Ana grinned. "Because they broke through the barrier some people put up like a wall of ice."

I was glad for once she'd explained the strange phrases she used. She got them out of books she found from Before. I was eager to learn some myself.

"What else have you kept from us?" Klar asked Saw.

He shook his head. "You've seen that. It's now your turn to show us one of your treasures."

Klar took a deep breath. He couldn't very well show Saw or his people the washing machine back at their building without giving away its location. Or perhaps he wasn't as anxious any longer to keep that a secret. Instead, he reached into a pocket of his pants and drew out six small beads, each in a different color. "This is a kind of medicine we've perfected. No, medicine isn't the right word. When you put it in the ground next to a young plant, it provides the nutrients to help it grow."

"It's a granular fertilizer! Ooooh!" Ana squeaked. "I know several people who'd love that."

Klar handed her one and she examined it with wide eyes.

Saw held out his hand. "I will show that to my people and tell them what you propose." He turned, and so did those with him. They left without another word.

"Well." Klar's mouth twisted. "Was he impressed, or even intrigued?"

"What if he and his people decide they don't want to cooperate with us?" Ana frowned. "What do we do then?"

"At least we agree with your group." Klar sighed. "We can do much without the Dedi."

"They won't come after you now, will they? Get what they want from you by force?" Lin asked.

"I doubt they could and hope to win. Although they probably number more than we do, with the addition of you twelve we're almost evenly matched. And the Borogo will side with us, if necessary. We've always treated them better than the Dedi do." He shook his head. "No, I think they'll agree. Even if they ask for conditions, I believe we'll reach a concord."

"And then what?" What would happen next?

"We'll work together to spread the word to everyone in Fartek." He must have seen my anxiety. "Don't worry. You'll be reunited with your people before long."

"Our journey was long, and somewhat perilous," Madoc pointed out.

Klar smiled at him then turned his gaze to me. "One of the machines we've perfected was used in the past to travel great distances."

I imagined it was something like the vehicles the Isty had in their domed city.

Lin must have had the same idea. "A kind of automobile?"

Klar narrowed his eyes at Lin. "Automobile? I've read

about those. Do you have one?"

Lin nodded. "So it isn't one."

"No. This is a flying machine." He pointed upward. "It's almost finished. It should be ready in a couple of days."

"Are they having a problem with it?" Donal was always ready to tinker with a new device.

Klar sighed. "Yes. I'm afraid so. Something about lift?"

"We've never attempted anything like that in Solwintor, but I've read about such machines. Do you think I could see what they're doing?" Donal's eyes gleamed.

Klar studied him. "When we get back, I will take you to the area where they're working on it."

"Great."

The Dedi returned. Saw continued to speak for them. "We have decided to work with you with certain considerations."

"What are they?" Klar leaned against a wall with his arms crossed.

"We will decide which peoples we give any of our knowledge, since we believe some are not prepared to use it."

"You do not know any besides the Borogo. How can you know what they're capable of understanding or using?" Madoc asked.

"We know many are savages who can barely survive." Saw's gaze swept over all of us. "They do not have the capacity to appreciate technology."

"So, we'll teach them." I folded my arms like Klar. "We can only show them what we have. True, some may consider the devices to be magic, but they can make their lives better and they will appreciate that."

Saw frowned at me. "Young woman, Henza said you were very outspoken. She was correct about that."

"Did she also say I knew what I was talking about?"

"You should listen to Nissa," Lin said. "The groups we've had contact with also have skills to share, even though they might not have any technology. The cataclysmic events a thousand years ago destroyed many aspects of civilization, not only technological advances."

"We still stand by our considerations." Saw waved a hand. "You can do whatever you like with the savages that inhabit this land."

Klar frowned and sighed deeply. "What if we don't agree to your conditions?"

A sly smile spread across Saw's face. "Why, we will have to fight you, of course. There can't be two groups ruling this land."

"We're not trying to rule anything. Our knowledge was shared freely in the past, and should be again."

"That was a long time ago." Saw rubbed his chin. "Perhaps when we've defeated you and your friends you will abide by OUR rules." He turned to leave.

Klar called him back. "I'm sure we can come to a compromise. We're all reasonable people here."

I hoped he was right, but Saw didn't sound very reasonable to me.

"I'm listening." But Saw remained in the doorway.

"We can start with the nearest peoples, the Borogo. If we each share some of our technology with them, we can study what they do with it. Then we can decide together how to proceed."

Lin nodded. "We're willing to go along with Klar's plan."

"As are we." Madoc spoke for our party.

Saw took a long time to decide. "Very well. If the Borogo agree to meet with all of us."

"Why shouldn't they?" Donal blurted.

"They may think we've combined forces to defeat them."

I shook my head. "From what I saw, they revere the Sion. If Klar or someone else from their group approaches the Borogo, they will be willing."

Klar smiled at me. "We can send a small party to converse with them." He looked at each person in the room. "Agreed?"

Saw sneered. "I wish you good luck in convincing them." He left the room and his people followed.

CHAPTER FIFTY-SEVEN

We waited until we knew Saw and the other Dedi had returned to their complex before we left the building. Klar kept the communication device to ensure Bin didn't contact them again until after negotiations with the Borogo.

"I won't tell them what you're doing," Bin protested, but to no avail.

Was it my imagination or was it colder outside than when we entered? I pulled my cloak around me as we walked the short distance to the Sion building.

Chan and Madi greeted us with expectant expressions.

"We have a tentative agreement with the Dedi." Klar detailed the conditions Saw had demanded. "We will send a party to talk to the Borogo, show them the simpler inventions we've perfected and gauge their reactions."

"They will be amazed as they always are with anything we do for them." Madi motioned for us to follow her. "We have prepared a meal for you, knowing you would be hungry after your trek to the small house."

Over a stew rich with vegetables and small amounts of meat, we refined our plans.

"We should show the Borogo devices from each group," Lin suggested. "And encourage them to share what they can."

Almost everyone nodded. The three who didn't looked thoughtful. One was Chan. "What could they have to offer?

Judging by their reaction to the crystal we gave them, they have no idea what those do."

"But they must have preserved something of their ancestors' way of life." Ana addressed the four tables of people with a question. "Were they farmers, skilled in growing plants? Were they skilled like Nissa in constructing clothing? Did they know secrets of herbal remedies we may have forgotten? Perhaps they kept histories from long before the second moon was launched."

I smiled at her and the excellent argument she made. Slowly, Chan nodded. "Those are good points, Miss."

"The name is Ana." She held out a hand to him.

His oddly shaped eyes widened as he took it. "Are you from the north or the other side of the world?"

"Well, not exactly the other side, but several days' voyage over the sea to the west. I'm from Solwintor."

Madoc continued for her. "A large group of people there, many more than you have here, have been working for years to reconstruct useful devices from Before. A few of us from Leara joined them not too long ago, and added our expertise to the mix."

"And that proves Ana's point." I chuckled. "My contribution is my sewing and altering skills. I'm sure there are skills like that among many people in Fartek."

"Don't let Nissa fool you." Ana put a hand on mine. "She didn't just mend clothing, she helped design waterproof diving suits with means to hold all of the devices the divers needed."

I'd only done what I was asked to do, but Chan and the rest of the Sion didn't have to know that.

"How did you know how to build machines?" Madi had been standing beside Chan and listening to the conversation.

"We had books from Before, like the two Madoc brought to Fartek and the Dedi took from him." Ana took a breath. "They gave instructions and pictures, although some were in languages few of us knew. Working together, we could recreate devices and machines of many kinds."

"During our travels we've demonstrated a few to people all over Solwintor and Leara, and then Fartek, although we weren't prepared for the divisions we've found here." I pressed my lips together.

"And you and your devices were welcome in your own lands?" Chan asked.

Donal tilted his head. "Several people thought our devices were magic, or the work of a devil, but yes, most of those we talked to were at the very least curious and often awed."

"If you pick items people can comprehend or find useful, they're more apt to accept them." Madoc pointed to the communication device Klar still held. "That may look simple, but it would be difficult to explain to anyone who has never seen one."

"So, we'll have to be careful what we show the Borogo." Klar put the device on the table. "And we have to decide who will go."

"Who has had contact with them?" I asked. "The party should include those they know. Strangers might make them wary, although they accepted us readily enough."

After a half hour of discussion, we agreed the party would consist of two Sion, Klar and Chan, two Isty, Lin and Vee, and Madoc and me to represent our group. We would show the Borogo the Sion's fertilizer and our image capturing device my brother called a camera, hoping those would be the easiest for them to understand. Lin didn't have anything with him we thought was appropriate.

"We can leave in the morning." Klar looked at my brother. "While we're gone, Donal can see what our people have accomplished with the flying machine."

Donal grinned.

That evening over a vegetable stew, we talked for a long time. The Sion and Isty had much to share about their history since the peoples of Fartek had been divided by the Fall.

"The Institute made every effort to collect all the documentation on the research they were doing, but some was destroyed by outsiders before we could build our protective dome." Lin put a forkful of carrot and potato into his mouth.

"But why did they want the plans, when there was no way to carry them out?" Chan asked.

"No one could understand their aim. Some were intent on destroying all technology."

Madoc nodded. "The same happened in Solwintor and other countries. Many people blamed the scientists and engineers for causing the disaster."

"Of course, they were right in a way." Lin waved his fork in the air. "It was scientists as well as governments who decided to launch the second moon, and engineers who made it happen."

"But there was also non-destructive technology," Klar said.

"Yes, that's what we hoped to preserve. Over the years since then, we've kept everyone out who might prevent us from carrying out the Institute's mission to improve the lives of people, although we knew we were keeping out the very people who would benefit from our research." He sounded regretful.

We told Klar, Lin and their people about books that formed the basis for the experiments at the Stronghold. "Luckily we had people who could read many of them, until Madoc arrived with his. The closest anyone came to understanding them were Katya and a few whose native language was also Ministic."

Once we finished eating, Madoc spread out the pages he'd copied before the Dedi took his books.

Klar was most interested. "These will be very helpful in reconstructing several devices. I'm curious about this one." He pointed to a picture of something with rows of letters encased in a black frame with what looked like a page of paper at the top. "I believe this was used to produce pages like the ones in this book, at least those with words. I don't know how they made the pages with pictures."

I looked at the diagram. "Someone at the Stronghold talked about printing plates, right Donal?"

He nodded. "They could make many copies of books that way."

"Let me see." Lin moved the paper closer. "That looks like a typewriter. We have a few, but the ink tape for it ran out years ago."

"If we're going to meet with the Borogo, we should start out before a storm develops."

"Snow?" I asked.

"Most likely," Chan said. "This time of year."

"If the flying machine was perfected you could use it," Donal suggested.

Klar shook his head. "We wouldn't want the Borogo to see it."

Sounded like some of the people at the Stronghold who wanted to limit what we shared with other people. He'd given some valid reasons for it, but I still thought it might cause problems in the future when the Borogo and others realized the Sion and the Isty were keeping devices from them that would be useful. Klar went off to arrange the supplies we'd need for our journey back to the Borogo.

Bin moved closer to me. "Nissa, I'm sorry for all the trouble I've caused. Can you make sure everyone knows that?"

"Why don't you tell them yourself?"

Her gaze swept the room and the people in it. "I doubt they'd believe me, but you do, don't you? And they'll listen to you."

"The best thing you can do is show by your actions that you want to help the Isty and the Sion, that you no longer believe what the Dedi told you."

"Oh, I will!"

Klar returned. "We will be ready to leave in the morning."

"Unless snow disrupts our journey," Lin said. "How deep does it get?"

"That varies greatly, but the deepest I've ever seen it was up to here." He held a hand at shoulder height. "That's rare, though. Most often it doesn't even reach our ankles."

I would need my warmest clothing. "I suppose I should wear my long divided skirt, longest foot coverings, and layers of tops and cloak."

"Do you see snow often where you come from?" Madi asked.

"No, but I learned how cold it can be when we crossed the Frozen Tundra of Sorn in a storm." I'd want a scarf to cover the lower part of my face.

"Where is that?" Lin asked. "I've never hear of it."

"It's in the southern part of Leara, always much colder than the surrounding territory." Visions of the ice bear we encountered flashed through my mind.

"But what were you doing there?" Bin's face blanched.

"Madoc had been abducted. I was on the way to find him with my brother, Blane, Madoc's brother and sister, and Rees." I indicated the big man.

He grinned. "Poor Nissa had nothing to protect her hands. We built a windbreak from ice. It was quite an adventure."

Neither of us mentioned Colm, who'd died later in the swamp.

Klar studied us. "So it was windy as well as snowy?"

"Yes. We were on horseback, and had to find a way to protect the horses as well as ourselves."

"At least here the wind is calm when it snows." Klar cupped his chin. "The flakes fall softly to the ground."

A wistful look filled Madi's eyes. "And it blankets the entire forest floor. Quite beautiful."

"Donal, perhaps you can take a picture of it, if it snows."

"Except you're taking the camera with you."

Madoc nodded. "True. We'll do it along the way."

"You'll have to take food for your journey. I'll go arrange it." Madi turned and left us.

The journey couldn't possibly be as treacherous as the one through the tundra, but it would be longer, especially on foot.

CHAPTER FIFTY-EIGHT

The Sion, Isty and the rest of our party saw us off the next morning after a hot breakfast of mashed vegetables. We carried inventions and food for several days. The air chilled me but it wasn't snowing. Klar led us, claiming he knew a shorter way than we'd taken from the Borogo to the Sion building. We'd avoid the Dedi complex completely.

We marched steadily through woods for several hours. Klar called a halt when the midday sun shone weakly through gathering clouds. Remnants of white from a previous storm dotted the ground, but it wouldn't be long before fresh snow joined it.

We ate carrots and a bread made from potatoes. I looked up from my food. "Can we find refuge anywhere between here and the Borogo village if it snows?"

Klar shook his head. "We'll have to go on."

Lin snickered. "Too bad you haven't invented an instantaneous shelter."

"Why? Have you?" Klar asked.

"We've seen pictures, but never thought it necessary to investigate. We've always had more important machines to build."

"Were they like tents?" I remember Gareth saying we should have brought one with us when we were searching for Madoc. We also had a temporary structure at Dulno Lake.

Lin scratched his chin. "I think they were. Do you have those?"

"Tents are actually quite primitive," Madoc said. "There's nothing mechanical about them. They're just poles that support fabric walls."

Klar stood from his seat on a rock. "We'd best move on if we want to make much more progress before the storm hits."

I collected the paper wrappers from the food we ate while everyone else got ready to leave.

We'd traveled another hour or so north when it began. The wind buffeted us from the west, then changed direction to blow straight at our faces. "We'll have to stop." Klar looked around. "Let's move into those trees. They'll provide protection from the wind." He pointed to a copse of evergreens, tall with branches like a skirt, dipping almost to the ground. The aroma of the needles was pleasant. They blanketed the ground, too.

The trees created a break like the wall of ice we'd built on the tundra, but soon snow joined the wind, blowing through the trees and coating everything. Klar spread a cloth for us to sit on. We huddled together, hoping to escape the brunt of it.

The storm intensified, then continued unabated for hours. I covered my face with my hands, and then pulled my cloak over it before my lips froze. Madoc's arm slipped around me to pull me closer, and I leaned into the warmth and familiar scent of his body.

Klar shouted above the howl, "We'll stay here for the night. Perhaps by morning the snow and wind will die down and we can move on.

At first the cold kept me from sleeping, but I must have slumbered because the next I remembered, I opened my eyes to the dim light of dawn. Was it my imagination or had the wind lessened? Snow continued to fall, but no longer blew through the trees.

By full light, everyone was awake. Without a way to heat our food or water, we contented ourselves with crusts from the potato bread and sips of water that was partially frozen. Somehow that warmed my insides enough that I could unbend from my position.

"We can move on now. Walking will heat us." Klar was first to leave our refuge among the trees.

As I followed, I became less and less stiff and much warmer. Madoc trudged beside me. The snow slowed our progress, but we developed a rhythm, and then were reluctant to stop at midday for another meal. By then, with the sun overhead, it wasn't as cold as during the night. But hunger forced us to halt briefly to eat more cold food.

We slogged on again without speaking. It was hard enough to breathe, let alone say anything. Every time we opened our mouths, warm, moist air was replaced by cold that seared our throats. I feared my tongue would never thaw completely.

Instead of words, we conversed by motions, Klar's hand pointing the way whenever we had to veer from the straight path in front of us, or Lin wanting us to look at something in the trees or on the path.

The snow's depth seemed to lessen. We sped up. Still, it was hours more before the first signs of the Borogo appeared, the remains of a campfire with snow accumulated in the center.

"Not much farther." Was Klar smiling? Difficult to tell with his head wrapped in a long scarf.

Two of the Borogo came to meet us. Their deference to Klar and Chan didn't surprise me.

Klar spoke to them. "We wish to meet with you and show you something new." He repeated it in Fartekana.

The two conferred, but soon agreed. We followed them to the building we'd been in days before and were told to wait. A woman I recognized as one of the three that had given us food, appeared in the doorway. She carried root vegetables, and gave them to us. We thanked her and gratefully ate what she brought.

It was warm in the building, protected from the wind. We sat on benches and waited, but not long. Mogo entered with the men who'd greeted us before. He spoke in Fartakana, and Klar translated, but I wished Katya were with us. Could we trust Klar to tell us what Mogo said without bending the words to his own needs? Still, the few words I knew corresponded to his interpretation.

Finally he told us, "They've agreed to see what we've brought. I didn't mention the Dedi, since that might have turned them against us."

"But they worship the Sion. I'm not surprised they will listen to you." Madoc rubbed his hands together. "So when can we demonstrate everything?"

"First they are insisting we share food with them. Come, they are already preparing it." He opened the door and led the way out to the next room where a table was filled with a limited selection of vegetables and some kind of dried meat.

I didn't bother to ask what it was, since I'd learned to eat whatever anyone offered me. It tasted like the snake we'd eaten.

As we ate, several Borogo, including Mogo, joined us. They didn't eat much and talked only about the snow and cold. But once we'd finished, they quickly cleared the table. "So, you have something to show us?" Mogo sat back in his chair expectantly.

Klar exchanged a glance with Madoc. "We'll start with this small fertilizer." He held out the pebble-like sphere.

"What does it do?" Reluctantly Mogo took it and rolled it around in his fingers.

"You put it in the ground with your seeds and plants, and they grow much faster. What do you think?"

"It sounds useful." Mogo put it down on the table, but it rolled toward the edge.

Klar reached out to catch it before it fell. "Of course we also have other items. Madoc, why don't you show him that picture thing."

Madoc reached into his pack and brought out one of my brother's favorite devices. "With this, I can capture your image and then produce a paper copy of it. It's called a camera."

Once Klar translated, stumbling over a word for camera, Mogo shook his head. "That is magic. We will not allow magic here."

"Tell him it isn't magic, it's a new invention that can help them..." I hadn't thought about how it might aid these people.

Klar smiled at me. He said something to them, then explained. "I told them it would help their children and grandchildren remember what they looked like."

Mogo examined the device, then handed it back to Klar who, in turn, gave it to me. I knew how it worked, even though I'd never used it. I motioned Mogo to stand close to one of the women. They eyed each other before complying.

"Klar, how do you tell them to smile?"

"Egao."

"Egao," I instructed and demonstrated.

They both giggled first, but finally smiled at me. I operated the device. The whir as it spit out the picture startled them, but when I showed them the image, they pointed to each other and giggled some more.

"I hope that means it's a success." I placed the camera on the table.

"I think we can truthfully tell the Dedi that the Borogo are open to trying our inventions. They understand the value, even if they don't know how they work."

I smiled. "I'm not sure I know how they do."

"Mogo insists we spend the night before returning home," Klar said.

We were shown more of their settlement first, fed another meal much like the first, and then sent to a large room with many beds, a kind of dorm for men and women to share. I was so tired, I didn't care who else was in the room. After washing my hands and face in a ewer like the one back in my much smaller bedroom at the manor, I stretched out on the lumpy mattress and fell asleep.

I woke in the middle of the night feeling a draft from a window high in the outside wall of the room. It hadn't been open when we went to sleep and was too high for someone to reach, so why was the wind whistling through it? Hunched down in my scratchy blankets, I drifted off again wondering about the window.

CHAPTER FIFTY-NINE

A shout woke me a second time. Mogo burst into our room. "The Dedi have attacked." He was out of breath.

Could the attack have been the cause of the noise I'd heard and the damage to the window? I looked up. In the dim light of early morning, the hole in the glass looked small. My eyes shifted to the ground. A rock the size of a small melon lay in the middle of the floor. "They threw something through the window last night."

"Oh, dear." Mogo wrung his hands like Glynis' mother used to when the roses or the cabbages had destructive beetles attacking them. "How will we ever fix that?"

By then, everyone in the room had wakened and they clambered to know what was going on.

Mogo repeated his first exclamation. "The Dedi have attacked."

"Was anyone hurt?" Chan asked. "Can we help you in any way?"

He pointed to the window. "You can use your magic to fix that window. I will go to make sure our defenses are holding." He rushed out as quickly as he'd entered.

Klar shook his head. "I didn't expect this, but maybe I should have. Are the Dedi so set on ensuring our plan can't work?"

"So it would seem." Madoc studied the window. "If we do fix that, I wonder who'll be more impressed, the Dedi or the Borogo?"

"Is it glass?" I asked. "How do you mend glass? Of course, if Ana were here she'd say, 'very slowly'." But joking didn't solve the problem. "Do you have an idea?"

"Do you have any of your yellow material with you?" Madoc asked me.

"The waterproof fabric?" I nodded. "There's some in my pack." I dug down to the bottom, under the clothing and other contents. My fingers felt the slick cloth, and I pulled it out. "What are you going to do with this? It's not transparent for one thing. How will you reach the opening?"

Madoc had Chan and Lin help him move over the table from the middle of the room to under the window, and then climbed up onto it. I handed him the fabric, still curious how he'd use it. He held one end to the wood frame and ran his forefinger along it. Somehow, it stuck even after he let go. Then he stretched the material across the window, running the same finger along the top and bottom of the frame.

I watched in awe. When he asked for my knife, I rushed to give it to him, realizing he intended to replace the glass with the fabric. It let in most of the light the glass had, and it would keep out the rain. He cut along that end and attached it to the frame as he had the rest.

Once he was on the ground again, he handed me the remaining material.

"How did you seal it to the frame?" I folded the piece and put it back in my pack.

He rubbed his thumb and forefinger together. "While you were finding that fabric, Lin gave me the special gum the Isty use for mending cracked wood.

Mogo had returned. He looked up with wide eyes.

"Of course, no one can see through the window any longer," Lin pointed out.

Madoc chuckled. "The window was so high we couldn't see out before."

Mogo inclined his head toward them. "Gentlemen, I believe this solution is acceptable to me and my people. No reason to argue, especially when we still have a larger problem."

Several of us said it simultaneously. "The Dedi."

"The projectile that broke the window was only the first of

several they fired our way. There are breaks in our outermost walls," Mogo said. "I'm afraid they won't stop."

"But first they have to have more projectiles." Madoc paced with his hands behind his back. "And how many machines can they have to propel them this way? They'd have to move each of them around to attack more than one side of your complex."

"Madoc, sit down. You're making everyone nervous." Lin patted the chair next to his.

Madoc glanced at Mogo standing near the table before taking the seat. "Do you have any defenses?"

Defenses? Why wasn't he talking about weapons? But then, that wasn't his way. He tried to avoid conflict. If the Borogo could fend off the attack, perhaps the Dedi would give up and leave.

Mogo pulled himself up to his full height. "Of course. My people have had to defend against many enemies over the years. We have catapults to send huge rocks into their midst."

Lin sneered. "So primitive." He drummed his fingers on the table.

"With your glass dome, do you even need fortification?" I asked him.

"In addition to our protective dome, we can create an electromagnetic field." He spread his hands out.

"What's that?" Chan asked.

Lin shook his head. "It would take too long to explain, but it repels any force used against it."

I thought of the shield Madoc created over our people when we went to Dulno Lake. Was it something like that? "Madoc, do you think..."

He smiled. "Klar, you said your people have learned to use the energy around us with your minds. Can you work with Nissa and me to form a defensive barrier?"

"We've never had to." He looked at Chan, who nodded. "We can try."

"I'll reach out to you first to form a connection." Madoc locked his gaze with Klar's.

I knew what was happening, but from the skeptical looks on the faces of the others, they were completely confused.

"Nissa?" I felt the familiar touch of Madoc's mind and joined the link. Klar's mind was different from any I'd ever touched, more intricate. Another mind joined us, Chan's. Somehow gentler than Klar's. Madoc took the lead, sketching the extent of the wall we were forming around the compound to keep the Dedi out. Before long, the protective web was complete, but we'd have to concentrate to hold it in place. How long could we maintain our link?

"Well?" Lin sounded impatient.

I ignored him, but Madoc was able to say, "We've created the shield we need."

I was vaguely aware when Mogo left again. My mind strained to do its part in maintaining the shield.

But when he rushed back in, he shouted so loudly we had to look his way. "They're retreating. Every time they came close they were rebuffed by the invisible wall you created. Well done! And thank you."

We held the barrier a while longer to be sure, but when we let it fall, Madoc said, "It protected us as well."

"So, now what?" Lin looked at each of us in turn. "We were here to..." He stopped before he revealed too much to the Borogo.

Klar held his hands palm out. "We've shown the people here the first of our inventions, and they want to see more. Our aim was to establish a relationship."

"But how can we repay you?" Mogo appeared more differential than ever.

I recalled some of the arguments back at the Sion house. "Your people have preserved skills others have not. I'm sure we can find those that benefit the Sion and the Isty, and exchange our inventions for what your people know."

"Skills?"

"Like weaving." I pointed to the floor. "I've noticed the fine rugs you have. The Sion don't have any."

"Oh. And you would find this skill of value?"

Klar nodded. "Most certainly. Like Nissa, I've admired some of the work your people do, not only the rugs but the hand-carved chairs."

Mogo cupped his chin as he regarded Klar. "Certainly, we would be honored to show you how we make our rugs and furniture."

"We'll leave early tomorrow morning, but we will return before long to bring more inventions." Klar clasped his hands in front of him. "Some of my people will come along later to talk to your artisans about their work. There is much we can learn from each other."

I reached over and tugged at Klar's sleeve. "Don't forget to ask about histories they might have."

"Histories?" Mogo repeated the word.

"Yes. Nissa is reminding me your people might possess other knowledge none of ours do. What do you know about the time before? Have you kept any of the old records?"

Mogo grinned. "Ah, yes. Our archives. But why would you want to look at any of those?"

"We can learn a lot from records of what was done by our scientists and politicians to cause the catastrophe, one we hope to avoid." Klar smiled. "And we should all know about our common ancestry."

"Not only were the peoples of this world divided by what happened, but each preserved something else," Lin said. "It's time to share it all."

"We will provide what we can." Mogo shook hands with each of us. "And tomorrow we will send you off with food for your journey. Now, let us talk of more pleasant things."

He never asked how we'd created the protection around the camp.

CHAPTER SIXTY

Our journey back to the Sion building was easier than the one going forth. It was still cold, but the snow had stopped. The existing snow was packed down and a bit icy.

Donal and Ana rushed out to meet us as we approached. "They did it!" My brother's eyes flashed as they only did when he was excited about a new discovery. "Come see their flying machine."

Ana put a hand on his arm. "Let them get their breaths. They've been traveling for days." She smiled at us. "C'mon inside. Plenty of time to see what Donal's babbling about."

We trooped into the building. Removing layers of clothing took time. Finally we sat down to soup and fresh bread. Then we told everyone about our adventures with the Borogo and their agreement.

"They're more likely to keep their word than the Dedi ever were," Chan said.

"Now will you come see the machine?" Donal pulled at my hand.

I smiled at him. "You've been so patient." We followed him to an open space protected on two sides by extensions of the main building, a bare courtyard.

Two men stood beside a huge basket, tipped over on its side. Ropes from the basket extended out to fabric spread out on the ground.

"They blow hot air into the balloon and when it fills, it rises in the air, pulling the basket upright." Donal grinned. "People get into the basket and the balloon lifts it up to float on the breeze."

"But how do you steer it?" I studied the machine. "How do you know where it will go? The wind blows wherever it wants."

"You wait until the wind is blowing the direction you want to go." Donal was too excited to see the dangers I did.

"Isn't there anything else you can do to control it?" Madoc asked. "Short of using the energy around us to change the wind."

"But that's just it!" Donal nodded vigorously. "We can control it better than most, right? We can use it to return to the domed city without that long trip by foot, and then to get back to the beach."

Madoc rubbed his chin as he walked around the thing. "But then someone will have to return it. I'm sure the Sion would want it back."

Lin stepped closer to the machine. "How many will the basket hold?"

"The twelve of us." Donal spread his arms wide. "All of us and all of you Isty."

"Won't we need a Sion to come along and control it? And then fly it back?"

My brother puffed out his chest. "I can do that. They've given me lessons."

Madoc lifted one eyebrow. "Well, it seems you've decided how we're going back."

"Madoc, I didn't decide, exactly." Donal shrugged but sounded irate. "If you can find another way to speed our return to the rest of our party, then by all means, tell us what it is."

Madoc stood facing him. "Donal, this is untested technology. Can we depend on it? If it fails midway, what will happen?"

"You never hesitate to use new machines." Donal's voice held a whine.

"Yes, that's true. Perhaps, though, we should make a shorter trip to see how it operates. If it works well, we should use it to return to the Isty city." Madoc turned to Lin. "Is that agreeable?"

"Oh, yes. Absolutely. We've accomplished even more than I'd hoped on this journey, but now I'm anxious go home."

Bin spoke up for the first time. "I'm staying here."

Every other head spun her way.

"One of the Sion can go in my place, but I'd prefer to remain." She clasped her hands in front of her.

I couldn't make sense of that. She'd complained our entire journey, but now we had means to return in an easier, quicker manner. What lure would keep her in this cold, dreary place?

"Bin, are you sure?" Lin put a hand on her shoulder.

"I find these people...sympathetic. This place," she separated her hands and waved an arm, "it suits me."

"And she's made a special friend." Ana smirked, causing Bin to turn a withering look her way.

Lin shrugged. "If you're certain, I won't try to convince you to come with us. But we're not ready to leave yet." He turned to Klar. "We have to make plans for the future."

Klar nodded.

We spent the next two days in meetings. The Isty agreed to provide the Sion with technologies they didn't already have. Klar decided to come to the domed city to see what they had, then to take us on to the beach. Donal, Klar, Madoc and Lin took the balloon and basket for a practice trip, and deemed it safe.

One night, Madoc, Donal, Rees, Katya, Ana and I sat alone in the dining hall. I'd been thinking about our friends and relatives who'd remained in the Isty city and on the beach. "I wonder what they've all been doing. What Blane, Carys and Morna have learned."

Ana nodded. "And Eva, Toren and Gareth as well as the others we left by the boats. We can speculate, but maybe we should wait until we see them and learn first-hand."

"I hope they're okay. I get so caught up in what's happening to us, I don't think about my sister, my brother and the others." I chuckled. "That happened when we were searching for Madoc, too. I rarely thought about my family at the Manor."

"We'll see them soon. The discussions between the Isty and Sion are winding down, and the flying machine is ready to go any time." Donal grinned. "I can't wait to see the look on Blane's face when he sees us in that basket."

"They'll all be amazed." Madoc stood and walked to the only window in the room. "Klar says it'll snow again soon. It's best if we can leave before that."

"How soon?" Ana asked.

Madoc came back to the table, but didn't sit. "Tomorrow. I'll go tell Lin we wish to leave then."

We went to the room where the Isty and a few of the Sion had been negotiating. "Lin, it's time for us to leave. Do you think you'll be ready by tomorrow morning?" He made it sound like a request rather than a demand.

Klar nodded. "Our talks are almost complete."

"Donal tells us the machine is ready," I said.

Lin nodded. "Then by all means we'll leave in the morning. This has been a fruitful visit and opened communication."

"What about communication with the peoples across the sea?" Madoc asked.

"Perhaps that too, before long." Klar rubbed his chin. "The pages you gave us have helped our people improve devices we already have, and one of our men has been translating the instructions into Solwinish for you."

"Thank you." Madoc smiled. "That will be most helpful."

"I hope when I bring the machine back here, I'll carry some of the devices the Isty have."

Lin nodded. "Our people have much in common, including our dedication to preserving and revitalizing the civilization that existed before the disaster that so divided our land."

"At least you are in agreement with us about what must happen in Fartek. I don't know whether we can ever convince the Dedi."

"Even after they see the cooperation between our people and between you and the Borogo?" Lin asked.

"They've shown their attitude with their actions." Klar shook his head. "We refuse to argue with a stone."

They all shook hands with each other and with us. Then we assembled all we hoped to take with us back to the Isty city. We decided what to leave for another time, since there wouldn't be enough room in the basket for everything Lin wanted. At a later date, when the basket would carry fewer people, there would be plenty of room for everything.

That night the Sion gave us a feast, including meat from an animal killed in the warmest time of year and cooked, then packed in huge plant leaves, dried fish from a river to the east of their settlement and stewed fruits and vegetables. I wished Carys were with us so she could teach their cooks some of her recipes, and learn some of their better dishes.

"She often improvises. If she doesn't have an ingredient she usually adds to her stews and other dishes, she'll substitute another." When I told them that, they nodded, as if they did the same.

"There are times during the year when the herb we prefer for fish dishes can't be found," Wen-Hsien said. She was a slight Sion woman who always wore a snow-white apron. "Instead we use wild onions. They don't taste quite as good, but most people don't notice."

I told her about the herbs my mother grew and those she gathered in the wild, as well as how she used them in making remedies and salves instead of food.

Wen-Hsien listened with wide eyes. "Do you know what plants she uses for what?"

My pack was in the room where we slept. "I'll return quickly with the ones I have. She writes on each of the packets what they should be used for."

When I came back and showed them to her, she asked me to translate what they said. We did our best with help from Terri and Katya. Wen-Hsien opened some and sniffed them.

"This one is like our lemon grass." She found several she knew or were similar to herbs she used for cooking.

"It's possible the Borogo also have plants they use for healing," Ana said. "That's something else they can share with you in exchange for your technology."

"I'll leave a few of these with you." I wrapped them again. "Perhaps you can duplicate my mother's salves for use by your people."

I went to bed well fed and full of ideas. I had paper in my pack and a writing instrument, so I wrote them down. I hoped I'd be able to share them with our new friends and my own people.

When I woke, the sky outside was steel gray. Would bad weather delay our trip? I hoped not.

CHAPTER SIXTY-ONE

I ate breakfast with one eye on the window. The gray hadn't changed. "Can the basket go up if it snows?" I asked my brother.

He shrugged. "As long as the wind isn't too strong, I think we can chance it."

"But do we want to?" Ana looked doubtful. "We can wait another day."

"Maybe we should have left yesterday." Rees shoved a spoonful of Sion porridge into his mouth.

"What do the people who built the thing think?" I asked Klar.

"I will go ask, but they didn't want to let us use their invention if the weather was bad." He pointed to the window. "Right now it is only threatening, but that can change quickly. I will also ask our weather prognosticators."

I hadn't known they had such a thing, and wondered what method they used to predict future conditions.

After we ate, we returned to our room to finish packing, assuming we would leave soon. We were almost finished when Klar walked in.

"The prognosticators confirm the weather will clear. There is no reason we shouldn't leave before midday."

We took our belongings out to the courtyard where the men were preparing the basket and envelope. The Isty, even Bin, met us there. She said farewell to the others, then went back inside. I still didn't understand why she wanted to stay.

We watched the men fill the balloon with air, heat it to expand it, and lift the basket. Then we climbed in with our packs. A few Sion appeared to say farewell. The ropes that tethered us to the ground were loosened, like pulling up the anchor of a boat. As the balloon and basket lifted into the sky, the gray dissipated and the sun shone through. There were no trees to block our ascent. Higher and higher we went.

I dared to look down. The building and people looked smaller and smaller as we rose. The sky around us was clear. A few clouds, fluffy and white, decorated the sky.

Klar and Donal worked a device that occasional shot a flame up into the envelope. "It heats the air inside," my brother told me.

"Why doesn't it burn?" I pointed to the fabric of the balloon.

"It's treated to keep it from scorching." Klar pulled on a cord and we floated in a different direction. "We're now heading north."

This high over the woods, all I could see was the crowns of the trees, dulnos and dulnos of them. We seemed to speed up.

"How long will it take to reach the dome?" Ana asked.

"Almost a day."

"As we get closer, I'll try to communicate with our people and let them know we're coming." Lin turned toward Madoc, slowly since we were so crammed into the basket. "Can you use your skills to reach your people?"

"I believe so. Between your methods and ours, they'll know we're on our way."

I hadn't realized we'd have to stand for so long in this cramped space. The view was so spectacular, I didn't mind for the first part of the trip. I could make out the lake we crossed and some of the hills. This was so much faster than on foot. I felt as if I was floating, gliding through the air like a bird.

Occasionally, we'd go up or down. My brother explained it was to catch winds going in our desired direction. Sometimes we even skimmed the top of the trees.

At midday, we took out the provisions the Sion gave us for the journey, fruit, dried meat, and water.

Unfortunately, we couldn't sit to eat. We could barely turn. Madoc stood next to me; his nearness was reassuring as always, not that I was nervous about being so high off the ground.

The basket came up to my chest, so there was little chance I'd fall out, and the balloon seemed strong enough to hold us up as it soared through the air.

I finished my lunch with a gulp of water. Looking in each direction as best I could, I thought I glimpsed the sea to the west. "I wonder where we are in relation to the beach where our ships are anchored."

"It's farther north, since we went almost due east to the Isty city." Ana pointed down. "We're over the place where the animals attacked."

"That would mean we're getting close to the dome." Donal looked northward. "I can't see it yet, though."

"It's still some distance away," Lin said.

A gust of wind, followed by another, pushed us off our route. To the west, the clouds grew larger and turned darker. "Is there a storm coming?" I had to shout to be heard.

"I hope not. But with this wind, it will be more difficult to hold our northerly course." Klar did something that caused us to descend a bit, but we were still buffeted by the wind. "We have to wait for the wind to abate so we can have more control of our direction."

"How far off course are we?" Madoc asked.

Donal took a small device from his pant's pocket. It looked almost like the watches some men wore at the Stronghold, but it had no band. He focused on it. "We're heading east. I think we can correct once the gale stops."

It continued for almost an hour. My hair flew until I tied it with some string. When we were no longer being pushed eastward, Donal and Klar consulted on the corrections they had to make.

"We'll be back on course before long." Klar took out a kind of telescope and scanned the horizon. "I still don't see your city."

We sailed on, our eyes trained downward to the ground and out to the north. As the sun began its descent we finally caught our first glimpse of the city. The sun bounced off the glass over the Isty city.

"We're close enough now to try to contact people." Lin

took out the small device he'd revealed as their communicator. He spoke into it, but all we heard was a crackling noise.

Madoc glanced at me. "Let's try."

I joined my mind with his and together we reached out, searching for Blane, Morna and Carys. I sensed Ana and Donal joining us, and then even Klar.

The others watched us with expectant expressions.

I gasped as Morna and Blane responded. At their end they linked with Carys. We told them to look to the south and high in the sky. We sent an image of the balloon and basket, and told them when they saw it approaching, to let the Isty know.

"What's happening?" Terry asked.

"We're telling our sisters and brother to let your people know we're on our way," Donal replied. "Will we bring this thing down outside the dome? Can they open the top?"

She shook her head. "The south side would be best, near where we left the city."

Donal listened with the rest of us to the messages from Morna, Blane and Carys. "The Isty want reassurance we are all well and safe. What might convince them?"

Lin shrugged. "Tell them 'mission accomplished.' Our people will understand."

We sent that strange thought, along with the instructions from Terry about where to meet us.

Morna seemed to shout, We see you. What is it like so high in that machine?

It's like floating. I hoped she'd also get a chance to experience what we were.

By the time Donal and Klar maneuvered the basket to the ground, night was near. While we waited for the Isty to open an entry to their city, we climbed out of the basket and deflated the envelope of the balloon, squeezing as much air out of it as possible. By the time we folded it and stored it inside the basket, an opening in the barrier appeared and several people came through it toward us.

When I saw Morna among them, I ran to her and threw my arms around her shoulders. She hugged back, burying her head in my chest. "I wasn't sure I'd ever see you again, Nissa. You were gone so long."

"It took some time to reach groups who could help us."

"Is that their machine?" She pointed to the basket, now on it's side again.

"Yes. It was so much faster coming back with it!" I held her away from me. "We have lots to show you, and hope you have plenty to show us."

"Oh, we do! These people have such amazing gadgets. They have one that freezes food better than a cold box, and another that curls your hair." She led me through the opening behind Blane, Donal and Carys.

"Besides the balloon, the Sion have a few wonderful machines, too. And some of the Sion can even mind speak."

"I thought there was someone I didn't know participating in the connection earlier."

I walked with her down one of the wide, paved streets toward a building I hadn't been in before. Three floors tall, it had bluish glass in the windows. The walls were made of a kind of metal.

"This is a school." Morna pointed to words over the double doors that seemed to be in the language of Madoc's books. "The kids learn so many things we never did, including where the different countries were Before."

"Are the lessons in Fartekana?"

"Most of them, but I've learned more of the language, besides so many other things. Do you know even people our ages still went to school Before? They didn't start to work until they were about Blane's age."

I climbed the broad stairs up to the doors with her. "I guess you've lost your interest in animals."

"Oh, no. There are lessons on those, too." She grinned as only Morna could. "All the species that are extinct. That means there aren't anymore anywhere in the world. But now there are new species that didn't exist Before."

New species? I wondered. "Like the ruda I killed."

"Yes, and your ice bear. And those tigers. There used to be animals like them, but not so big and not so fierce."

"We ran into people who'd been attacked by others on this trip." I pointed to the doors. "Do they have any baby animals like Gita had back at the Stronghold?"

"Yes, of course. I'm learning the names both in Solwinish and Fartekana."

"So you've enjoyed your stay here?"

She nodded. "But we'll have to leave now you're back. Did you find anyone who could read Madoc's books? Is it ancient Fartekana like we thought?" Her questions were as rapid as ever.

"Yes. A group took the books from us, but Madoc had copied them, and some of the Sion read them. They're using them to perfect machines they were already working on." I was so happy to see my sister and brother and Carys. "But where are the rest of our people?"

CHAPTER SIXTY-TWO

Morna bit her lip. "The rest are in the infirmary."

"That's like a hospital, right?" That was where they'd taken Eva.

She nodded. "The medics told us they were exposed to something here that affected them badly."

"Then why didn't you get sick?" This didn't make sense. "And why didn't any of us who traveled south?"

"It's something in the air here, they said. Blane, Carys and I don't come from Solwintor, and somehow that allowed us to resist the substance that made the others sick."

"And Gareth?" I hadn't seen Madoc's brother.

"Oh. He's okay. But he's spent most of his time talking to the people in charge here." She pointed to another building. "That's where they have offices."

"What are they doing for the patients?" When we left Eva was being treated for her wounds. She remained in the infirmary, but now for a different reason. "Can we visit them? I'd love to tell them about all we saw in our travels."

"We're allowed to visit once a day just before evening meal. They appear to be recovering, but it's slow. Meanwhile, Carys, Blane and I are learning all we can from the Isty." She led me into a classroom, filled with the first children I'd seen since we originally arrived in the Isty city. A teacher stood in front of them, speaking in Fartekana about cities and countries that had changed or disappeared since the Fall.

My understanding of the language had improved so I could follow what he said. He was talking about a place called Tailong, not far from where we were now, but few of the buildings had survived a tidal wave.

Morna and I listened for a few minutes and then moved on. I walked slowly as I thought through everything I'd heard since we'd arrived in Fartek. "Each of the people we've met have different stories about what it was like Before. I suppose it's no wonder, since contact between all the splintered groups is so infrequent, and communication so difficult."

"But now we've brought at least some of the groups together." Morna grinned. "Fong was so astonished by what he saw here that, at first, he believed it wasn't real. But now he spends every day with the historians telling them what he knows about his people's history."

"And I believe the Isty and the Sion, as well as the Borogo, another group we met, will exchange not just technology, but also whatever they've each preserved."

"I guess that means we've accomplished more than we set out to." An unusually serious look filled my sister's face.

"What's wrong?"

"Once everyone's well again, I suppose we'll leave."

"Don't you want to go home? Either to the Manor or the Stronghold?" We'd reached the doors again.

She frowned. "I'm not looking forward to the trek back."

"I don't think that's the total reason you don't want to leave, but Klar, the Sion man who came with us, agreed to take us to the beach in the balloon."

"I'll get to fly in it?" A bit of her gloom lifted.

"Yes." We walked out into the bright sunshine. "I'd like to spend a little more time in this city before we leave, though."

"Can we? Oh, Nissa, I so want to see as much as I can. We'll probably never come back here."

Donal, Blane and Carys sat on the steps to the building. Donal's hands were flying. He was probably regaling them with tales of our trip, or maybe some of the wonders the Sion had.

"Where's Madoc?" I asked.

"Lin took him and Klar to talk to some of the Isty leaders."

Donal grinned. "And Rees went to find Gareth. I just told Blane and Carys how we helped the Borogo fend off the Dedi."

I explained about the different groups to Morna.

"So there are still people who don't want to cooperate?"

I nodded. "The Dedi are also the ones who took Madoc's books."

She frowned.

Carys put a hand on her shoulder. "Morna, you know not everyone always agrees. Did you tell your sister about the illness that's afflicted some of our party?"

"Yes. Let's go see them, let them know you're all back."

The Isty who'd traveled with us had all wandered off. No one mentioned Bin's absence, and I wasn't going to bring it up. Whatever her reasons for staying behind, it wasn't my business.

I knew where the infirmary was from our short stay in the city before we left. As we walked towards it, I asked Carys what she'd learned from the Isty cooks.

"They have the most amazing spices they use in their food. Some of it is very hot, made with a kind of pepper. I hope they give me ingredients before we leave."

"We had some different foods, too." I told her about a few.

Ana was already standing by Eva's hospital bed. "Nissa, some of their medical equipment is amazing. You should see how they inject a substance under Eva's skin to fight her illness."

Eva had completely recovered from her earlier wounds, but her face was still pale. The part of the bed under her shoulders and head were raised somehow. She greeted us with a wan smile.

"Is their medicine working?" I took her hand.

"I think so because I couldn't hold my head up three days ago and now I can." She touched her forehead with the hand not holding mine. "My fever's gone, too."

"My mother always used yarrow to bring down fever." Morna turned to me. "Right, Nissa?"

"Yes. What do they use here? Is it something..." I tried to think of the word I heard people here use. "...artificial?"

"Well, synthetic, anyway. It's a chemical similar to the natural substances that can lower the body temperature. And, as Ana said, some of their medicines are injected and others are pills we take in our mouths and swallow."

A woman rushed in. "Time for your next shot, Eva." She had a tray in her hands and on it was a very long and thick needle as well as a tube and a few other items.

I'd been using needles to sew all my life, but never saw one like it. I watched in awe as the woman used it with some of the other items to force the liquid from the tube into Eva's arm. She patted the spot afterward and covered it with a strip. "What's in that?" I pointed to the needle.

She said a word I didn't understand, and not because it was in Fartekana. Then she laughed. "Don't try to pronounce it. They make it in the laboratory. It seems to be helping Eva and your other friends who came down with this bug."

Morna wrinkled her nose. "Bug?"

"Infection, viral probably. It wasn't an allergic reaction like we originally thought. We call all such bugs, even though they're much smaller than the insects you know." She'd finished with Eva and took off the hand coverings I hadn't noticed she'd worn. She held out her right hand. "I'm Flava, by the way. I've been caring for them all since they became ill, and trying to determine why some of you didn't."

I took the proffered hand. "Maybe it's because we come from a different land. My brothers, sister and I are from the continent of Leara. Madoc, Gareth, their sister and Rees all come from an island off our eastern coast."

She nodded. "That could explain the differences in immunity."

"And our trip isn't over." Morna shook Flava's hand, too. "Do you also take care of the animals when they're sick?"

I grinned. "My sister loves animals, maybe even more than humans."

"We have special medical personnel for the animals. They understand the illnesses they get that are different from ours."

Morna nodded.

"I'm surprised you haven't found the animal infirmary yet." I tilted my head.

A touch of pink on Morna's cheeks warned me I'd touched a tender subject. "Well, I guess I've been spending so much time with the healthy ones, I hadn't thought to ask before."

I knew there was more to it and vowed to find out what that

was. Meanwhile, I watched as Flava put an instrument to Eva's forehead. "Good. The fever is already coming down."

"You can tell that from your stick?" Morna's eyes were round, and she pointed to Flava's instrument.

"Yes. We used to have many more devices for monitoring a person's body. Sadly, we still haven't been able to duplicate them."

"Were they powered by crystals?" I asked.

She chuckled. "Isn't everything?"

"Flava, when can I get out of this bed?"

"Perhaps later today you can try to walk a short ways. I wouldn't do too much at once, though."

"No, I suppose not. But how will we make the long trek back to our companions on the beach?"

"Oh, Eva. Has no one told you about the marvelous machine that brought Nissa, Ana and the others back?" Morna didn't wait for an answer, but described the balloon and gondola as only she could with lots of hand gestures and facial expressions.

Ana and I exchanged smirks as she tried to tell Eva about our descent just outside the dome.

Eva, and Flava, too, listened intently. Then Eva turned to us. "Is it true?"

"Yes. And Klar has promised to use the balloon to bring us back to the beach." Ana grinned. "Wait until you feel that floating sensation and look down on the tops of trees. There's nothing like it."

"I know they used to have flying machines Before, but our scientists haven't succeeded in making one of those either," Flava said.

"That's why Klar and Lin plan an exchange of information. The Borogo, too."

"What about the Pin-Shing?" Eva asked.

I'd almost forgotten Fong and his people. "Of course. They have skills and knowledge the others don't. Whether they'll accept modern technology is debatable, though."

"Fong seems fascinated by everything here." Eva smoothed the blankets over her body. "If we can convince him, he could get his people to agree to share, too."

CHAPTER SIXTY-THREE

Our other sick companions weren't doing as well as Eva. They were in the same room in beds like hers. Flava showed us how to elevate part of their beds. Toren looked weaker than I'd ever seen. Holt wasn't his usual energetic self. "You should have seen me last week." He tried to sit up straighter.

"I understand when we've recovered we'll be leaving." Toren lifted one eyebrow.

"Yes, that's true." I stepped closer. "Meanwhile, the Isty and Sion are making arrangements for an exchange of knowledge among several groups in Fartek."

He nodded, closed and opened his eyes. "Will we be able to communicate with the people here?"

"We hope so," I replied. "Toren, these people have many inventions to share, but so do the Sion. And groups like the Borogo and even the Pin-Shing have skills everyone else can learn from."

"If I stay, is there a way for you to bring Berel here?"

The young woman he'd rescued had been left on the beach. From his request, Toren must have formed more of an attachment to her than I'd thought. "You'll have to talk to the Sion man, Klar, about that. He'll pilot the balloon to take us back to the beach. He'll probably return to his own conclave after that."

He clasped his hands and wrung them. "I'll talk to him. I heard about the balloon, but didn't know the plan."

"You should see it. Even you'll be amazed." I smirked.

"Once everyone's well, we'll leave for the beach. Did you want to stay to learn more about the Isty? Or you can come with us, and then return to the Sion with Berel and Klar."

His hands unclenched. "Do the Sion also have advanced technology?"

"They constructed the balloon, and they're also building devices from Madoc's book. Why don't I bring Klar to you, so you can talk?"

Morna came over from talking with Holt. "What are you talking about?"

"Toren has an idea to discuss with Klar. Let's go find him." I took my sister's arm. Toren probably didn't want his personal wishes known.

"Where are you going?" Carys asked.

"I'm going to look for Klar. Thanks, Flava, for your care of our friends."

Morna decided to stay with Holt, and the rest had other things to do, so I walked across from the Infirmary to the office building.

I finally found Klar, Lin and Madoc talking to Chou, the man who'd introduced himself as the leader of the Ist y when we first arrived.

Madoc smiled at my approach.

I returned the smile, then turned to Klar. "I'm sorry to interrupt you, but when you have a few moments, Klar, I have a request."

"I believe we're finished here for the time being. We can reconvene after our evening meal." Chou stood and bowed first to Klar, then Madoc and finally Lin. He turned and left.

"What is it, Nissa?" Klar motioned to a chair next to Madoc.

"One of our party, who's still ill, wishes to return with us to the beach, but then, along with another companion, return with you either here or to the Sion building." I sat on the edge of my chair and waited.

"Why?" Klar asked.

"Nissa, are you talking about Toren?" Madoc took my hand.

I nodded. "He's fascinated by everything they're doing here

and won't be satisfied returning with us unless he has an opportunity to learn more."

"But he wants Berel to remain with him." Madoc pursed his lips.

"Exactly." I squeezed his hand.

"Klar, the man Nissa's talking about is considered a mage like me. He's a very learned man from Solwintor." Madoc paused.

"Who's Berel?" Klar looked between us.

I replied, "On our way here, he rescued her and feels responsible for her." He probably felt more than that, but it should be enough to convince Klar.

"Alright. I will speak with him."

"He's in the infirmary." I pointed in the general direction.

"I understand your companions will recover in the next couple of days. We will leave the day after that. I hope you'll help me make the arrangements, both of you. I'll go find Toren and speak with him." He left.

"So, we'll be going home soon."

"Will you be sorry to leave?" Madoc walked closer. He put his hands on my shoulders.

"You know I'm always reluctant to leave a place that still holds more for us to learn, but I'm also anxious to get home."

"And what do you consider home these days?" He pulled me closer.

"Well...First off, anywhere you are." I laughed. "More specifically, I don't think I can be content to return to the manor, not to stay. I want to see my parents, but I believe the Stronghold is where I can make more of a difference."

"Yes. I agree. Others from Solwintor can bring knowledge back from here, but I want to be with them." He brushed my cheek. "Nissa, I believe we've found our place at the Stronghold."

I pressed my lips to his. "Then it's settled. We can leave it up to our siblings to decide for themselves, but I expect they feel the same way." I took his hand. "Come, we should decide with our companions what we bring back with us."

We walked out into the sunlight again. It was so much warmer than at the Sion compound. "Do the Isty have a way of controlling their weather?"

Madoc shrugged. "We'll have to ask. Their technology goes

far beyond anything we've found anywhere, even among the Sion."

Donal, Blane, Carys and Ana sat on the steps of the infirmary. "Is Morna still inside?" I asked.

"She took Katya to show her something." Donal stood and offered me his spot on the stone next to Carys.

I sat, and Madoc took the place on my other side. "We'll be leaving for the beach in three days. We should decide what we still want to see and what technology we should carry back with us."

"The three of us have been talking about that, and about where we want to go." Carys pointed to Blane and herself. "Once we're wed, we'd both like to settle at the Stronghold. There's still so much to do there and we want to do our part, even if it's only cooking and guarding the place."

"Me too." Donal bounced on his feet. "I can't wait to tell the people there about all we've seen! And the ideas it's given me about some of the devices we could never perfect."

"Will Eva, Toren and Holt be ready to travel in three days?" Blane asked.

"Yes, but Toren might not be coming all the way with us." I grinned. "Once he's collected Berel from the beach he wants to come back here or continue to the Sion compound with Klar."

Blane nodded. "He hasn't had as much time watching demonstrations by the Isty as we have."

"Or by the Sion." I scanned all the buildings around us. "I wouldn't mind seeing more of this place before we go. Where do you suggest I start?"

Carys took my hand. "Come on. There are a couple of things that should interest you especially."

She took me down a couple of streets, turning enough times that I wasn't certain I could find my way back. The buildings looked so much alike. Finally, she led me into one with a sign over the door: Clothing Manufacture.

"Do they have the kind of machines they're trying to perfect at the Stronghold that sew fabrics?"

She beamed. "Almost all the clothing people wear here is made in this building. They have dozens of the machines. Some work automatically, and others need an operator. They sew skirts and dresses, shirts and pants, even items made from heavier fabrics, like jackets or protective gear."

Excitement coursed through me, especially after we entered one huge room ten times the size of the sewing rooms at the Stronghold, Filled with similar tables, each held a silver and black machine tapping away as a needle went in and out of fabric, pulling thread through to create a perfectly straight seam.

A woman working with a machine stopped as we approached and allowed me to examine the work it produced. I thought my stitches were fine, but the seam was even finer.

"I wish I could bring one of these machines home with me! Wert, the man in charge of making clothing, would be so amazed." And the colors of the fabrics ranging from blues and purples to bright reds and pinks were almost as surprising. "We make mostly green clothing although at the manor I wore blues and deep reds. How do you get these colors?"

"With many synthetic dyes." The woman held up the blouse she had finished in a vibrant shade of yellow, not like the waterproof fabric I used for the diving suits, but sunnier. "I'm sure we can gift you with this. It complements your complexion and brown hair."

I held it against me to see whether it would fit.

Carys nodded. "It's even more becoming than your white blouses."

"The dyes do not come from plants?" I asked.

"This one comes from minerals found here, but enhanced by our scientists by mixing the powders with chemicals."

"I wonder whether I could also bring back some of the dyes."

"Thanks, Tan." Carys pulled me away. "Let's go ask Chou or one of the others."

Still clutching my new blouse, I waved to the seamstress and went with my friend. The clickety-clack of the machines faded as we left the room and went back outside. This time, we walked only one street over to a lower building than most. It wasn't made of the same glass and metal as most of those in the city. Still, it was imposing by it's construction from a variegated material Carys called marble.

"The original buildings in this town were all made of marble." She pointed to the carved columns holding up a small portico. "This was the headquarters for the research institute and became an archive for knowledge after the Fall."

We entered and walked down a cool and quiet hall. Towards the end was a door with Chou's name on it. I hoped he'd agree to my requests.

CHAPTER SIXTY-FOUR

I knocked on Chou's door. Rather than a response, it was opened by Lin. He smiled at us. "Nissa and Carys, Klar and I spoke to your friend Toren and made arrangements with him. I'm here to report to Chou."

"That's wonderful. I'm afraid I'm here to make an additional request." I looked past Lin to Chou and swallowed before making my appeal. "Chou, Carys took me to see your clothing manufacturing methods."

"Did you want to take back a machine?"

"Oh, I'd love to. But what I want more are the dyes used for the fabrics. We have nothing like them."

Carys stood next to me. "You know Nissa is a seamstress and has introduced several innovations at the Stronghold."

"Dyes? Is that all you want?" Chou flung back his head and laughed. "But of course! That's easy."

"Thank you, Chou. Thank you so very much." My grin threatened to crack my cheeks.

"If you have any further requests, continue to come directly to me."

Carys chuckled. "Let's go see what else we can come up with."

Chou and Lin laughed even more as we left.

"Carys, this is amazing! Can you imagine what I can do with those dyes?"

"I'm sure you'll come up with all sorts of things. Now let's find your sister. She's probably in the animal nursery."

"That's not surprising."

"Honestly, if it wasn't for Holt she might choose to stay here, too."

Two streets over, an open corral contained four horses. It extended from a wooden building, unlike any others in the city. Carys pulled open the door to reveal the sounds of many animals combined with a few human voices. We followed them to an area containing a lamb and it's mother, as well as my sister and two Isty women.

"Nissa, Carys, do you know Ila and Ting?"

Ila, as blond and tall as many Solwinish women, held out her hand and I shook it. Ting was short, with dark hair and eyes like many people we'd met in Fartek..

"We're showing Morna our newest babies." The shorter woman rubbed a hand over the lamb's back.

"My sister loves animals and always gravitates to them."

Morna was in her element. "Ila and Ting are veterinarians like Gita."

"They have all sorts of babies here. There's a foal down that way, a real darling." Morna pointed behind us.

"Our people were able to collect many species from this area when the floods came." Ila waved a hand. "There's even a place where we keep wilder animals, and they're quite happy as long as they have enough to eat."

Ting nodded. "They haven't mutated like the large cats and predators outside our dome."

"Mutated?" Another new word.

Ila explained. "Over time, exposure to crystal dust from the satellite fall caused some animals to change, become larger, more aggressive."

"Like the tigers just outside?" Carys asked.

"Yes." Ting frowned.

My eyes opened wide. "That's what we thought happened to the megatanners at the bottom of Lake Dulno."

"And maybe to the ruda you killed in the sea or even the ice bear," Carys said.

Ting nodded. "So you've seen the result of some of the

mutations."

"Oh, yes we have."

"The animals here in our city are still the same as before." Ila put an arm around the lamb.

"Our horses and cows haven't changed as well," Carys said.

I nodded. "And cats and dogs. There's even a dog called Raj with the companions we left on your western shore."

"Did you ever prove the mutations are due to exposure to crystal dust?" Carys asked.

"Our biologists studied what animals we could capture over many years," Ila replied. "They could only conclude it is likely the dust causes accelerated growth. They could never say whether it contributes to the increased ferocity of the animals. That could be due to climate changes or a loss of natural predators."

I understood most of what Ila said. Perhaps my sister could explain the rest to me later. "May I come see the babies again?"

"Of course, Nissa. Come with Morna any time."

"I might turn you into an animal lover after all." Morna chuckled.

"I love animals, only not as much as you, little sister." I hugged her with one arm.

"Yes, Morna. I've seen how the black cats at the manor loved Nissa," Carys said.

I chuckled. "Morna's always been jealous they loved me more than her."

"I was not!" She pulled out of my arm, frowning at me.

Carys and I both laughed at her protestation.

"Well, maybe a little. But they liked me too, didn't they?"

"Of course." I patted her back. "They loved you."

Her smile returned. "C'mon. I'm hungry and it's almost dinner time." She led the way to the building where we ate when we arrived in the Isty city.

People streamed in from each of the three outer doors. Instead of just a few Isties, about fifty of them joined us for the evening meal. But it was Klar they wanted to ask questions. He told them all about the Sion, their community and those of the Borogo and Dedi. We added all we knew about the smaller groups living in the areas we crossed.

"Most know nothing about the existence of the Sion,

Borogo and Dedi, let alone the Isty and the groups between here and the coast," Ana added.

Our meal was much more varied than the diet we'd been eating with the Sion. In addition to bread, fruit and vegetables, we ate fresh meat, possibly chicken but I wasn't certain, and some cheese. Some of the animals they were raising certainly contributed to the Istys' food supply. I smeared a spreadable cheese on my bread and took a bite. It tasted almost like home.

I still hadn't seen Fong-Wei since we'd returned to the Isty city. Did he know all that was happening among the various groups? It would affect his people as much as any. "Is anyone making arrangements to take Fong-Wei back home?" I asked Terry, next to me.

"I understand he's spent all of his time here talking to some of our historians."

Leong, the man sitting on the other side of her nodded. "He is trying to trace the migration of various sects before and after the catastrophe." Leong looked around the room. "I can take you to see him if he doesn't join us for this meal."

"Thank you. I wanted to be sure he could return to his mother and the other Pin-Shing without being attacked by the tigers."

Terry grinned. "Nissa, you worry too much about other people."

"He brought us to you, despite his own misgivings." I expected he was as fascinated by this place as any of us. "The least we can do is help him find his way home."

"He told us about the woven fabrics the women of his tribe make." Leong put down his fork on his empty plate. "I would like to see them. Perhaps there is a way I can accompany him back to his village."

Klar laughed. "I believe I will have to make a stop on the way to the beach."

I recalled the village site. "There's a clear spot on the plateau above the chasm. The weavers are at the bottom, but there is a stairway down the side."

"Klar, you can use your balloon like transportation means from the past, making stops at defined locations." Terry eyes twinkled. "I suppose you can even charge for the service."

"Oh, I won't do that for our Solwinish friends or any Isty who wish to visit my home."

"What is the range of your machine?" Leong asked.

"Tens of thousands of dulnos, I expect."

"So, not enough to take us all the way back to Solwintor." Morna shrugged. "There's too many of us anyway."

"And don't forget the ships and their crews." I shook my head. "We can't abandon them."

"Well, if you're finished, Nissa, I'll take you to find your Pin-Shing friend." Leong stood.

I drank one last gulp of my juice and joined him. My sister and Ana decided to come with us.

The building Leong took us to was a library or archive. Several of the rooms were filled with shelves of books, each the size of the library at the Stronghold. Leong took us to one where Fong-Wei sat at a table in the center beside a young woman. In front of them was a large book opened to a page with beautiful illustrations of a kind of church. They looked up when we entered.

Fong-Wei pointed to the picture. "Midori and I were talking about the different religions that used to exist in this part of the world. There are also some practiced in Solwintor and Leara."

"The churches in my part of Leara are now ruins, visited as architectural wonders." I looked again at the picture. "The one near my grandmother's home looks a lot like this, but is in disrepair."

"The Borogo seemed to worship the Sion, or at least the stone the Sion gave them." Ana said.

"Fong-Wei, we'll be leaving here in a few days in the Sion machine that brought us back. Klar can stop on the way to the coast to leave you with your people."

He shook his head. "There is still so much to learn from these people. Perhaps I will return to my people another time."

"If you are staying, there is much I would want to discuss with you," Leong said. "And when you finally return, I wish to accompany you to see for myself the woven fabrics your women make."

"There is so much the different groups here can learn from each other. I only wish we from Solwintor could share with you all more than we have."

"Perhaps in the future there will be ways to communicate

over such great distances, as there were so many years ago." Leong waved an arm. "All of the knowledge we have in this library should be shared."

"This place is much larger than the library at the stronghold." I walked around the periphery of the room and examined the titles on the books. Many were in languages I couldn't read. "Would it be possible for me to take any of these with me?"

CHAPTER SIXTY-FIVE

Leong watched me examine the books in the library. "We can ask Midori whether there are any books we can spare. Perhaps there are duplicates we can send with you."

I wouldn't know where to start in selecting any we could use. "I'll consult with my companions and find out what books they'd find interesting."

We left the library and Leong waved to a vehicles. It stopped, and he spoke to the driver, then ushered me inside. He let me off in front of the building where I'd slept the last time I was there.

My packs had been placed in the room. I thought through all I'd seen since I was back in this city. Half a year earlier I wouldn't have believed any of this existed. But I didn't belong here any more than I did at the manor.

Carys came in carrying a package wrapped in a brown paper, slightly larger than the packs of salves and medicines my mother gave me. "Netsui gave me these powders. The two of you haven't met, but she creates these to make the dyes you wanted. Each packet inside is marked with the color it gives. She said mix the powder with water and a little vinegar to make the dying bath."

"Oh, how wonderful." I examined the neat writing on the outer wrapper. "We are going to have fun with these! Wait until Rani sees the colors." I clutched the package to my chest. "You must introduced me to Netsui so I may thank her."

Carys nodded. "I promised her I'd bring you by later today or tomorrow."

"What are you talking about?" Ana asked. Neither of us had heard her come in.

Carys brought me this package. It contains the powders they use to dye clothing here."

She laughed. "You've wanted to change the color of our jumpsuits since you arrived at the Stronghold."

"And now I have the means. If Wert will allow me to."

Morna burst through the door. "Everyone, come quick. There's been an accident!"

We rushed out of the room and building, not needing Morna to show us the way. Smoke billowed from the building where we'd eaten our meals, and people were running this way and that, but mostly away from the scene.

Ana stopped one of them as he went by. "What happened?"

"One of the old stoves in the kitchen exploded. No one knows whether it was because it was so old or due to an act of sabotage."

"Was anyone hurt?" Morna asked.

He shook his head. "I don't think so."

"But who would purposely blow up a stove?" Carys frowned. "And how will they prepare food?"

"I don't know, but I have to find Chou to tell him." The man ran on.

"I'm going to make sure there are no injuries." I moved against the flow of people toward the kitchen.

"Nissa!" Carys called after me, but I didn't heed her.

I found a handful of people still in the doorway. One had burns to her hands, while another was wrapping one of them. "I have salves for that."

They turned to me. "I've already treated her hands." The young man smiled at me. "We've perfected the treatment of burns and cuts based on texts found in the hospital and recorded by the doctors in the past. Perhaps we medics can share them with you."

"That would be wonderful." I couldn't wait to tell my mother about this. "All I have are salves and medicines derived from natural plants."

"A few of ours are derived from plants too." The medic

started on the second hand. "But also, several medicines were developed by our scientists."

"Artificial." I used a word I'd heard often since I arrived.

"Synthetic." He lifted one shoulder. "I suppose that means the same thing. They synthesize medicines in the laboratory based on analysis of natural herbs and other materials known to heal, but also from those books I mentioned." He tapped a tube next to the patient's arm. "This one works wonders on many kinds of wounds." He capped it and slapped the patient on the back. "See ya, Hiro." He moved on to a woman holding a wet cloth around her hand.

I felt there was nothing I could do for anyone injured in the blast. Donal approached with one of the Isty men.

"We're going to investigate why the oven exploded." My brother sounded excited. He was working with the people here, just as Morna was helping the veterinarians. Madoc was often involved in talks with the people who made the decisions here. It was much like at the Stronghold where I had little to contribute beyond the use of a needle and thread. Even those were useless here.

"Nissa, do you know what happened?" My other brother appeared around the building.

"An oven exploded. Donal's in there now with the people investigating it." I sighed. "I tried to help with the few injured people but their medicines are so much more advanced than ours."

"Feeling like there's no place for you here?" Blane sat down on a stone step, and I joined him.

"Definitely."

"Join the club. None of my skills apply here. Carys and Morna can fit in anywhere, and Donal's mechanical knowledge is perfect for a place like this. People always learn they can consult Madoc. But you and I...our abilities are great in less advanced societies, but not here."

I turned and looked back into the building through the still open doors. "I could probably join Carys in the kitchens, learning new recipes, although I don't find cooking as interesting as she does."

"I'm glad neither of you were there when the explosion happened."

"We have to acquire some new knowledge, big brother." I

smiled at him. "The hard part will be deciding where to start."

He studied me, but not for long. "Great idea, and this is a wonderful place to do it. I know just the thing I want to learn to do!"

"What's that?"

He grinned. "Fly the balloon."

"That should help Klar when he takes us to our companions on the beach, but how will you use that skill when we return to Solwintor?"

"If I learn how it works, perhaps we can build one at the Stronghold. Wouldn't that be wonderful?" He sounded enthused by his idea.

"Yes, of course. But that still leaves me with nothing useful. I could learn to use a sewing machines, but since I won't be bringing one back with me, what use would it be?"

"Nissa, just as my learning to fly the balloon will include studying how it was constructed, maybe you can learn something about the sewing machines. Seems to me the engineers at the Stronghold have been working on a machine like that for ages. If you study the ones here, you'll be able to help our people."

"You're right." But I still wasn't satisfied. There had to be something.

Blane stood. "I'm going to find Klar and arrange my first lesson."

I nodded. "Go ahead." Something the medic had said earlier was stuck in my mind. They'd created medicines they could share with us, but it was the preparation of those medicines that intrigued me. Would anyone be willing to explain to me how they did that?

CHAPTER SIXTY-SIX

I raced to catch up with Terry, walking across the square, before she entered a building. "Terry!"

She turned at my voice, stopped and waited. "Nissa, did you want something?"

"Which building houses the laboratories where they make medicines? I'd love to see how they're manufactured."

She pointed to the end of the row where a particularly tall steel and glass structure stood. "Go to the third floor. Ask for Chihiro."

"Chihiro. Thanks." I left her and strolled to the building she'd indicated.

It was cool inside, as in all of the buildings. A stairway rose in front of me but before I reached it, the woman sitting at the table in the center of the large entryway called to me.

"Where are you going, and whom do you wish to see?" She looked like many of the short, dark-haired Isty.

"I was told I could visit Chihiro in the laboratories." Chihiro could have been male or female, not that it mattered.

"Second floor, room two oh seven. You're one of the visitors, aren't you? Name please." She took out a square of thick paper and a writing instrument.

"My name is Narissa Day."

"Please write your name on this card." She handed it and the instrument to me.

I wrote my full name, and she took the card back, placing it inside a clear holder with a metal clasp on the back.

"Attach that to your..." She looked me over. "The waistband of your pants should be adequate."

I did as she said, and she sent me on my way. "You can use the stairs or the elevator." She pointed to a door without handles. But buttons were on the wall next to it.

I could figure out how that worked another time. Instead, I climbed the stairs. The second floor hallway was lined with closed doors. Pungent and acrid odors escaped around a few. I found the one with 207 on a plaque next to it and knocked. A high-pitched voice bade me enter.

Cabinets and counters encircled the room. The tables in the center held the most interesting assortment of bottles and long glass tubes, mortars and pestles, and instruments I'd never seen before. A sink was set in the middle of one table and over the other was a device that looked like a huge upside-down funnel. A short women with black hair and eyes wearing a pair of spectacles stood in front of one of the tables, a small open-topped tube in one gloved hand and a pitcher in the other.

"May I help you?" she asked.

"I'm Nissa, Nissa Day. One of the medical people responding to the explosion in the kitchen earlier told me you make medicines from plants." Looking around, I saw a few sprigs of what looked like tansy. I pointed to it. "My mother uses that to make her salves and remedies."

"Yes. It has medicinal properties, but we improve on the natural ability of the plant by compounding it with synthetic substances, either in powdered or liquid form."

"Could you show me some? I'm very interested in all methods of healing."

She put down the pitcher and swirled the contents of the tube before putting it in a clever wooden holder that kept it from spilling it's contents. "Let me show you how I make the salve you most likely saw used on burns." She picked up a plant I didn't know. "We grind this to a powder. It has the ability to heal and cool the skin at the same time." She used the mortar and pestle to turn the plant in fine particles. Then she took a small container of a liquid and sniffed it before adding a few drops to the powder, creating a paste. "The liquid helps the medicine penetrate the skin and keep it from drying and cracking."

"That's not too different from what my mother does."

"Ah, but does she add this?" Chihiro found a tiny envelope containing grains of another substance and added a few to the paste. "This is a synthetic substance that accelerates the ability of the skin to restore itself. Do you do any cooking?"

"Some."

"Have you ever added yeast to dough so it will rise faster?"

"I've seen Cook do that. And my friend Carys."

"It's based on the same principle although it doesn't act in the same way."

Over the next hour or so, she demonstrated more amazing things including a small sphere an ill person could swallow that would help them fight a fever and six different remedies for various illnesses.

My eyes must have grown wider and wider as she showed them to me. "My mother would be even more fascinated than I am with the work you're doing here."

"It's no more than recreating the medicine available to people in all lands before the launch of the second moon and the destruction that followed. I guess we're one of the few facilities that could preserve and restore the pharmaceuticals that had been developed, just as your facility and ours have safe-guarded and found ways to recreate other technologies."

I was thrilled with all I'd learned in just one afternoon. I promised to return the next day for another lesson. "Unless I'm in your way."

"Nonsense. I love to talk about my work and what we're accomplishing here. I'm happy to pass along what we've developed to help others." Chihiro put down the things she called 'pills'. "I am curious about what your mother was able to accomplish as a herbalist."

"I'll bring some of her salves when I return." I grinned. "It's good to know what she's done is unknown to you, even as what you've accomplished seems so strange to us."

I left her where I found her, busy with her work on new and improved medicines, and I felt much more useful than before. Blane joined me on the steps of the building. "You look the way I feel, as if I know what my purpose has become."

"We all have had a similar purpose for a while, to collect the knowledge and technology kept and developed all over this country and bring it back across the sea." He'd just sat down, but I stood. "I'm going to visit the invalids and see how they're doing." I held out a hand. "Coming with me?"

"Absolutely." He grinned.

We strode together to the building where Toren and Holt were recovering. They both looked better than the last time I visited. Toren sat up reading a book, and Holt was examining a device I'd never seen before.

"What's that?" I pointed to the small box in his hands. It had knobs on one side and a piece of metal that extended into the air.

"It's a music machine. You turn this." He grabbed a knob and spun it. "And music comes out of it. I don't know how it works, but it's great." I wasn't sure I'd call the sound coming from it music, but Holt grinned. It was more like bells of different tones played in sequence over and over. "This is the music people here used to listen to."

"I bet the people of Leara or Solwintor listened to different music. I doubt it was that." Blane was a musician himself. "Does it play anything else?"

Toren spoke up. "Unfortunately, it's all pretty much the same. And I've been subjected to it over and over since someone brought him the machine."

"If it disturbed you, you should have said something." Holt's voice was defensive.

The mage shrugged. "We'll be out of here soon and going home, or at least you all will. I've made other arrangements."

"So we heard." I moved closer to his bed. "What's the book about?"

"It's a history of the cultures of this part of the world. They were divided even Before."

"So the current divisions aren't new?" I thought about the various groups we'd met, how they'd each kept different pieces of the world Before, and how some were more willing than others to share. In the Stronghold, people from different places in Solwintor and surrounding areas had gladly come together to rebuild. "Why are they so insular, much more than people where we come from?"

"Think about your own home, the almost feudal society in Leara, despite the fact you all came from the same stock. Think of the resistance to recreating the way of life from before the launch of the second moon. Why, you have only to look at Duke Alec and the difficulty you had with him. Even his own son couldn't convince him about the devices we brought to the manor." He shook his head. "There's no rhyme nor reason to it."

"So what was it like here Before?" Blane asked.

"Long, long ago there was a society much like Leara that was destroyed by revolt of the poorer, working classes. Only in a few areas of Fartek. Elsewhere, conditions were even more primitive. The people in the different sections of the country were believed to be of different racial stock, as different say as you are from Katya or Mai or Gita."

"Granted, we look different, but so what?"

"In some societies, it meant a lot. And though Chou and Klar may look to be the same race, historically they aren't." He opened the book to an early part and showed a page to us.

Blane and I read it together, about a war fought between two groups of people, not over race but over land. Still, they identified themselves as being different racially.

Toren took back the book. "That was one of the divisive concepts that led to distrust in the past. Just before the launch, most of those issues were resolved."

"Do you think we can avoid those issues as we move forward?" I asked.

"I'm afraid it could lead to problems in the future. That is, if we don't learn from our mistakes."

CHAPTER SIXTY-SEVEN

Toren rubbed his unshaven chin. "Some say it's human nature."

"Well, I think we should do everything we can to help people see that differences among people don't matter. What matters is that the world survives."

His crooked grin had become familiar. "Spoken by an idealistic young woman."

"Is that an insult?"

"No, Nissa. I'd never insult you or your motives." He sounded amused. "I think they're grand, fine, and, as I said, idealistic. I only hope you're prepared to see people won't all go along with you."

"Oh, I've seen enough to know that."

Blane changed the subject. "Chou and Klar said you've made arrangements to return to the beach with us, but then continue on with Klar."

"Yes. I'll never have an opportunity like this again. Perhaps some day his machine can fly all the way to Solwintor and take me and Berel home, but meanwhile, there's so much to learn here. And I promise to make every effort to carry out Nissa's lofty goal." His mouth quirked again. "I'll be happy to get out of this bed. Hopefully I can see more of this place before we leave."

I thought of my tour. "Perhaps we can take you around in one of their vehicles."

My brother nodded. "When Nissa and I left home six

months ago for the first time, I hadn't any idea of the diversity of sights we'd see."

"And now you won't be content to return to your provincial manor, will you?" Toren propped himself up on one elbow.

Blane and I shook our heads. "I've decided my place is in the Stronghold. My brother feels the same." I looked to him for confirmation.

"Most assuredly. The manor is so static. Oh, it's alive, but not growing and changing."

I frowned. "Duke Alec will be slow to accept anything new, so conditions at the manor will remain the same for many years to come."

"So you're certain you wish to live at the Stronghold when you return to Solwintor?"

"Yes. I want to share the many things I've learned about here with everyone there."

Blane nodded. "I agree with my sister. The goal of our trip was to find the source of Madoc's books, but the underlying aim was to contact people and exchange knowledge. To complete that task, we must return to the Stronghold."

"And what of your princess?" Toren's grin had transformed into his usual sardonic sneer, but I'd come to recognize it as a facade. He wasn't as cynical as he pretended to be.

"We will marry on our voyage west. Her parents agreed, and we want it more than ever. She'll return to the Stronghold as my wife."

I grinned. "Of course, she also wants to share the recipes she learned from the cooks here."

"I'm surprised she hasn't passed on the recipe for making Meecham cookies."

"Who says she hasn't?" I chuckled. "You've been cooped up in this hospital too long. A lot has happened outside these walls."

Toren laughed. "Yes, I suppose the little news I hear doesn't reflect that. None of you has been idle."

"Neither have you, even here."

"The more I read about these people, the more I want to know. Has anyone told you about the mystics who were revered here two thousand years ago? Perhaps there was a time when magic was more prominent."

"Before the people understood about the energies around us."

"Oh, it went beyond that, Nissa. Now I believe those energies were enhanced by all the crystal dust that covered large sections of land after the fall of the artificial satellites. But before that, there were different forces at work." He smiled. "So much to investigate in this part of the world."

As usual, I didn't understand half of what he said, but thought it wonderful he'd found a new purpose. I suppose we all had to one degree or another.

Blane and I left the invalids and searched for Madoc and Carys. They sat with Morna and Gareth under an odd tree. The trunk twisted around itself and the leaves were like those of a fir tree back home.

I sat next to Madoc. Since we'd returned, I hadn't seen him much, but knew he had been included in discussions with the Isty in charge and with Klar representing the Sion.

"I finally did it." Carys grinned. "Finally convinced the bakers to try the Meecham cookie recipe."

Blane and I both laughed. "We were beginning to wonder why you hadn't yet. Toren brought it up. What do they think?"

"They love them as much as we do, of course. So different from most of their sweets."

"I suppose we're leaving this place on a positive note." Gareth seemed much more relaxed than I'd ever seen him.

"What have you learned from your time with the Isty?" I hadn't thought before about how boring it might be for him.

"You won't be surprised to learn, with all the ethnic groups in this land, they've perfected various forms of warfare but also of defense." He leaned back against the tree. "It's been many years since an all out war, but some of the young men and women learn the defense maneuvers as discipline for the body and the mind. Nothing like any exercises we know. Quite fascinating. I can adapt them as part of the training of my palace guards."

"I hope we can carry everything we've collected on the ships back home." Carys tucked her hair behind an ear. "And I wonder what our companions have been doing on the beach all this time. We've been away from them for well over a month."

"They wouldn't have spent all that time looking for us, would they?" I searched the faces of the others. "They could have done so much more, learned about the cultures and knowledge of the people along the coast."

"I've tried to reach out to them with my mind, but so few of them had the training to receive our thoughts."

I nodded. "And I certainly haven't received any of theirs."

"The sooner we return, the better," Carys said. "There's not much more any of us can do here."

I smirked at her. "Now you've passed on the recipe for Meecham cookies and learned about some of their foods, you're done."

"Well, no, not done. But one of the cooks gave me a recipe book and it's even written in a language I can read."

"Have you all explored the library?" I pointed to the building. "So many books on so many topics."

Blane nodded. "It makes the library at the Stronghold seem tiny and limited."

"Too bad we can't take more than a few books with us." Carys sighed.

Madoc tilted his head. "We have to be very selective."

"Except the Isty aren't going to give us the chance to pick and choose." Gareth sat up straighter again. "We take what they allow us to have."

Morna had been quiet during our discussion. "Do you think I can bring an animal back with me?" The plaintive note in her voice touched my heart.

"Nothing too large, not a baby that'll grow into something enormous or dangerous," I warned.

"Oh, no. I was thinking of one of the ringtail lemurs."

"Won't it be lonely without another lemur?" Carys asked.

She frowned. "Maybe. I'll talk to the vets about what animal I can take."

"It would have to get along with Raj." I loved to tease my sister.

Her smile was back. "Everyone and everything gets along with that dog."

"It'll be hard to leave this place, but good to see our friends again." Madoc took my hand.

I nodded. "Won't they be surprised by all we have to show them!"

Rees approached with Donal and Ana. "We've talked to Klar about where we should take off from."

"Outside the city, I presume. Otherwise the dome will prevent us from leaving."

Ana sat down beside Gareth. "The Isty have had people out by the gondola since we arrived to prevent anyone or any animals from harming it, but Klar brought the folded envelope inside."

Donal was the one who'd learned something about flying the machine, so I turned to him, but before I could ask what he knew about it, he nodded. "Earlier today Klar took me out to show me how the controls work."

"So we're almost ready to go." Gareth stood and dusted off his pants. "Chou seemed to think we required a send-off dinner tonight." He smirked.

Carys stood as well. "Yes, that's why the bakers agreed to try the Meecham cookie recipe. I should return to the kitchens to see whether they need any help."

"Did anyone ever determine what went wrong with the oven that exploded?" I asked.

"I hate to say it, but it appeared to be sabotage." Donal shook his head. "Not something we have to worry about since we're leaving."

Alarm bells went off in my head. "You don't think anyone here would try to prevent our departure, do you?"

"I doubt it had anything to do with us." Gareth dismissed it with a shrug.

"What makes you say that?" Madoc's right eyebrow rose an inch. "Couldn't our presence have ignited a feud that was already brewing?"

Rees nodded. "From what I've heard, that's likely what happened, but it would have eventually flared up even without us. It's like the arguments you've described that occurred at the Stronghold. Heated discussions over whether or not to share technology."

"Does every more advanced group include a few dissenters who prevent progress?" Donal probably spoke for all of us who believed keeping knowledge from others could only lead to problems.

"But how do we convince those naysayers?" Carys asked.

I shook my head. "It's not our place to do that. All we can do is support any Isty factions who've called for sharing technologies with other groups. If we become too vocal, though, it might hurt their cause."

"Nissa's right." Madoc put a hand on my shoulder. "We should stay in the background, not give the opposition anything they can use against the majority of the leaders here."

"It's obvious Chou supports the sharing of information and devices, but do you know who else does? And who doesn't?" Blane asked.

"The main objections come from two people, a man called Ho Minh and a woman. I'm not sure of her name." Gareth took a breath and let it out. "They argue the Isty were charged with protecting all knowledge from what they term outsiders. I'm sure there was a reason for that soon after the fall, but they persist in holding to that foundation tenet of the city."

"That's a strong argument."

"Have they considered the scientists and engineers who were here at that time came from different parts of Fartek, and even from other continents?" I thought of people like Terry, who was descended from people from Solwintor.

"That's what Chou and another leader say." Gareth shook his head. "It's not enough to sway Ho Minh and the woman."

"Is that Gia? She has very strong opinions about everything." Rees rolled his eyes.

"Let's hope they don't have enough followers to stop our departure." Gareth walked off with Rees and Ana at his side.

CHAPTER SIXTY-EIGHT

After the lavish dinner the night before, including almost everything I'd eaten in Fartek, I had no appetite for the breakfast the Isty cooks served us in the morning. We didn't know when we'd have another meal, though, so I made an effort to eat some eggs, bread and the local fruits, similar to melons we ate in Leara.

We gathered our belongings and everything we hoped to take back with us. Chou insisted he had enough time to show Toren parts of the city before leading us all to the section of the dome that could be open to allow passage outside.

But as we approached the site of our exit, a man and woman approached. "We have no objection to these *ngoila* leaving, but we cannot allow them to take anything from our city." The man grabbed two books out of my hands as I tried to stuff them in my pack.

The woman also pulled at our packages, carefully tied up by our friends in the city. "You cannot take!"

Chou stepped between the woman and Carys. "That is no way to treat our visitors. These were gifts for them to carry home to show their people our appreciation and goodwill. This young woman is a princess in her land, yet all she requested was to learn our recipes." He retrieved the cookbooks and returned them to Carys with a slight bow. "We have been honored to receive you."

"It was my pleasure to meet such wonderful and interesting people. Thank you, Master Chou, for an enlightening stay in your glorious city." Carys returned his bow and turned to the two, bowing even more deeply.

Chou and Carys' diplomatic words seemed to calm the man and woman, but they still frowned as we stepped out toward the gondola. Klar and my brother were already examining it to ensure it would carry us to the beach.

Then we began to inflate the balloon, just as we had near the Sion enclave. The man and woman who'd objected to the items we were taking watched from inside the dome. Their frowns changed first to curiosity and finally to amazement. The inflated balloon was about a third as tall as the dome.

We tied down the basket so we could fill it and climb in ourselves. With help from Chou, Terry and a couple of others, we lifted off the ground and ascended into a clear blue sky.

As we rose, the domed city and especially the people became smaller and smaller. We watched for as long as we could, exchanging wistful waves with the Isty.

"You'll have to direct me to the beach." Klar had to shout above the roar of the burner. "Then Toren, the girl and I will head back to my home."

We flew over forests. The mountains appeared as hills. From up here we couldn't see the Mora village but knew it was under the canopy of green.

After a couple of hours, Morna pointed down. "Look, there's the chasm we had to cross to reach Fong's people."

The trek across Fartek that had taken us a few days on foot would be accomplished in several hours. My heart raced as we neared the beach. What would we find? So much had happened to us while we were away, and I imagined the same for those we'd left there.

White sand and blue sea appeared. Something inside me relaxed at the sight of two boats still remained offshore. As we descended, moving dots on the beach resolved into people. I wondered what our friends would make of this machine that brought us back to them.

One by one the people stopped and turned their faces up to us. As we neared the sand, they stepped back away from the huge basket and balloon. Voices erupted into cheers and shouts. But we didn't have time to respond. It took everyone in the basket to deflate the balloon, move the basket on its side, and fold the envelope.

The people on the beach formed an irregular oval around us and watched with large rounded eyes.

Once we finished, we greeted our friends at last. Everyone spoke at once until Gareth held up a hand. "We'll take turns speaking and asking questions, but first, let me introduce Klar, a leader of the Sion and our pilot."

Each of our companions stepped forward, saying his or her name, and bowing slightly to Klar.

Then we were bombarded with questions ranging from what happened to us at the chasm to whether we found the source of Madoc's books to how the balloon and basket operated.

When we satisfied everyone, we asked about what had happened on the beach in our absence. I pointed out to sea. "The ships are still offshore, but what happened to the crews?"

"They spend part of each day aboard, keeping everything ready for us to leave." Glynis grinned. "We decided to wait one more week for you to return, and then give up and sail off. I'm so glad you showed up today." She grabbed me in a hug.

As I hugged her back, I asked, "Is everyone in our party well?"

"Oh, yes. This place is beautiful, and the water is wonderful for wading and even swimming." She pointed to a structure near one end of the beach. "We built a house to eat and sleep in, but mainly we're out here all day."

Her face and arms were tanned. She looked healthier than I'd ever seen her.

While we talked, the others became reacquainted. They gathered in laughing groups as they traded stories.

Toren found Berel among our companions and pulled her to the side for a private discussion. When he finished talking, she smiled and nodded, and he steered her toward Klar to introduce her again.

"What is Toren planning?" Glynis asked.

"He's staying and wants Berel to stay with him. Klar will take him back to the Sion conclave."

"So you met many different groups."

"Yes, and we learned something from each of them. Most

now realize they can exchange their knowledge and the devices they've created." I took her hand. "I only regret you won't be able to see all of the wonders we have, particularly in the Isty city, built where a vast research facility used to stand. But we've brought back books and a few other items we plan to share with the people in Solwintor and Leara."

"You're not going home to the manor to stay, are you?"

I shook my head. "It's no longer my home."

"I understand. Adair and I will return there, if only to prevent Larena from taking her father's place in the future. Both of us know Kerr won't return."

"At least Adair will be more apt to accept innovation than Duke Alec." I squeezed my friend once more. "It is so good to see you again. As many new people, places, ideas and things as I've seen over the last few weeks, I've missed you and everyone else who wasn't with us."

The native people who'd visited our companions after we left were no where in sight. "What happened to the Min?"

"They've come and gone. I think they feared the Panshee would attack if they stayed here, but it's been very peaceful."

I felt disappointed. "So you didn't have much opportunity to learn more about their culture?"

She shook her head. "No we didn't. You said the Panshee, or Pin-Shing, are peaceful?"

"They're very protective of their territory and their people. The women and children are kept down in the chasm, where they weave beautiful mats and baskets, while the men hunt. They have differences of opinion about whether they should communicate with other groups, what the Isty tend to call tribes. Fong-Wei, the man who took us to the Isty, is one of the more progressive of his group but he had issues with what they call the Tektek, and call themselves the Isty." I took her two hands. "Oh, there's so much to tell you!"

"You mentioned you gained knowledge and more devices from some of these people. Like what?"

"For one, I have synthetic dyes and instructions on making them so we can have clothing and other items in many colors." I grinned. "Oh, and of course Carys has some new recipes."

"What are those?" She pointed to my sister who was

introducing the lemurs to Raj. He seemed to be studying them, but not in an aggressive or defensive way.

"They're called lemurs and they love to climb trees. She couldn't resist bringing one home, but a veterinarian insisted she take two so the first wouldn't be lonely. She also reassured Morna they'd get along with a dog."

"Raj gets along with everyone."

I nodded. "That's what I said." But it was Wim I studied. "Has that boy grown again?" The pants Gita bought him at the beginning of our journey only came to the bottom of his calves, and his head was almost on a level with my sister's.

Glynis laughed. "Gita has remarked about it several times. But what did she expect? He's a growing boy."

The horses had been kept in a make-shift corral with plenty to eat and water to drink. I spent a few minutes greeting Gallin. I couldn't tell whether he was happy to see me or annoyed I'd left him for so long.

That evening, we had a big dinner with all of our friends including Klar who'd remained on the beach. The two ships' captains and their crews joined us.

The people on the beach had gathered many fruits and nuts from the trees nearby and the sailors brought freshly-caught fish that they cooked over a huge bonfire. Nothing ever tasted as good as that meal.

In the morning before we sailed west, we bade farewell to Klar, Toren and Berel. With a lighter load in the basket, the balloon rose higher and faster, up over the trees toward the chasm.

The rest of us spent the morning loading our treasures onto the two ships.

"You'll be happy to see we've mended both ships for the voyage home." Captain Woryn pointed to his Flying Dragon.

We split up into two groups as we had when we left Fairhaven. Once everyone was settled, the captains and their crews cast off. We were going home at last.

*

Thank you for reading Beyond the Sea, the third book in The Crystal Odyssey series. If you enjoyed this book, please leave a review on Amazon and Goodreads.

ABOUT THE AUTHOR

Retiring in 2008 after forty-five years in the scientific literature publishing business, Joyce Hertzoff moved from the dreary mid-west to the sunny southwest where she and her husband love their mountain view and spicy food.

She wrote a romantic mystery for the 2008 NaNoWriMo that's still in the editing phase. *The Crimson Orb*, the first novel in the Crystal Odyssey series, was originally published by the Phantasm Books imprint of Assent Publications in June, 2014 and republished in 2017, followed closely by the sequel *Under Two Moons*. The flash mysteries, Natural Causes and Say Cheese were published in the anthologies *The Darwin Murders* and *Tasteful Murders*. A short story, Princess Petra, appears in *The Way Back* anthology. Her young adult fantasy novella *A Bite of the Apple,* published in 2016, won the New Mexico Press Women's fiction contest prize in the YA category and second place in the National Federation of Press Women's contest.

Joyce acts as a mentor and facilitator at Writers Village University and as managing editor for fiction for the MFA certificate program ezine. She's also a member of Southwest Writers.

Please visit Joyce online at:

www.joycehertzoffauthor.com

www.fantasybyjoycehertzoff.com

www.hertzoffjo.blogspot.com

https://facebook.com/joycehertzoff.3

https://twitter.com/JoyceHertzoff

Cast of Characters

From the manor in Holmdale by way of the Stronghold:

Narissa Day – 18-year-old 3rd Day child. Clothing constructor at the Stronghold and motivator for everyone. In love with Madoc.

Blane Day – the oldest Day child at 21. A defender at the Stronghold. Blond. About to be engaged to Carys

Morna Day – the youngest Day child at 16. Redhead. Loves animals, worked with the baby animals at the Stronghold.

Donal Day – the second oldest Day child at 19. Redhead. Fascinated by devices, he found uses for the ones developed at the Stronghold.

Madoc – Former science and magic teacher at the manor in Holmdale. Third son of the King and Queen of the East Islands. Planner at the Stronghold.

Kerr – son of Duke Alec at Holm Manor, works with Donal on new devices.

Carys – Madoc's sister, Princess of the East Islands, about to become engaged to Blane, master chef.

From the manor at Holmdale:

Glynis – Narissa's childhood friend; recently married to Adair

Adair – second son of Duke Alec; recently married to Glynis

Duke Alec Holm – Duke of Holm manor

Tavish Day – father of Blane, Donal, Nissa and Morna, swordmaster at Holm manor

Edana Day – mother of Blane, Donal, Nissa and Morna, herbalist and apothecary

From the East Islands:

Gareth – Second son of the King and Queen of the East Islands. In charge of the Royal Guards

Elwyn – Eldest son of the King and Queen of the East Islands and heir to the throne

Captain Woryn – Captain of the merchant vessel the Flying Dragon

Lem – seaman on the Flying Dragon

Rees – Royal Guard

Captain Trahern – Captain of the Royal ship the Queen Bronwyn

Queen Branna

King Owen

The Stronghold

Col Ramin

Wim – Col's adopted son

Gita – Col's wife, a veterinarian

Rani

Katya

Toren - mage

Holt

Ana

Eva

Mai

Dreas

Raj – the Ramin's dog

Others

The Great White – ship to Leara

The Dolphin – ship to Leara

Captain Simon Felden

Berel – Toren's rescue

Village of Teyab in Fartek

Karf

Panshee = Pin-Shing

Fong-Wei

Ying – his mother's

Tektek = ISTY

Terry Olson

Dai Moon

Pim Boa

Chou Caw

Dens

Bin

Vee

Lin

Flava

Ila

Ting

Chihiro

Dedi Enclave

Worgu Fami

Riman Saw

Henza Kel, Resto Eng, and Nata Wend – assigned to Nissa, Ana and Bin

Borogo

Mogo

Sion

Klar

Chan

Madi

Wen-Hsein

91578871R00238

Made in the USA
Columbia, SC
19 March 2018